North of 9/11

North of 9/11

a novel by
David Bernans

Cumulus
P R E S S

M O N T R É A L

Dépôt légal, Bibliothèque nationale du Québec, 2e trimèstre 2006.
Legal Deposit, National Library of Canada, 2nd quarter 2006.

Library and Archives Canada Cataloguing in Publication

Bernans, David, 1969-

    North of 9/11 — David Bernans.

ISBN 0-9733499-6-4

    1. September 11 Terrorist Attacks, 2001—Fiction. 2. War on Terrorism, 2001—Fiction. I. Title.

PS8603.E698N67 2006   C813'.6   C2006-901105-2

designed, typeset and cover photograph by
Chester Rhoder @ Typo-Pawsitive

Printed in Gatineau, Québec by Imprimerie Gauvin on
100% post-consumer recycled paper.

Cumulus Press acknowledges the support of the Canada Council for the Arts for its publishing program.   Canada Council   Conseil des Arts
                                                           for the Arts   du Canada

DISCLAIMER: This novel is a work of fiction. Although real people and events form a non-fiction backdrop, the plotline and the characters portrayed in this work are purely fictional. Any resemblance the story and its characters may have to reality is purely coincidental.

Cumulus PRESS
P.O. Box 5205
Station B
Montréal (Québec) H3B 4B5
Cumulus
P R E S S www.cumuluspress.com

This book is dedicated to all victims of terror before, during, and since 9/11. It is dedicated to victims of terror everywhere: in the North, South, East, and West. It is dedicated to victims of all forms of terror: religious fundamentalist terror, military terror, state-sponsored terror, economic terror, imperialist terror, corporate-sponsored terror, and war-on-terror terror.

It is also dedicated to my son Sasha who was in his mother's womb on September 11, 2001.

SPECIAL THANKS TO Lillian Robinson, Helen Hudson and David Widgington. Their frank advice and merciless criticism were good medicine. It was often difficult to swallow but in the long run, it made the story much stronger.

There are also many people who, directly or indirectly, with or without being aware of it themselves, helped bring this project to a successful conclusion: Anne-Frédérique Provencher, Helen Riordon, Brandi Heeren, Susana Vargas, Tom Keefer, Laith Marouf, Marina Tarantini, Chadi Marouf, Sabine Friesinger, Trish McIntosh, Al Revesz, Dennis Soron, Margot Brennan, Belinda Ageda, Mia Brooks, Jaggi Singh, Sunera Thobani, Dave Austin, Rocky Jones, Martin Bracey, Rosie Douglas, Ezra Winton, Noah Stewart-Ornstein, Patrice Blais, Sabrina Stea, Svetla Turnin, Philip Ilijevski, Tom Price, Victoria Natola, Christina Xydous, Rob Green, David Noble, Al Gunderson, David McNally, Rob Albritton, Taien Ng-Chan, Chester Rhoder, Maude Prud'homme, Catherine Charron, Shannon Bell, George Comninel, Leo Panitch, André Munro, Geneviève Page, Jean-François Hamilton, Monique Laramée, Jessica Lajambe, Samer Elatrash, Yves Engler, Ethan Cox, Maria Peluso, Tim McSorley, Sophia Southam, Erika Shaker, Tania Tabar, Patrick Shorey, Anita Rau Badami, Sharon Fraser, Bianca Mugyenyi, Wendy Kraus-Heitmann, Aimee van Drimmelen, Magnus Isaccson, Fiona Becker, Macdonald Stainsby, Dolores Chew, Misha Warbanski, Maria Abi-Habib, Sobia Virk, Larissa Dutil, Cybel Chagnon, Anastasia Voutou, Alexis Lagos, Andrew Thompson and Ken Heckman.

There were also many groups whose support was indispensable: Solidarity for Palestinian Human Rights (SPHR), Block the Empire, Convergence des luttes anti-capitalistes (CLAC), Concordia Urban Lacrosse Team, Peoples' Potato Food Collective, Concordia Student Union (CSU) Executive Committee (1999-00, 2000-01, 2001-02, 2002-03), CSU Council of Representatives (1999-00, 2000-01, 2001-02, 2002-03, 2003-04), Collective opposé à la brutalité policière (COBP), Québec Public Interest Research Group (QPIRG) Concordia, Simone de Beauvoir Institute, Jewish Alliance Against the Occupation, South Asian Women's Community Centre, Voices of Conscience, Emergency Coalition Against War Hysteria and Racism, Uberculture, Canadian Union of Public Employees (CUPE) 4512, CUPE 3903, Agence Amen, and the Concordia University Archives Office.

SUNDAY, SEPTEMBER 23, 2001

"Wherever he wants me to line up, just tell me where.
And he'll make the call."
— CBS NEWS ANCHOR DAN RATHER SPEAKING ABOUT
PRESIDENT GEORGE W. BUSH ON DAVID LETTERMAN, 9/17/2001

"IT LOOKS LIKE RENÉ-LÉVESQUE is blocked by the protest, sir," the cabby advised. He knew the businessman in the back seat could barely hear his traffic report over the tumult of conflict all about them: honking horns of irate drivers and police sirens squaring off against drums, whistles and cries of demonstrators. In any event, his fare's mind was elsewhere. The well-dressed executive sat restlessly, glancing out his backseat window at the flashing lights of the police cars surrounding the protest and blocking streets. He kept looking at his watch, then verifying the papers in his briefcase. A few tiny beads of sweat had formed between the worry lines on his forehead.

It's Sunday, thought Jack, glancing again at his watch. Like most men in his profession, he had a love-hate relationship with his timepiece—always in constant dread of displeasing his merciless master, yet admiring its precise regularity and absolute impartiality. He observed the date this time, to verify what he already knew. How could there be a traffic jam on a Sunday? As usual he had planned everything to perfection, and as usual, outside factors beyond his control had found their way into the gears of his day's precision operations. Why couldn't the rest of the world be as orderly and as rational as he? He was sure it was not always this way. The conduits of this city must have moved with clockwork precision before all the trouble. He didn't know when the trouble started. History was not his strong suit. Yet he was sure North America had once been as serene and as sublime as *Leave it to Beaver*, but somehow everything got mixed up. Western civilization—morality, rationality, the work ethic—it had all been contaminated. He could smell the contamination, even in this cab. It came from the cabby. He only saw the back of a balding head with black hair around the edges and a pair of dark eyes and bushy eyebrows in the rearview mirror. An Arab? But he wasn't wearing one of those Arab scarves... What were they called again? His daughter had made quite a point of mentioning that name yesterday. Kaf..., kaf, kaf-something or other.

"I'll have to take de Maisonneuve," said the driver as he forcefully edged his cab through heavy traffic into the right lane to turn.

Jack heard the accent. Yes, definitely an Arab. But the cabby's words did not register in the form of sentences or ideas in Jack's mind until the car began to veer from its predestined course. He was thinking about the meeting he had to get to, about his client: an aerospace manufacturer. Civilian aerospace was taking a nosedive but there was definitely potential in the military sector. All of this was beyond his control—nothing could be done to reverse the 9/11 factor. His job was spin. What does this mean for his client's image? was the question Jack had been asking himself for the past few days. And he was pretty sure he had the answer, but this damn cabby was not going to get him to his meeting in time.

"I'm in a hurry," Jack reminded his driver. "An important meeting."

"Of course sir," replied the cabby. His eyes squinted a smile at his fare via the rearview mirror. Hassan Mohamed chuckled to himself under his breath. Look at him squirm. Imagine how he'd be squirming if he knew...

With the driver's window open a couple of inches, he could hear the barbarians at the gates of the American consulate. One minute the slogans were in English, then Arabic, then French. Hassan chanted along under his breath, *George Bush, terroriste! Canada complice!* He knew the daughter of the man in his back seat—Jack's daughter—was in that crowd, putting her body in front of the war machine gearing up for action in Afghanistan. Did Jack know about Sarah? Did he have any idea what his own daughter was up to?

Hassan wanted to honk his horn, stick a raised fist out of the window, and join in the protestors' chants. The small band of rebels was completely outflanked by a sea of police cars. The cabby felt guilty for passively betraying his embattled comrades, but he could not afford to be too conspicuous at the moment. Since September 11, he had to become somebody else—somebody less dangerous. No more kaffiyeh around his neck. A clean close shave at all times. No more political discussions with his fares. To do otherwise would be bad for business, or worse. He had already seen a friend get his car windows smashed with "Arab go home" painted on the hood. After the Twin Towers fell, he and other cabbies like him had to become "good Arabs," at least while they were on the job. Raj, a Sikh cabby Hassan sometimes played chess with, was also targeted, but there was not much he could do. He could not stop wearing his turban or cut his beard. They were essential to his religion. Raj couldn't become a good Sikh. Nobody was publicly accusing Sikhs of having anything to do with 9/11 but that didn't matter. To North Americans, Sikh men fit the image of terrorists. They were quintessentially non-Western in appearance. So Raj's tips went down, he lost a few customers, and he started to take more abuse.

Look at that cabby smile. It was a good-natured don't-worry-be-happy smile but it would not ease Jack's agitation. He knew being a cabby was tough, but somebody in such a menial position could never understand the pressures faced by the top-consultant of an important PR firm. There had to be a way to communicate to ordinary people what it meant to be late for a crucial meeting with a Fortune 500 client.

"Nice weather we're having," offered Hassan in a careless tone.

Jack nodded with a forced smile and cleared his throat, casting yet another malevolent glance at his watch.

"*George Bush, terroriste! Canada complice!*" Jack heard the chants as the taxi turned the corner.

"How can they say that?" asked Jack in an accusatory tone. His indictment was not directed at the cabby. As much as the driver's good-natured smile and polite conversation annoyed the businessman, they also sent a clear and comforting message.

The Arab driver bore no malice towards Jack or his Western ways. He was not like those marauding Arabs on the street, calling for an anti-American Jihad. "Everybody should be behind our President at a time like this," Jack said confidently—a statement of fact, not an opinion.

"With all due respect sir," replied the cabby in a voice that was a shade short of respectful yet just shy of impertinent, "he's not my President. I'm a Canadian." It was a visceral reaction. He knew it was a mistake even before the words came out of his mouth. But Hassan could not accept having a bloodthirsty President foisted on him without even getting a chance to vote. Well, he said it. Now he would have to keep his mouth shut no matter what reactionary thing Sarah's father said. He had to admit it. She was right. Listening to him was like watching Dan Rather. He even had that same paternalistic yet matter-of-fact news anchor way of speaking.

Did I say "our" President? thought Jack. I was sure I said "the" President.

September 11 was Jack's star-spangled rebirth. He left Jersey more than thirty years ago and, until now, he had never looked back. He avoided talking about those days as much as possible. The bitterness of betrayal remained, made all the more distasteful because he was both betrayer and betrayed.

Although Jack knew very well he was no longer the same naïve draft-dodger who drifted into Montréal back in 1968, he was only beginning to realise how profoundly American he had actually become. He got a brief glimpse of his transition thanks to a chance encounter with his old friend, Mordecai Dingleman. It was on the metro back in the early eighties, before Jack swore off public transportation for good.

JACK SAW MORTY STEPPING ON AT ROSEMONT STATION AND IMMEDIATELY BURIED HIS HEAD IN A NEWSPAPER, PRETENDING TO READ. HOW WAS HE GOING TO GET TO BERRI-UQAM WITHOUT MORTY SEEING HIM? THERE WERE ONLY TWO OTHER PEOPLE IN THE CAR: A LEATHER-CLAD PUNK STARING OUT THE WINDOW (PROBABLY STONED ON SOMETHING), AND AN OLDER WOMAN SHAKING OVER HER FOUR-PRONGED CANE. MAYBE MORTY WOULDN'T RECOGNISE HIM.

MORTY STILL LOOKED THE SAME, WITH HIS JEANS AND HIS "U.S. OUT OF LATIN AMERICA" T-SHIRT. MAYBE HIS HAIR WAS A BIT THINNER ON TOP AND HE HAD A FEW MORE GRAY HAIRS BUT HIS MUSTACHE LOOKED THICKER AND BLACKER THAN EVER. DEFINITELY STILL THE OLD MORTY. BUT JACK WAS DECIDEDLY MORE CLEAN-CUT THAN HIS FORMER 1969-SELF. MAYBE IF HE JUST SLOUCHED A LITTLE LOWER...

"JACK? JACK MURPHY?" A SURPRISED VOICE EXCLAIMED AS JACK LOOKED UP FROM THE STOCK PRICES INTO THE GOOD HUMOURED FACE OF HIS OLD HOUSEMATE. WITH HIS THICK GLASSES AND MUSTACHE, HE STILL LOOKED THE PART OF THE "GROUCHO MARXIST." THAT WAS WHAT HE USED TO CALL HIMSELF, BACK THEN.

"MORDECAI DINGLEMAN," JACK RESPONDED WITH THE ENTHUSIASM OF AN ACTUARY AT A TAROT READING, WHILE HIS OLD FRIEND SHOOK HIS HAND, PUMPING MADLY.

"WOW MAN," MORTY MARVELED AS HE LOOKED JACK UP AND DOWN FROM HIS NEATLY TRIMMED HAIR TO HIS POLISHED BLACK SHOES, "LOOKS LIKE YOU'VE COME INTO SOME SERIOUS CASH. WORKING THE STOCK MARKET NOW?" HE GESTURED AT THE STOCK PAGES IN JACK'S HANDS.

"ADVERTISING."

"OOOOH," MORTY WINCED IN EMPATHETIC PAIN. "WELL, GOTTA MAKE A LIVING SOMEHOW I GUESS. AT LEAST YOU CAN GIVE TO THE CAUSE SO DIEHARDS LIKE ME CAN KEEP THE STRUGGLE GOING, EH?"

JACK STARED BACK BLANKLY. WHAT CAUSE, WHAT STRUGGLE COULD MORTY POSSIBLY BE TALKING ABOUT? DID PEOPLE REALLY STILL TALK LIKE THAT? AT LEAST THERE WAS NOBODY HE KNEW IN THE SUBWAY CAR TO SEE THE COMPANY HE USED TO KEEP.

TAKING JACK'S BLANK STARE AS A PLEA FOR REVOLUTIONARY EDUCA-TION, MORTY SAT DOWN BESIDE HIM AND STARTED TO EXPLAIN "THE CAUSE." LIKE EVERYBODY ELSE JACK KNEW FROM THE 1960S, MORTY HAD LEFT THE MAOISTS IN DISILLUSIONMENT. BUT UNLIKE JACK'S OTHER MAOIST FRIENDS WHO HAD GONE ON TO BECOME PART OF THE ESTABLISHMENT, MORTY SOLDIERED ON. OVER THE PAST FEW YEARS, ESPECIALLY SINCE THE 1979 NICARAGUAN REVOLUTION, HE HAD BEEN ACTIVE IN LATIN AMERICA SOLIDARITY WORK AND JUST RECENTLY HE HAD STARTED TO GET INVOLVED WITH YESH GVUL SOLIDARITY.

"YESH GWHAT?"

"IT'S SOMETHING I FELT I HAD TO DO," MORTY EXPLAINED. "AS A LEFTIST AND AS A JEW. IT'S FINE FOR ME TO CRITICIZE WHAT UNCLE SAM'S

DOING IN EL SALVADOR, BUT LOOK WHAT'S BEING DONE IN MY NAME OVER THERE IN ISRAEL: THE INVASION OF LEBANON, SABRA AND SHATILA MASSACRES, AND ALL THAT SHIT. PRETTY SCARY STUFF, MAN. YESH GVUL IS A MOVEMENT OF ISRAELI MILITARY RESERVISTS WHO ARE REFUSING TO SERVE IN THE OCCUPATION AND OPPRESSION OF PALESTINIANS."

"OH," JACK LAUGHED. "YOU'RE SUPPORTING ISRAELI DRAFT-DODGERS. WHY DIDN'T YOU JUST SAY SO? MAKE LOVE NOT WAR, MAN." HE PUNCTUATED HIS LAST SENTENCE WITH HIS TWO FINGERS HELD UP IN A PEACE SIGN.

MORTY DIDN'T LAUGH. "NOT DRAFT-DODGERS. THEY'RE WAR RESISTERS. THEY'RE RESISTING AN UNJUST WAR OF OCCUPATION."

"YEAH RIGHT," JACK LOOKED OUT THE SUBWAY WINDOW INTO THE BLACKNESS. "WHATEVER YOU SAY MORTY."

"I CAN'T BELIEVE I HAVE TO EXPLAIN THIS TO YOU," MORTY SAID, LOUDER THAN JACK WOULD HAVE LIKED. "YOU OF ALL PEOPLE, MAN. YOU WERE LIKE ONE OF THE BIGGEST WAR RESISTERS BACK IN '69. I REMEMBER. *JE ME SOUVIENS* JACK."

"PLEASE, MORTY, DON'T..." JACK SAID SHAKING HIS HEAD.

"OH DON'T TELL ME..." MORTY'S HAPPY-GO-LUCKY PERMA-SMILE WAS SLOWLY DISAPPEARING UNDER HIS MOUSTACHE. "NOT YOU TOO JACK. COME ON MAN. YOU TOLD ME YOURSELF. YOU DIDN'T WANT TO GO 'KILL PEASANTS RESISTING AMERICAN OCCUPATION'."

DID I REALLY SAY THAT? JACK THOUGHT. AND HE KNEW HE PROBABLY DID. HE SAID A LOT OF THINGS BACK THEN. BUT SO DID EVERYBODY. ALL THOSE MAOISTS GOING ON ABOUT "DECADENT BOURGEOIS HABITS" OR "LAPDOGS OF IMPERIALISM." IT WAS JUST WHAT PEOPLE DID. IT WAS A FASHION, LIKE WEARING BELLBOTTOMS. HE SAID IT, BUT HE DIDN'T MEAN ANYTHING BY IT. HE WOULD NEVER SAY ANYTHING LIKE THAT NOW—ESPECIALLY NOT TO THE AEROSPACE CLIENT HE HAD JUST LANDED FOR THE COMPANY. THEY WERE THE ONES WHO MADE THE PLANES USED TO "KILL PEASANTS RESISTING AMERICAN OCCUPATION."

"THAT WAS A LIFETIME AGO MORTY," JACK CHUCKLED, PUTTING HIS HAND ON HIS OLD FRIEND'S SHOULDER AS HE GOT UP. "THIS IS MY STOP. SO TAKE CARE..."

MORTY GOT UP TOO AND FOLLOWED JACK OUT OF THE CAR INTO THE CROWDED BERRI-UQAM STATION, SHOUTING HYSTERICALLY ALL THE WAY. "SO THAT'S IT? TOO BAD JACK! YOU REALLY MISSED YOUR CHANCE. THINK OF ALL THE GOOKS YOU COULD HAVE KILLED BACK IN '69! MAYBE

YOU COULD'VE GOT A MEDAL! YOU COULD'VE HELPED WIN THE WAR AGAINST THE GODLESS COMMUNISTS! THE YELLOW HOARDS! THE RED MENACE!"

JACK TURNED ON HIS TUNNEL VISION, MAKING STRAIGHT FOR HIS GREEN LINE TRAIN, PRAYING NOBODY HE KNEW WOULD SEE THE SCENE MORTY WAS MAKING. HE COULD FEEL HIS FACE FLUSHING IN THE BREEZE CREATED BY THE SUBWAY WIND TUNNEL. THE HAIR ON THE BACK OF HIS NECK WAS STANDING ON END. THANKFULLY, MORTY DIDN'T FOLLOW HIM PAST THE ESCALATORS. HE QUICKLY SAT DOWN AT HIS NEXT STOP AND BURIED HIS HEAD IN THE SAFE ANONYMITY OF THE FINANCIAL PAGES ONCE AGAIN.

AS HE WAITED, THE EMBARRASSMENT FADED, BUT HIS FACE REMAINED FLUSHED. THE SHAME WAS SINKING IN. IN THE SIXTIES, DODGING THE DRAFT WAS COOL. BUT EVEN THEN, JACK KNEW IT WAS WRONG. OUTWARDLY, HE WAS A HIPPY, BUT INSIDE, THE GUILT GNAWED AT HIM. IN 1968 NOBODY, EXCEPT HIS FATHER AND THE U.S. GOVERNMENT, THOUGHT ANY WORSE OF HIM FOR NOT GOING TO WAR IN VIETNAM. BUT THERE WAS NO GETTING AROUND IT. IT WAS WRONG. DAD WAS RIGHT, LBJ WAS RIGHT, AND JACK WAS WRONG. BUT THAT WAS 1968, AND THIS WAS 1983. DRAFT-DODGING HAD GONE OUT OF FASHION. RAMBO WAS IN. JACK WISHED HE COULD BE RAMBO, BUT HE WAS JUST COWARDLY JACK—THE EX-DRAFT-DODGING AD MAN, CLIMBING THE CORPORATE LADDER.

AFTER THE ENCOUNTER WITH MORTY, JACK PROMISED HIMSELF HE WOULD NEVER TAKE THE METRO AGAIN. ON HIS SALARY HE COULD AFFORD TAXIS. AND HE TRIED NOT TO THINK ABOUT MORTY OR THE OTHERS LIVING IN THAT PSEUDO COMMUNE HE CALLED HOME IN 1968 AND '69. BUT EVERY ONCE IN A WHILE, MORTY'S GOOD-NATURED FACE, TWISTED INTO AN EXPRESSION OF ANGRY CONDEMNATION, WOULD MAKE A BRIEF APPARITION—AN ILLUSORY GLIMPSE ON A CROWDED STREET, A DEMONSTRATION ON THE 6 O'CLOCK NEWS, OR IN A DREAM. NO, IT WASN'T MORTY. JUST A MISCHIEVOUS GNOME FROM JACK'S OWN MIND, PLAYING TRICKS. AND JACK WOULD FORGET ABOUT HIM AS QUICKLY AS HE HAD APPEARED.

And now more than a decade later, the purifying fire of 9/11 helped Jack exorcize his ghosts. Even though it was a terrible tragedy, it brought him closer to his American brethren. Everybody rallied to the flag, singing *God Bless America*. It was his chance for redemption. What could he do to make his daughter Sarah see the light? She was too Canadian, even anti-American. She was being used by the Arabs. What would it take to bring her into the fold? He knew it would happen eventually, the same way his Maoist friends from the sixties would later join the establishment except for the crazy Mordecai Dingleman. But he was afraid Sarah would make a big mistake she would regret for the rest of her life.

"What I mean is that no matter what our politics, after the bombing nobody can oppose what the [he did want to say 'our'] president is doing," explained Jack in a tone that was more patronizing than he meant it to sound.

You're either with us, or you're with the terrorists, Hassan mentally continued Jack's line of thought. He kept reminding himself this was not the time to pick a fight. Just let it go. He would be caught in the war on terror's grip soon enough. To keep in view the importance of his mission, he put his hand in his jacket pocket and gripped the cool metal that was so essential to the plan. The emotions he felt towards this particular American became less intense. He and Sarah's father were just pawns in a much larger chess game. Their moves were only important insofar as they had a strategic impact on more powerful interests.

"Really, it's like Bush said. You're either with him, or you're with the terrorists. There's no middle ground. That's true whether you're an American, a Canadian, a Pakistani or an Afghan. Whether you're black or white, or yellow or blue, or whatever. We have to get the people responsible for this terrible crime. Calling Bush a terrorist is only helping the criminals. These protestors are helping the terrorists."

"I thought they were just protesting the bombing of Afghanistan," offered Hassan in an empty voice. Playing dumb. Just a dumb Arab. That's all I am. What do I know? thought Hassan. And Jack is just a pawn, and so am I, and so is Sarah. There's a bigger picture. Remember the big picture. Still, he couldn't help wondering how Sarah could be so politically astute, especially at her age, when her father was such a blind patriot.

"What do they suggest we do then?" retorted Jack. "Just keep asking the Taliban, 'can you please give us Osama bin Laden? Pretty please?' I mean, get real."

As each predictable argument was lobbed his way, Hassan clinched his teeth into a muzzle, keeping his frustrated sense of justice in check. It was that same maddening internal censor that he thought he had left behind when he evaded the draft of the al-Assad dictatorship in Syria back in the early 1970s. Hassan wanted to reply that the Afghan authorities were only asking to be presented with evidence that bin Laden was responsible for the attacks before handing him over, which is normal procedure in international law. Bombing innocent civilians with high-tech weapons might be considered terrorism too, even if it was to bring an international terrorist to justice. But Hassan simply nodded and smiled.

Taking the cabby's silence as agreement, Jack continued with his treatise on international relations in the age of global terrorism. "When you're dealing with a dangerous maniac like Osama, diplomacy goes out the window. Anybody standing in the way of justice, whether they're giving active support to Osama by aiding his terrorist network, or passive support by selling supplies, will face the consequences." Jack looked at his driver expectantly for a sign of approval. Any rational human being would have to agree with these simple statements of fact. His daughter resisted the truth—that was only to be expected from a rebellious teenager. But how could Shirley, his own wife, question the burning revelation staring them in the face every night in their living room? The Twin Towers falling, falling, falling.

Hassan's teeth-clenching was giving way to gritting. He wanted to counter the argument using Jack's own definition of "support for terrorists." The way that Hassan figured it, many CIA operatives and their superiors would have to be arrested and tried for their support for bin Laden and his ilk during their insurgency against the Soviet-supported Afghan regime of the 1970s and 80s. Maybe even George Bush Senior would be caught in the dragnet. But all that the cabby could do was continue to smile and nod like the bobbing lapdog head on his dashboard. He confined his anger to the muscles in his jaw, not allowing it to escape through the rearview mirror's reflection towards the paying customer. He's just a pawn, only a pawn. Later, when it was safe, his anger would leak out, and then it would turn to shame for not speaking his conscience, shame for not wearing his kaffiyeh, for not teaching his kids Arabic, for abandoning his parents, for his failure as a husband...

"Afghanistan is bringing this war on itself," Jack explained. "This is a just war if ever there was one. Now if you excuse me, I've got to call my assistant. Since I am going to be late for this meeting [he emphasized the word 'late' as he glared at Hassan's eyes in the rearview mirror] I have to give her instructions on how to deal with our client."

It is often said that the customer is always right. In this case it was not only the last word that went to the client, but even the final judgement: a just war if ever there was one.

Jack's attention turned to the meeting he was missing. He barked orders into his cell phone as the cab moved through the uncharacteristically heavy Sunday traffic. The PR man wanted to make sure his assistant didn't unwittingly sabotage the account while waiting for him to show up.

Hassan was happy not to have to listen to the patriotic drivel spouted by his friend's well-connected father. As he listened to the increasingly vitriolic rantings of his fare, he gripped the object in his pocket tighter and tighter until it became as hot as his temper. Better not risk any small talk. Getting into an argument could ruin the whole plan. These days talk on any subject always came right back to 9/11. Sports: game cancellations and tighter security. Travel: fear of flying. Fashion: red, white and blue is in. Music: 9/11 benefit concerts. For two weeks now television, radio and newspapers had been completely saturated with the Twin Towers tragedy. Smoke, rubble, and stars and stripes colonized airwaves and print.

Hassan spent the rest of the fare thinking about something that could not get him into any more trouble with Sarah's father: the chess game he would continue with Greg tomorrow afternoon. The lad was putting up more of a fight than usual, or was it Hassan whose strategy was becoming over-cautious? Chess was the one thing that had gone well in Hassan's life of exile. When he played the game he was a different man. He still had a balding crown and an age-worn face, a potbelly, nicotine-stained teeth and fingers, and a generally frumpy appearance, but when he played his eyes lit up with an intensity that impressed onlookers and intimidated his opponents. One could, as more than one observer remarked, "hear the wheels turning." That is what Genviève, his ex-wife, saw when she met him at a café in Paris.

When the cab pulled up to the Innomonde Building office complex, the fare was $24.55. Jack handed him a twenty and a five, and said, "keep the change."

Serves me right for that "I'm a Canadian" comment, thought Hassan. Who do I think I am? Wayne Gretzky?

Jack grabbed his briefcase and jumped out of the cab. The cabby was half way through saying, "Have a nice day," as his fare disappeared through the rotating door of the glass complex. Jack was twenty-two and a half minutes late by his calculations. Hopefully his assistant was holding down the fort.

Hassan looked around for a parking spot. He was not in a hurry and Sunday parking downtown was easy to find. There was about five minutes to kill before he was supposed to follow Mr. Murphy into the building. He was only a little nervous. There was no commitment at this stage of the plan.

Still, Hassan had his doubts. What was the most effective arm in such a lopsided propaganda war? Would throwing their bodies into the gears of the war industry have any more impact than today's mass action?

It looked like there were less than a thousand people mobilized to stand in the way of the increasingly militaristic posturing of Canadian/American authorities, but at least today's ragtag gathering got some media attention. On the other hand, would the protest really be drawing attention to the right issues?

Nobody could seriously accuse the protestors of being in league with bin Laden, although some, like Sarah's father, would give it a shot. It was a respectable organizing job on such short notice. The Emergency Coalition Against War Hysteria and Racism was only about one week old. Most mainstream unions and citizens groups were too shell-shocked by recent events to mobilize resistance to the coming war, but there was still an impressive diversity. Afghan community members, the Voices of Conscience (a group opposed to sanctions against Iraq), the South Asian Women's Community Centre, the Jewish Alliance Against the Occupation, various Palestinian human rights groups and student groups had pooled their forces. Still, it would be an understatement to say that the anti-war and anti-racism movements were fighting a rearguard action. They needed something to focus attention on what was unspeakable in the more jingoistic than usual media: the long history of US-led imperialist oppression and terror that had brought the world to this sad state of affairs. Demonstrating against the post-9/11 racist backlash and against knee-jerk war response was necessary, but getting people to see any kind of long-term alternative to simply going after the bad guys would require a more creative approach.

Hassan found a parking spot right away, which allowed him enough time to smoke a cigarette. He checked his jacket pocket to make sure he had what he needed, then made his way through the same doors by which Sarah's father had passed into the antiseptic environment of corporate wellbeing. Hassan went straight to the security guards' desk and pulled the object from his pocket. "Mr. Murphy forgot this in the taxi this afternoon. I believe Mr. Murphy is in a meeting with the firm executives on the third floor. I am his driver," he said. In his hand was an impressive looking gold and silver pen. He handed it to the security guard who looked like he was in charge: a young, freckled, redheaded man with far too much neck muscle—the kind of security guard who wanted to be a cop but didn't make the cut. Hassan would have liked to give it to the young woman beside him, but her mind was elsewhere. She had a glazed-over look on her face that inevitably sets in whenever an intelligent human being is asked to be a property-protection device. She appeared to be staring intently at something just underneath the desk.

The male guard examined the pen and read the inscription:

Jack Murphy, communicator. The pen is mightier than the sword. Love Shirley.

The guard's lips moved as he read. Then he went through the logbook to verify that Jack Murphy had in fact signed in.

"I'll take this up to Mr. Murphy," said the guard in his police captain's voice.

"I'm sorry," said Hassan apologetically, "I have to take it to Mr. Murphy myself. Company policy."

The guard's face reddened. That was the downside of being a corporate guard. There was nothing his bosses hated more than violations of company policy, even if that company was not one of the tenants. Still, this guy looked like he could be an Arab. Maybe a terrorist. He would note it in his book. He handed the pen back and said, "You have to sign-in."

Hassan signed using Mr. Murphy's pen. Its nib spread an even trail of deception as it glided across the page. It felt heavy.

"Follow me," the guard ordered.

Hassan followed the swaggering guard to the elevator and up to the third floor. The guard kept glaring at Hassan, but the middle-aged cabby was not to be intimidated. He polished the pen on his coat sleeve and responded with a nicotine-stained grin.

The elevator doors opened to a hallway with a door at either end and an exit to the stairwell opposite the elevator. The door at one end of the hall had the corporate name on it, while the door at the other end read "employees only." The guard led him through the company door and into a reception area. Hassan was surprised to see a receptionist sitting at the desk. How did they manage to get her to come in on a Sunday, and why would they bother for just one executive meeting? The receptionist flashed pearly white teeth at the pair, "Good afternoon. How can I help you gentlemen?" With her perfect hair and Channel air, the receptionist was at one with the office décor. All that was missing was a flight attendant's uniform to go with all of the model airplanes and murals adorning the immaculate waiting room.

"I have a valuable belonging to Mr. Murphy that I must return to him. He left it in my cab." The security guard had opened his mouth to say something but Hassan was too quick. The guard's face started to redden again.

The receptionist smiled at the frowning guard and at the frumpy cabby as she pressed the button on an intercom system. "Yes," came the response of a disembodied male voice.

"Mr. Tremblay," responded the receptionist. "I have a cabby here who says he has a valuable item that Mr. Murphy left in his cab."

There was a pause for about thirty seconds. The receptionist continued to smile at the odd pair before her. Hassan glanced around the reception area as the security guard kept his eyes glued to the interloper. On the coffee table in front of a leather couch was a huge scale replica of an F16 fighter jet. It caught Hassan's attention because he recognized it as the model used by the Israeli military. He remembered stories he heard from Palestinian refugees who had seen family members torn to pieces or buried alive by the bombs dropped from war-birds just like that one. He knew that this company made component parts for those very planes. And there it was, decorating a coffee table, like a vase of flowers. There it is, thought Hassan, that's the big picture. The image of the fighter jet set off an instant chain reaction: expensive military technology, occupation, US interests in the Middle East, three-billion dollars in annual US military aid to Israel, Canadian corporate participation, weapons of mass destruction, human rights violations, collateral damage, the cutting edge of military technology and great decorative ideas for any corporate office. At that moment he was convinced that the plan had merit.

Disembodied laughter filled the reception area for an instant followed by, "Okay, send him in."

"Right this way," said the receptionist as she pressed another button to buzz open the offices behind her desk.

Hassan followed her into the plush office where the pawns were waiting in their fifteen-hundred-dollar suits.

TUESDAY, SEPTEMBER 11, 2001

"What was more important in the world view of history?... the Taliban or the fall of the Soviet Empire? A few stirred-up Muslims or the liberation of Central Europe and the end of the Cold War."

— U.S. SECRETARY OF STATE ZBIGNIEW BREZINSKI, 01/98

AS SARAH WALKED INTO AL-TAÏB, the restaurant's typically animated clientele had become zombies, hypnotized by the big-screen television in the corner. On her way to the counter to order a zatar, she glanced in the same direction as the mesmerized herd. She too was brought under the power of the flickering images. Her afternoon hunger was forgotten.

The Twin Towers attack was on everyone's lips that morning on Concordia's downtown campus, but actually seeing it on the screen was another matter. It became real.

She gaped at the slow-motion replay of the plane crashing through the South Tower and the fireball coming out the other side. Her grip loosened on her cumbersome bundle of textbooks and notes. A few sheets of paper drifted out of her file folder and down to the floor beside her army boots. The tip of her tongue toyed with the ring on her lower lip. Screams of panic, confusion, smoke, dust, blood; it was a war zone. A black woman was stumbling about. White ash covered her face, her eyes vacant—a ghost. This was New York? But these things didn't happen where people like Sarah and her family lived. They happened in far off Third World countries, not a day's drive south of Montréal. Wasn't Brent in New York? She would have to ask her mother. If Brent was killed or injured in this thing... And then it really hit her. The attack had touched, however peripherally, her own life.

SHE REMEMBERED BRENT AS A BOY TWO YEARS HER SENIOR, SHOW-
ING HER HOW TO PLAY MONOPOLY ONE RAINY EASTER SUNDAY IN NEW
JERSEY IN THE BASEMENT OF HER AUNT'S SUBURBAN HOME. HE LET
HER WIN. AS BRENT'S FRIENDS WOULD SAY, SARAH, THE SIX-YEAR-OLD
"BABY" DIDN'T "GET" MONOPOLY. WHAT THEY MEANT, WITHOUT UN-
DERSTANDING IT PRECISELY IN THESE TERMS, WAS THAT SARAH HAD
YET TO ABSORB THE BASIC PRINCIPLES OF CAPITALIST COMPETITION.
SHE WOULD HAVE TRADED PARK PLACE FOR BALTIC AVENUE BECAUSE SHE
LIKED PURPLE BETTER THAN BLUE. MOST EIGHT YEAR OLD BOYS WOULD
HAVE GROUND THE LITTLE GIRL INTO POVERTY AND THEN LAUGHED AT
THE NAÏVETE OF HER STRATEGY. BUT BRENT WENT OUT OF HIS WAY TO
LET HER WIN.

HER FATHER ADMONISHED BRENT AND SPOILED THE ILLUSION FOR
SARAH, "HOW'S SHE GOING TO LEARN THE GAME IF YOU JUST LET HER
WIN?" HE ASKED THE BOY.

"IF SHE ALWAYS LOSES IT WON'T BE ANY FUN," HE REPLIED. "SHE
WON'T WANT TO PLAY ANY MORE."

Although Sarah saw Brent only during rare family occa-
sions, she had a certain comfortable familiarity with him, like
revisiting an old friend. And now she didn't know if he were
dead or alive.

"You dropped this," said a young kaffiyeh-wearing man
standing beside her in line at the counter. He held up a few
pieces of paper. Notes from her Women and Religion course.

Sarah grabbed them quickly before he could decipher
their significance. The last thing she wanted at the moment
was a discussion on women and religion with this young Arab
man. At first Sarah had an unquenchable thirst for intellectual
debates about feminism and the Muslim religion. Concordia
offered a rich feast of scholarly debate following the lean years
of *CÉGEP* that were supposed to prepare her for university. But
after a few days of calorific discussions with people in the Muslim Students Association she had her fill of argument on that
particular question. Sarah had savoured those talks, but now
she needed some time to digest them. "Thanks," said Sarah.
And then realizing she was blocking his view of the television,
she moved closer to the counter to place her order.

The four men working the counter were pushed to the limit today. The frantic pace, the din, and the heat of the pizza ovens made it a tough job on the best of days, but on September 11 the customers were simply too shell-shocked to respond to efforts at communication. *"Suivant, next. Pardon madame. Est-ce que je peux vous aider?* Can I help you please?" The entire clientele was mesmerized by CNN. They couldn't even liberate their minds long enough to place their orders. Customer indecision became the bottleneck in what was normally an exceptionally efficient fast food machine. Sarah was as absent as the rest. She had to be asked twice to place an order. She even walked away with her zatar and coke without paying. The cashier had to come out from behind the counter, to bring her back to reality long enough to pay for her meal.

She took her tray up to the second floor and looked around to see if anybody she knew was there. Sure enough, Hassan was watching CNN just like everyone below as he nervously tapped out an S-O-S with his cigarette package on the table. "Hi Hassan."

"Oh Sarah," said Hassan in a surprised voice, turning to look at her as if she had just passed through a solid wall. The spell of CNN was broken. He was no longer in New York's smoldering skyline, but back in Al-Taïb, smiling yellow teeth up at his friend. Even though she was young enough to be his daughter, he found Sarah to be attractive—dark wavy hair, green eyes, and a very nice body. She would be even better looking if she didn't wear those army pants and boots, if she stopped wearing bandanas in her hair like the protestors in the Québec City FTAA protests, and if she took those silly piercings out of her eyebrow and lower lip.

Sarah didn't notice Hassan looking her up and down today. She was too distracted. In any event, she was used to guys doing that. It bothered her, but she was used to it. Occasionally she would lash out at one of the more obvious gawkers, but not a helpless frumpy little old guy like Hassan, and not today. She sat down at the table beside him. "What's up?"

Hassan simply gestured with his head towards the television. He continued to tap his cigarette package on the table. He had been meaning to go on the balcony for a smoke for three hours now, but he was held in place by his eyes which refused to let go of the screen. Sarah furrowed her brow and nodded in response.

"Dude," Sarah burst out, her voice muffled slightly by the zatar that filled it, "that is some fucked up shit. Who did it?" She had cultivated the habit of speaking with her mouth full ever since she noticed how much it bothered her father.

"Why is that always the first question?" Hassan complained. "Well, at least you didn't ask, 'what Muslims did it?'..." he drifted off pensively. Palestinian street celebrations were being shown, once again, on the screen as if to illustrate his point. "Of course it may very well have been a radical Muslim group. I don't know. Osama bin Laden seems to be a likely candidate. But all Muslims and Arabs are going to pay the price. There's going to be a backlash. It'll be worse than it was during the Gulf War."

"What's going to happen with the bazaar and rally on Saturday?" asked Sarah.

The Concordia club, Solidarity for Palestinian Human Rights, had been planning a rally and a bazaar to commemorate the September 1982 massacres at the Sabra and Shatila Palestinian refugee camps under Israeli occupation in Lebanon. The university administration had already been giving SPHR a hard time, refusing to let the group book an empty lot for the event. Rector Frederick Lowy had even written an open letter to the Concordia community, citing "the magnitude of the proposed events and the risk of confrontation and possible violence." Much had been made about an article in a local pro-Israel newspaper, *The Suburban*. The headline:

The whole idea that terrorists were somehow involved in a student club was laughable, but nobody was laughing. And now Hassan was talking about the beginning of a new backlash. If there was going to be a backlash after the World Trade Center attack, then what had they been experiencing up to now? And how could the situation get any worse? Sarah knew Hassan had much more experience in these matters than her, and she respected his opinion, but it seemed hard to believe.

"I don't know," admitted Hassan. "Maybe it'll end up being cancelled or postponed. It depends on how militant people are and how belligerent the administration is."

"But dude, this is like the perfect opportunity to underline the similarities between the terrorist bloodshed in New York and the Sabra and Shatila massacres. Isn't it?" she demanded. "In both places thousands of people were killed in cold blood. Now North America is seeing what this kind of violence is really like. I like totally understand you want to avoid backlash but come on. You guys have got to stand up for yourselves."

There were more parallels that could be made. Hassan knew about them and Sarah would soon learn. If bin Laden was behind the World Trade Center attack, then in both cases, the US played a role in the massacres. The training and equipping of Osama bin Laden's network was co-funded by the CIA when he was fighting the Soviets in Afghanistan, and the US was implicated in the Sabra and Shatila massacres as well. Uncle Sam was giving more military aid to the Israeli military than to any other country in the world. But Hassan did not mention any of that today. There was no reason to encourage Sarah on this issue. It would only make her more pigheaded. Did she really understand how SPHR needed to avoid a backlash? How could she? A white girl living in Westmount?

"There are a lot of connections," Hassan admitted, "but nobody will understand. I've been watching TV all morning. People are being brainwashed to think this thing just came out of the blue for no reason, and the US is just a victim. They just see these images of death and destruction in New York. They see these innocent victims, and then they see an American flag.

And the obvious conclusion is that the whole United States, even the government and the army, is like these innocent victims. Nobody's going to understand."

"We can make them understand," Sarah persisted unconvincingly. She had to admit it would be difficult.

On the bottom of the image of the black cloud hovering where the Twin Towers used to be, the following words crawled across the screen:

State Department calls today's attacks "worst act of terrorism on US soil."

Even with the smattering of US history Sarah had picked up in *CÉGEP*, she could have easily disproved the State Department's assertion. The worst act of terrorism? Really? What about the hundreds of thousands of slaves kidnapped from Africa and dragged to American soil against their will to be forced into degrading labour, raped, tortured and murdered? Doesn't that count? What about the millions of Native Americans killed in genocidal wars on American soil to make way for white settlers? Doesn't that count either? But what could she do, call up the State Department or CNN and demand they print a retraction? There had to be something she could do. There had to be a way around this backlash.

Sarah felt some invisible force slowly pressing down on her. She couldn't define it, or even talk about it. Movement became increasingly difficult. Her lungs squeezed shut. It was impossible to cry out. And it was all happening so quickly. A few short months ago she thought she had all the answers. But suddenly all those activist teach-ins, the songwriting workshops, the mass actions—they all seemed insignificant next to this.

DESPITE THE TEARGAS AND THE STORM-TROOPER GOON SQUADS, THE MASS ANTI-FTAA (FREE TRADE AREA OF THE AMERICAS) PROTEST AT THE SUMMIT OF THE AMERICAS IN QUÉBEC CITY THE PREVIOUS APRIL WAS THE MOST LIBERATING EXPERIENCE OF HER YOUNG EXISTENCE. SARAH WAS PART OF A LARGE AND GROWING "ANTI-CAPITALIST" MOVEMENT THAT WOULD SOMEHOW GIVE BIRTH TO A BETTER WORLD. MONTHS AFTER THE RAGTAG SIEGE OF THE 34 SOVEREIGNS HOLED-UP IN THEIR

FENCED-IN FORTRESS, THE RHYTHMS OF PROTEST DRUMS OVER THE THUNDERING POLICE HELICOPTERS WERE STILL IN HER EARS. HER SKIN STILL BURNED FROM TEARGAS, AND SHE COULD HEAR THE BOISTEROUS CHEERING FOR THE ANTI-CAPITALIST WAR ENGINE SUCCESSFULLY CATA-PULTING TEDDY BEAR PROJECTILES INTO THE CORPORATE STRONGHOLD. MOST OF ALL, SHE FELT THE COLLECTIVE POWER OF THE BARBARIAN HOARDS AS THEY BROKE THROUGH THE RANKS OF ARMOUR-CLAD KNIGHTS AND TORE DOWN THE "WALL OF SHAME" PROTECTING GEORGE BUSH AND HIS VASSALS.

HER AFFINITY GROUP, THE RAGING GRANDDAUGHTERS—THE YOUNG, ANARCHISTIC VERSION OF THE RAGING GRANNIES THAT SERENADED AC-TIVIST RALLIES ACROSS CANADA—HAD SENT HER TO THE QUÉBEC CITY CONSULTA WEEKS BEFORE THE SUMMIT. THERE, SHE PARTICIPATED IN DISCUSSION GROUPS AND PLANNING SESSIONS WITH MORE EXPERIENCED ACTIVISTS. SHE MET HASSAN AND OTHER MILITANTS FROM CONCORDIA, WHO INTRODUCED HER TO THE ANTI-OCCUPATION STRUGGLE FOR PAL-ESTINIAN HUMAN RIGHTS. IT SEEMED STRANGE TO GO TO QUÉBEC CITY TO MEET PEOPLE FROM A UNIVERSITY THAT WAS WITHIN WALKING DIS-TANCE FROM HER *CÉGEP*, DAWSON COLLEGE, AND TO MEET PALESTINIAN SOLIDARITY ACTIVISTS. BUT THAT'S HOW THINGS WERE CONNECTED. U.S.-SUPPORTED MILITARY CAMPAIGNS IN COLOMBIA, OR ISRAEL/PALESTINE, COULDN'T BE SEPARATED FROM ECONOMIC GLOBALIZATION. THE WHIRLWIND OF TEACH-INS, MEETINGS AND PROTESTS—ESPECIALLY THE 50,000-STRONG PROTEST IN QUÉBEC CITY—OVER THE PAST EIGHT MONTHS HAD OPENED HER EYES TO A WORLD OF GLOBAL POLITICS THAT SHE HAD ONLY GLIMPSED IN HER WORLD ISSUES CLASS AT DAWSON. IT ALSO SHOWED HER THAT IT WAS POSSIBLE TO ORGANIZE THINGS DIFFER-ENTLY, LIKE THE QUÉBEC CITY PROTEST ITSELF, WITH NO BUREAUCRATIC LEADERSHIP, BUT INSTEAD WITH DEMOCRATIC SELF-ORGANIZED AFFIN-ITY GROUPS WHICH SENT REPRESENTATIVES TO LARGER MASS MEETINGS, OR SPOKESCOUNCILS.

ORGANIZED YET SPONTANEOUS, POLITICIZED YET ANTI-DOGMATIC, A POWERFUL TIDE WAS SLOWLY SHIFTING LIFE ON *CÉGEP* AND UNIVER-SITY CAMPUSES ACROSS QUÉBEC. IT SEEPED THROUGH THE INTERNET, SPILLING INTO MASS MEETINGS AND TEACH-INS. THE NEW CURRENT WAS STILL BEING CALLED THE 'ANTI-GLOBALIZATION' MOVEMENT, BUT THE TERM DID NOT DO IT JUSTICE. IT WAS MORE THAN AGAINST GLOBALIZA-TION. IT WAS FOR A WORLD WHERE LIFE MATTERED—SOCIAL JUSTICE, DEMOCRACY, FREEDOM, CREATIVITY, HEALTH, ECOLOGY. THE NEW SO-CIAL FORCE WAS STILL EMBRYONIC, ITS FEATURES UNDEFINED. BUT ITS LIFE FORCE WAS PALPABLE TO SARAH AND HER FRIENDS.

THE RAGING GRANDDAUGHTERS WERE PART OF A RENAISSANCE OF FEMINIST THINKING AND PRACTICE. IN THE COURSE OF THEIR ACTIVIST

ADVENTURES, SARAH AND HER FRIENDS MET WOMEN WHO TALKED ABOUT HOW FEMINISM WAS CENTRAL TO THE STRUGGLE FOR HUMAN LIBERATION. ONE OF THOSE WOMEN WOULD HAVE A DECISIVE IMPACT ON SARAH'S ACADEMIC FUTURE: LILLIAN ROBINSON. SARAH MET ROBINSON AT A TEACH-IN ON THE FTAA HELD AT CONCORDIA A COUPLE OF MONTHS BEFORE THE PROTEST. THE PRINCIPAL OF THE UNIVERSITY'S SIMONE DE BEAUVOIR INSTITUTE SHOWED THE FUTURE CONCORDIA STUDENT THAT HER STUDIES COULD GO HAND-IN-HAND WITH HER ACTIVIST WORK. THEORY AND PRACTICE WERE NOT OPPOSITES. THERE WAS EVEN A WORD TO DESCRIBE THE UNITY OF THE TWO: PRAXIS. SARAH WAS NOT ONLY STRUCK BY THE KNOWLEDGE OF WORKING CLASS AND FEMINIST HISTORY THAT ROBINSON DEMONSTRATED AT TEACH-INS AND CONFERENCES, BUT ALSO BY THE DEPTH OF HER PERSONAL COMMITMENT THAT LED HER TO TAKE DIFFICULT POLITICAL STANDS. THE OLD JEW FROM NEW YORK WAS ALSO A MILITANT AND INCREASINGLY VISIBLE SUPPORTER OF THE PALESTINIAN LIBERATION STRUGGLE. SHE WAS THE MAIN REASON SARAH DECIDED TO GO TO CONCORDIA TO DO A DEGREE IN WOMEN'S STUDIES. THE ANGRY REACTION THAT IT PROVOKED IN HER FATHER SIMPLY CONFIRMED FOR HER THAT SHE HAD MADE THE RIGHT CHOICE. HE WANTED HER TO GO TO McGILL. "YOU WENT TO CONCORDIA," SARAH THREW BACK AT HIM, "WHY CAN'T I?"

"I WENT TO SIR GEORGE WILLIAMS," HER FATHER CORRECTED HER. THE NAME "CONCORDIA" WAS CREATED IN 1974 WITH THE FUSION OF THE DOWNTOWN SIR GEORGE WILLIAMS UNIVERSITY AND THE JESUIT LOYOLA COLLEGE IN NDG. "AND I WENT THERE BECAUSE I HAD TO. YOU HAVE A CHOICE."

"AND I CHOOSE CONCORDIA. I DON'T CARE ABOUT McGILL'S REPUTATION. I'M NOT GOING TO UNIVERSITY TO MEET A NICE YOUNG DOCTOR HUSBAND. I WANT AN EDUCATION IN FEMINIST POLITICAL ECONOMY!" SHE KNEW HER FATHER DIDN'T HAVE THE SLIGHTEST IDEA WHAT FEMINIST POLITICAL ECONOMY WAS. IN FACT, SARAH WASN'T TOO SURE WHAT IT WAS HERSELF, BUT SHE KNEW SHE WANTED TO LEARN ABOUT IT.

JACK THOUGHT HE KNEW PRECISELY WHAT FEMINIST POLITICAL ECONOMY MEANT: WOMEN'S LIB. AND HE DIDN'T LIKE IT. WHERE DID SARAH GET IT FROM? SHIRLEY WASN'T ONE OF THOSE WOMEN'S LIBBERS. IT MUST HAVE BEEN THE TEACHERS AT DAWSON COLLEGE. ANYWAY, SHE WOULD OUTGROW IT. WOMEN'S LIB WAS *PASSÉ*. BUT WHY DID SHE HAVE TO SABOTAGE HER CHANCES BY GOING TO CONCORDIA? McGILL WAS A BETTER SCHOOL. EVERYBODY KNEW THAT. HE WOULD HAVE GONE TO McGILL IF HE COULD HAVE. JACK JUST WANTED HIS DAUGHTER TO TAKE ADVANTAGE OF THE CHANCE HE NEVER HAD: A CHANCE OF A LIFETIME. RICH PARENTS FROM THE STATES SENT THEIR KIDS TO McGILL FOR MEDICAL SCHOOL. IT WASN'T JUST ABOUT MEETING A GOOD HUSBAND,

BUT REALISTICALLY, WHAT KIND OF A HUSBAND WOULD SHE MEET IN WOMEN'S STUDIES? THEN FOR A BRIEF INSTANT JACK CONSIDERED THE POSSIBILITY THAT HIS DAUGHTER MIGHT BE A LESBIAN. HE PUT THE IDEA OUT OF HIS MIND AS SOON AS IT APPEARED. NO, SHE WAS JUST NAÏVE, NOT DEVIANT.

SARAH'S FATHER WAS A NUISANCE, BUT HE COULDN'T STOP HER FROM THROWING HERSELF INTO THE DYNAMIC CRUCIBLE OF SOCIAL MOVEMENTS THAT WAS CONCORDIA UNIVERSITY.

But now, as of September 11, Sarah was up against something far more formidable than Jack Murphy. The shadow caught her from behind, slowly suffocating her, leaving her immobilized and aching with fear—the backlash. It was a force much bigger and more powerful than that name, but it would have to do.

"You can't just make people understand," said Hassan shaking his head and throwing up his hands. His Arab accent became more evident when he was upset. Does she think I want to allow the backlash to wipe out the massacres of more than 2000 living human beings from the slate of history? Then he reminded himself what a kid Sarah was. How could she know any better? Sometimes she seemed so much older. The kid was a born leader—forceful and articulate, commanding respect, dominating every political meeting. But she was only 19, just a bit older than his own daughter.

He took a deep breath, then laid out all the facts like the pieces of a chess game. "Okay," he conceded, "it looks bad. How can we accept that the Sabra and Shatila memorial can't happen out of respect for the today's victims? Why should respect for one set of massacred victims demand the denial of respect for another?"

Sarah nodded, and started to respond, "That's just it, you can't..."

Hassan cut her off, "But you've got to understand how hard it was even to get people living next door to the massacres to admit they happened, and then it took even longer to get people to admit that Israel was responsible for them. And they still don't understand the US role in the whole thing. Right now the historical conditions are making it impossible to 'make' people understand this. You can't fight history."

HASSAN STILL REMEMBERED HIS YOUTHFUL IDEALISM BACK IN 1982 WHEN THE MASSACRES HAPPENED. HASSAN AND THAT YESH GVUL-INSPIRED MORTY DINGLEMAN WERE CONVINCED THEY COULD MAKE A DIFFERENCE. AS THE MOST ACTIVE (SOME SAID OBSESSED) PART OF THE QUÉBEC-PALESTINE SOLIDARITY COMMITTEE, THE PAIR WAS FOREVER PORING OVER DOCUMENTS AND CORRESPONDING WITH ACTIVISTS IN ISRAEL AND PALESTINE—HASSAN IN ARABIC AND FRENCH AND MORTY IN ENGLISH AND HEBREW. FOR MONTHS AFTER THE MASSACRES, THEY WORKED FEVERISHLY TO COLLECT THE NECESSARY DOCUMENTS, EYEWIT-NESS TESTIMONY AND FORENSIC EVIDENCE, AS IF THEY WERE RUNNING THEIR VERY OWN INDEPENDENT INQUIRY HERE IN CANADA. AND THE MOHAMED-DINGLEMAN REPORT WAS ONLY A FOOTHILL AMONG THE MOUNTAINS OF OFFICIAL INQUIRIES AND INVESTIGATIVE JOURNALIST REPORTS PRODUCED WORLDWIDE. AT FIRST THE ISRAELI DEFENSE FORCE (IDF) HAD DENIED KNOWING ANYTHING ABOUT THE MASS MURDER BE-ING CARRIED OUT DAY AND NIGHT BY THEIR LEBANESE PHALANGIST ALLIES RUNNING THE DETENTION CAMPS. THE IDF TROOPS STATIONED LESS THAN 100 YARDS AWAY, JUST OUTSIDE THE CAMPS, APPARENTLY DID NOT NOTICE THE CONSTANT GUNFIRE OR THE TRUCKS PILED WITH DEAD BODIES LEAVING THE CAMPS FOR THE TWO-DAY PERIOD. BUT EVENTUALLY, THROUGH PUBLIC PRESSURE, INCLUDING MASS PROTESTS BY ISRAELI ACTIVISTS IN THE STATE OF ISRAEL ITSELF, A PUBLIC INQUIRY WAS UNDERTAKEN BY THE ISRAELI GOVERNMENT—AN INQUIRY THAT CONDEMNED THE MINISTER OF DEFENSE, ARIEL SHARON. HASSAN EVEN READ ABOUT IT IN *THE GAZETTE*:

THE GAZETTE, Montreal, Wednesday, February 9, 1983

EDITORIALS

Ariel Sharon must go

One thing we can be sure about as a result of the special Israeli inquiry into the mas-saxrre at two Palestinian refugee camps in Lebanon last September: Defence Minister Arel Sharon must go. Whether Prime Minis-ter Menachem Begin leaves as well or de-cides to tough it out or call new elections should be known soon.

with a "certain degree of responsibility."

The conclusions contrast sharply with the government's early rejection of suggestions of responsibility as a "blood libel" to be re-jected "with contempt." Mr. Begin, who fi-nally appointed the commission under pressure, at the time indicated he would re-sign if senior offic

AND STILL, FOR THE 33 YEAR-OLD HASSAN, THAT EDITORIAL DIDN'T GO FAR ENOUGH. LIKE SARAH, HE DEMANDED THAT THE TRUTH COME OUT. THE NUMBERS CITED FROM THE OFFICIAL ISRAELI REPORT WERE WRONG. IT ONLY ACKNOWLEDGED 328 CONFIRMED DEAD AND 991 MISSING. INDEPENDENT REPORTS, USING PHALANGIST OFFICERS AND INTERNATIONAL RED CROSS AND RED CRESCENT SOURCES, PUT THE BODY COUNT WELL ABOVE THE 2000 MARK. BUT IT WASN'T THE NUMBERS THAT BOTHERED HASSAN THE MOST. WHAT BOTHERED HASSAN WAS THE WAY THE BLOODY MASSACRE OF MEN, WOMEN AND CHILDREN WAS TREATED AS AN ISOLATED CASE OF HUMAN RIGHTS ABUSE. NOBODY WAS LOOKING AT THE BIGGER PICTURE OF THE BRUTAL OCCUPATION SPAWNING THE MASS MURDER: AMERICAN-BUILT IDF-OPERATED TANKS AND JET FIGHTERS BLASTING AWAY AT A STATELESS POVERTY-STRICKEN PEOPLE.

HE PHONED EDITORS AND JOURNALISTS AT *THE GAZETTE* AND *LA PRESSE*. HE EVEN STARTED A LETTER-WRITING CAMPAIGN, DEMANDING THAT THE MEDIA TALK ABOUT U.S. RESPONSIBILITY IN THE AFFAIR. HASSAN WROTE THE FRENCH LETTERS AND MORTY WROTE THE ENGLISH ONES. IT TOOK SO MUCH OF HIS TIME HE SAW MORE OF MORTY THAN HE SAW OF HIS OWN INFANT DAUGHTER, HE WAS FAILING HIS COURSES, AND HE HAD TO DROP OUT OF UNIVERSITY. IT WAS ALL IN VAIN. THE MEDIA ACCEPTED THE OFFICIAL U.S. LINE. AT THE TIME, IT OUTRAGED HASSAN. BUT NOW HE REALISED THAT'S WHAT JOURNALISTS DO. THEY HAVE TO ACCEPT THE VERACITY OF OFFICIAL SOURCES.

AS MORTY SAID, "IF THEY DIDN'T HAVE CREDIBILITY, THEY WOULDN'T BE CALLED 'OFFICIAL SOURCES,' RIGHT? OR IS IT, IF THEY WEREN'T CALLED 'OFFICIAL SOURCES,' THEY WOULDN'T HAVE CREDIBILITY? THE CHICKEN OR THE EGG? SUCH A CONUNDRUM. JOURNALISM'S A TOUGH RACKET HASSAN."

THE U.S. ENVOY TO THE REGION, MORRIS DRAPER, DID IN FACT PROTEST TO ARIEL SHARON IN A PUBLIC STATEMENT:

> YOU MUST STOP THE MASSACRES. THEY ARE OBSCENE. I HAVE AN OFFICER IN THE [SHATILA] CAMP COUNTING THE BODIES. YOU OUGHT TO BE ASHAMED. THE SITUATION IS ROTTEN AND TERRIBLE. THEY ARE KILLING CHILDREN. YOU ARE IN ABSOLUTE CONTROL OF THE AREA AND THEREFORE HAVE RESPONSIBILITY FOR THAT AREA.

BUT WHY DID DRAPER MAKE THIS STATEMENT ON SEPTEMBER 18, TWO DAYS AFTER THE KILLING HAD BEGUN, AND AS IT WAS FINALLY WINDING DOWN? JUST TO ASK THE QUESTION WAS ENOUGH FOR JOURNALISTS TO CALL HASSAN A CONSPIRACY THEORIST.

And the 51-year-old Hassan knew that asking the question now would result in far worse insults.

The Gazette would soon be printing pictures of President Bush and Prime Minister Sharon, two respectable heads of state, smiling and shaking hands, warriors in the fight against terror. Backlash was a powerful thing. And, for the moment at least, it was too strong to fight.

"Sometimes," said Hassan with a carefully cultivated patience, "you have to take two steps backward before you can take one step forward."

* * *

Carla kneeled in the cool shadows of the church on that sunny and clear Tuesday morning as she had done every September 11 ever since she was eight years old. For a long time, she thought she did it for her mother. But her mother had been dead for two years now, yet she returned on her own. Carla was not religious, yet she came to the church and she prayed.

She thought of her mother, Margarita Rodriguez, when she lit the candle but she did not light it only for her. She lit the candle for all of the victims of terror, for all the dead. Carla considered her mother one of the victims because she died before her time. Breast cancer. That premature death must have had something to do with the terrible events they had lived through. She prayed such an awful thing would never happen again.

Her father, not a religious or a sentimental man, was always careful to make sure she had a clear understanding of the political contradictions that led to the September 11 attack. Carla's mother, on the other hand, reminded her of wounds it had left: the friends and relatives whom they had lost, and the terrible blow suffered by the whole country. Carla herself had only the vaguest of memories of those dark days. But she made the pilgrimage here to try to bring those painful memories back. And in front of the candle that her mother did not need to tell her to light, she felt her mother kneeling beside her, as it had always been.

She could still hear her mother whispering in her ear the names of those who fell, of their important contributions to their country, and how the violence of arrogant, jealous men could never erase them from the hearts of those who loved them. In fact, it was Carla who found herself whispering those names, looking very much like Margarita would have looked twenty years ago. Tears rolled from her dark almond-shaped eyes down her cheeks to be swallowed up by the sleek black hair coiling down to Margarita's cross around her neck. She was so absorbed in this communion that she did not notice the others filing in to light their own candles.

A woman a few years younger than her mother touched her hand. Carla thought she had seen this woman somewhere before, but she could not quite place those teary green eyes. "They are in a better place now dear," said the vaguely familiar mourner. Her voice quivered into an unconvincing smile. Carla had not seen that face recently. The woman was from a long time ago, maybe from her adolescence. Where had Carla seen her before and what was she doing in this church on a Tuesday afternoon?

How did this woman know Carla's suffering? And what had brought this crowd into the church? Many of them were weeping and consoling each other. Had she stumbled into a funeral ceremony?

"I'm sorry," Carla stammered. "I probably shouldn't be here." She got up off of her knees to stand.

"Oh of course you should," said the familiar stranger, putting her arm over Carla's shoulders and sitting her down on the pew. "At a time like this, people must come together in faith and hope."

"At a time like this?" asked Carla.

"Yes, I mean, with the bombing..." Now both of them were confused.

"But that was twenty-eight years ago," replied Carla weakly as she tried to shake the cobwebs from her mind. She touched her face and realized that her cheeks were wet with tears. The woman offered her a tissue.

"Twenty-eight years ago?" the woman slowly repeated, trying to bridge the gap between their two worlds of grief. "I don't know what happened twenty-eight years ago. I'm here because of what I saw about twenty minutes ago." Her tone became less steady and her tempo increased, the words spilling out her own anxieties, "The Twin Towers were hit by planes. Both of them collapsed. It's really terrible. When I saw the second one fall, I came straight here. I didn't know what else to do. I just couldn't watch the TV anymore. It's too horrible. It looks like thousands of people are probably dead. I don't know how anybody could survive that. My nephew is in New York and..." Her voice wavered and her lips trembled. More tears to dab after taking her arm from Carla's shoulders.

"The World Trade Center?" Carla was incredulous. How could anybody manage to inflict that kind of damage to such an important building in New York City? How many people did she say were killed? "That's terrible," said Carla. She put her arm around the woman's shoulder. "I'm sure your nephew is probably okay." But Carla was not focused on this woman's nephew. She was still unable to conceive the World Trade Center attack.

THE UNITED STATES WAS THE SUPERPOWER THAT BACKED THE MILITARY COUP IN CHILE ON SEPTEMBER 11, 1973. ON THAT DAY BOMBS RAINED DOWN ON THE PALACE OF LA MONEDA IN SANTIAGO WHERE THE DEMOCRATICALLY ELECTED PRESIDENT SALVADOR ALLENDE AND SOME OF HIS SOCIALIST ENTOURAGE HAD BARRICADED THEMSELVES, REFUSING TO SUBMIT TO THE VIOLENT USURPERS. THAT DAY, A NEW MONSTER EMERGED FROM THE SHADOWS OF CARLA'S CHILDHOOD: U.S.-BACKED GENERAL AUGUSTO PINOCHET. WITH CONTROL OVER TANKS, PLANES AND WARSHIPS, HE SEEMED OMNIPOTENT. HE WAS MADE EVEN SCARIER TO THE LITTLE GIRL BY THE DARK GLASSES HIDING HIS MYSTERIOUS INTENTIONS. WHAT MADE HIM ROUND UP THOUSANDS OF UNION LEADERS, LEFTWING STUDENTS, PROFESSORS, PEOPLE LIKE HER PARENTS WHO DISAGREED WITH THE NEW ORDER? THEY WERE ALL ARRESTED, HERDED LIKE CATTLE INTO DETENTION CENTRES. MANY WERE NEVER SEEN AGAIN.

WHEN CARLA GOT OLDER, SHE LEARNED WHAT HAPPENED TO THOSE WHO DISAPPEARED. HER FATHER THOUGHT IT IMPORTANT TO TELL HER THE TRUTH ABOUT THE TORTURE AND MURDER OF INNOCENT PEOPLE. HE WANTED CARLA TO UNDERSTAND THAT THE MEN DOING THE BLOODY WORK WERE PART OF A LARGER PROBLEM. MANY OF THE SOLDIERS UNDER PINOCHET'S COMMAND LEARNED THEIR VIOLENT TRADE IN THE U.S. MILITARY TRAINING FACILITY IN PANAMA CALLED THE SCHOOL OF THE AMERICAS.

AS CHILE FELL INTO THE HANDS OF THE U.S.-BACKED REGIME, CARLA FLED THE COUNTRY WITH HER MOTHER, FATHER, AND YOUNGER BROTHER. HER AUNT, AN ANTHROPOLOGY PROFESSOR, AND HER AUNT'S HUSBAND, A HISTORY PROFESSOR, DISAPPEARED SHORTLY AFTER. THEY WERE THOUGHT TO BE AMONG THE 12,000 PRISONERS HELD IN THE SOCCER STADIUM BETWEEN SEPTEMBER 11 AND NOVEMBER 7. HER GRANDFATHER WAS ALSO TAKEN THERE AND TORTURED. HE SURVIVED. HE NEVER SAW CARLA'S AUNT OR UNCLE BUT HE HAD HEARD THEY WERE IN THE STADIUM TOO. HE NEVER TALKED TO CARLA ABOUT WHAT HE LIVED THROUGH IN THE GALLOWS.

"You have family there too?" asked the woman sobbing in her arms.

"No," said Carla absentmindedly, "the family I lost was in Chile. That's what I meant when I said it happened 28 years ago."

The woman stopped sobbing, and she fixed those familiar eyes on Carla. "It's funny you know," she said with a furrowed brow. "You look just like the Chilean woman who ran the corner store down the street in NDG where we had our first house. What was her name?"

"Margarita," Carla spoke softly, offering the precious name of her dead mother.

"Yes, that's it," said the woman. "That was her name. And her husband..."

"Jesus," said Carla with a smile.

"Yes, that's right," laughed the woman, wiping away her tears. "Jesus. My daughter thought she was so cleaver when she'd say 'His name is Jesus, like Jesus Christ in the bible, but it's pronounced Hey-soose'."

The memory momentarily chased away the grief that brought Carla to the place of solace. She laughed, "Yeah, those were my parents."

"So you're..."

"Carla."

"Their teenage daughter? You're so grown up now. You look just like your mother! Such a beautiful woman... I'm Mrs. Murphy. Shirley."

Carla smiled back at the kindly Mrs. Murphy from down the street, back in the 1980s.

"And how are your parents? Do they still run the store?" asked Shirley.

"My dad does," answered Carla. "My mom..."

Shirley saw the tears forming again in Carla's eyes, and offered her another tissue. "Jesus and Margarita probably saved my life."

"How's that?" asked Carla.

"They refused to sell me cigarettes when I quit smoking. They told me my money was no good at their *dépanneur*. I'd have to walk ten more blocks to the grocery store. By the time I walked all that way, I would change my mind."

Laughter spilled out from Carla's tears. Mrs. Murphy was so sweet to cheer her up at a time like this. Carla could not allow herself the luxury of any more weeping. Mrs. Murphy's suffering was fresh. It took precedence over her own.

Carla felt no joy of revenge with the news of the World Trade Center attack. She was filled by empathic grief for Mrs. Murphy's nephew. In any event, Carla's father had always said what was needed was *justicia*, not revenge. The criminals responsible for the terror visited on Chile, whether in the Chilean military, in the CIA, or in the United States government, should be arrested and brought before an international court. Carla was convinced that justice could not be found by bombing innocent people in the country whose government had served as the terrorists' training ground. She wished the bombers could see the face of this worried aunt and all the people like her.

"Your nephew..."

"Brent."

"Brent," said Carla, promising herself to remember the name this time. "You can't jump to any conclusions. New York is a big city."

"I'm sure you're right," said the woman with a brave sniff. "Brent never mentioned anything about going anywhere near the World Trade Center. He's probably watching the whole thing on TV just like everybody else." She laughed nervously, clearly not convinced of her nephew's safety. "But it's so terrible not knowing for sure."

"You'll find out soon enough," said Carla reassuringly. She was more composed now. "He'll call you as soon as he gets a chance. Have faith."

CARLA REMEMBERED HOW HARD THE WAITING WAS FOR HER PARENTS. SHE DIDN'T UNDERSTAND THE TURMOIL THE COUNTRY WAS IN, BUT SHE KNEW HER FAMILY FACED TERRIBLE DANGERS. HER FATHER CAME HOME EARLY THAT SEPTEMBER II MORNING BEFORE HIS SHIFT WAS OVER. HE GRABBED HER OUT OF BED, STAINING HER PINK NIGHTGOWN WITH BLACK GREASE. HE LEFT WORK WITHOUT EVEN WASHING HIS HANDS. HE TOLD HER IN THE MOST REASSURING VOICE HE COULD MANAGE, "WE'RE GOING ON A LITTLE TRIP, TO CANADA." THE NEXT THING SHE KNEW SHE WAS IN A CAR, THEN IN A CHAOTIC AIRPORT, THEN IN ANOTHER AIRPORT WHERE NOBODY SPOKE SPANISH.

THOUSANDS OF PEOPLE DISAPPEARED AFTER SEPTEMBER II. MANY OF THEM WERE NEVER SEEN AGAIN. HER FATHER WAS A SHOP STEWARD IN HIS UNION, SO A LOT OF HIS COLLEAGUES WENT MISSING. SOME, LIKE HIM, HAD GONE UNDERGROUND AND FLED THE COUNTRY. OTHERS WERE NOT SO LUCKY. CARLA REPEATED THE EXACT STORY HER MOTHER TOLD TO MRS. MURPHY. "HAVE FAITH," HER MOTHER WOULD SAY. CARLA REMEMBERED TRYING TO HAVE FAITH, PRAYING TO GOD WITH

HER MOTHER, BUT THE DAYS OF WAITING TURNED INTO WEEKS, THEN MONTHS. EVENTUALLY THEY HEARD ABOUT SOME FRIENDS AND FAMILY WHO HAD RESURFACED OUTSIDE THE COUNTRY, OR ABOUT PEOPLE WHO HAD BEEN RELEASED, BUT AS THE MONTHS TURNED INTO YEARS THEY GRADUALLY GAVE UP HOPE FOR THE OTHERS.

IT WAS HARD FOR CARLA'S MOTHER TO ADMIT THAT HER SISTER ROSITA, AND HER SISTER'S HUSBAND OSCAR, WERE GONE FOR GOOD. THERE WERE NO BODIES. THERE WAS NO DEFINITIVE PROOF. MARGARITA COULD NOT IMAGINE THAT SHE WOULD NEVER HEAR THEIR VOICES AGAIN.

CARLA REMEMBERED PLAYING HIDE-AND-SEEK WITH HER AUNT AND UNCLE, WHO DID NOT HAVE ANY CHILDREN OF THEIR OWN. THERE WERE LOTS OF GOOD PLACES TO HIDE IN THEIR HOUSE. MANY CLOSETS, A WARDROBE, THE CELLAR. THERE WAS ALSO A BOOKCASE THAT CARLA COULD FIT BEHIND BUT THE ADULTS COULDN'T. THAT WAS HER FAVORITE HIDING PLACE. SOMETIMES SHE WOULD TAKE ONE OF HER AUNT'S ANTHROPOLOGY BOOKS FROM THE LARGE COLLECTION, AND SHE WOULD SIT BEHIND THE BOOKCASE, LOOKING AT PHOTOS OF THE CANADIAN INUIT AND THINKING ABOUT LIVING IN AN IGLOO AND EATING SEAL BLUBBER. WHEN HER PARENTS TOLD HER SHE WOULD BE GOING TO CANADA, THAT'S WHAT SHE THOUGHT THEY WERE GOING TO DO. WHAT AN ADVENTURE! WHEN CARLA'S MOTHER TOLD HER THAT HER AUNT AND UNCLE MIGHT BE HIDING FROM PINOCHET'S MEN, SHE IMAGINED THEM CROUCHING IN THEIR WARDROBE, WAITING FOR THE SOLDIERS TO PASS. SHE DID HAVE FAITH THEN. SHE THOUGHT AUNT ROSITA AND UNCLE OSCAR WOULD COME OUT OF HIDING AND RUN TO SANCTUARY. HER MOTHER HAD AN IMPRESSIVE FAITH—NOT THE FAITH OF A LITTLE GIRL. SHE HELD OUT MUCH LONGER, WHICH MADE THEIR PASSING MUCH HARDER. SOON AFTER SHE FINALLY LET THEM GO, CAME THE DIAGNOSIS: BREAST CANCER.

Carla hoped Mrs. Murphy, now sobbing in her arms, would not meet the same fate as her mother. "Let's pray together," she suggested, "for Brent." It was what her mother would have done.

Shirley nodded. And they both knelt and prayed to a God neither was sure existed.

* * *

Jack whistled as he walked into his Sherbrooke Street office building. He was always cheerful in the morning—definitely a morning person. Sharply dressed, closely shaven, jacked up on coffee, he was always ready to motivate his subordinates and impress his superiors—a first-rate corporate soldier. But Jack hadn't always been that way.

In his university days Jack was more of a night owl, drinking and partying until dawn. Such antics were why his father called him a longhaired communist-hippie-draftdodger. He may have had longish hair back then—just above the shoulders—but he was not much of a hippie and he certainly wasn't a communist. He was a draft-dodger, but that was just because he didn't want to get killed. It had nothing to do with his politics. His irresponsible diversions got him kicked out of NYU and onto the draft list. Montréal looked like it could be a fun place to evade the draft, and it was, except for all the politics.

But now, thankfully, all those battles had died down. The *québécois* were not going on about American or English imperialism any more, feminism was back out of style (he wished somebody would tell his daughter), and the Black Power movement was a thing of the past. As was his enjoyment of the Montréal nightlife. Still, he liked his job. And he liked the morning view from his office window, especially while poring over the headlines with a fresh espresso. And of course there was the money, lots of money. He had a house in the ostentatiously wealthy municipality of Westmount with a swimming pool and all the amenities. Plus it was within walking distance from work. On a nice day like today he could leave his car in the garage.

But something was amiss on this beautiful Tuesday morning. He strode passed that nice young black security guard, Greg, and he did not hear "Good morning Mr. Murphy." He had always been politely greeted ever since Greg had started working here. That was what he liked about Greg: he was nice and polite, clean-cut in his pressed blue uniform. And now he let Jack pass as if he were not even there. There's respect for you!

Jack looked back towards the security desk as he pressed the elevator door button. He saw the back of Greg's brown shaved head. Greg was staring at a portable television screen on his desk and there was a wire running from the television to an ear-piece he was wearing. It looked like he was watching a news report on a fire. There was a building ablaze on the screen. Why would his attention be so captivated by a fire? Then he made out some of the letters on the bottom of the screen and he saw the words "World Trade Center." Oh my God.

"Ping," the elevator door opened. Transfixed, Jack did not even turn around. Unable to step onto the elevator, Jack was pulled towards the television set on Greg's desk. It seemed impossible that the Twin Towers could be burning like that. They were indestructible.

HE WAS GOING TO NYU IN THE SPRING OF 1968 WHEN THOSE UNMISTAKABLE SYMBOLS OF MODERN DAY NEW YORK CITY WERE UNDER CONSTRUCTION. HE REMEMBERED GAZING IN WONDER AT THOSE COLUMNS, SHIMMERING IN THE DAWN LIGHT AUGMENTED BY THE LSD COURSING THROUGH HIS VEINS. HE WAS ON THE ROOF OF HIS DEALER'S GREENWICH VILLAGE APARTMENT. HE LIKED TO HANG OUT WITH THE DEALERS MORE THAN THE HIPPIES. HE UNDERSTOOD WHAT THE DEALERS WERE ABOUT: MONEY AND PLEASURE. HIPPIES WERE TOO FULL OF ART AND PHILOSOPHY BULLSHIT. THEY WERE LIVING IN SOME KIND OF UTOPIAN DREAM. BUT JACK COULD SEE THE REALITY, AND WHILE THE LSD BROUGHT THE HIPPIES CLOSER TO THEIR HIPPIE UTOPIA, IT JUST BROUGHT JACK CLOSER TO REALITY. LSD PEELED AWAY ALL THE BULLSHIT AND LET HIM SEE WHAT WAS UNDER IT: THE ESSENTIAL, THE REAL, THE RATIONAL KERNEL OF THE MATERIAL WORLD. WHEN HE LOOKED AT THE TWIN TOWERS HE SAW THEIR REAL MEANING. THEY WERE MORE THAN TWO NEW COLUMNS IN THE NEW YORK SKYLINE. THE TOWERS WERE QUINTESSENTIALLY MODERN: REFLECTIVE METAL AND GLASS, PERFECTLY UNIFORM, ERECTED BY THE MOST ADVANCED ENGINEERING AND CONSTRUCTION TECHNIQUES, REFINED OF ALL MATERIAL IMPURITIES THAT CAN BE SEEN IN BRICK OR CONCRETE. THEY REPRESENTED THE DAWN OF A NEW ERA. AS HE WATCHED THE GIANT MACHINES BUILDING THE TOWERS EVER SKYWARD, AND THE GLITTERING SHOWER OF SPARKS SPOUTING FROM THE STEEL SKELETON OF THE UPPER FLOORS, HE WAS POSITIVE THE ERA OF THIS NEW ARCHITECTURE WAS AN EPOCH THAT WOULD BE MEASURED IN MILLENNIA.

And thirty years later, one of them was ablaze and spewing smoke. No wait, a camera shot from another angle showed that both of them were on fire! And then another shot, a plane crashing into one of the towers in slow motion and exploding.

"What the hell is going on?" asked the executive.

Greg jolted upright for a second, startled by what he perceived as someone sneaking up behind him. Greg turned around to see the concerned executive staring at the television he had been watching so intently. "Oh, good morning Mr. Murphy."

Ah, there it was, his "Good morning Mr. Murphy." Jack found the words reassuring. The Twin Towers were burning, but in Montréal all was well. The black security guard at his office was still a nice and polite young man.

"Some terrorists hijacked two planes and crashed them into the Twin Towers," Greg explained. "The second one hit just a couple of minutes ago."

"Holy shit," was all that Jack could say. And he gaped at the television screen in disbelief. He watched the billows of smoke coming out of the tower on the screen. Since there was no sound of an announcer to tell him what to think, his mind wandered.

The image triggered a memory of black smoke billowing out windows of another edifice Jack had been looking up at over thirty years ago. The building he recalled was smaller, maybe 14 stories high. Unlike the image on the screen, his memory came with sound, "Let the niggers burn! Let the niggers burn!"

PEOPLE WERE CHANTING ON DE MAISONNEUVE BOULEVARD BELOW. JACK WASN'T CHANTING WITH THEM. HE WAS NOT MUCH OF A CHANTER, BUT HE WAS THINKING IT. HE WAS MAD AS HELL.

IT WAS 1969 AT SIR GEORGE WILLIAMS UNIVERSITY WHERE JACK WAS A STUDENT. HE WANTED TO GO TO McGILL. THERE WERE BETTER LOOKING GIRLS AT McGILL, BUT HE DIDN'T HAVE THE GRADES. SIR GEORGE WILLIAMS WAS WHERE A LOT OF CARIBBEAN STUDENTS AND UNDERACHIEVERS LIKE HIMSELF TOOK CLASSES. AND NOW A BUNCH OF THOSE CARIBBEAN STUDENTS, A BUNCH OF "NIGGERS"—HE NEVER CALLED THEM THAT, BUT HE THOUGHT IT—HAD TAKEN OVER THE COMPUTER CENTRE ON THE NINTH FLOOR OF THE MAIN BUILDING. THEIR RACISM CHARGES AGAINST THE UNIVERSITY FACULTY WERE DRAGGING SIR GEORGE'S ALREADY TARNISHED REPUTATION THROUGH THE MUD.

FOR THE PAST FEW WEEKS, THEIR STORY WAS ON THE RADIO AND THE TELEVISION AND IN ALL THE PAPERS. IT WAS ALL STUDENTS WERE TALKING ABOUT. BIOLOGY PROFESSOR PERRY ANDERSON HAD BEEN ACCUSED OF RACIST GRADING PRACTICES, BUT CARIBBEAN STUDENTS COULDN'T MAKE THE CHARGES STICK. UNABLE TO ACCEPT THAT BLACK STUDENTS MIGHT JUST BE MORE STUPID (WHAT KIND OF AN EDUCATION SYSTEM DID THEY HAVE DOWN THERE IN THE CARIBBEAN ANYWAY?), THE BLACK POWER RADICALS WALKED OUT OF THE SPECIAL HEARING SET UP JUST FOR THEM IN THE HALL BUILDING AUDITORIUM. THEY IMMEDIATELY WENT UP TO THE NINTH FLOOR TO OCCUPY THE COMPUTER CENTRE.

FOR TWO WEEKS THEY HAD BEEN HOLED UP IN THERE, AND HE HEARD THAT THE UNIVERSITY HAD EVEN WORKED OUT SOME KIND OF A DEAL WITH THEM, AGREEING TO THEIR DEMANDS. BUT THAT WASN'T GOOD ENOUGH FOR THE RADICALS. THEY THREW COMPUTER PROGRAMS OUT THE WINDOW. PROGRAMS WERE ON PUNCH CARDS IN THOSE DAYS, SO THE RAIN OF CARDS HAD LITTERED THE STREET BELOW. THEY REPRESENTED THOUSANDS OF HOURS OF PROGRAMMING WORK. THE BOULEVARD WAS WHITE WITH THEM. AND NOW THEY WERE BURN-ING THEM ON THE NINTH FLOOR. AS CLOUDS OF SMOKE POURED OUT OF THE WINDOWS, IT BECAME CLEAR THAT THE FIRE MUST HAVE GOT-TEN OUT OF CONTROL. WELL, IT SERVES THEM RIGHT, THE NIGGERS! THEY WERE RUINING SIR GEORGE'S REPUTATION. LET THEM BURN. FIRE TRUCKS HAD COME, EXTENDING THEIR LADDERS AND HOSES TO DOUSE THE FLAMES, BUT A LOT OF GOOD WHITE STUDENTS BELOW WHO JUST WANTED TO GET AN EDUCATION, AND DIDN'T WANT ALL THAT POLITICAL CRAP, WERE FED UP. "LET THE NIGGERS BURN! LET THE NIGGERS BURN!" THEY WERE CHANTING.

"Do you want sound, Mr. Murphy?" asked Greg.

Now there was a nice young black man. Why weren't the Caribbean students at Sir George Williams nice and polite like him? That whole mess could have been avoided if they had been more like this Greg. "Yes Greg, would you turn on the sound please. Let's see what mess those terrorists are causing now. Have they said who did it? Was it the Arabs?" If it was a suicide attack, it had to be the Arabs.

"No, Mr. Murphy," replied the security guard in a hol-low voice. "Nobody knows who's responsible at this time." Greg Phillip consciously ignored the racist motives behind the question. His first thought of who the bombers might be was coloured by the recent events of the Unabomber attacks and the Oklahoma City bombing. Both of those white guys faced the death penalty for their actions, even if the Unabomber got off with life. A black man would have gotten the chair for sure. The attackers were suicidal. But Greg said nothing more to Mr. Murphy. In his experience, initiating arguments about racism was a way to get into trouble. That's what happened to his mother back in 1969 when she took part in the computer centre occupation at Sir George. Greg was not born yet, but he had heard all the stories. Many times. His mother insisted on telling them over and over.

BETTY PHILLIP WAS WORKING AS A NANNY IN WESTMOUNT AND TAKING COURSES AT SIR GEORGE ON THURSDAYS—HER ONE DAY OFF. SHE WAS ABOUT HALF WAY THROUGH A BACHELOR'S DEGREE IN ENGLISH LITERATURE WHEN ALL THE TROUBLE STARTED. THE WHOLE THING ENDED UP COSTING HER A DEGREE AND ALMOST GOT HER DEPORTED BACK TO JAMAICA. SURE, THE PROFESSOR WAS RACIST AND CARIBBEAN STUDENTS WERE OPPRESSED, BUT WHAT DID ALL THEIR POLITICAL BRAVADO AND ACTIVISM ACCOMPLISH?

SHE WAS LUCKY TO FIND ANOTHER JOB WAITING ON TABLES IN A ROSEMONT DINER. IT WAS HARD ENOUGH FOR A BLACK WOMAN TO FIND ANY JOB IN MONTRÉAL, LET ALONE A BLACK WOMAN FIRED FROM HER LAST JOB FOR SUCH A SCANDALOUS REASON. AND FINDING AN APART-MENT WAS ALSO TOUGH. SHE WAS TOLD RIGHT TO HER FACE ON MORE THAN ONE OCCASION, "I DON'T RENT TO NIGGERS." SHE ENDED UP IN SOME KIND OF HIPPIE COMMUNE HOUSE WITH SOME OTHER ARRESTEES. OF COURSE, MOST OF THE OTHER ARRESTED STUDENTS, MANY OF WHOM WERE WHITE, COULD TURN TO PARENTS FOR SUPPORT SO THEY DIDN'T NEED TO TAKE THAT KIND OF A JOB AND THEY ALREADY HAD APART-MENTS TO GO HOME TO.

BUT THAT'S ALL HIS MOTHER GOT: A JOB IN A DINER, SAVING TIPS TO FINISH HER DEGREE. IN 1971, AFTER THE ORDEAL OF A TWO-YEAR TRIAL, THE NANNY TURNED PROTESTOR GOT OFF WITH A $1000 FINE. ALL SHE HAD TO DO WAS SIGN A STATEMENT SAYING THAT SHE WAS TAKING PART IN A PROTEST AGAINST RACISM WHICH SHE THOUGHT WAS LEGAL, WHICH WAS TRUE ENOUGH ANYWAY. BUT PAYING THAT FINE ATE UP ALL HER SAVINGS.

THEN SHE GOT PREGNANT WITH GREG. HE WAS NOT IN HER PLANS EITHER. HE NEVER KNEW WHO HIS FATHER WAS, BUT HE HAD A SUSPICION

THAT IT WAS SOMEBODY HIS MOTHER NEVER REALLY LIKED. SHE NEVER TALKED ABOUT HIM.

WITH ALL THAT HARDSHIP, YOU WOULD THINK SHE WOULD HAVE RE-GRETTED HER ACTIONS. YET SHE TALKED ABOUT THE BLACK LIBERATION STRUGGLE WITH GREAT PRIDE AND AT GREAT LENGTH. GREG NEVER REALLY GOT THE MESSAGE. THE PAIN ETCHED ON HER WEARY FACE SPOKE LOUDER THAN HER WORDS—THE BAGS UNDER HER EYES FROM LONG HOURS OF WORK, AND THE WAY SHE WINCED WHEN SHE STOOD UP WITH HER HAND ON HER LOWER BACK. SHE WOULD COME HOME IN HER PINK WAITRESS UNIFORM AFTER DARKNESS HAD FALLEN, HOURS AFTER GREG HAD RETURNED FROM SCHOOL. AND EACH DAY, THERE WAS A LITTLE MORE PAIN ETCHED ONTO THAT BEAUTIFUL BLACK FACE. SHE WORE HER PAIN WITH THE SAME PRIDE AN OLD SOLDIER WEARS HIS BATTLE SCARS, AND SHE TOLD HER WAR STORIES TO ANYONE WHO WOULD LISTEN. THAT WAS NOT THE KIND OF OLD AGE GREG WANTED TO LOOK FORWARD TO.

THAT WAS WHY GREG WENT OUT OF HIS WAY TO ACCOMMODATE HIS BOSSES. HE DIDN'T WANT TO ROCK THE BOAT LIKE HIS MOTHER DID. LOOK WHERE IT GOT HER.

So Greg did not say anything for the rest of the time he and Mr. Murphy watched the Towers burning, President Bush talking to reporters in Florida, the Pentagon getting hit by another plane, the first tower falling, the smoke and the debris. Mr. Murphy was muttering something about the fall of Western civilization and lax border security and how this would be a wakeup call for the sleeping giant. The lamb would become the lion. America would rise from the ashes and would lead a crusade against this evil. It was Pearl Harbor all over again. Greg tried hard not to listen. He just wished Mr. Murphy would leave him alone and watch it in his own office upstairs.

But then, as people were walking by the security guard's desk on their way to lunch, out of nowhere Mr. Murphy exclaimed, "I knew it was the Arabs, I knew it! Didn't I say it was the Arabs earlier?" He was clearly pleased with himself as he clapped his hands together and pointed to the screen, as if he were watching a baseball game and his favourite player just tagged the runner stealing second. People turned to look.

Greg simply smiled faintly and nodded. He felt like getting up and glaring down at Mr. Murphy. Greg was about six foot six and well-built, so he would have towered over the executive. He resisted the urge to smack Mr. Murphy across the face and tell him this wasn't a game of pin the blame on the minority. But Greg grit his teeth and said nothing. There was no sense in arguing.

On the screen were Arabs, Palestinians to be precise (not that it made any difference to viewers like Jack) who were celebrating in the streets of the West Bank at the news of the World Trade Center attack. And the announcers were talking about Osama bin Laden and how he had tried to bomb the World Trade Center back in 1993. It was still too early to say who was behind the attacks today, but there was speculation. Jack didn't need to speculate any further. He knew who was responsible.

"This whole suicide bombing thing is part of their cultural tradition," Jack said in his authoritative news-anchor voice.

Greg stirred in his chair. Mr. Murphy had stepped over a line. It was the line that had been hardwired into Greg's brain by his mother without him even realizing it. His mother's solid stance was stiffening his own spine, and he was determined to speak his mind. Greg knew it would be a mistake. He could already see the want ads and the rejection letters on his kitchen table, all the difficulties confronting a young black man looking for a job in Montréal. His mother's legacy repeated. Nothing could stop his visceral reaction—an instinctive, emotional and empathic defense of human dignity that was the basis of every revolt the oppressed had made against their oppressors from the beginning of history. Clearing his throat, he stumbled over the first words, "Mr. Murphy, I don't think... I mean Arab culture is not..."

Jack's cell phone rang. Saved by the bell.

"Hello... Oh, hi honey. Yes I saw... Yes it's horrible... Brent? Is he in New York?"

Shirley had always kept track of the comings and goings of all their nieces and nephews. She sent them Christmas cards every year and called them on most important holidays. She was good at that kind of thing. Jack couldn't be bothered. He was too busy making the money they needed to maintain their lifestyle, and besides, he only saw most of their relatives once every two to three years or so. Until his father died in 1988, it was very difficult to see his family at all because the patriarch refused to be in the same room with the draft-dodger. Jack never got back into the habit of seeing his family after that. Brent was Jack's sister's son, but Shirley knew more about him than he did. She knew he was working at a video store in Manhattan and trying to get some kind of funding for an independent film he wanted to produce.

"He's so talented," said Shirley, her voice was shaking. "It would be such a shame if..."

"Oh, don't worry honey," Jack reassured her. He heard the emotion welling within her. "New York's a big city."

"I know, Jack. But what if he had some kind of business in the financial district? You know he's looking for funding..."

He hated when she got like this. She was simply incapable of listening to reason—such a worrywart. She was always anticipating the worst case scenario. When the mad-cow scare first hit the UK, she wouldn't cook him steak for months. When the millennium bug was supposed to make all the computers crash on New Year's Day 2000, she had weeks' worth of canned food, candles and bottled water stocked in their basement. What was she going to do this time? "Why don't you try calling him?" asked Jack. At least that would keep her busy for a while, and maybe she would talk to Brent and everything would be fine.

"I've been trying to get him all morning. I left messages on his machine but he's not home!"

Should have thought of that one. Of course she would have called Brent. That's the first thing she would have done. "He's probably at work, dear. Really, you shouldn't worry so much." But as the words were coming out of his mouth, the second tower was falling on the screen before his eyes. Should he try to prepare her for this, or was it better to leave her to find out on her own so that he wouldn't have to deal with her irrational panic?

"Ohh, ohh, oh my God. Did you see that Jack?!" she shrieked.

He hadn't considered that she was watching the whole thing on television too. "I didn't know you had a TV at your work," said Jack feigning interest. Changing the subject was a long shot but it might work. Jack really didn't know that there was a TV at his wife's workplace. In the ten years she had been working there, he had never visited. He thought of it as a hobby. It wasn't real work. It was in a youth centre in NDG. The job paid less than a tenth of Jack's salary. But she said it was for a good cause. It was like charity. That's what Jack told his business friends. His wife worked for charity, to help poor kids in NDG. It sounded good.

"Jack. The other tower fell! There were still people in there! Oh my God!" She was hysterical.

Greg watched as Mr. Murphy winced the phone away from his ear. Even with the TV on, he could hear Mrs. Murphy shrieking on the cell phone. He had forgotten what he was going to tell Mr. Murphy, and was now thinking about the poor woman on the phone who had the misfortune of being married to this asshole.

"Pull yourself together Shirley," said Jack. "This is what the terrorists want you to do. They want you to panic. Don't let those Arab bastards win. Stay strong. Stay in control of yourself."

Greg remembered what he was going to say.

"Oh Jack," said his wife in exasperation. She was starting to calm down. "You just don't understand. I don't care about the hijackers. I care about Brent, and the others like him. Look at this destruction Jack. Look at it. It's... it's like in the bible. You know, Armageddon. I think... I'm going to go to church."

"You're going to church?" Jack said in a mocking tone. He was sure Shirley had not been to church since Sarah was baptized.

"Yes Jack. I'm going to church. I just don't know what else to do."

"Um, okay," said Jack hesitantly. He was confused but happy to get her off his back. "Say a prayer for me while you're there."

"I'll be praying for Brent," she sighed. "And for the others... Goodbye Jack."

MONDAY, SEPTEMBER 24, 2001

*"The most potent weapon in the hands of the oppressor
is the mind of the oppressed."*
— STEPHEN BIKO, 1971

AS USUAL, GREG WAS PREPARED at their regular back corner table, the top of his shaved brown head aimed toward Hassan as he walked in. The giant was gazing down at the game pieces carefully laid out in front of him, a steaming bowl of *café au lait* at his side. The old cabby admired the young guard's tenacity. It must have been fifty games straight that Greg had lost, but he kept persevering. Every Monday evening in the smoky dimly lit Café Stratagème, from 6:00 to 7:00 p.m., he subjected himself to the punishment of Hassan's superior strategic knowledge.

The first day he lost four games in one hour. That was the novice's first lesson: how to avoid the scholars mate—a four-move manoeuvre with the queen and bishop, used handily by Hassan to trap Greg's immobile king in the opening game.

Even after that, it took a long time before Greg could manage to last more than seven or eight moves into the middle game. Hassan's years of experience, all the chess literature he had digested, and his natural knack for the game, gave him a seemingly insurmountable advantage.

But Greg read all the books that Hassan had generously lent him, and he played other opponents who were regulars at Stratagème—an old stone-walled cellar. The smoke hung in the air as it must have done in the days before central heating was installed and the fireplace was the only source of warmth. The yellow pages of the books that lined the walls would never rid themselves of the nicotine odour they had absorbed over the years. Although Greg did not partake of that evil weed, the time spent breathing in second hand smoke as a regular at

Stratagème must have given him a better than average chance of developing lung cancer. After a couple of months, Greg had managed to beat some of the more worthy players who hung out in the old Ontario Street café. The games with Hassan grew longer, beyond their traditional one-hour limit. So Hassan and Greg noted the placement of the pieces on the board and the play would continue from the same point the following week.

This was the first game to last into a third week. Both the old master and the novice were intrigued.

"*Salut* Greg," Hassan greeted his protégé. Hassan, who spent a decade living in Paris before coming to Montréal, spoke French better than English and Arabic better than French, but he was comfortable in all three languages. Like many Montréalers, Greg and Hassan often switched back and forth between French and English mid-conversation—even mid-sentence.

Greg stopped looking down at the pieces and raised his head towards his teacher. Even though Greg was sitting down and Hassan was still standing, they were almost at equal height. There was a foot and a half difference between them when they were both upright. "It's your move old man," said Greg with a cocky smile as he gestured towards the empty chair facing him.

Hassan had never seen such presumptuousness from the lad. If Hassan were to win this game—and this time it really was a question of "if" not "when"—it would likely have something to do with the youngster's overconfidence.

In the opening game, on September 10, Hassan had an excellent start, managing to control the centre of the board and force Greg into trading his bishop for one of Hassan's knights. But Greg had developed a solid defense, castling at just the right time behind a row of protective pawns while his queen and remaining bishop hunted. Hassan had some opportunities to go on the attack, but he would always react one move too late, his concentration thrown off. And as the game progressed, the earlier trade started to work in the novice's favour. As the pieces became more dispersed, the range of the lost bishop was compensated for by the dexterity of the knight that the apprentice had kept in the trade.

Hassan sat down, took out a cigarette, and started tapping it as he surveyed the board. He didn't need to look, he remembered exactly where all the pieces were. He had even thought of a whole series of possible game scenarios nine or ten moves into the future. Still, he made a show of re-familiarising himself with the board. And shaking his head with disapproval for what he observed, he lit his cigarette. "How's your mother doing?" The middle-aged cabby felt a certain affinity with Betty. Greg's mother was a fellow immigrant in a dead-end job.

Although Hassan mastered the abstract strategies of chess, his real life was strewn with wreckage. He had bombed out at two universities, in Paris and Montréal respectively, and had started a restaurant that crashed along with his marriage in the mid-nineties (too much drinking with his female waiting staff and not enough attention to the books). So now he had taken refuge in a taxicab. He wished he had done something as heroic as Betty had done to deserve such a fate, but Hassan was not a hero. He was just irresponsible.

"She's okay. The doctor says she should have foot surgery to remove her bunions, but she says it's not that bad."

Greg didn't have to mention the real reason. When foot pain was "not that bad" for a waitress, Hassan knew that meant she couldn't afford to take the time off work for the corrective surgery. "She's a tough woman, your mother. That must be where you get it from. All that study is finally paying off, eh?" Hassan then gave his full attention to the board, absent-mindedly blowing his billows of smoke into Greg's face.

After about two minutes of concentration, Hassan moved his queen just as he had planned to do yesterday, forcing Greg to move his queenside rook to avoid a diagonal attack.

Greg shook off the comparison, "I'm not like her." He loved his mother dearly but Greg wished Hassan would stop seeing her in him. "I'm not political. I didn't get kicked out of Concordia. I dropped out. University is just too damn expensive right now." Greg had dropped out in the middle of his second year in 1996. Tuition had just doubled due to government cutbacks. There were a lot of student action committees organized across the province to fight the increases, but Greg didn't have time for politics. "What's the point in getting a university education anyway? It's not like employers are bending over backwards to hire guys like me." The security guard saw there was only one move for him—the rook—and he made it, moving it towards Hassan's side of the board. Could Hassan draw it out further, removing his opponent's queenside defensive capabilities?

"I don't know," admitted Hassan. "I don't think I'll get a job if I finally get my math degree. But I kind of like solving problems. And the university milieu, it's... stimulating. Don't you miss it a little?" Hassan wanted his protégé to get an education in something a little more promising than amateur chess. He would have to give Greg some bait to get him to bring his rook out. How about a bishop on Hassan's kingside?

"What's to miss?" asked Greg. "It's just a bunch of professors giving lectures that have no basis in reality, and a bunch of students taking notes and memorizing that bullshit because they know it'll be on the exam. Concordia says it's about "Real Education for the Real World." That's their slogan, right? But it's an ivory tower just like the rest of them. It's like McGill, only your degree is worth less."

"So all university is about is taking courses and studying?" Hassan asked. "What about all the debates and stuff? I mean, look at our society right now. In all the newspapers and television, all we see is war propaganda. My daughter was watching a program the other week. One of those entertainment programs, you know? On an American station. And it was all about how the fall of the World Trade Center had affected the personal lives of American Hollywood stars. There was some TV actress talking about how one of the assistants on her set had a husband who was in the World Trade Center. The way she cried for him, you'd think it was her own husband. She'd never even met the man. I guess those Hollywood stars have stronger emotions than us mere mortals. But anyway, that's what most people see. At least in the university there's more of a rational discussion about the issues. There's more freedom of speech. It's not perfect, but..."

"Freedom of speech, is that what my mother had? Is that why she went to jail for fighting racism?" Wasn't Hassan always complaining about how there was no freedom of speech for pro-Palestinians at Concordia? Hassan's bishop was ripe for the taking, and Greg's rook would be putting him into check at the same time. There must be a trick, though. Better look at all the possibilities.

"No. She didn't have freedom of speech. Just like Tom and Laith don't have freedom of speech today." Tom Keefer and Laith Marouf were elected student representatives active in Palestinian solidarity work. They had recently been expelled on some trumped-up charges of assault. There were eleven eyewitnesses who said they did not assault anybody, but the rector had refused to set up a hearing to consider their testimony. "Freedom of speech is an abstract principle, not reality. Still, Tom, Laith and your mother had more freedom of speech than they would've had outside the university setting. Imagine if Betty, an immigrant nanny, had confronted the racism of her boss the way she confronted the racism of the university. She wouldn't have lasted in Canada very long, I'll tell ya! The university is a place where young people can experiment with new ideas. People are generally more organized and thoughtful there than the rest of society. There are still consequences for challenging the status quo, but they're less severe within the university setting. That's why all kinds of new revolutionary ideas and movements have come out of that milieu."

Hassan had lived through some formidable political tempests incubated in the university environment like the successive waves of student movements in post-1968 France. Even the Montréal student anti-war movement of the 1991 Gulf War managed to fill the streets with an impressive tide of activists. But Greg had no personal experience of such things. He knew his mother's story, and it didn't seem too glorious to him. The rest was just history—it had nothing to do with the present context. "You're going to need some revolutionary new ideas to get out of this one, Hassan," Greg smiled broadly, suppressing a giggle, as he moved his rook kingside to take Hassan's bishop. "Check."

"Don't take anything for granted, Greg," the master advised his student. "Sometimes an opponent may appear weak, but he may have a strategic advantage you don't see. Sometimes things are not at all as they seem." He moved his second bishop between the rook and his own king. "The Sir George administration underestimated the black students at Concordia back in 1969. They thought that charging some of them with kidnapping and extortion, and sticking the RCMP on them would scare the rest from taking radical action. But students like your mother fought back. They put themselves at risk for the community as a whole, and they achieved a lot. There were a lot of little changes after the riots. Eventually they created the Ombuds office and the Office of Rights and Responsibilities to deal with student complaints and campus conflicts."

Was Hassan giving him a hint about this chess game, or was he just trying to shake Greg's confidence? Was he talking about the game at all, or was it all about Concordia politics? Since September 11, Hassan's play had deteriorated. He was distracted. The more Greg looked at the situation on the board, the more he became satisfied that he made the right move. Now Hassan's queen was immobilised because it had to protect his bishop. His bishop was immobilised because it had to protect his king. Kingside knight takes pawn. The next move will put Hassan into check again. "The Office of Rights and Responsibilities? Isn't that the outfit that refuses to give Tom and Laith a hearing because they weren't considered students? Like most students, they weren't registered over the summer when the assault was supposed to have happened. And since they weren't students they don't get a hearing. And by pure coincidence, they're also pro-Palestinian activists. Tell me, great wise man, how is the Office of Rights and Responsibilities supposed to be some kind of extraordinary advance in the struggle against racism at Concordia?"

"The Office has a lot of problems," Hassan admitted. "It mostly does what the Rector wants it to do because its head is appointed directly by him. But just the simple fact that the Office exists, and the fact that Rights and Responsibilities disciplinary hearing panels exist gives people the impression that there are supposed to be some kind of procedures followed before students are expelled. Tom and Laith are exploiting that. They're taking the university to court, they're doing press conferences, and so on. It may appear right now that the post-September 11 backlash is too strong for Palestinian solidarity activists to get a fair hearing, but the administration's going to regret expelling those boys, let me tell you. And their victory will be built on the past achievements of people like your mother. Oh, and that is checkmate."

Hassan's queen, the one that was supposedly immobilised by the necessity of protecting the bishop, had moved in on Greg's queenside, where his rook had been protecting earlier, trapping his king behind a row of pawns. The one spot where Greg could get out from behind that row was covered by Hassan's bishop—the piece that was supposedly immobilised by the need to protect its king from Greg's rook. He had underestimated the capabilities of Hassan's queen and bishop. And Hassan had all but spelled it out to him. He saw that now. "Well played old man." He shook his hand, as gracious in defeat as always. Greg had a lot of practice at that.

The waitress, a tall woman with black-framed horn-rimmed glasses, came to take Hassan's order. *"Pour le gagnant?"* she asked.

"Un allongé s'il vous plait," Hassan replied. *"Bientôt tu vas prendre la commande de Greg en posant cette question. Il s'est beaucoup amélioré."* He made an appreciative nod in Greg's direction.

"Yes he has ameliorated himself a lot," she said with a strong French accent as she patted Greg on his shoulder. "You never passed so much time in a game before."

Greg smiled sheepishly as he arranged the chess pieces on the board.

"I don't think we should start another game just yet," Hassan advised. He saw Sarah had just walked in the door and she was heading over to meet him as they had planned. "Greg, this is Sarah. Marie-Pierre, *je te présente Sarah.*" The waitress and the chess companion looked with interest at the pierced bandana-clad teenager. She was not one of his usual opponents.

As Greg twirled his fallen king on the board, he cast his gaze toward Sarah. Very few men could pull off a smile like Greg's, confident of his intrinsic worth as a human being even though he had been routed in a contest of strategy by another man.

"Do you want something?" asked the waitress.

"I'll take a glass of cold water please," Sarah said, slightly out of breath. "Dude, I just biked straight from the Emergency Coalition Against War Hysteria and Racism meeting. I'm pretty thirsty." Marie-Pierre looked at her with her head slightly askew before she walked away to fill their orders. Sarah was not at all typical of the clientele at Café Stratagème. She was the type of person one would find at Café Chaos about six blocks closer to the Université du Québec à Montréal.

"Just saying the name of that group is enough to make you thirsty," said Greg, his humble demeanor transforming itself into a mischievous smirk. "It's a mouthful."

"Yeah, well it's like an emergency coalition," Sarah explained, pulling a third seat up to their chess table. "We didn't have time to refine the name down to something more manageable. Anyway, I kind of like it. It's long, but it also covers all the bases. The name explains exactly why the group exists. We need an emergency coalition to react to the post-9/11 situation, which is like totally war hysteria and racism—the things we're against. Yo, Hassan, can I have one of your death sticks?" She was in the habit of calling cigarettes 'death sticks' ever since she realised the profound stupidity of her addiction to them. She hoped the cultivation of such a cynical attitude towards the substance would eventually give her the will to butt out entirely. The irony was that she started smoking to fit in with the protest counter-culture of Montréal—the same counter-culture that denounced corporations profiting from death. Somehow tobacco companies had escaped their critique.

Hassan obliged Sarah with a cigarette, as he had done countless times before. She hardly ever bought cigarettes herself. Still, she couldn't stop herself from smoking socially.

"How you doin' Hassan?" Sarah gave a meaningful look to her friend as she lit her cigarette.

Hassan understood she wanted to talk about their plans, but she felt uncomfortable with Greg's presence. And he knew she was right to be cautious. At this stage, the fewer people in the know the better. "I'm fine," he replied.

"How'd it go yesterday?" she asked.

"Fine. No problem."

Greg could see that they were speaking in shorthand, and that he was in their way. As he got up to go to the washroom, Sarah was taken aback by his towering figure. She didn't realise how big he was until he was upright.

"He would be great to have with us if there was any kind of a situation," Sarah whispered as she pointed to the giant retreating into the dark recesses of the café. He had to duck under the beams of the low ceiling.

"Forget it," Hassan advised. "He wouldn't want to get involved. And besides, he's a security guard, so he can't risk getting arrested."

Sarah nodded in agreement. She didn't trust security guards anyway. Still there was something about Greg—his almost overbearing, confident humility.

Hassan saw Sarah's eyes lingering. "He is single though..." chided Hassan with a playful nudge to Sarah's shoulder.

"But dude, he's a security guard," Sarah objected in an offended tone. Why couldn't he have any other job? she thought. Why not a janitor, a bartender or a garbage man? Why did somebody so damn charming and attractive have to be an armed thug for the ruling class?

"Hey," said Hassan, taking offense at Sarah's activist more-radical-than-thouism. "It's a job. He punches in, does his time, and punches out. Think I'd hang out with him if he were one of those wanna-be cops? Give me some credit!"

Just a job? Funny, she had never thought of it that way. She had never really met a security guard until today, unless you count the confrontation between protestors and guards outside the boarded-up bank in Québec City. The blue uniform and ramrod posture of the typical guard, even if he didn't always have a gun, seemed to make him a subspecies of the cop. She knew security guards enjoyed significantly lower pay, authority and social status than their more dangerous brethren in blue, but it never occurred to her that guards could simply be working stiffs punching the clock. She looked down shamefully and picked up a black castle from the chessboard, fiddling with it absentmindedly. "Sorry, I didn't mean-"

"I know you didn't," Hassan assured her. "But that's exactly the kind of attitude that will keep crazy activists like us [he wanted to say 'white activists like you' but thought better of it] isolated from the normal population at large. You can't expect everybody to be a flag-waving anarcho-communist. You don't know anything about Greg, so don't jump to conclusions. You know who his mother is? Betty Phillip. She was one of the occupiers in the 1969 computer riots."

The game piece dropped out of her hand and she looked wide-eyed at Hassan to make sure he was serious. How could the offspring from the vanguard in the black liberation struggle grow up to be a straight-laced man in blue? "Sorry, I..."

Hassan silenced her excuses simply by wrinkling his eyebrows well into his worn forehead and looking sternly into her eyes.

Sarah changed the subject, "So it went okay with my dad?"

"Yeah, I had to bite my tongue a few times not to get into an argument, but I got in." Hassan hesitated about telling Sarah what an ugly American her father was. She knew what he was like. She had even warned Hassan about him. But just the same, he felt that complaining to her about Jack's reactionary politics would be rubbing salt in her wounds.

"And it's a go?"

"Yep. Here are the plans." He handed her a couple sheets of crumpled folded papers from his jacket pocket. Sarah put them directly into her backpack without looking at them.

"It should be possible to get in the back way around closing time," Hassan explained. "You just need somebody to leave from the parking lot exit."

"Well, my dad was right about one thing," said Sarah with an ironic laugh.

"What's that?"

"He always said that one day I would be glad he has the job he does, working for the companies he does, and making the connections he does."

Her comment sent Hassan into suppressed laughter, hissing between his teeth for discretion's sake. "Yeah, I'm glad too. And all the families shredded by daisy-cutter anti-personnel bombs will be really happy. *Qui sera dans le coup?*"

"There are a few people in the Coalition Against War Hysteria and Racism and a couple of the more radical women from the Raging Granddaughters. I'm still working on the wording of our manifesto. Thanks for helping me with the research, although I had trouble making sense of some of your notes. My Arabic is pretty rusty."

"Oh," Hassan laughed. "I do that sometimes when I'm writing about the Middle East. Force of habit. I wrote a few words in Arabic off the cuff, but I translated everything."

"Dude, it's an awesome manifesto! Maybe that's what we should call it. The Awesome Manifesto. And we'll print out a few thousand copies at the student union office once everybody agrees with the statement." She loved using the word "manifesto." It made what they were doing sound so important—like they were changing the course of history. Finally she would relive that exhilarating sensation she had been infused with as part of the pulsating chanting, drumming tear-gas-doused mass in Québec City. She could still recall the feeling, tearing down the monstrosity of a fence surrounding the Summit of the Americas.

She inhaled the smoke deeply into her lungs, letting the nicotine rush mingle with her natural high.

Hassan did not like the manifesto idea at all, not as a manifesto anyway. It was a good didactic exercise for the two militants. It helped them hone their analysis and their rhetorical skills, but it would be of no use as a document for mass distribution. So while he discouraged Sarah from going forward with it right from the start, he couldn't help but participate in the reworking of some of Sarah's more simplistic and naïve formulations. It was part of her political education—and his. Despite her relative inexperience, there were still some things the teenager could teach her middle-aged comrade. But the manifesto would not teach the public at large much about anything. A press release would be much better—more practical, more accessible, and it would not make them look like a radical fringe group. Manifestos were all the rage at Université Paris VII back in the '70s, but very few of them were anything more than hot air and wasted energy. But he didn't have time to throw metaphorical cold water on her enthusiasm because Marie-Pierre had arrived with a glass of water, and a long espresso for Hassan.

As Sarah drank deeply, Greg came back and sat down.

"Ahhh," she said with satisfaction as she put the empty glass on the table. She looked directly across the table into Greg's eyes. Those eyes that had been humble and good-natured when he left had become dark and mysterious by the time he returned. "Greg, tell me about your mother..." She rested her head on her hand, prepared to listen to some war stories from a time when radical youth like Betty Phillip were on the offensive, challenging the establishment. Besieged as Sarah was by the war on terror backlash that had even taken hold of her own father, some '60s nostalgia was exactly what she needed.

Greg closed his eyes and opened them again slowly, checking his vision. He was taken by surprise both by her question itself and by the attention Sarah was suddenly showing him. When he had left the table he was a third wheel, getting in the way of a private conversation. Now he had become an object of marvel and wonder. Tell me about your mother, she had asked. He never would have guessed that such a question could be used as a pick-up line. It was what psychiatrists asked their patients. Yet, from Sarah's mouth, the question had been posed in a particularly engaging way. She was in search of a lustrous and beautiful treasure. Sarah had the mistaken impression that concealed somewhere within him was a fascinating anecdote that had to be coaxed out. Sarah's green eyes were looking at him from under those full dark eyebrows with such eager anticipation and admiration—admiration he knew was undeserved. He didn't want to disappoint her, but he was certain he would. She wanted to hear about a glorious fight against a racist and corrupt system, but all he could offer her was the story of a young woman full of promise and potential reduced to unhappy single parenthood, chronic pain and poverty. Greg turned to his chess partner with a pained look, "You told her about my mother?"

"Um..." Hassan glanced about him uncomfortably as if looking for somebody else to put the blame on. Not finding anybody, he took a sip of coffee, nervously examining his watch. "Oh, look at the time. I should get going," he lied. "Got a nightshift again."

"Oh," said Sarah with mock disappointment. "Too bad you boys can't continue with your war games. Looks like such fun."

"Chess is not a war game," Hassan protested, gulping down the rest of his espresso. "It's a game of skill and strategy. Its abstract rules have nothing to do with real war. Real war is a lot messier and unpredictable, and it's connected to politics, ideology. Any well-connected idiot can be a General, but very few of them could beat me in a game of chess."

"Dude, just teasing. See you soon. I'll send an e-mail about our meeting." With that she turned her full attention to the mysterious security guard sharing her table. She was determined not to let him out of her sight until he told her something about 1969.

* * *

Walking back from the *dépanneur* with the beer and cigarettes, Greg wondered how he had been conned into introducing Sarah to his mother. But deep down he knew he hadn't been conned at all. He wanted Sarah to meet the most important person in his life. Sarah was cute, and persistent, and persistently cute, but he could have said no. Greg didn't say no because he felt she just might be worth the gamble.

It was obvious Sarah wanted to meet Betty *qua* 1969 hero of black liberation. And if it were just a question of activist tourism, Greg would have never brought her. But Sarah's questions at Café Stratagème were as much about Greg—his childhood, his intellectual development, his life—as they were about Betty. And Sarah was so intensely engaged in their conversation that he had to conclude there was something more. It seemed Sarah genuinely believed that Greg's mother had an intrinsic worth beyond her role in history. He often disparaged his mother's political strategy, but never his mother. So he took a leap of faith, giving Sarah, the radical politico, all the ammo she needed to make his life hell.

Every time his mother met anybody politically active at Concordia, she would gossip for hours, offering all her old war stories and getting all the more recent dirt in return. With Hassan that was okay. He was just an old cabby Greg played chess with, but with Sarah it was different. Greg would have liked to know her a bit better before she became his mother's new best friend.

Within five minutes the two were cackling at the kitchen table over the latest university administrative fumbling of the Tom and Laith expulsions. Then his mother sent Greg to the store for beer and smokes. He knew that meant they would be gabbing until the wee hours. His first instinct was to find a pretext to break it up, but when he looked into his mother's eyes and saw that fire in them again, he smiled in spite of himself. She had little joy in her life. How could he rob her of this one harmless pleasure? Let her have her fun, Greg thought as he took the beer money from her purse. By the time he got back, Betty was telling Sarah the story of the occupation.

"Everybody knew Professor Anderson was racist," said Betty. "There was never a question about that. Oh, here's our alcohol. Open up a beer for your mother dear. He'd call white kids by their first names, 'Samuel, what did we talk about last week?' while blacks were systematically called by their family names, 'The mid-term exam will take place on March 5ᵗʰ Ms.

Grace.' In the Caribbean Student Association the word was *ste we from dat Anderson*," she repeated in its original Caribbean idiom. Then moving on, switching effortlessly back to Queen's English, "So when the committee looked like it was going to whitewash the whole thing, that was the straw that broke the camel's back."

Then she painted the historical background of the Anderson affair, first with broad strokes, then in intricate detail. That was how his mother brought willing explorers into her world. She started with the latest Concordia events and regressed ever backwards, painting larger and larger concentric circles. It wasn't just one racist professor. The issues behind the occupation were much deeper. They had to be understood at the institutional level. But racism at Sir George University couldn't be understood outside of the broader historical context. By the end of the night, she and Sarah would find themselves on the high seas of the African slave trade.

But first the racism at Sir George. As her son dutifully provided her with a basin of hot water and Epsom salts for her sore feet, she explained how Vice Principal John O'Brien had laid charges of kidnapping and extortion against three black students who had stood up to him in his office.

Ironically, the trio was charged because of an incident where they complained to Dr. O'Brien about his referring to a "risk of violence" against Professor Anderson where only peaceful tactics had been used. In that meeting Dr. O'Brien denied ever having written a letter mentioning violence. When the letter was produced from O'Brien's files, the students called him a liar and refused to leave without a written apology. He wrote an apology, but he later claimed it was written under duress and he laid the charges.

"Oh, I'm sure he felt threatened alright!" Betty laughed. "The poor man was probably not used to black students standing up for their rights. But kidnapping and extortion? Kidnapping and extortion? I mean, honestly."

"Dropping the charges against the three students was one of the occupation's demands," Betty explained. "But the occupation was about more than that. People were talking about racism, oppression, exploitation, imperialism and capitalism. It was about respect for black students and respect for human life. There were student revolts in Paris and many parts of Québec the previous May. The anti-war movement was creating a climate of confrontation on campuses all across the United States and Canada. The occupation was part of the spirit of the times. A spirit of liberation." Betty paused, swigging her beer. Then she added bluntly, "And it was about racism," poking Sarah in the shoulder with her bony finger, almost in an accusatory tone.

And as a resident of the white and ruling class neighbourhood of Westmount, Sarah couldn't help but look back at her host guiltily and speechlessly. Betty wore a knowing smirk as she looked back at her scandalized guest. The white guilt dynamic became even stronger when Betty told Sarah what her Westmount employer did to her after the occupation.

It was in the early hours of the morning that Betty finished spinning her yarn of the occupation, historical context and all. Only after that could she be coaxed into talking about the aftermath: the story of her arrest, and that of 96 other students.

At her arraignment she saw the pursed lips and angry eyes of Mrs. Whitmer, her boss's wife. In her pearls, mink coat and beehive hairdo, Mrs. Whitmer was obviously embarrassed to be sitting there with the parents of other arrested students. She even explained to many of the white parents, who looked an awful lot like her, and who probably wished they were not parents of the accused either, "I'm not a parent. I'm here because our nanny was arrested."

Mrs. Whitmer was allowed to see Betty briefly after she was denied bail at the arraignment.

"And all that woman said to me was 'Of course we can't keep you on after this. What would the neighbours say? You can come and pick up your things as soon as you get out of jail.' I lived with that woman for two years, taking care of her five-year-old son, day after day. And that's all she could say?" demanded Betty from across the kitchen table as the shell-shocked Sarah apologetically gulped her host's beer.

Most of the other students had lost their jobs after the occupation as well. They were, after all, as all the newspapers had reported, a bunch of communists who had caused two million dollars in damage to their university. Of course most of the student arrestees were white kids from middle class families and they could go to their parents for help. Not Betty. She, and eventually, her son, would have to live on her minimum wage job.

Obviously, that was difficult for Betty but she accepted her fate defiantly. For Greg, however, Sarah could tell it was a bitter pill to swallow.

When Greg was in the bathroom and Betty had a few beers in her, she admitted to Sarah in a hushed tone, "I don't blame him for being the way he is. It wasn't his idea for me to throw away my academic career like that. But I had to do it. It just had to be done. Eventually, he'll understand."

WEDNESDAY, SEPTEMBER 12, 2001

"I will never apologize for the United States. I don't care what the facts are."
— GEORGE BUSH SENIOR, COMMENTING ON THE ACCIDENTAL DOWNING
OF AN IRANIAN AIRLINER BY USS VINCENNES, A CRUISER STATIONED IN THE PERSIAN
GULF. 290 CIVILIAN PASSENGERS WERE KILLED, 7/3/88

SARAH BREATHED A SIGH OF RELIEF as her mother hung up the phone. "I'm so glad that Brent's okay," said Sarah as she put the salad on the table.

Shirley wiped her tears of joy as she bent to open the oven. "He could have called earlier. Didn't he realise we were worried sick?" The sweet odour of cumin-spiced squash filled the kitchen and spilled into the dining room where Jack sat looking over some files. "Dinner's ready!" announced the matriarch.

Sarah dimmed the lighting and put flame to the candles on the dining room table. Her father glanced up at the dimmed chandelier with annoyance as he tried to continue working in obscurity.

"Put that away Jack," his wife ordered. "If ever there was a time for a family dinner it's now."

"Just a minute," snapped Jack glancing in the general direction of the kitchen over his reading glasses. He was making a few post-it notes to remind himself what he was thinking about as he read the first reports on the financial outlook for American Airlines and United Airlines, the two carriers involved in the September 11 highjackings. Neither of those companies were his clients, but he was worried that their possible bankruptcy through lawsuits could also lower the altitude of the aerospace manufacturer he worked for. In the wake of the attacks, there was bound to be turbulence in the market, and he had to make sure his client's image was best suited to weather the shocks. To do that, they had to react quickly to the tempestuous market, more quickly than the competition.

"I won't have you working through dinner again tonight," she said adamantly, undeterred by the glacial expression on her husband's face. She was determined not to let his obsession with work spoil the good news. "The thing about these tragic times is that they make you realise what's important in life. What's more important to you Jack? The image of the corporations you work for or your family?"

"You go mom!" whooped Sarah. Her mother's newfound leftist outlook was a bright spot for Sarah in a sea of post-9/11 gloom. She had not reacted at all as Sarah had expected when smoke from the Twin Towers fire darkened other peoples' hearts. Usually Shirley let her husband decide what political opinions she ought to have, but for some reason she was not following his lead this time around. Her unwifely demeanor was all the more astonishing given that most of their Westmount friends and neighbours had suddenly become almost as hysterical about "the Arab and Muslim terrorist threat" as Jack. Shirley did not typically contradict popular wisdom, but now she was Sarah's first political ally in the richest, whitest and most anglo enclave of Montréal.

"Those corporations pay for the food on our table," Jack countered as he reluctantly closed the file he was examining and put it on the buffet behind him. He knew Shirley would not stand for him keeping the file on hand over dinner. There was plenty of room since the oak table could easily seat twelve, but it had to be free of "clutter" so they could eat in "serenity."

Shirley put the casserole dish on the table and started to fill their plates. "What good is the food your corporations pay for without a family to share it with?" she countered as she set the plate down in front of her husband.

"Vegetarian again?" Jack complained. "Just because our daughter is a granola-crunching hippie doesn't mean we all have to be. Why don't we have meat anymore?" Even after the mad cow scare had passed, Shirley never went back to cooking the quantities of meat Jack was used to. It bothered him, not enough to start making dinner himself, but enough to produce incessant complaints.

"It's a vegetarian loaf," Shirley explained. "Sarah gave me the recipe. It has squash and grains, and cumin..."

"Cumin?" Jack's question had an accusatory sound to it.

"Yes Jack, cumin. You like cumin."

"That's an Arab spice. Arabs use that spice."

Shirley looked at her husband with wide eyes, dumbfounded. Sarah's piercing glare was one of unmitigated anger. Jack's eyes sped nervously back and forth from wife to daughter as he realised that he had just stepped over their political correctness line. He would be in for a two-on-one debate. Okay, fine, bring it on. He was a PR expert. "Sure I like cumin," he explained. "But don't you think it's a bit profane to be eating Arab food the day after the terrorist attacks? Wouldn't it be more respectful to eat a good American meal like steak and potatoes?"

Blood was rushing to Sarah's red-hot face. She tried to speak but was only able to stutter, "Bu, fu, wha?" Shirley was going frigid white, completely speechless.

Finally, Sarah overcame her rage long enough to spit out a challenge to her father, "How the hell can you say that?! First of all, this isn't Arab food! It's a recipe from the People's Potato food collective at Concordia. Second, who cares, even if it was an Arab recipe! You can't blame an entire race for the attacks! That's so goddam racist. I can't believe you said that."

Jack's head jolted back from the verbal slap. He had rarely seen his daughter this hysterical, but then maybe that was because he had rarely seen his daughter at all for the past few years. He was too busy with work, and she was too busy with... well, whatever she was busy with. "Look dear, it's not that I think all Arabs are terrorists, but there's obviously something in the Arab culture that promotes suicide bombing as a solution to political problems. And maybe we shouldn't be celebrating that culture, especially now. And there's no reason to swear at me." Jack was speaking in a calm tone, that matter-of-fact journalistic fashion he taught his clients to use in their press conferences. He was convinced he would win Shirley over to his side if he appeared calm and rational while his daughter engaged in histrionics.

"There is too! You're being a fucking bigot!"

"Now how am I supposed to respond to that?" Jack shrugged his shoulders, appealing to his wife's sense of reason.

Shirley composed herself with a drink of water and a deep breath. She had no idea Jack was so, so, so... "I don't know how you're supposed to respond to that Jack. It seems to me Sarah's right. You are being an effing bigot," she said.

"But, I-"

"Do you know who I met in church yesterday? Remember the Rodriguezes who ran the *dépanneur* down the street from us in NDG? The Chilean family? I met their daughter, Carla. She told me about the friends and family they lost to terrorism. Only this terrorism was supported by the United States."

"The US doesn't support terrorism-"

"Let me finish!" Shirley interrupted him.

Sarah was looking on with as much admiration for her mother as with disgust for her father. An analysis of US terrorism? Who would have thought her mother had it in her?

Shirley continued, "You see, September 11th is the anniversary of another terrorist attack: a US-sponsored attack on the democratically elected government of Chile. Don't shake your head at me Jack! It was sponsored by the US. Look it up. It's been declassified. And Carla was praying, just like her mother prayed before her, for the victims of that attack. She lost an aunt and an uncle. Her family became refugees and fled to Canada. But she doesn't say, 'oh, I can't eat American food because Americans are terrorists.' Listen to yourself Jack! You sound like your father!"

Suddenly Jack's annoyance was consumed by dread. Beads of sweat formed on his brow. He rubbed his clammy palms with his napkin, trying hard to be casual and nonchalant as he put it down on his lap, preparing to eat as if nothing was wrong. "My father never met an Arab in his whole life," said Jack in a voice made hoarse by the dryness of his throat. In the back of his mind he knew she was onto something, and it scared him. He didn't want to be like his father, but he was also starting to see, more and more, that his father was right about many things.

Sarah's eyes narrowed as she tried to pierce through her father's nervous facial ticks to see what was really going on in that conservative head of his. The dead grandfather she had never met was always a source of mystery. Jack simply refused to talk about him. But now he was being put on the spot and at least some of the truth was bound to come out.

"No, your father wasn't an Arab-hater. He was a Jew-hater, but the comparison is valid."

How did Shirley know about his father's anti-Semitism? It must have been Jack's sister who told her. Jack remembered it quite vividly despite all the years he had been putting it out of his mind. "Now you're really talking nonsense. I don't hate Arabs. I just have some problems with Arab culture. And even if I did, everybody knows that being anti-Arab is nothing like being anti-Semite. The Arabs and the Jews are at war for Christ's sake!"

"Yes, they are," Shirley admitted. Funny, she hadn't even thought of that aspect of the comparison. She never paid much attention to the fighting in the Middle East. It was all so confusing: holy sites, thousands of years of history, different religions and customs. How could anybody make sense of that? She was starting to lose her train of thought. "But, but..." She knew that there was some way to make sense of the comparison between the father and son, but Jack had thrown her off. The Middle East was not her strong point.

Jack smiled and leaned back in his chair. He could see that Shirley was stumped.

"Wasn't grandpa mad that you came to Canada?" asked Sarah.

Jack snapped back to attention, looking nervously between his daughter and his wife. The question caught him by surprise. His father was supposed to be out-of-bounds, but this was not a normal argument. The daughter saw the division developing between her parents, the opening it provided to some information she had always been curious about, and she took it. Jack looked at Shirley with puppy-dog eyes. Please don't go there, his eyes said.

Shirley looked back at her husband with a frown, shaking her head, not this time Jack. "Yes dear, that's right. Grandpa was mad because your father was a draft-dodger."

"A draft-dodger?" Not her father. Impossible. She knew he came to Canada during the Vietnam War but it had never occurred to her that he was avoiding the draft. Even now, it seemed they were talking about somebody else—her dad's previous life. She could never imagine the man she saw every day in fifteen-hundred-dollar suits with patent leather shoes and red suspenders, as a draft-dodger. He was a businessman, not a hippie. But then again, the past two US presidents had avoided serving in Vietnam.

"Yes. Your father was quite the hippie," Shirley giggled.

"I was not a hippie! That's what my father called me, that's all."

"It really bothered you didn't it?" asked his wife suppressing a giggle.

Jack looked away. He did not want to talk about this.

"He said you were a 'longhaired-hippie-communist-draft-dodger.'"

Jack was totally unresponsive, pouting. But Shirley would not stop this time.

"And he thought there was some kind of a Jewish-Communist conspiracy."

THE MEMORIES FLOODED PAST THE CAREFULLY CONSTRUCTED BAR-
RIERS IN JACK'S MIND. ANTI-SEMITISM WAS AS AMERICAN AS APPLE PIE
BACK IN SUBURBAN NEW JERSEY OF THE 1950S AND '60S. NOBODY WAS
WORRIED ABOUT BEING POLITICALLY CORRECT. JACK'S FATHER TALKED
OUT LOUD ABOUT A JEWISH-COMMUNIST GLOBAL CONSPIRACY. HE WAS
ALWAYS SAYING HOW THE JEWS WERE CONTROLLING HOLLYWOOD, OR
STIRRING UP TROUBLE IN THE SOUTH, OR SELLING SECRETS TO THE SOVI-
ETS. HE ALWAYS SAID THAT HIS BROTHER, JACK'S UNCLE, DID NOT DIE IN
KOREA SO THAT THE JEWS COULD BUS THE NIGGERS INTO OUR SCHOOLS
AND TURN US INTO COMMUNISTS. AND AT THE TIME IT MADE SENSE TO
JACK. HE REMEMBERED WHAT THEIR PARISH PRIEST SAID ABOUT THE
JEWS EVERY EASTER, BECAUSE IT WAS THE JEWS WHO CRUCIFIED CHRIST.
THE PRIEST CALLED THEM "PERFIDIOUS JEWS." HE NEVER KNEW WHAT
PERFIDIOUS MEANT BUT HE KNEW IT WAS BAD AND ANTI-CHRISTIAN. AND
MEN LIKE HIS FATHER AND JOSEPH MCCARTHY AND RICHARD MILLHOUSE
NIXON WOULD STOP THEM. HE REMEMBERED SEEING JEWS AS A KID ON
A DAY-TRIP TO NEW YORK. THEY WERE ALL DRESSED IN BLACK WITH
THEIR BEARDS AND THEIR CURLS ON THEIR TEMPLES. THEY WERE DIF-
FERENT. THEY HAD THEIR OWN SHOPS, THEIR OWN LANGUAGE, THEIR
OWN CHURCHES. IT MADE PERFECT SENSE THAT THEY HAD SOME KIND OF
PERFIDIOUS PLAN TO SABOTAGE THE REST OF US.

BUT AT SOME POINT, HIS FATHER'S ANTI-SEMITISM STOPPED MAKING
SENSE. MAYBE IT WAS WHEN HE LEARNED THAT HIS NINTH GRADE CLASS-
MATE RACHEL (ON WHOM HE HAD A CRUSH) WAS JEWISH. MAYBE IT WAS
WHEN HE REALIZED THAT LOTS OF PEOPLE IN NEW JERSEY WERE JEWISH
AND THEY LOOKED JUST LIKE EVERYBODY ELSE. THEY WORE THE SAME
CLOTHES, WENT TO THE SAME RESTAURANTS AND WATCHED THE SAME
TV SHOWS. IN ANY EVENT, AT SOME POINT JEWS LOST THEIR PERFIDIOUS-
NESS AND BECAME MORE LIKE HIM. HE WOULD NEVER GO OUT ON A DATE
WITH RACHEL, BUT HE DIDN'T THINK SHE WAS A COMMUNIST EITHER.

YEARS LATER, IN THE 1980S, IT WAS THESE NON-PERFIDIOUS JEWS
THAT JACK SAW BEING TARGETED BY SUICIDE BOMBERS IN ISRAEL. JEW-
ISH PARENTS AND CHILDREN, WEARING WESTERN CLOTHES, LISTENING
TO WESTERN MUSIC, IN CAFÉS AND MALLS. SOME OF THEM EVEN HAD
BLONDE HAIR AND BLUE EYES. THEY WERE BLOWN TO BITS BY CRAZED
SUICIDAL MILITANTS WITH DARK SKIN AND BEARDS, CITING STRANGE
RELIGIOUS TEXTS. OF COURSE JACK KNEW THAT ISRAELI SOLDIERS ALSO
KILLED PALESTINIAN CHILDREN, WOMEN AND MEN IN REFUGEE CAMPS
AND OCCUPIED TERRITORIES. BUT SOMEHOW THOSE DEATHS SEEMED
LESS SIGNIFICANT, EVEN IF THERE WERE FOUR TIMES MORE OF THEM.

Arabs were different, non-Western, perfidious—and they were attacking people like us even if the victims were Jews. They wanted to destroy civilization. He had always suspected it, and 9/11 proved it. And now the victims were Americans like him.

"Okay Shirley, Sarah's grandfather was a crazy old McCarthyite. Are you happy now? Do you really think she needs to know this?"

Shirley put her hand over her mouth and looked at her daughter. Maybe she had gone too far. Would her daughter be able to handle this? There was a lot more baggage than even Shirley knew about, more than 30 years worth, to be dumped on Sarah all at once, and right after the World Trade Center attacks. When Shirley looked at her daughter's naïve young countenance, she felt like she was looking in the mirror 25 years ago. Despite the contrast between Shirley's bleach-blonde hair and Sarah's bandana-covered head, there was quite a resemblance. They both had the same green eyes, the same overbite, same dimples. Sarah also inherited some of her father's features, and her grandfather's: dark wavy hair, thick eyebrows (which Sarah had pierced) and the prominent chin.

"Actually dad, this like totally explains tons of stuff. Now I see where your politics come from." Sarah wore a knowing grin that widened the more her father squirmed in his chair. "Like your defense of the cops at the Summit of the Americas. Dude, they fired more than 900 rubber bullets and 5,000 canisters of teargas. They arrested over 400 protestors just for protesting. Jaggi Singh was detained for 17 days on the pretext that he was assaulting police officers with teddy bears. And you said 'There was reasonable use of force given the threat to public safety.' No concern for free speech or the right to protest."

"I stand by that statement," said Jack defiantly. "There's nothing McCarthyist about protecting world leaders from a bunch of thugs. People have a right to demonstrate but that doesn't mean they have a right to be violent. And I'm sure that Mr. Singh was doing a lot more than throwing teddy bears."

"So you're calling me and my friends thugs now? We were trying to stop our so-called democratic governments from handing over all the power to a bunch of multinational corporations through the FTAA."

"Oh, now who's the conspiracy theorist! Honestly, Sarah, do you really think these CEOs get together in secret to plan the takeover of the whole hemisphere?" Jack smiled glibly, a victorious general posing for a portrait. He was sure he had the upper hand. Shirley was put out of commission with guilt and Sarah was running herself into the ground with the irrational radicalism that seemed to be endemic to Sir George/Concordia. The subject of his father safely sidetracked, he dished salad onto his plate. "Let's dig in. Supper's getting cold. Pass the bread, would you dear?"

Shirley and Sarah made eye contact, sharing a meaningful look. Jack carefully avoided their gazes, going on with his dinner as if nothing had happened. Would they let him get away with it? Shirley looked away from her daughter and passed her husband the bread. It was up to Sarah. Their daughter could decide for herself how far she would push her father, and how much she wanted to know.

Sarah couldn't help but feel betrayed by her new ally. She was encouraged by how far her mother had come but it was disillusioning to see, when push came to shove, her mom was still letting her dad run the show. "So the vegetarian loaf isn't spiced too un-American now dad?"

"As I said dear, I like cumin."

"It's true," confirmed his wife. "It's one of his favourite spices."

"I can't believe this!" Sarah cried, her blood boiling again. "You're such a hypocrite!" she shouted at her father as she got up from the table and stormed away. The sound of boots tromping up the stairs was followed by the slamming of Sarah's bedroom door.

"What's got into her?" asked Jack just before he bit into the vegetarian loaf.

"You know very well what's gotten into her Jack." Shirley shot him a piercing gaze while he sat chewing the unpatriotic mouthful.

He looked blankly back at her, a cow chewing its cud. She shook her head and started putting salad on her plate.

The middle-aged couple sat eating their meal in silence when, about ten minutes later their daughter stormed down the stairs clutching a huge tome. She wore a triumphant grin as she slammed the encyclopedia down on the table. "Dude, cumin is an Indian spice!"

"What are you talking about?" asked Shirley.

"Cumin. It's an Indian spice," she said catching her breath. "Well, it's a spice of the world actually. The only places it's not really that popular are North America and Europe." She looked down at the book quoting from passages she had underlined. "The spice is 'of Western Asian origin.' Today it's mainly produced in 'India, Iran, Indonesia, China and the South Mediterranean.' It's popular in 'Latin America, North Africa and all over Asia.' Cumin is totally not an Arab spice dad! But I guess that doesn't make any difference to you. Africans, Asians and Latin Americans are probably all terrorists too, right?"

"Nothing you quoted contradicts what I said," Jack said defiantly. He could be just as stubborn, self-righteous and competitive as his daughter. Only Jack, with years as a PR executive, had learned to hide his emotions and speak dispassionately whatever the topic. "The book says that cumin is used in North Africa and the South Mediterranean. Who do you think lives there dear? Arabs."

"Yeah, but it's not an 'Arab spice' dad."

"Well if Arabs use it, it's an Arab spice. Anyway, all I was saying was that we should be eating American in respect for the victims of Arab terrorism. And you just said, it's not a spice widely used in North America but it is used by Arabs."

"I can't believe we're arguing about this!" Sarah cried in frustration.

"I don't want to be arguing about it dear," Jack was speaking matter-of-factly again, in his deep authoritative newscaster voice. "You see dear? I've eaten the casserole your mother made. It's quite good. You should sit down and have some with us." He gestured towards her chair and the cold vegetarian loaf on her plate.

"Dad, the point isn't that you should eat or not eat the dinner, the point isn't whether cumin is an Arab spice or not, the point is your racism towards Arabs." She slammed the encyclopedia shut and sat down with a sigh of frustration.

"I'm not racist towards Arabs," he countered as calmly as he could manage, but Jack was loosing his cool. How dare she call her father a racist? "I just don't appreciate their culture of Jihads and suicide bombings that's killing thousands of my fellow Americans." As Jack pronounced the word "Jihads" his voice became much louder and his face started to redden, much like his daughter's. "Think about your cousin Brent for the love of God."

"Brent is fine dear," his wife jumped in. "Didn't you hear us talking when he called?"

"Oh really?" Jack's eyes widened with surprise. The perfect victim of terrorism to illustrate the savagery of Arab culture was okay? The tears Shirley was wiping from her eyes at the beginning of the meal suddenly made sense. He was too occupied with his American Airlines file to notice the pre-dinner mother-daughter conversation about Brent. "That's just super. I'm sure you must be very relieved." He offered Shirley a nervous smile.

"Yes, I was relieved Jack," his wife's reply was caustic. "Twenty minutes ago, when we received the call from Brent. When you were sitting right there!"

"Dude, you don't care about Brent," accused his daughter. "You sooo just want to blame the Arabs for everything."

"Of course I care about Brent," claimed Jack. "I didn't hear you talking, that's all. I have a lot of work these days, so you'll have to excuse me if I'm a bit distracted at times. It's not that I 'want to blame' the Arabs. I'm just admitting the obvious fact that the terrorists were Arab. All the terrorists were Arab. They were from Saudi Arabia. It said so on the news. What more evidence do you need?"

Sarah had become so exasperated with her father's inability to listen that she no longer had the energy to yell. She managed to sigh a few rhetorical questions, "So I should stop being involved in SPHR? I should stop hanging around with Hassan and Hakim, and my other Arab friends? They're all a bunch of terrorists, right?" As she spoke, she saw her father's mouth opening to respond to her rhetorical questions. Would he dare to answer in the affirmative? Was he that far gone? There was more that she wanted to say yet the urge to cry was overwhelming. She wouldn't give her father the satisfaction. She closed her eyes to stop the tears. She stopped speaking to prevent the sobs. And she pushed aside her untouched dinner to rest her head in her arms, exhausted.

"What?" asked her father. Jack must not have heard her correctly. It sounded like she was associating with Arabs and some Arab organisation. What did she call it, "SPHR"? That name sounded familiar.

Sarah did not lift her head from the table. She did not answer her father. Only her red bandana was visible.

"What group did you say you were involved with? SPHR?" her father persisted.

"Solidarity for Palestinian Human Rights," his daughter said reluctantly, her frustrated voice muffled by her arm.

Solidarity for Palestinian Human Rights—that name was in the news recently, he was sure of it. Where had he heard that name?

"You really are a piece of work Jack," said Shirley. "You know how to ruin a perfectly good non-American meal don't you?" She started clearing the table.

Jack wasn't listening to his wife. He was thinking about that mysterious acronym—SPHR. Then it hit him. He got up from the table, leaving his plate for his wife to pick up, and went into the kitchen to sift through the recycle bin.

Shirley didn't pay any attention. After clearing the table except for Sarah's untouched dinner, she pulled up a chair beside her daughter and put her arm around her, placing her head beside Sarah's on the table. "It's okay dear. We all deal with tragedy in different ways."

Jack had removed a mountain of newsprint from the bin and was sifting through it page by page on the kitchen floor. Then he found it. The article was in the *Suburban*:

GEST ENGLISH WEEKLY NEWSPAPER

AUGUST 15, 2001   48 PAGES

Rally, terror groups linked

A park owned by Concordia University is being advertised across

According to noted Mideast terrorism expert Steven Emerson, many of the groups connected with the many of the

Consulate to the United States Consulate on St. Alexandre Street, then back to Concordia.

The anger he felt towards his daughter evaporated as his mind clouded with fear. What was she getting herself into?

"The fact that there is only an indirect connection between Dow [Chemical Corporation] recruiting students and napalm dropped on Vietnamese villages, does not vitiate the moral issue. It is precisely the nature of modern mass murder that it is not visibly direct like individual murder, but takes on a corporate character, where every participant has limited liability. The total effect, however, is a thousand times more pernicious, than that of the individual entrepreneur of violence. If the world is destroyed, it will be a white-collar crime, done in a business-like way, by large numbers of individuals involved in a chain of actions, each one having a touch of innocence."

— HOWARD ZINN, "DOW SHALT NOT KILL," *THE NEW SOUTH STUDENT*, 12/68

JACK MURPHY'S ASSISTANT WAS HUNCHED over the computer, typing up her boss's scribblings on airline industry forecasts. She was absorbed in the task of deciphering the post-it-note hieroglyphs, cryptic allusions, circles, arrows and personalized shorthand laid out on her desk in careful order. Janet was the only one able to make sense of this brainstorming jumble. She knew her employer's thought processes better than her own. Her identity had been erased by his. It was part of the job.

"Janet." Her fingers jumped off the keyboard as her muscles constricted. At the sound of Mr. Murphy's static-filled voice she shot upright in her chair. She zeroed in on the intercom with a scowl of hatred and fear that can only be bred from years of abuse.

"I need you to come in here right away," ordered her employer.

"Yes, Mr. Murphy," she answered promptly. Smoothing her gray skirt with the palms of her thin white hands, taking a deep breath, she wondered what Mr. Murphy wanted. She hoped it was just coffee. The last time he called her in like this, it was to ask her to come in on Sunday to prepare a presentation for an important client. As if she had a choice.

Janet left her cramped cubicle, and walked into her boss' bright and spacious office. She paced with carefully measured steps, a soldier on her way to stand before the firing squad. She stood directly before his massive oak desk, looking at him on his leather throne as he tapped his gold pen against his prominent upturned chin.

Jack glanced at his assistant out of the corner of his eye. Janet's face was ordinary. That's what Jack liked about her. There is nothing more useful to a PR executive than an ordinary person.

"Mr. Murphy?" she asked.

"Oh, yes," said Jack in a surprised tone, as if he had just noticed her standing there. He looked directly at her for a long second without saying a word. Janet nervously picked at the skin on her right thumb with her index finger. The rawness of its skin had come back with a vengeance after her summer vacation. Those all to brief careless days were rapidly fading from memory.

Jack didn't notice the thumb-twitches of his assistant. His eyes were focused much lower, on Janet's legs. They seemed soft and supple. His wife used to have legs like those, a long, long time ago. "Yes," he repeated as he closed his eyes and put his pen on his temple, letting the women's legs fade from his mind. His other hand was lying on the bible of his industry, the O'Dwyer's PR newspaper on his desk.

"Cappuccino?" offered Janet nervously to fill the silence. Waiting in front of the firing squad was always the worst part.

"No!" he shot back, annoyed. He had lost his train of thought. But then it came back. "Star Wars!" he exclaimed, followed once again by silence.

Janet knew by his utter stillness that a response was expected. And it had better be good. But she had no idea what he was talking about. Was it the movie? Seventies retro was in, and that was a 1977 film. It was also an important movie in the PR biz because it was the first to spend more money on promotion than on production. But somehow she knew he was not talking about the movie.

She looked at the PR newspaper on his desk, and read the headline of the editorial, upside-down from her perspective:

PR Needed To Keep Consumers Spending

The full headline would have read, "PR NEEDED TO KEEP CONSUMERS SPENDING IN THE WAKE OF 9/11" but the last few words were redundant. Everything in the PR industry was now post-9/11. What did Star Wars have to do with 9/11? Unless, it was the Star Wars defense system...

"Oh yes, Mr. Murphy," replied Janet in a serious tone. "That's very good sir. Definitely a green button." She gestured with her right hand as if her reddish raw thumb were pushing the button on a remote control. Their focus groups always pressed the green button when something in an ad produced a positive reaction, red when it was negative. "Star Wars is the kind of comfort we need now. We need to feel secure from threat. Terrorism, rogue states, and so on. It's scary. Star Wars anti-missile defense is the ultimate cocoon."

"Yes!" he spun around on his chair. "I knew it, I knew it!" Jack had been chewing on this problem for two full weeks now: how to get a terrorized public to start spending on his clients' products again. He knew that people were concerned for their own safety and that of their family. Just as Shirley and Sarah had freaked about Brent. Just as he was now worried about Sarah's involvement with Arab radicals at Concordia. From travel to shopping, terror had slowed down consumption as people stayed home and took care of their families. But that fear was also a potential resource for PR consultants like him. He just had to figure out how to harness it and hitch it up to the product lines of his clients. Terror could be his salvation, if he could sell people the sanctuary they so desperately needed. And now he had a found a big piece of the puzzle. Attitudes about key big-ticket defense items were changing. He looked up at her ordinary face, and prepared to pose another question.

Mr. Murphy's wide eyes and seriously pursed lips told his assistant that he wanted her to answer honestly and in her own words, but also to answer the right way, his way. "You wouldn't have said that before now would you?"

"No sir," she admitted. She wasn't even sure if she would say it today. She just knew that was what her boss wanted her to say, right here and right now.

Hallelujah. Everything was falling into place. "Mark my words Janet," he pointed at her with confident authority. "9/11 will be to the aerospace industry what the Gulf War was to the auto industry! This will win Mr. Tremblay over for sure." The rival PR firm vying for the aerospace account had given Jack just the push that was needed to drive him to obsession. And obsession was the mother of innovation. Even after Jack's presentation last Sunday, the competing firms were still running neck-and-neck. But this would put Jack's company in the lead.

"We just need to find a way to get individual consumers to vicariously participate like the SUV drivers did," he said as he paced back and forth like a General at HQ. "We need an Arnold Schwarzenegger, and of course, we need a Hummer!"

Arnold Schwarzenegger was the action hero who popularized the Hummer, a civilian version of the armored Humvee used in Operation Desert Storm. He insisted that AM General produce his very own Humvee. The SUV craze of the 1990s was widely credited to this innovative PR maneuver. Billions of North American consumer dollars spent on gas-guzzling aggressive-looking family vehicles, and all thanks to a patriotic feel-good hero who insisted on his very own larger-than-life military car from a feel-good war.

"Genius sir," she said with bowed head. Stroking Mr. Murphy's ego was 90 per cent of her job. Stroking ego was 90 per cent of the public relations biz. Janet kissed Mr. Murphy's ass, Mr. Murphy kissed Mr. Tremblay's ass, and Mr. Tremblay was bound to be kissing some older, fatter and richer ass higher up on the corporate ladder. As she bowed her head, Janet looked at the family photos on Mr. Murphy's desk. She wondered if he were as demanding on them as he was on her. The careless smile of his daughter standing in front of a picturesque grove of pines suggested otherwise. "Make people feel good about the war on terror. Get them buying. Brilliant."

"Terrorists thought attacking the World Trade Center would ruin the economy," said Jack. "It'll only make it stronger. Get me a list of our client's product lines and do your best to think of civilian spin-offs for them. I'll look at it when I get back from lunch."

"Yes Mr. Murphy," Janet responded. "I'll get right on it."

* * *

"Sure, people have to eat," Sarah admitted. "But, dude, there's more to life than getting a job with some multinational corporation to pay for your house and your DVD system and your SUV. What if the corporation you're working for is producing engines for the Israeli F16s raining terror on Palestinians?" The television camera crews had left the Hall Building lobby about half an hour ago. But as students filed out of the General Assembly, a knot had formed around Sarah and Hassan squaring off against Abdul and Gord. The real debate was just beginning. Abdul and Gord were engineering students who voted with the majority against the anti-corporate motions put forward by the leftwing student union leadership. Sarah and Hassan continued to defend the assembly's losing side.

Abdul threw up his hands in disgust. "Oh, come on. Let's not talk about a theoretical debate. Let's talk about what was actually on the table." Had he left behind the sterile religious debates of the imams in Saudi Arabia only to find himself in the middle of equally sterile academic debates in a second-rate Western liberal arts university? This white activist had a lot of nerve using the struggle of his Palestinian brothers and sisters to get him to support a student union that was driving away corporate employers. It was hard enough already for a young Arab engineer to find a job.

"It's not a theoretical debate," Hassan insisted. "There's a corporation at Concordia that produces Israel's F16 engines: Pratt and Whitney." Unlike the engineers who had shown up en masse for the assembly, mobilized by the Engineering and Computer Science Student Association, Sarah and Hassan had actually read about the issues on the table. The student union newsletter had one article in particular that spelled out some of the most questionable corporate dealings of the University:

Concordia University and the Corporate Commur

Making a Killing

by David Bernans, CSU Researcher

Millions of people in Africa are dying from AIDS while millions more are HIV positive with no acces sive drug treatments. Over the past decade, more than 35 000 Colombians have been murdered in politi vated violence while millions have been displaced as a result of this military and para-military violenc years, hundreds of Palestinians have been killed and thousands have been injured by Israeli occupying f

What does all of this have to do with Concordia University? The corporations that profit from these ca murder are part of Concordia's "corporate community".

"Pratt and Whitney?" asked Abdul. His voice had shrunk almost to a whisper and he was scratching his head. He didn't want to believe it. Pratt and Whitney had been a major sponsor of Engineering at Concordia for as long as anybody could remember. And it was an important employer of graduates. Yet Hassan wouldn't lie about F-16 missiles regularly blasting Palestinian houses, and the families inside them, to rubble.

"But that's not the point," Gord jumped in. From his baseball cap and his Computer Science and Engineering T-shirt, he showed that he was a real team player. A stocky kid, just a tad too short to be a football player, but with the right build. He had been recruited to fight along side his fellow engineers against the student radicals who were taking over the campus. He experienced the power of his team today, and it felt good. Today's gathering was more like a football game than a General Assembly. He and about 500 fellow engineers filled the auditorium and dominated the proceedings. Engineers were a minority of the predominantly liberal arts student body, but it didn't feel like that today. Abdul was also a member of Gord's team, but that punk chick had found his Arab teammate's weakness: the Palestinian question. He had to get the debate away from the Israel-Palestine conflict to keep Abdul in the game. "This G.A. wasn't about Pratt and Whitney, it was about telecommunications corporations. They don't produce anything for Israeli F16s now do they?" He adjusted his baseball hat, a pitcher on the mound who had just thrown an impossible curve ball. Strike one.

"No they don't," Hassan admitted in a careless tone. His strategy was not about winning or losing a debate. His end game was to open one or two people's minds to a different perspective. "But that doesn't mean those corporations are good guys. The reason the student union called the assembly was to propose that students take a look at the human rights abuses those corporations are involved with in Colombia. And then suggest appropriate measures for the administration to deal with the situation."

"And just look at what those corporations are doing in Colombia and you see why action should be taken!" said Sarah, her finger just a little too close to Gord's nose. The fire in her eyes and her heavy breathing showed that she cared very much who won the debate. She was a sore loser and she wanted revenge. Sarah came to Concordia to be part of a leftwing tradition. She didn't come to see a bunch of rowdy engineers yell misogynist insults at women. But that's exactly what the Women's Studies major witnessed in the auditorium they had just left. "We're not talking about cutting a few corners on worker safety. We're talking about rightwing paramilitary death squads going around and kidnapping, torturing and killing union leaders in the public telecommunications industry. Just to pave the way for IMF-imposed privatization!" As she pronounced the words "death squads" Gord tried to respond, but Sarah yelled louder and finished her last two sentences without stopping to breath. Her face had turned pink by the time she had finished.

The camera crews had left, but there were still about ten security guards making the rounds outside the auditorium, keeping an eye on the stragglers. Sarah's vitriolics caught the attention of a young female guard. She gestured for her male colleague to join her as she waded into the small circle of onlookers surrounding the confrontation.

"But students want to work for those companies," Gord shot back, doing some finger pointing of his own. "That's why they voted against the CSU motion. We're the majority. You're the minority. We won. You lost. Get over it." Strike two.

Sarah was not about to let the sports fan taunt her like that. Hassan could see the anger in her eyes and her face was getting redder by the second. "Wha... fu... uhh," her voice revving up for a race. Hassan grabbed her sleeve, to pull her finger out of Gord's face.

"The security guards are coming," he whispered into her ear. Then he turned to Gord and told him in a calm voice, "You had the majority today, but that doesn't make Colombian public sector union leaders any less dead. It doesn't bring back Palestinian children from their graves. Think about that. That's all I ask. You should think about it."

From the frown on Abdul's brow, and the way he was rubbing his beard, it seemed like he might be doing just that. He was about to ask what would happen to their programs if the university stopped getting money from these companies when Sarah shook her sleeve loose from Hassan's grip and shoved her finger back in Gord's face. Those bastards stole the General Assembly, and she couldn't let Hassan concede so easily.

"You and the rest of your mengineer friends were in the majority," she shot back. "But that's because your Dean gave you the day off, and I even heard he sent out an email spouting all kinds of lies about the CSU." In fact Dean Esmail did send an email to his faculty claiming that the CSU was trying to "destroy a cornerstone" of the Engineering faculty by criticizing corporations, and that the CSU sent nasty letters to Montréal corporate leaders to stop them from coming to job fairs. No such letters were ever sent. "But the majority of students are women, Liberal Arts students. The people you were shouting obscenities at in there. They didn't get out of classes this afternoon."

Smear job

At Concordia University, students have been learning a valuable lesson outside the classroom about the nature of free speech. One is that free speech doesn't take place in a vacuum. As Sir Issac Newton put it, for every action, there is a reaction. Some of the largest employers in Montreal, including Merck Frosst and Bell Canada Enterprises (BCE), have been bailing out of Concordia job fairs th:

The motion, if supported, will not be binding on the university. But it has already had its consequences, as the Merck Frosst and BCE withdrawals have shown. "We're all extremely upset," said Michael Nimchuk, president of the Engineering and Computer Science Association. The

Hassan got hold of her arm, pulling Sarah's finger out of Gord's face again. He started to push his friend back to a safer distance, more with moral force than physical might. The diminutive Hassan could not push the teenager anywhere she was not willing to go. He gestured to the approaching security guards to keep back. Everything was under control.

"Plus you had the propaganda machine of *The Gazette* on your side!" Although she was being forced back, Sarah continued her verbal assault unabated. "That 'Smear Job' editorial yesterday, you know the one that the mengineers plastered all over the campus, telling students to take back their student union from the radicals who are driving corporations away? Dude, how are we supposed to compete against that? The student union newsletter doesn't exactly have the same kind of power as a major city newspaper. But at least the student newsletter had some facts! It's so ironic that *The Gazette* called the accusations thrown at Concordia's corporate partners a 'smear job.' The real smear job was in *The Gazette*. That was like totally a smear job. Did you read the article? Did you actually read it?"

Gord wasn't sure how to answer her question. He glanced over the article as he posted it up in poster format all over the Hall Building, but he couldn't really say that he had read it carefully. He was pretty sure it claimed the CSU had said bad things about corporations and that made employers stay away from job fairs this fall, but he couldn't remember specifics. If he said anything about it, he was sure that this man-eating feminist would tear him to shreds. He looked around at the crowd watching them. It was growing larger as Sarah created a scene. Stage fright was setting in on Gord. He didn't want to be made a fool of by a girl in front of all these people.

"Did anybody read the article?" asked Sarah, looking around at the crowd that now numbered about twenty. Nobody answered her question. The tension between Sarah and Gord had been broken by their physical separation. Now that Sarah was addressing a larger audience, Hassan let go of her arm and gave her free reign to finish what she had started. "Well, you're not missing much. All it said was that the CSU 'smeared' good Concordia corporate partners. But dude, how did it smear them? It accused them of 'corporate crimes.' But for that to be a smear, those charges would have to be false. Nowhere has anybody challenged the facts as they've been presented! Pratt and Whitney does make F16 engines. Telecommunications corporations are like totally involved in privatization enforced by death squads. Biotech corporations are letting people die of AIDS in the Third World. It's soo true dude. The people killed couldn't be any more dead. It's not a smear."

"But there was nothing in the General Assembly about Pratt and Whitney and the F16s," Abdul countered. He was not really arguing with Sarah. He was just confused about this whole process. "Why didn't we talk about that today?"

Sarah was about to respond, but Hassan beat her to the punch. He agreed with everything she was saying. It was just the way she was saying it that was problematic. Abdul was close to coming around. He just needed a push in the right direction. "Two words," Hassan replied. "September eleventh."

Abdul looked at Hassan in confusion. "What? I..."

Hassan unpacked his shorthand explanation, "You know what people are starting to call Concordia? Gaza U. You can't talk about Middle East politics right now. That's why the SPHR rally the weekend before last had to be cancelled. You saw all those television cameras in there today? Imagine how crazy the situation would be if we were talking about Palestine. But still the cameras were there. And, when you really think about it, we were still talking about Palestine. At Concordia, you can't not talk about the Middle East either. All corporations at Concordia are Pratt and Whitney. All Third World countries are Palestine. That's why you have the university administration, *The Gazette*, and the corporate community on one side and the student radicals and the Arab 'terrorists' on the other. As Dubya says, 'you're either with us or you're with the terrorists.' You were on the wrong side today, my friend." He put his hand on Abdul's shoulder, giving it a friendly shake. "You were duped."

Abdul laughed and shook his head. "Oh, I don't know if it's as simple as that."

After that, discussion and debate continued in a much more civilized manner. Gord had had enough of Sarah, and went to join his teammates for a few celebratory rounds of beer at the student pub. Sarah didn't need to lash out any more. She had vented the frustrations she felt sitting in the General Assembly. It didn't matter that the vote was over and the motion had been defeated. The issues still needed to be discussed or they would fester. The debate in the G.A. could not be called a rational exchange of ideas. People lined up at the 'Yes' and the 'No' microphones on opposite sides of the auditorium like some kind of tug-of-war match. The engineers cheered every time somebody spoke against the motion and heckled and booed every time somebody spoke in favour.

"The CSU is hurting our future. We want jobs with these corporations!" Hooray!

"We should not be letting these private corporations, who only care about profit, run our public university!" Boo!

What had really damaged Sarah's psyche, however, were the sexist and racist catcalls from the peanut gallery. At one point, a Mexican woman stood up and tried to talk about the injustices and hardships faced by people in her country, and how university students there were fighting back. "Go back to Mexico!" yelled a heckler.

It didn't matter what people said at those microphones. The whole thing had already been decided in advance, at the mini-pep-rallies in every engineering class across the campus that morning.

It was all part of the backlash. There was a sense of urgency, but at the same time, total impotence, as the clouds of war in Afghanistan became clearly visible on the horizon. Activists were like ants scurrying in all directions in an effort to save what they could of their colony, as a giant foe kicked at their little hill. There was the Tom and Laith defense committee trying to get the expelled pro-Palestinian student leaders reinstated; there were people working on getting SPHR space for its bazaar and rally from an obstructionist university administration; and there were people working on the more general anti-war/anti-racism front.

After about a half-hour of discussions in the lobby of the Hall Building, Hassan tapped Sarah on the shoulder, "I've got to go up to the Dean of Students office to do some bureaucracy, then I've got to study for a math quiz tonight. Did you want to discuss our plans?"

"Sure," Sarah croaked. "I'll walk with you. Just let me get a drink first."

As they walked to the water fountain beside the escalator to the second floor mezzanine, they passed under the balcony where they couldn't help but notice a ten-foot star-spangled banner hanging just above their heads. Sarah made out the words:

> **Our hearts go out to all the Americans who lost their lives in the World Trade Center Terrorist Attacks... God Bless...**

"Dude, please tell me, why does the American Students' Association have to put that thing up?" pleaded Sarah, as if Hassan could do something to change the situation. It wasn't the omni-present mourning of the victims that bothered her. Anybody who cared about human life could get behind that. It was the equally omni-present US flag. Was she the only one to see the glaring contradiction?

"I know, I know," said Hassan, patting Sarah on the back as they walked under the tribute to Uncle Sam's kids and she bent over the water fountain. "What can you do?" He made a frustrated gesture towards the ceiling with his hand.

Sarah took a break from drinking to breathlessly answer half of Hassan's question. "If it was just the US flag, you could burn it."

"Right," agreed Hassan. "Well, maybe you couldn't burn it right now. You used to be able to burn it. But the banner has that message of righteous sorrow and mourning. Burning that is the ultimate disrespect. I guess that's why we can't burn the American flag anymore. The flag itself has become a sacred symbol of US 9/11 victimhood. It's as if every US flag has that tribute to the 9/11 victims written on it in invisible ink."

On the way up the escalators to the sixth floor, Hassan tried to talk Sarah out of the manifesto idea. Except for a few stragglers, students had cleared the hallways and the escalators. The last class change was about twenty minutes ago, so the noise level was low enough that they could discuss these sensitive matters without having to yell. The corridors of the Hall Building were very much like those of the city's underground metro system. There was the constant hum of fluorescent lighting, the kuchunk-kuchunk and scraping of metal from the escalators, punctuated by rushes of commuters at peak hours making their way through the recycled air past the back-lit mega-ads taking up all the prominent visual space. Unlike the subterranean corridors of the metro there were also hundreds of less noticeable posters of a commercial, artistic, cultural or political nature. Today there were several posters advertising the General Assembly, many of them with reproductions of *The Gazette* "Smear Job" editorial, calling on students to reject their leadership.

"We're an ad-hoc group," he pleaded. "Ad-hoc groups don't issue manifestos. They do press releases."

"But we set out to deliver a clear, unadulterated and radical message, remember?"

Those were the exact terms that Hassan used when they conceived the idea, but he did not put the same emphasis on the word, "radical."

"Dude, my father does press releases," Sarah insisted. "I do manifestos."

"This is not about you and your father," Hassan countered. "This is about exploiter and exploited, oppressor and oppressed, bomber and bombed. We'll not be doing any favours for the exploited, oppressed and bombed if we come off as a neo-Leninist vanguardist cell. Nobody will take us seriously, and it'll be that much easier for the cops to throw the book at us. What kind of public sympathy are we going to get?"

Does he think I'm just a spoiled white girl from Westmount rebelling against daddy? Indignant, Sarah raised her voice louder than she should have, "But the whole idea was to target the corporate bastards that are feeding the state-terrorist machine. Of course they'll call us terrorists. Everybody's being called terrorists. 'You're either with us or you're with the terrorists.' Okay, dude, so we're fucking terrorists. But we're right, and we can prove it!" All eyes turned towards the anarchist youth and the frumpy old cabby—a pair of deer caught in a camera crew's spotlight at the top of the escalators.

Hassan wished he could disappear. The media had been scouring the corridors of the campus for weeks now in search of sensationalistic images of Concordia's "ethnic tensions" in the wake of September 11. For the past couple of weeks Hassan had seen more camera crews on campus than credit card vendors. The media vultures swooped in anywhere and anytime, trapping unsuspecting victims under the cold lenses of their oversized microscopes.

"Calm down," said Hassan under his breath as he led her down the hallway, out of the camera's field of vision towards the Dean of Students office. "Everybody's looking at us. This is not how you organize an illegal action."

Sarah's face, which was already red with anger, turned a shade redder with embarrassment. She looked around to see who was listening. Except for a surprised camera crew down the hall, there was just a bunch of students like her. A kid with dreadlocks from the People's Potato returning a foldout table used to serve food at the G.A. smiled at the pair and laughed. That reassured her. She also caught a glimpse of a guy with a baseball cap reaching the top of the escalator behind them. He was looking down so she couldn't see his face, but she seemed to remember seeing him in the crowd surrounding their discussion in the lobby that afternoon. Could he be following her? He turned and walked in the opposite direction, towards the classrooms.

Once the surprise had worn-off, Hassan had to laugh. "We're a really serious revolutionary cell here, eh Sarah? All that screaming about our manifesto in public places is just a way to throw them off our track! Anyway, think about it this way. Look at this General Assembly today. The CSU is right about all the terrible things these corporations are doing but they haven't got that message out to students. That's their most important job as a student union. Since they failed to do that, they lost the vote. They did a couple of articles in their newsletter and passed out a few flyers. That's enough to get the Dean of Engineering really pissed off, but it's not enough to inform students. Your manifesto is likely to produce the same result. We need to deliver a clear, unadulterated and radical message about corporations profiting from death. Like it or not, that means dealing with the mainstream press. You can't simply hand people a manifesto and re-educate the public just like that. It's a good manifesto. Believe me, I know how hard you worked on it, and I was glad to help. But sometimes the chief value of these things is self-clarification. Like Marx and Engels' *German Ideology.*"

Sarah sighed with exasperation, wishing she had time to get beyond the *Communist Manifesto* in her Marx and Engels Reader. Without having read *German Ideology*, she felt incapable of arguing further and, in any event, further argument was not an option in their current locale. "I'll think about it," she said.

As Sarah made her way down the escalators, tearing 'Smear Job' posters the whole way, she considered whether a mere press release could make history like a manifesto. She loved that manifesto. So much of her own life-energy had been channeled into it, devoting the better part of a weekend poring over it in meticulous detail, reorganizing paragraphs for maximum rhetorical effect, retracing the logic of every argument looking for even the smallest contradiction. And there was a lot of Hassan in it too. She kept calling him and pestering him to help her with historical details, especially on Middle Eastern history. Didn't Hassan feel the same ownership of the work as she? Some adjustments would probably have to be made since it was supposed to represent the collective will of their group. But so far she had not received any commentary on the 5000-word essay beyond the advice painfully extracted from Hassan. She doubted anybody had even bothered to read the email she had sent out, which, of course, only leant credence to Hassan's argument. If nobody in their group of activists had bothered to read their comrades' work, how could she expect average people to make the effort to relate to it? Maybe she needed to hire a PR consultant to market their revolutionary new ideas.

"You don't want me as a PR consultant," Greg persisted. "You wouldn't like my advice." He should never have admitted his activist sympathies to Sarah. All she could hear was how he agreed with the morality of his mother's actions. She couldn't seem to understand that his support for the ideas of the occupiers was in the abstract. Sarah was deaf to anything he said about the futility of the whole computer centre occupation as a strategy for change. If he had been less candid about his secret passive support for illegal occupations, she would have never told him about their crazy plan. She would never have trusted him. On the other hand, if she hadn't trusted him, she would never have revealed anything about herself, and the closeness they had established over the past three days would never have blossomed. "How about this one?"

She looked up to see the image of a gun-toting Keanu Reeves, cloaked in a black trench coat, peering down at her from the VHS box in Greg's hand: *The Matrix*. "Already seen it," Sarah sighed. "Dude, you don't have much selection at this store do you?"

"Unless you're into porno," said Greg shrugging his shoulders apologetically, "it's the place with the best selection in my neighbourhood."

Sarah wrinkled her nose in disgust. "I'm sure we'll find something," she replied with a forced smile. "You like Godard?"

"Mmm, sometimes," Greg mused, "but not tonight. It'll put me to sleep." He was looking beyond the aisle they were camped in, surveying the nearby aisles from his position above the shelving. In the comedy aisle he caught sight of a respectable Woody Allen selection. "What would you say to Woody Allen?"

Sarah put the Godard film back on the shelf, relieved to be rid of it. "Sounds good to me!" she chimed enthusiastically as she jumped up from the floor. "You see, I like your advice. Just tell me what you think we should do, as somebody who doesn't 'give a shit' about politics, as you say. That's the kind of advice we need. We're trying to convince people this is something worth giving a shit about."

As they strolled over to the Woody Allen corner Greg winced. "Promise you won't get mad?" he begged.

"Promise."

"Ditch the manifesto," he said in a voice totally devoid of expression. "Go with a press release."

"I knew you'd say that," Sarah sighed.

Greg turned in her direction, head slightly askew, "Then why did you ask?"

"Because I had to hear you say it," Sarah said touching his arm. "You're right, of course. And I'm glad you said it."

"Funny," Greg commented. "You don't look glad."

"No, I am glad, but glad..." she trailed off pensively and then her eyes lit up. "Glad in a sad kind of way. I spent the last half-hour telling you how important the manifesto is to me, how hard I worked on it and everything. So you knew I wanted you to tell me to use it-"

"And I told you to ditch it," Greg glumly finished her line of thought. "Not exactly great encouragement."

"But that's what you honestly think," said Sarah as they found themselves in front of the shrine to Woody. There had to be about thirty of his films, capped with a cardboard cutout of the actor/director's comical face, eyebrows raised above his dark-rimmed glasses as if to say, well I know it's not much but here's my life's work. "You told me what you really believe, not what I wanted to hear. That's what's important." And then, almost as an afterthought she added, "plus, you're right."

Greg was hunched down to ponder the Woody Allen films. He wasn't giving careful consideration to *Bananas* and *The Purple Rose of Cairo*, but to the meditations Sarah had just offered.

With his head at a reasonable height, Sarah took the opportunity to give him a well-deserved kiss on the lips, placing her hands on the back of his head so he was unable to escape. "Always be like that Greg," she whispered. "Don't you ever tell me what I want to hear just to shut me up."

At Sarah's insistence, they rented *The Front*, a 1975 film about blacklisted screenwriters during the red scare of the 1950s. Since she had learned about her grandfather's McCarthyist political leanings, she had become fascinated with that particular dark stain on American history. How could anybody write a comedy about such draconian measures bred from political paranoia? She had to find out. Greg had already seen the film, but it was a classic, so he didn't mind watching it again.

After viewing the film on the overstuffed couch in Greg's dingey apartment, they talked—argued mostly, to Sarah's great pleasure—until 2 a.m. about the collective paranoia of the red scare, the current racist paranoia, and the best strategy to bring people to their senses. Comedy or tragedy? Reform or revolution? Or was it even possible to make a difference at all?

Barricaded from the world by cushions, blankets and intense affection for each other, they quarreled, snuggling closer all the while. The thrusts and parries of their conflict were guided by unspoken rules each knew would be respected. Each wanted to push things as far as he or she could go while respecting the limits of the other.

They talked about Greg's mother and Sarah's father because in the minds of this unlikely young couple, the lives of Betty and Jack were irretrievably intertwined in all of these politico-philosophical questions. At one point Sarah retorted defensively, "I'm not an anarchist just because it drives my dad crazy." And despite her defensiveness, Greg believed her, almost fully. She was too advanced in her political-economic analysis, and she was too committed to her political principles, for it to be a simple question of youthful rebellion. But there was no getting around it, her father, in a very real sense, was the system. She had to be rebelling against him, at least a little bit.

"I thought you said 'the personal is political' is a feminist principle," Greg laughed. "What's more personal than your relationship with your father?"

"I don't deny I have a political relationship with my father that is also personal," Sarah agreed, carefully considering her own words in the new light Greg had cast on them. "I have a feminist critique of his attempts to dominate me. But that doesn't mean my political analysis is simply the result of a rebellion against him."

"Oh," Greg nodded, "okay." He flashed a lighthearted smile to let her know that he accepted her explanation, but not entirely. And he really did know it was true. But he also knew there was another level of "the personal is political" beyond the political analysis of father-daughter domination, on the level of "feeling." "So when am I going to meet the old man anyway?"

"Dude, are you sure you want to do that?" Sarah asked. "I'm like, very concerned for your psychic well-being."

"Hmm," Greg mused nervously. "Maybe not just yet. I should let you resolve some of your father-daughter tensions before we play 'guess whose coming to dinner'."

"Yeah, we have some... issues," Sarah agreed in self-conscious understatement.

"I guess I just feel at a bit of a disadvantage," Greg admitted. "You've already met my mom, and on our very first date, no less!"

"What would you say to my dad anyway? What would you talk about?"

"I guess, I would say, 'Mr. Murphy...'—hey, you know it's funny, there's a Mr. Murphy at work. He's a PR guy. Really tight-assed."

"That's funny. My dad is a really tight-assed PR guy. His office is in-"

Greg finished her sentence, "the Réelvision Building!"

"Get out of town!" Sarah attacked Greg with her pillow. He shook his head, which prompted more cushion whacks. "No! It can't be! This is not possible!"

"So that Mr. Murphy is your dad..." Greg was trying to picture the two of them together but it didn't work, like two objects trying to occupy the same physical space. "I thought you were exaggerating about him. But Mr. Murphy is... hmm, how can I put this?"

"Closed-minded?" Sarah offered.

Greg tilted his head in a gesture of indecision.

"Opinionated? Arrogant? Pompous? Overbearing? Domineering?"

"Yeah," chuckled Greg.

"Prejudiced? Intolerant? Xenophobic? Racist?"

Greg's smile faded, and he bowed his head in somber confirmation.

"Yeah," sighed Sarah. "He is, isn't he?"

Neither of them could say anything more. Sarah couldn't apologize for her dad. There was no excuse for him. Greg knew it was impossible to say anything to make Sarah feel any worse than she already did about her father's racism.

"I wish my parents were like your mom," Sarah sighed longingly, holding tightly to Greg's hand.

"No you don't," said Greg softly, gently squeezing back. "You think you do, but you don't. Believe me, growing up in Westmount is better than Rosemont."

"Sure, I know I'm like totally lucky with all the advantages I have, materially speaking. But your mom's cool." Greg laughed, trying to interrupt, but Sarah continued, raising her voice slightly. "No, I don't mean she's cool because of her activism in 1969. I mean she's cool because she knows what's important in life. She values friends and family. She values you. That's the solidarity that made her do what she did. That's what made her who she is. And that's why you live in Rosemont and not in Westmount."

"Okay," Greg agreed. "She's cool. But, there's solidarity and there's foolhardiness."

"It couldn't have been easy to do what she did..." Sarah hesitated. She could feel Greg's hand tensing up, but she thought she should at least put the matter out on the table so they could deal with it at some point, when he was ready. "I mean putting her job and her academic career at risk to stand up against injustice. And she paid a heavy price. And even though she didn't mean for it, you had to pay the price too-"

"Look, you really don't know anything about the price we paid," Greg shot back with more venom than he intended. "I know you're trying to be understanding and everything," he continued in a softer tone, "but you just don't know. You don't know what it was like."

And Sarah could tell he was right. How could she know what it was like for him? Still she knew one thing, and she knew it because his mother told her so. If Greg could move on from those old wounds and accept all the positive things that came from his mother's actions, he would be a lot happier. He was his mother's son and if she had sold out he would have been somebody much less attractive to Sarah. If he could stop being a spectator in the struggle that loomed so large in the path his mother had taken, his life would be more complete and have more meaning.

"Racism, capitalism, patriarchy," Greg listed the trinity of evil that had always been his mother's nemesis. "They all suck. And they suck the most for those of us on the bottom of the social ladder, especially the uppity ones like my mom. But don't expect me to be cleaning up your dad's mess."

Sarah smiled sympathetically, closing the door on the topic that made him so uncomfortable, "It'd be nice if he'd clean up his own damn mess, wouldn't it?"

THURSDAY, SEPTEMBER 13, 2001

"'It's a poor sort of memory that only works backwards,' the Queen remarked. 'What sort of things do you remember best?' Alice ventured to ask. 'Oh, things that happened the week after next,' the queen replied in a careless tone. 'For instance, now' she went on, sticking a large piece of plaster on her finger as she spoke, 'there's the King's Messenger. He's in prison now, being punished: and the trial doesn't even begin till next Wednesday: and of course the crime comes last of all.' 'Suppose he never commits the crime?' said Alice. 'That would be all the better, wouldn't it?'"
— LEWIS CARROLL, *THROUGH THE LOOKING GLASS*, 1871

IT WAS AN AFTERNOON LIKE any other, but when Sarah walked into her World Issues *CÉGEP* course she did not see her teacher, Mrs. Martin. Instead her father was standing at the front of the class. "Dude, what are you doing here?" Sarah asked in a whisper.

"I'm teaching the class today," he responded in an authoritative voice, much louder than she would have liked "and please address me as Mr. Murphy, not 'dude'." The snickering of her adolescent classmates was burning Sarah's reddening ears. Jeff MacAuslin wore a silly smirk. Sarah knew he would be teasing her after class about this one. She took a seat at the back and tried to slouch down so that nobody would notice her.

"Hello students. My name is Mr. Murphy and I will be teaching World Issues today." Mr. Murphy spoke down to the students, more like a private school headmaster than a *CÉGEP* teacher. "Your old professor Mrs. Martin will no longer be teaching here. She will be appearing before the Special Committee on Un-American Activities. As part of your re-education, you will be watching the whole hearing process on television. Karin and Jeff, could you take this form down to the Audio Visual Department and bring us a television please?"

Karin and Jeff simply obeyed the new headmaster's orders as if nothing were wrong. Sarah looked around at all the other students. Some were watching their new professor. Others were talking amongst themselves about the hockey finals or the latest *Star Wars* movie. Everyone seemed oblivious to anything out of the ordinary.

"Dad?" Sarah started incredulously. She knew he didn't like the stuff that Mrs. Martin was teaching them about the Free Trade Area of the Americas, but he was taking this way too far.

"Uh, uh, uh!" He gave her a stern look and raised his finger.

"Okay, Mr. Murphy. What do you mean Mrs. Martin is appearing before the Special Committee on Un-American Activities? We're in Canada!"

Mr. Murphy laughed down at his deluded student, and all Sarah's classmates joined in. "Obviously, Mrs. Martin has had quite an influence on your impressionable young mind. Canada is part of the United States my dear. That is why we are blessed with freedom and liberty. They are bestowed on us by our Constitution. Of course terrorist evil-doers are jealous of our blessings and are trying to take them away, but we know how to deal with the evil-doers, don't we?"

"I don't want to be part of the United States," Sarah protested. "I don't want the Constitution."

"Then you are a terrorist," the headmaster said matter-of-factly. He walked to the wall and spoke into the intercom. "Mr. Tremblay please..."

Her eyes started to open, and she rolled over and pulled the covers above her shoulders. "That was a really fucked up dream."

"Yes, it's Jack Murphy, I would like to speak to Mr. Tremblay please." Sarah could hear her father's voice from the next room. She looked at the clock by her bed: 7:45. What was her father doing talking on his office phone at 7:45 a.m.?

"Ah, Mr. Tremblay, finally we connect."

Pause... Sarah could not hear the voice on the other end of the phone.

"Yes, I've been very busy as well... Of course. Yes it does. It changes everything... That's right. The civilian sector is bound to go through some tough times, but as you say, there's an unprecedented opportunity to expand in defense... Sure, obviously the US is key. NATO too, of course... No. Canada's a joke. Damn Liberals... Oh well, that's something I hadn't even thought about. But it makes perfect sense, sure. War on drugs, war on terrorism."

As her father talked about military buildup, Sarah looked at the photos of the Québec City protest on the wall opposite her bed. She was still lying down, so the photos appeared sideways. In one of them the police were firing a water cannon straight up at protestors. She imagined the water raining right back down on the cops afterward.

"Well, yes. I have some ideas. I would love to discuss them with you... Of course, I understand. I would do the same thing in your situation. It never hurts to get a second opinion, ha, ha." Sarah could tell her father's laugh was forced. No doubt Mr. Tremblay wasn't being fooled either. The confidence he had in her dream was lost. She found it reassuring somehow.

"How about next week sometime in the morning...? The afternoon too?"

Long pause.

"Of course Mr. Tremblay, I understand completely. Restructuring and all. The evening then?"

Long pause.

"You didn't mention anything on Thursday night. Maybe we can meet then... Oh yes, I forgot to mark that in my calendar. The President's speech. Right. That should be a good one. Can't wait to hear it. I'm sure it will be good news for military spending... How about the week after...? Of course you're right. We need to move fast... Sunday? Sure, we can meet on Sunday. Just name the time and place and we'll be there... Your office will be open on a Sunday...? You bet! I look forward to it... "Yes, see you there! Goodbye, and have a nice day."

Sarah was disgusted and yet intrigued by the half-conversation she had just heard. She rubbed her eyes wondering if she wasn't still dreaming. Once in an upright position, she felt lightheaded, and fought the urge to lie back down. It wasn't normal for her to get up this early, but there seemed to be some kind of opportunity here.

Her father had been talking to a client that had military production contracts. They were doubtlessly involved in building the military hardware used to terrorize people the world over. She was ashamed of her father's mercenary involvement. There must be some way she could sabotage the operation.

She heard her father get up from his desk and walk down the stairs to the kitchen.

In a flash, she jumped out of bed, threw on her bathrobe and went into the next room. It was not out of the ordinary for her to use the office. She used her father's computer to do homework. But it was unheard of for her to be in there this early. They were able to share the same office without conflict precisely because their hours were so different. Sarah usually wouldn't do any work until after 8 p.m. Sometimes she would be putting the finishing touches on an essay as her father put on the morning coffee.

As luck would have it, Jack's agenda was sitting open right beside the phone.

It was open to September 23, a Sunday. There were two appointments. One was with his mechanic on Papineau St. in the East: "Oil change and tune-up, 14:30." The other was a 15:00 downtown appointment with a company whose name Sarah recognized right away—it was a major multinational aerospace corporation. Sarah fumbled for a pen and paper and wrote down the information.

"What are you doing up?"

Sarah jumped. The pen leapt out of her hand and hit the computer screen. "Huh? Oh, dad. You surprised me." She turned around to see her father standing in the doorway looking at her over his reading glasses, with a cup of coffee and the morning paper.

"I hope you don't need the computer," her father advised. "I've got to check my email before I go to work."

"Sure dad, no problem. I can wait." Sarah walked out of the office, putting her hands into her bathrobe pockets as she passed Jack, the slip of paper tucked safely within her left hand. She went down the hall to the bathroom to brush her teeth. There was no way her nerves would let her get back to sleep now.

* * *

"Could you spare a death stick Hassan?" Sarah asked. Hassan sat smoking with a couple of punks on the front steps of the Beaudry Street community centre in Montréal's rapidly gentrifying Centre-Sud neighbourhood. The meeting was called for 6:00 pm, but she knew it wouldn't start on time. They never did. There was something different about Hassan today, but she couldn't put her finger on it. He was a little bit more subdued than usual.

It was a much more relaxed place to have a meeting than the bustling Hall Building of Concordia's downtown campus. The community centre was converted from an elementary school in the midst of what was, until recently, a multi-ethnic lower-income neighbourhood of brown-brick triplexes, all tightly stuck together like rows of milk cartons in a supermarket. Hassan and Sarah didn't know if the punks with them on the steps were waiting for the meeting as well, or if they were part of some other community centre-based group. Even though the neighbourhood residents were rapidly becoming decidedly upward in their mobility, the clientele of the community centre still included squeegee kids, welfare families and blue-collar workers. The economic laws of supply and demand, helped along by land speculators and condo developers, were beginning to force the eastward migration of lower income residents, but the community centre and its services had so far resisted the tide.

Even though the meeting was called just two days ago, hours after the World Trade Center attacks, dozens of activists walked past the smokers into the centre where the meeting had yet to begin.

Activists needed to decide on some kind of common direction. People were completely disoriented by the sudden onslaught of blind patriotism and racism mixed with genuine grief. The only means of advertising the emergency gathering was a brief email sent out to various lists:

```
[Montréal, PQ]
[Please forward and post]

EMERGENCY MEETING
in opposition to racism and war hysteria

Thursday, September 13 at 6pm
1710 Beaudry (metro Beaudry)
Montréal

Concerned individuals in the Montréal-area
are convening an emergency meeting this
Thursday. This meeting is in clear opposition
to the racism and war-hysteria that is being
promoted and fostered as a result of today's
events in New York, Washington and elsewhere.
We are calling this meeting in clear
opposition to Arabophobia and war mongering,
and with the goal of _organizing_ a concerted
response by Montréal-area individuals.

Please join us this Thursday to help
collectively plan a local response.
```

About halfway into her cigarette, Sarah recognized what was different about Hassan, "Dude, you're not wearing your kaffiyeh today."

He shook his head and took one long drag on his cigarette, then put it out under his foot. "Not a good idea for a cabby right now," he said as he exhaled. "Don't tell my parents back in Syria. They're already upset with the fact that their grandchildren don't speak Arabic or go to the mosque. They think I'm too Western." Hassan stood up, emphasizing with upturned chin, "Keeping a clean, close shave too."

Sarah put her hand on his unusually smooth face, "like a baby's bottom."

"It sickens me to have to do it, but it's my job. I don't have a choice. Pretty soon cops will be stopping us on the streets and we'll have to show our papers, like in France a few years ago."

"*Ostie de fascistes!*" said the punk, as an exclamation point to Hassan's sentence.

"Oh, you haven't seen fascism yet my friend," Hassan laughed. "But you might just get a chance, very soon. There are some important interests, a lot more important than your standard redneck racists beating us up on the metro. It'll be those big boys that'll be pushing for a serious law and order agenda. Arms manufacturers, the security sector, private prisons... Look out."

"So they, the big boys, should be our target?" asked Sarah.

"Ultimately..." Hassan raised one of his bushy eyebrows, "ultimately, yes. What are you up to, you naughty girl?" He saw the mischievous look on her face and knew that no good could come of it.

"What would you say if I could get us into the head office of one of those military industry multinationals here in Montréal?" She was bobbing up and down on the sidewalk like a puppy, unable to contain her excitement.

"I would say you are full of shit."

"And you would be wrong."

Hassan was smiling in spite of himself, "Which one? What kind of military production? What do they do?" Sarah's excitement was contagious. He knew he was going to regret it, but the idea of sabotaging the war machine just as people were getting worked up for a new imperialist campaign was just too tempting. It was like tying a bully's shoelaces together just as he was getting up to punch out the fat kid for his lunch money. There might be some potential in Sarah's idea. "Wait, before you answer any of those questions, let's take a walk. Fill me in on the way." Sitting outside of a widely publicized political meeting was probably not the best place to talk about such things.

They walked around the neighbourhood, smoking half a pack of Hassan's cigarettes, then stopping at a 99-cent pizza joint to get *une pointe* and a Pepsi. Hassan made an effort not to look at the prostitute with the super-short miniskirt plying her trade outside the pizza joint. He was easily distracted by such things.

"How do you know your father's going to want a cab?" Hassan asked as they sat down. "He could just as easily take the metro."

"I know my father," said Sarah in a reassuring tone. "And he never takes public transportation. That's soo not Jack Murphy. That would mean dealing with the unwashed masses. I considered the possibility that he'd get his assistant to drive him, but he wouldn't do that either because he doesn't trust her to do anything important. He'd be afraid that she'd make him late."

"Hmmm..." Hassan was mulling it over.

"I've done all the research," said Sarah. "I talked to Project Ploughshares and the Polaris Institute. They have good intelligence. It's just like all the other aerospace companies here in Montréal. Really, it doesn't matter which one we go after—Bombardier, SNC Lavalin, Lockheed Martin, CMC Electronics, Pratt & Whitney, or CAE. Dude, they're all involved in supplying the US and US allies with weapons for their dirty little wars. They're all Warmonger Inc. You can bet their equipment will be used in Afghanistan. And I can tell you that they also make component parts for Israel's F16s. Buuurp. Excuse me, it's the Pepsi."

"If we do this..." As Hassan spoke, Sarah became jittery and her smile widened. "Hey, I said, if!"

Sarah forced herself to settle down, wiping the smile off her face, trying her best to look serious.

The frumpy old man fought the urge to smile. In this state of mind, Sarah reminded Hassan of his daughter who he did not see nearly as often as he would like since the divorce. "If we do this, it'll have to be carefully planned. If I don't like what I see in there, the whole thing's off."

"Of course."

"Obviously, I'll help with the scouting and planning, but I won't be part of the action."

"Obviously," said Sarah, suppressing a giggle.

"I'm getting too old for this."

"Far too old."

"Hey, you don't have to agree with me about everything you know." They both laughed.

"No, seriously. It's not 'cause you're old. You've got responsibilities. And I bet the cops will treat Arabs way worse."

Hassan nodded. "It's very serious. I've been looking at a report that a grad student friend of mine is putting together on the backlash that's just starting. It's pretty scary." He pulled out a set of typed sheets of paper from his jacket pocket. "The reports from the mainstream press so far. Makes me afraid for my life." Hassan's Arab accent was now more apparent and his voice was becoming weaker.

"Want to read out a couple?" asked Sarah. "If you're comfortable with it," she added, after she saw Hassan's hand that was holding the papers start to shake.

"Okay," he agreed. "We don't have time to go through the whole list but here's just a brief selection..."

He read out loud:

> During the night, vandals attacked a parked car with a "Free Palestine" bumper sticker. By morning, the sticker had been written over to read, "F*** Palestine" and the body of the car was scratched and vandalized. The car's owner was cut off several times while driving, and

motorists made obscene gestures at him. (*The San Francisco Chronicle*, 9/13/01)

> A man armed with a baseball bat in Cooper City, Florida confronted a cleaning crew at Nur-Ul-Islam mosque and academy. When police arrested him he explained that he intended to use the bat to scare the mosque leaders so that they "would tell the congregation not to bomb New York." (*Miami Herald*, 9/13/01)

"Oh and here's one from New Jersey," said Hassan as he glanced at the next page. "Isn't that where your father's from?" He read the Asbury report:

> A Sikh man in Asbury, New Jersey reported that his car had been vandalized after someone pelted it with garbage and stones. (American Press, 9/12/01)

"My dad's family is not in Asbury," Sarah thought it important to make the distinction. "They're in Collingswood."

"Collingswood?" repeated Hassan. "Oh here's another one from there." And he continued:

> In Collingswood, New Jersey, vandals spray-painted the walls of two Indian-owned businesses with the message, "Leave town." (American Press, 9/13/01)

"I guess they didn't like the smell of cumin coming from their house..." Sarah mused. Sarah felt somehow responsible for the Collingswood incident. Her family was from there. It made her think about how racist her father was. Was he always that way, or was it because of the attacks?

"What?"

"Oh, it was just something my dad said. He got all mad because my mother cooked with cumin last night. I pointed out that it originated in India, but he didn't care." She looked at Hassan's confused frown, then shamefacedly down at the table. "Of course, not that it would be okay if it was an Arab spice."

"Of course," said Hassan. If he weren't so preoccupied by fear of racist violence, he would have been amused by her discomfort. "These reports are filled with stuff like that. It's not just Muslims and Arabs being targeted. Sikhs are fair game too. There was even a Brazilian targeted." And he read a report from Bridgeport:

> In Bridgeport Connecticut, a Brazilian writer was attacked on the street by eight men who taunted him and accused him of being an Arab. The group badly bruised the victim's face and broke his arm. (Deutsche Press-Agentur, 9/13/01)

"Here's one that scares the hell out of me," said Hassan. And he read the report:

> In Manassas, Virginia, somebody threw a bottle at a Muslim taxi cab driver who escaped injury but did not report the incident to police. After the bottle incident, the driver was chased through traffic by another car. (*Alexandria Journal*, 9/13/01)

"Now you see why I'm not wearing my kaffiyeh?" Hassan asked. He really felt the need to justify it. Even though he knew it was for personal safety, he felt guilty about denying his culture.

"Of course," said Sarah reassuringly. "Anybody in your situation would do the same thing."

"Listen to this one," Hassan continued. "It's insane."

> Members of the Sterling Virginia Islamic Community Center gathered at their worship center early to board a chartered bus they had rented. The group had planned to go to a Red Cross center to donate blood. As they arrived at their worship center, they found their hallway spray-painted in thick black letters, several feet tall, spelling out, "Die Pigs" and "Muslims Burn Forever." (*Washington Post*, 9/13/01)

"Oh and they show Palestinians celebrating on the news, but do we hear about this?"

> In Birmingham Alabama, several women dressed in hijabs were harassed and spat upon hours following the terrorist attacks. (American Press, 9/13/01)

"Or this one."

> Two men drove a car through Brooklyn with a sign taped to the rear window that read, "Kill all Palestinians." (*New York Post*, 9/13/01)

"I need a cigarette," Hassan said. His hand was shaking again as he put down the stack of papers to take out his cigarettes.

Sarah looked wistfully at the package. It didn't seem like the proper time to ask.

Hassan didn't even need to look at her face to know what she was thinking, and he offered her one.

As they both sat smoking and musing, Hassan said, "Okay, one more and then we should get back to the meeting. This one's a killer." He searched through the papers to find the pièce de résistance of all the racist attacks.

> A Sikh American took a taxi to the World Trade Center and witnessed the second plane as it slammed into the South Tower. He and hundreds around him fled as the rubble from the crash showered down on the streets below. After distancing himself from the building, he caught the attention of two young men in the crowd who shouted at him, "Take that turban off!" The Sikh crossed over to the opposite side of the street. The men crossed as well and repeated their order, "You terrorist, take that f****** turban off!" The Sikh man broke into a run again and the men chased after him. He managed to outrun them and ducked into

the subway to escape. (*Newsday*, New York, 9/13/01)

"Instead of trying to help the people who were injured, they go after a guy wearing a turban," said Sarah ironically. "Dude, it makes perfect sense. How many reports do you have there?" she asked admiring the stack.

"Must be about a hundred or so," Hassan estimated. "Imagine how big this stack'll be after a few more days of news coverage."

"It's scary," observed Sarah. "It's surreal, like something out of a horror movie—*Invasion of the Body Snatchers*. Our society is going collectively insane."

"More scary than I thought it would be the day before yesterday. That's why we should get back to the meeting."

There were more than 100 people in the cramped and hot meeting room on the third floor of the centre, that had seating for thirty. They spilled out into the hallway where Sarah and Hassan sat listening for an hour before the crowd dispersed enough for them to get into the room. People there were discussing much the same thing that the two friends had talked about earlier, only with a much higher degree of tension and argument.

There were disagreements over what course of action to take, whether they should be using the word "imperialism" and so on. The stifling heat, the cramped quarters, unbreathable air, and the frustration at being bombarded with racist propaganda, led to people taking out their frustrations on each other. It was a mini refugee camp of victims in the new war on terror. Religious and social groups, friends and family had suddenly become targets of hatred and violence. Finding themselves in a cramped room, hot and angry, there were bound to be skirmishes. They knew their real enemies—the ones fanning the flames of the racist backlash—were making plans in air-conditioned comfort. The generals in the war on terror were immune from attack, so aggravations ended up boiling over into infighting among the victims. Nevertheless, folks were offering the same critique of the recent barrage of jingoistic nationalism, and expressing the same fears about reactionary violence, as Hassan and Sarah did in their informal conversation. It was a political meeting, but it was also group therapy—a collective decontamination of the ideological pollutants ingested over the past two days. And it went on for hours.

*"...the mission is to fight and win war,
and therefore prevent war from happening in the first place."*
— GEORGE W. BUSH, FIRST PRESIDENTIAL DEBATE, 10/3/00

HAKIM, SAYED AND OMAR SPILLED out of Hakim's downtown apartment and makeshift SPHR office along with a cloud of smoke and laughter. It wasn't something they discussed or even thought about consciously, but they felt most comfortable walking in threes. A kaffiyeh-wearing dark man with facial hair strolling on his own, or even with one friend, was a target. Four or more of them were a threat. Three was just the right number—enough to give a measure of security, but not so many as to pose a challenge. They still got a few dirty looks from Saturday morning shoppers on Ste-Catherine Street, but not one of the onlookers verbalized their hatred.

Omar was happier than he had been in days. They were finally about to come out of hiding, to assert themselves in a positive action—the first one since 9/11. In the sunshine, flanked by his friends, Omar felt like he was finally waking from a bad dream. "Finally some fresh air," he said with a charming Parisian accent. The trio had been cooped up in Hakim's smoky residence all morning while he sent out faxes. "You guys smoke far too much," he complained. Of the three, Omar was having the most difficult time adjusting to the post-9/11 wave of hatred. He had led a sheltered childhood, growing up in a privileged family in Tunisia, going to the best private French schools and consorting with the children of the ruling class. When his father took them to Canada where he got a job as an engineer, everything changed. In Tunisia, Omar was lighter skinned than most of his fellow Africans. Here he was a dark-skinned immigrant, darker than Arabs like Sayed and Hakim. And in the past two and a half weeks, Omar had felt people's fear and hatred intensify under the scorching heat of the Twin Towers' flames, which burned continually on every television set in every North American living room.

Sayed bowed his head apologetically but said nothing. He would have put out his cigarette without even a murmur of protest, if Omar had asked him to. Sayed hardly ever spoke, and when he did people rarely noticed the low rumble of his voice and movement of lips behind the dark wilderness of his beard.

"Too much fresh air is bad for you," Hakim shot back, wearing a mischievous grin framed by a thick, well-kept goatee and moustache. "Don't turn into a hippie on us now! You've been eating granola haven't you? Admit it."

It was precisely the kind of remark that Omar would expect from Hakim, but Sayed, who had known Hakim longer and had been on the butt end of that sarcasm more than once, was as usual, completely scandalized. Maybe Omar had asthma or some kind of allergy or condition. And as usual, Sayed said nothing. He didn't want Hakim to turn his rapier wit on him.

"I don't know what things are like over at McGill, but at Concordia, the hippies and the anarchists are running rampant all over campus," Hakim continued. "You know what it was? That Summit of the Americas thing. That's what started it! How are we supposed to organize a serious political movement with these activist tourists everywhere?" Omar and Sayed knew Hakim was not seriously upset about "hippies" or the Summit of the Americas protest, but they could also tell he was making a point—one that he made often—that levels of sacrifice, commitment and personal stakes varied greatly amongst what was often assumed to be a homogenous group of activists. Hakim, a second-generation Palestinian immigrant, barred from returning to his homeland, was more than a little annoyed by activists picking and choosing their struggles like clothes at the Gap. Is Palestine in this year, or will it be baby seals? Sarah was the one white activist that Hakim thought could be almost fully trusted—almost. Strange as it seemed, that white girl was more uncompromising in her Palestinian solidarity than many of Hakim's Arab friends.

To most white activists, Hakim talked about Palestinian human rights in the abstract—violations of the Geneva Convention, collective punishment, arbitrary arrests, systematic torture, and so on. But Sarah was able to get him to go further.

ON THE THREE-HOUR BUS TRIP TO QUÉBEC CITY LAST APRIL, SHE WAS ACTUALLY ABLE TO PRY OPEN HIS PROTECTIVE SHELL, COAXING HIM TO SHARE WITH HER WHAT THE OCCUPATION HAD DONE TO HIS FAMILY. SHE REALLY SEEMED TO CARE ABOUT HIS FIVE-YEAR-OLD COUSIN WHO DIED AT A CHECKPOINT IN AN AMBULANCE ON THE WAY TO THE HOSPITAL, OR HIS AUNT WHO REFUSED TO LEAVE HER FARM EVEN AFTER THE ISRAELIS HAD BULLDOZED HER OLIVE TREES TO THE GROUND. HE REMEMBERED HOW WIDE-EYED SHE HAD BEEN OVER THE COURSE OF THAT RIDE. HE REMEMBERED HER TELLING HIM HOW IMPRESSED SHE WAS THAT HE WAS TAKING THE TROUBLE TO GO TO THE PROTEST IN QUÉBEC CITY AGAINST INJUSTICES IN THE WESTERN HEMISPHERE. CLEARLY HIS FAMILY HAD ITS HANDS FULL JUST TRYING TO HOLD THEMSELVES TOGETHER WHILE THE TROOPS, TANKS AND PLANES OF OCCUPATION WERE DOING EVERYTHING THEY COULD TO KEEP THEM APART. SHE WAS THE ONLY WHITE PERSON WHO HAD EVER SAID ANYTHING LIKE THAT TO HIM. STILL, HE WAS WAITING FOR THE OTHER SHOE TO DROP. THERE HAD TO BE ANOTHER SHOE. THERE ALWAYS WAS.

"Sure, we have our own hippies," said Omar. "Here comes one of them now."

Dave was walking behind the trio for some time, but he didn't notice them at all until he almost bumped into Omar when they stopped at Bishop Street to cross northward to Concordia's campus. He was looking at his feet and the cracks in the sidewalk. For some reason, one that even Dave himself could not explain, he had decided to avoid stepping on cracks in the sidewalk today. Dave did things like that. Chalk it up to the strange algorithms found only in the neural networks of certain McGill graduate students in computer science.

"Oh," said the surprised Dave as he looked into the smiling face of Omar inches away from his own. "Didn't see you there. Sorry. So, are you guys going to Sarah's meeting?"

Omar nodded as the trio smirked at the space cadet. Even Sayed was grinning in spite of himself. But then he bowed his head, looking at the sidewalk that Dave had been watching so intently. But instead of a reasonable explanation for Dave's behaviour there on the ground, he saw that Dave was wearing one green sock and one white sock. With great effort, Sayed was able to keep his lips from spreading into another disrespectful grin.

"Good," said Dave, not at all ill at ease for being caught in a child's game. He liked the attention. "I'll walk with you then..."

* * *

"What do you think?" asked Melanie, in her high-pitched squeaky voice as she held up her protest sign for Sarah's approval. She was so sweet and cute, like a little Lisa Simpson, only with more piercings and bright blue hair. The placard she held up read:

ON SEPT. 11

35 615 CHILDREN DIED OF STARVATION

- UN Food and Agriculture Organisation

Underneath the slogan she had painted a colour-coded graph representing the death totals in New York and the rest of the world on September 11.

Sarah turned from a computer screen where she was checking her email to look at the sign her fellow Raging Granddaughter was displaying. Melanie was sitting cross-legged amidst a clutter of paint, markers and bristol board strewn about the floor of the CSU "communications office"—a computer room on the sixth floor of Concordia's Hall Building that officially belonged to the student union but had been commandeered by leftwing campus groups to do posters, zines, leaflets and the like. It was also the room that Sarah had told people in her *ad hoc* group to congregate in to discuss their plan of action.

"That's awesome Melanie," Sarah radiated goodwill in Melanie's general direction. Melanie was always so cheerful and sweet; not smiling back at her would be like squashing a kitten. "It's really obvious but it's something we don't even think about. I mean, everybody knows that millions of children are starving or malnourished all over the world but we never talk about it so we forget. It puts the World Trade Center attacks in perspective."

Alex, another Raging Granddaughter, read off more statistics from another computer screen her coke-bottle lenses were glued to. "Twenty-two per cent of Palestinian children are suffering from acute or chronic malnutrition according to the UN Relief and Works Agency." Alex's much huskier voice contrasted markedly with the squeaky Melanie. "You can put that statistic on the opposite side." Alex didn't bother to turn away from the computer screen she was slouching in front of. Her extreme nearsightedness, only partially corrected by her thick glasses, meant that she always had to work in a hunched-over position. Her straight jet-black hair hung down to the keyboard where her bony white fingers were typing away. She and Melanie made a good team. Alex would research the information, and Melanie would lay it out artistically on the protest sign. They had been inseparable ever since their Québec City protest experience five months ago where they had spent a night in jail.

"That's terrorism," said a muffled voice from underneath a jacket on the couch by the window. It was a male voice, a bit hoarse, like a vacuum cleaner picking up tacks. That's how an old smoker's voice sounds when its owner wakes up on a couch on a Saturday morning.

"Dude, I thought you were asleep," laughed Sarah.

"I just woke up," said Hassan taking his jacket off of his face. "The chronic malnutrition of Palestinian children is not a natural disaster. It is an intended consequence of the occupation. It's terrorism." The ruffled hair around the edges of his bald head made him seem even frumpier than usual. "Ohh, that's goood!" he exclaimed as he saw Melanie's sign.

Hassan looked at his watch. It was 11 a.m. He had been sleeping for two hours and he didn't even hear the Raging Granddaughters come in. The Friday all-night shift was killer. Wasn't the meeting supposed to start at 10:30? "Where is everybody?" he asked.

"Yeah, where are all the boys?" asked Melanie as she made a note of Alex's suggestion for the verso of her sign on a scrap piece of paper.

"I knew they'd be late," said Sarah in an accusatory tone, "so I told them 10:30 instead of 11."

"Well, if they aren't here within the next hour or so we're going to be invaded by people getting ready for the demo," warned Alex. "And from the cryptic messages you've been sending us up to this point, I get the idea that you don't want a lot of people knowing about our plan."

"I've got it!" exclaimed Sarah, who had been reading over some quotes from Bush's most recent speech. "Dudes, listen to this one, for a slogan on one of your placards... If you're with Bush, you're with the terrorists!"

There was a pause while people let it sink in. Hassan nodded in agreement, "It works. It does work. It's perfectly reasonable, but..."

"I knew there was a 'but' coming," said Sarah in disappointment. "Ever since the attacks, we've been censoring ourselves."

"I know," Melanie agreed. "It's insidious."

"But there's nothing we can do about it," answered Hassan, ever the strategic realist. "All we can do is to soften the rhetoric without softening the critique. How about, If you're with Bush/bin Laden, you're with the terrorists?"

There was another pause as everybody tried on the new slogan.

"I don't know," Hassan was now second-guessing himself. "Maybe you should stick to your original idea. Of course everybody knows bin Laden's a terrorist. The point of your slogan is to show that Bush is one too, so maybe putting bin Laden in is just redundant. It's just that..."

"I know," Sarah said in an uncharacteristically soft and reassuring voice. She wanted to be understanding, especially now. Sarah knew she had a tendency to be brash at times, which was fine for the rightwing mengineers at the General Assembly, but it could be debilitating as hell for the people closest to her.

It was Greg who had helped her take a step back from the political arguments she was having with Hassan and Hakim, to look instead at the personal camaraderie that held their friendship together. In an ironic twist, Sarah was getting tips on activism from a security guard who claimed to be a-political. There was potential in him yet, she was sure of it. He wasn't ready to join their little group, but he was coming around. Greg just needed a little more friendly persuasion. Maybe they could rent a heart wrenching leftwing political drama tomorrow night: *Reds, 1900, Matewan...*

She had consciously refused herself the luxury of being offended by Hassan's suggestion. As the backlash grew, especially after the disastrous CSU General Assembly, people were becoming much more hesitant about expressing themselves too unequivocally. Protest signs, brandished with pride last April in Québec City, were now being discretely put into storage. Anti-imperialist T-shirts found their way to the bottom of dresser drawers. Sarah didn't like it. She was frustrated as hell by it, but she forced herself to be as accommodating as possible to people's fear of backlash without succumbing to it herself. As Greg had said, she couldn't scare people over to her side because it was her class enemy who had all the guns. He told her it was one of the few things his mother used to say that actually made sense. Two weeks ago Sarah had argued adamantly against canceling Sabra and Shatila remembrance activities. Today, with conscious effort, she acknowledged the reactionary pressure that called for a different approach. The new tactic rubbed her the wrong way. It was like listening attentively and patiently to fingernails on a chalkboard sending shivers down every confrontational bone in her body. "SPHR is being branded a 'terrorist' organisation in the press," she reminded her friends in a subdued and unassuming tone. "They couldn't even book university space to do their bazaar. If we're too over-the-top at this protest it could be fun for us, but damaging as hell for SPHR as an organisation."

As she was finishing her sentence, Sayed, Dave, Hakim and Omar walked in.

"What could be damaging as hell to SPHR?" Hakim asked feigning serious concern. "You're not bringing your anarchist flags and Molotov cocktails to the demo today are you?"

Sarah shot back a nervous smile. She was never quite sure when he was being ironic. Hakim's dark eyebrows in a permanent frown gave him an emphatically serious bearing. And she knew he had a bit of a chip on his shoulder about young radical chicks like her.

Hakim was always teasing Sarah and the other Raging Granddaughters about their anarcho-anti-globalization ideology and tactics. Although he and other SPHR activists had been involved in the Québec City anti-FTAA protests, they were skeptical about the seriousness of the "fly-by-night" affinity groups that converged on international conferences like deadheads at Grateful Dead concerts. He, Sayed and Omar were dressed much more clean-cut than the Raging Granddaughters. They wore short hair, jeans or slacks and button-down shirts, and they lacked the piercings of their anarchist counterparts. And today, in preparation for the protest, all three were wearing their kaffiyehs.

"This is your student union office?" asked the wide-eyed Omar. It was his first time on the Hall Building's sixth floor—his first time in the nerve centre of Montréal student protest. Looking over the clutter on the floor, the overflowing recycling boxes, the Coke cans, pizza boxes, the state-of-the-art computers, and the grafitti painted on the walls, he laughed and said, "I can't imagine our student society at McGill allowing this in their offices." His father, who had sent him to private schools, both in Tunisia and Montréal, insisted that he continue his first-class education at McGill. Omar wanted to go to Concordia because the SPHR chapter seemed more active, but he couldn't bear disappointing his father. The young activist looked at the radical-friendly environment of his Concordia comrades with a certain envy.

"No, the SSMU offices are for professional student politicians, not mere students," Dave jumped in as he raced to the one computer that was not in use. "Their security system is probably tighter than Warmonger Inc.'s. You have to convince the receptionist you have official business with somebody important before she'll buzz you in." The keyboard was already clattering under the able fingers of the computer geek as he finished uttering his last sentence. He grinned and laughed through his nose at something on the screen. If anybody made the mistake of asking him what was so funny, few would have understood his explanation of the humourous idiosyncrasies of the CSU office's computer network. He would have followed the explanation with an equally incomprehensible joke about that system and then would have laughed far too loudly about it, knowing full well that nobody else understood the humour. He seemed to take pride in maintaining a quixotic appearance, like he wanted people to wonder about what made him so weird. That must have been why he had decided to part his straight blond hair right down the middle of his head and to wear two differently coloured socks at all times. Today he wore a T-shirt with his official mascot on it—Albert Einstein. It got a lot of compliments at McGill. For some reason people thought Einstein was cool. Whenever anybody said how great Einstein was, Dave would immediately agree and add, "Yeah he had a great anti-capitalist political analysis. I loved his 1949 article 'Why Socialism?' published in *Monthly Review*." After that, according to Dave's expert calculations, 99.9 percent of McGill students changed their opinion about Einstein, while 0.01 percent changed their opinion about capitalism.

Seeing the grad student step out of line, Sarah cracked the whip. "Dude, before you get too comfy there, we've got to have our meeting. You guys are late, and there are going to be people coming in pretty soon to prepare for the 2:00 demo."

Without any argument the friends grabbed chairs from the desks and placed them facing the couch where Hassan was seated. Hassan watched with appreciation. It never ceased to amaze him how Sarah, a 19-year-old first-year university student straight out of CÉGEP, was able to order guys around who were ten years her senior without any opposition. Melanie remained cross-legged on the floor in the middle of the group, painting away.

Sarah took a large roll of paper from her backpack and spread it out on the floor over top of one of Melanie's protest signs. It was the plans that Hassan had given her, redrawn in a larger and easier to read format than the crumpled papers from the cabby's pocket.

"The action itself might sound a bit far-fetched, but it'll actually be the easy part," she explained. "The hard part will be getting past the 9/11 propaganda machine to reach the hearts and minds that it's holding hostage. That's what Hassan will be trying to do while we're putting ourselves on the line."

With that everybody turned to the surprised, half-asleep and disheveled cabby whose small form was half-sunken into the cushions of the couch. Hassan looked blankly at the friends around him for a few seconds before it occurred to him that he was expected to speak. "Um, yeah. Since I won't be in on the action I'll be doing media work. Sarah has done a draft press release in English, which I'll translate into French. If anybody wants to help do the press releases, that would be great. I'm also going to do a call-out for activists in English and French for the day of the action so they can engage in some kind of solidarity demonstration involving masses of people. That'll be very important in drawing attention to what you guys are trying to do. It'll also make it more difficult for the cops to come down too hard on you."

"Is the non-violence of the action part of the message?" asked Hakim. "We don't want any of this 'diversity of tactics' stuff. It'll make us look like we really are terrorists."

Diversity of tactics had become a rallying cry for the radical left ever since the Summit of the Americas "riot." The idea was to allow space at mass mobilizations for all forms of protest including controversial property destruction (mostly painting of political graffiti and window-smashing at banks and corporate retail outlets) and "violence" (fighting back when police use crowd-control techniques). The rationale was that it would be impossible and undesirable to employ a stage-managed and disciplined non-violent resistance to combat a violent system of global oppression. Genuine mass resistance was, of necessity, messy and destructive. Furthermore, polite non-threatening protests were unlikely to produce a substantial change from the normal course of global governance—what amounted to corporate-sponsored mass murder. The powers that be had to be threatened with the real possibility of an ungovernable population.

The Raging Granddaughters and other radical anti-globalization groups were known for their support of a diversity of tactics position. As he posed the diversity of tactics question, Hakim looked directly at Sarah, as the unofficial leader of the Raging Granddaughter tendency, raising his right eyebrow while frowning with his left. This was a make-or-break issue for him and the SPHR boys. Either the whole action would be explicitly, and entirely, non-violent, or they would not participate.

"Don't worry," said Sarah reassuringly. "Diversity of tactics, I think we can all agree, totally does not apply here. The risks inherent in this kind of illegal action are already bad enough without 9/11. We don't need to, like, add fuel to the fire. We don't have the means to destroy any weapons-industry infrastructure, and even if we did, there's no way we could do that without risking innocent lives, including our own. I think the press releases and call-outs should be as explicit as possible about our non-violence. For our own safety, if nothing else." People were nodding in agreement. Hakim's right eyebrow slowly reestablished its equilibrium with the left one.

"Anyway, the press releases and call-outs are not the only way we'll be communicating. Dudes, you should be checking out our manifesto too," Sarah reminded the group.

"Oh right, yeah," Hassan had forgotten about the manifesto, once Sarah admitted the press release was the way to go with the mainstream press. "We all got it on email. I helped put it together, but it's kind of long..." He looked around at others in the room to see if anybody would jump in to talk about the document.

There was an uncomfortable pause that seemed much longer than the five seconds it lasted. "I read it," Dave finally said with a proud grin as others guiltily avoided Sarah's glare.

"At least one person read it," a dejected Sarah gave an appreciative halfhearted smile to the grad student. "The weekend that I spent writing it wasn't entirely wasted." It wasn't quite true that only one person had read the manifesto. Hassan and Sarah's mother had also looked over the document, but Sarah didn't count Hassan because she dragged him and his big old brain into the writing process and she couldn't count her mother. She had to read it. It was her motherly duty.

"Actually," murmured Sayed. His words were articulated very clearly, but his voice was only slightly louder than a whisper. "I read it too." Somehow Sarah was surprised every time that subdued voice slipped out from behind his beard. It always seemed to her that a barrel-chested man like Sayed should have a booming voice. Sayed wouldn't have said anything at all about reading the manifesto if Sarah had not been so insistent. He hated the feeling of eyes burning into him. And now that he opened his mouth, he had become the focus of attention. "It was good," he offered, hoping that they would stop staring at him.

After a few more seconds of hushed stillness had passed, and it was clear that Sayed had said his piece, Dave jumped back in. "I have a few suggestions about wording. With a bit of tweaking it could be made more appealing to a broader base of people. I'll send them to you. Also I could put it up on the Internet as a PDF file so people can download it. I know people will read it once we make a splash."

"Thanks that would be great," Sarah's smile broadened. "Anyway, while Hassan is on standby waiting to press the 'send' button on the press releases and call-outs, it'll be Dave's job, as our token white boy," she gave the white boy a wink, "to get us all into the Innomonde Building. Their security system is pretty tight on the whole building because all the corporate tenants are like totally big player high-security clients. Besides Warmonger Inc., there's an electronics manufacturer, a software developer, and some other stuff like that."

"At about ten minutes to five, dressed as a nice respectable business dude with matching socks and everything, he'll go through the front entrance here," she pointed to the map on the floor. "He'll give the security guard a letter for our friend Mr. Tremblay on the third floor in an envelope with some bank's letterhead on it to make it look important. Then Dave, the respectable business dude, will ask to use the washroom, which is on the ground floor, here. But instead of returning to the main entrance when he's finished, he'll go out the back way. If the security guard asks, Dave, your 'car is in the garage' down this stairwell, here."

"Which means he can let us in the rear stairwell," said Hakim.

"Yes, but not right away," said Sarah. "There's a security camera in the stairwell that the guards might be watching when Dave leaves. That's why he's just going to nonchalantly plug the latch hole in the automatic lock with something. Hassan will be waiting out front with a cell phone to see when the security guards are distracted enough for everybody to go in."

"Cool," said Melanie, painting the other side of her child hunger placard. "We're like spies in a Hollywood movie."

"Except this time the Arab terrorists are the good guys," added Omar.

Everybody laughed except the old cabby tucked away on the couch, but nobody seemed to notice him.

"That's really a new twist," said Hakim briefly suppressing his own snickering. "Maybe we can film everything and get Al-Jazeera to run it."

It took about twenty minutes for Sarah to bring them up to speed on the whole plan in all its detail. Ten minutes would have been enough for a full run-down but people kept making jokes or humming the theme song from *Mission Impossible*. The cloak and dagger aspect of the whole operation was a novelty to the student activists, and despite the dangers involved, it was fun. And there was so little fun in those early days of the recently declared "war on terror" that they had to savour every delicious moment of it. And they all did savour it—everybody except Hassan. He was simply incapable of sharing their youthful excitement. Ironically, as the only one who was not putting his body on the line in the action, it was Hassan who was seriously worried about the grave consequences that might befall his friends. But they chalked up his sour expression to morning grumpiness.

People were talking and joking about how surprised the Warmonger Inc. executives would be as Hassan was deep in his own dark thoughts, brooding on his corner of the couch. It seemed that the meeting was ending, but it appeared to Sayed that there was one more important question that needed to be dealt with. He looked around to see if anybody else would bring it up, but everyone seemed oblivious. "So when do we hit them?" asked Sayed.

Nobody heard him. Sarah, however, noticed he was trying to get a word in. She gestured for everyone to quiet down, which people did.

"What's that Sayed?" she asked.

"When are we going to do the action?" he reluctantly asked again.

"That's a totally important question," Sarah replied. She took out her agenda and started to look over the next couple of weeks, "I don't know about the specific day. Obviously the

whole plan depends on going in at the end of a workday, so it has to be sometime between a Monday and a Friday, but it could work on any Monday through Friday."

Omar caught a glimpse of her agenda cover, "Oh my God, is that-"

"Yes it is," Sarah said before he could finish his question. She was proudly holding her agenda for all to see. "The famous *Uprising 2001-2002 CSU Agenda*. 'This is not an agenda called uprising: it is an agenda for uprising.' Let me tell you, it was sooo hard to get. I had to keep coming back every day. They got a few hundred copies from the printer every day or two but students kept nabbing them up. Fifteen minutes after a new shipment came in they were all gone. Last week I was here at the right time when they wheeled in about 20 boxes of them. You should've seen the free-for-all that erupted."

"Is it as radical as they say?" asked the awestruck McGill student.

"My only problem with it is that there's no space to write appointments with all the political stuff in it," Hassan commented. "That's why I don't use it. It's not much more radical than last year's agenda. There's more Palestinian content and that bothers a lot of powerful people here. Plus there's the September 11 factor. There was no way the student union could've known about that when they sent the thing to print back in August."

"Yeah, but there was some guy that came to my class," Hakim jumped in, "who was saying the CSU exec knew about the attacks beforehand."

Incredulous laughter irrupted, but Hakim maintained a straight face. "No, I'm serious. He said that on the date of September 11th there was something in the agenda about the bombing."

The laughter died out, and Sarah's brow became furrowed as she leafed through the agenda to find the date of September 11. On the top of the section devoted to that date it read: ➤

SEPTEMBER

Monday
10

ORIENTATION EVENT: 7pm H-
Bringing the Struggle Home

Tuesday
11

1812 Luddite Potato riot in England

ORIENTATION EVENT: 7pm H-
Splitting the Sky

Wednesday
12

Last Day to add two-term (/3) and
(/2) courses
1918 Eugene Debs sent

"He couldn't be referring to 'Splitting the Sky' could he?" asked Sarah.

"Yeah, that's it!" exclaimed Hakim. "He said the CSU was having an event called 'Splitting the Sky' on September 11, so they knew it was going to happen. He said that we should sign the petition to kick the radical executive out of office."

"Oh my God," said Sarah. "This is crazy. 'Splitting the Sky' is the name of the native speaker who they had scheduled to speak on that day. I'm like so sure he changed his name just to speak on September 11th at a CSU event."

"Just when you thought it couldn't get any weirder..." said Alex as she shrugged her bony shoulders.

Sarah tried to shake the ridiculous thoughts loose so she could concentrate. "Okay, dudes, we still have to decide on a date."

"You know what would be cool?" asked Alex. People looked at the lanky student with a glint of excitement behind her thick glasses. "What would be cool is if we had all the research on the technologies Warmonger Inc. produces that are being used to bomb the shit out of Afghanistan and we put that in our press stuff, and we hit them the day after the bombing starts."

There was general agreement in the room, except Dave who asked, "Okay, but what if the bombing starts on a Friday or a Saturday?"

"Oh, that shouldn't be a problem," Sarah answered. "We can just do it on the following Monday anyway."

"What's a likely timeframe for the bombing to start?" asked Melanie, and all eyes turned to the cabby.

"Who do I look like, Donald Rumsfeld?" asked Hassan in perfect deadpan delivery. He waited for the laughter to die down before answering the question. "Okay, the way things are going now, I would say early to mid October. They don't want to wait too long, because they don't want to get caught in the field in the middle of the Afghan winter. The Soviets didn't have much fun with that one."

"So people should be ready to go any time in early to mid October," Sarah advised as she looked through her calendar. "Dude, that's next week! So we should be ready to go next week. Put all the stuff on your checklists in a bag somewhere handy. As soon as the bombing starts, check your email and I'll give a meeting time and place."

"Why don't we meet at Al-Taïb at 12 noon, on the day after the bombing starts, no matter what?" suggested Hakim. "I don't know if everybody will be able to check their email."

"Good idea," Sarah agreed. "And remember, don't do anything at the demo today that might get you arrested. We can't risk having anybody in jail at this point. And don't talk about this plan to anyone. It's top secret."

"This message will self-destruct in 30 seconds," added Dave, and with that, people started humming the theme song to *Mission Impossible*.

The group continued to make placards for the SPHR demo, and as the 2 o'clock departure time approached, the office became a beehive. More and more activists added their bodies to the clutter of the small communications office, tripping over the placard facings and sticks that littered the floors, squawking frantically on cell phones, and taking care of last minute organizational details.

The realization that a war was imminent, in the next week or two, spurred the organizers to continue despite the storm of slander, threats and racist violence sweeping North America. Nevertheless people were worried. How would the police treat Arab protestors wearing kaffiyehs or hijabs while carrying Palestinian flags in a demonstration organized by a group labeled "terrorist" in the mainstream press? And when these protestors were joined by the *Convergence des luttes anti-capitalistes* (CLAC)—a ragtag group of anarchists and anti-globalization activists that had been involved in organizing the Québec City protests against the Summit of the Americas—what then?

It was a lively crowd of over 500 that assembled in front of Concordia's Hall Building. There were Palestinian flags flying along side the black and red of anarchists. People were drumming on homemade instruments, chanting anti-war slogans and "free, free Palestine" in English, Arabic and French. The pro-Palestinian slogans and flags were not appreciated by a group of Zionists who confronted the protestors as they marched down Ste-Catherine Street, but the demo's marshals—provided by SPHR—were able to control the situation, separating the two groups and keeping the police at bay.

Hakim, Sayed and Omar pitched in as marshals. They kept discipline in the ranks of the mobilization as the Zionists tried to provoke a confrontation, hurling the racist slogan, "Arab terrorists, go home." The marshals blocked the small incendiary group from mixing into the crowds of demonstrators by forming an immobile chain of human bodies. Refraining from any reaction to the epithets, the three men radiated a sense of calm to their fellow protestors. Their expressionless faces told their friends these fanatics are not worth the trouble.

Sarah, Melanie and Alex all hung together, singing from their Raging Granddaughter repertoire. Hassan and Dave simply walked and chatted. They talked about everything from the Israeli-Palestinian conflict in the post-September 11 context, to Sarah's manifesto, to chess. They talked a lot about chess.

The CLAC's anti-globalizationist radicals joined the protest as it arrived at Phillips Square on its way east. With over 600 protestors now, the march continued in an eastward direction until St. Alexandre, a back-street that led them to the American consulate. The marshals, surprised that the street was not blocked by riot squads, kept a close watch on the more adventurist protestors and their police escort, fearing a trap. As the protest passed the consulate, various anti-American slogans could be heard, *"George Bush terroriste, Canada complice!"* But there was also a prepared speech given by a representative from SPHR mourning the loss of innocent lives in the September 11 attacks. There were some that clearly wanted to stay and vent their frustration at the American consulate—protected by a single line of Montréal police in riot gear. Nevertheless, the SPHR marshals kept the protest moving south along St. Alexandre and then west along René-Levèsque Boulevard.

The protest "ended" at a park on the west side of downtown. That was the official termination of the event, but once the SPHR marshals had hung up their armbands a few members of the crowd began rallying people for an unofficial protest that would head back to the American consulate for an impromptu flag-burning ceremony. At that point, the *ad hoc* group members decided to leave the protest. They couldn't afford to risk arrest right now. That could totally ruin their whole plan.

Just over a hundred protestors stuck around for the ill-fated anti-American fireworks. They had a right to free expression. It was the United States that didn't have the right to bomb whomever it felt like just because people wanted revenge. Nevertheless, it was clear that in the post-9/11 climate of security overkill, the finer civil-libertarian niceties were all but forgotten. The white anarchists who led the unofficial protest back to the consulate for a short-lived star-spangled bonfire, unwittingly gave SPHR's enemies precisely what they were looking for—an excuse to label the demonstration "violent" and to make more insinuations about SPHR "terrorist connections." Concordia Rector Lowy would mention the arrests as evidence after-the-fact for the pre-emptive actions taken to deny SPHR the right to hold its activities on Concordia's campus.

It was the flag-burning combined with some graffiti written in black marker on a McDonald's that provided the ideological justification for the mass arrests that followed—eighty in total. Suddenly the protest became a "riot." As Montréal Police spokesperson André Durocher told reporters, "Obviously when people come to demonstrations with slings, gas masks and paintballs, one can, at least, question their intentions."

* * *

"This is the place dad," said Sarah insistently, as if by sheer force of will, she could overcome his skepticism about the Rosemont diner.

"Not exactly my idea of ambiance," he replied, dutifully parking the car.

"It has ambiance," Shirley chimed optimistically, "just not the kind you're used to. We used to hang out at places like this when we were your age dear." She gripped her husband's arm and gave him a meaningful look, "Remember Jack?"

And then he did remember. He remembered why they were here, and how he was supposed to act. "Oh yeah, sure. We didn't always have money. Took me a while to work my way up the corporate ladder." As they entered the greasy spoon he was careful not to comment on the bright lighting or the failed effort at simulating 1950s décor, just as he had refrained from making any disparaging remarks about the spectacle of abstract modern dance they had experienced earlier that night.

The family sat at a window booth in the small no-smoking section. Their waitress, a black woman in a pink uniform with close-cropped gray hair, gave them menus. "Hello dear," she said to Sarah in a warm voice, "so these are your folks?"

"Oh hi Betty," said Sarah, feigning surprise. "Yes this is my dad, Jack Murphy and my mom, Shirley. Mom, dad, this is Betty."

"Hi Betty," her parents said politely. Jack buried his head in his menu while Shirley smiled at her daughter and her unlikely friend.

"Dad," said Sarah, pulling his menu down to lay bare his face, "you might know Betty from back in the 60s. She went to Sir George Williams you know..."

"Is that right?" asked Jack in an uneasy surprised tone.

"Yeah," Sarah replied smugly. "Well, she finished before you did, in February of 1969."

There was a restless silence as the not-so-subtle hint about Betty's past sunk in. Nobody "finished" university in the middle of winter session, and February 1969 just happened to be the date of the Sir George Williams computer centre riots.

Jack finally broke the silence with a forced laugh. "It was a crazy time," he said shaking his head.

"I bet it was," Sarah agreed, with a triumphant grin. "Hey, maybe you two have some old friends in common."

"Sure," said Betty in an amiable tone. "How about Rocky Jones? Everybody knew who Rocky Jones was."

Jack only shook his head, still wearing his ridiculous forced smile. But Shirley touched his arm and laughed. "Sure you knew Rocky Jones. I remember you talking about him. Didn't he give some kind of speech on the Mezzanine?"

"Oh boy, did he ever!" said Betty. "I had such a crush on Rocky back then. A lot of us did. He gave such great speeches and he had those deep-set eyes. He didn't wear sunglasses like the other black leaders. I first saw him speak at the Black Writers Congress at McGill back in 1968. But it was his speech on the Mezzanine that everybody remembers. He told all those white students and professors right to their faces that they were 'pansies'..." And with that Betty started shaking with uncontrollable laughter. When she finally caught her breath again she continued. "He said, 'White men are pansies, because they won't even fight for white folks. They allow their own society to exploit their own people, and black people have become the vanguard of the revolutionary movement to overthrow that whole thing that's exploiting everybody. You're pansies.' And then all those white students and professors applauded..."

Her resumed laughter was contagious to Sarah and Shirley, but Jack merely bobbed his head with its painted smile that hid his tightly clenched teeth.

JACK REMEMBERED THAT SPEECH TOO, BUT HE WASN'T ONE OF THE "PANSIES" WHO WERE APPLAUDING. HE SAW THE TRUTH IN ROCKY'S WORDS AT THE TIME, BUT HE JUST THOUGHT EXPLOITATION AND INJUSTICE WERE THE WAY OF THE WORLD AND IT WAS BETTER TO GET AHEAD THAN TO RISK HIS OWN HIDE TO "LIBERATE" THE CARIBBEANS WHO WERE PISSED OFF ABOUT BEING ON THE BOTTOM OF THE SOCIAL LADDER. JACK HAD ALWAYS THOUGHT OF HIMSELF AS "NON-POLITICAL," BUT HEARING ROCKY'S SPEECH MADE HIM REALIZE THAT, IN THE EYES OF STUDENT RADICALS, HE WAS "REACTIONARY":

NOW A LOT OF REACTIONARY STUDENTS THAT EXIST IN THIS CAMPUS AND EVERY CAMPUS WILL REJECT THAT CONCEPT OF FIGHTING CAPITALISM BECAUSE THAT'S THE OLD MAN OUT THERE WHO OWNS THE STORE THAT IS EXPLOITING THE PEOPLE. IF THE OLD MAN IS THE BOSS, AND SOME OF THE PEOPLE ARE THE WORKERS, YOU'LL SAY I CAN'T FIGHT THAT BECAUSE

THEN I WON'T BE ABLE TO COME TO THIS UNIVERSITY
AND PLAY MY GAME, AND GO ON MY TRIP, AND
SMOKE MY POT, AND SCREW MY WOMEN...

OKAY, SO I'M A "REACTIONARY" THOUGHT JACK. SO WHAT? BUT IT
BOTHERED HIM BECAUSE HE KNEW THAT BEING A REACTIONARY WAS
CONSIDERED OUT OF FASHION IN THE 1960S AND JACK LIKED BEING
IN STYLE. YOU WERE ALLOWED TO SCREW AND GET HIGH BUT THERE
SEEMED TO BE SOME RULE ABOUT A HIGHER PURPOSE—PEACE AND LOVE.
IT WAS ALMOST LIKE RELIGION. JACK LIKED THE SEX, DRUGS AND ROCK-
AND-ROLL AND HE HAD THE GROOVIEST OF FASHION SENSE. HIS BLUE
AND WHITE STRIPED BELL-BOTTOMS WERE TIGHT AROUND HIS GROIN, HIS
HAIR CAME DOWN TO JUST ABOVE THE SHOULDERS OF HIS SIR GEORGE
JACKET, AND HE HAD THE RESPECTABLE BEGINNINGS OF A LOVELY JET
BLACK FU-MAN-CHEW ON HIS UPPER-LIP AND CHIN. BUT JACK'S POLITICS
WERE OUT OF STYLE—THEY CLASHED WITH HIS THREADS. OF COURSE,
THE POLITICS OF THESE RADICALS WERE SO EXTREME HE REALLY DIDN'T
THINK THAT MOST OF THEM EVEN BELIEVED THEIR OWN RHETORIC. HE
WAS SURE HIS MAOIST FRIENDS WHO HE SMOKED UP WITH WERE JUST
IN IT FOR THE CHICKS—THEY WEREN'T REALLY POLITICAL. THEY WERE
REACTIONARY, JUST LIKE HIM. WHEN HE MET A REALLY SEXY GIRL, SOME-
TIMES JACK WOULD PRETEND TO BE A COMMUNIST TOO, BUT HE ALWAYS
FELT GUILTY ABOUT IT THE NEXT MORNING. HE WOULD REMEMBER
HIS FATHER CALLING HIM A LONG-HAIRED-HIPPIE-COMMUNIST-DRAFT-
DODGER AS HE TALKED TO HIM ON THE PHONE FROM THE NEW YORK
BUS STATION. THAT WAS THE LAST THING HE WOULD EVER HEAR HIS
FATHER SAY. HIS MOTHER WOULD STILL SEND HIM HIS FATHER'S MONEY,
BUT HE WOULD NEVER HAVE HIS FATHER'S APPROVAL. HE WOULD ALWAYS
BLOW OFF THOSE GIRLS THE NEXT MORNING, NO MATTER HOW PRETTY
OR HOW NICE THEY WERE. ROCKY MUST HAVE SCORED A LOT WITH THE
CHICKS...

"So what's old Rocky up to now?" asked Jack.

"Oh, he's got a successful law practice over in Halifax," said
Betty wiping the tears of laughter from the corners of her eyes.
"A lot of those 'student radicals' have become real success stories.
Rosie Douglas was deported from the country in leg irons but he
went on to become the Prime Minister of Dominica! But here I
am, still working as a waitress... So what can I get for you folks?"

They all looked at the menus again. Sarah, who had been
entirely pleased with herself about this whole "accidental"

meeting she and Betty had arranged, suddenly saw the flaw in her plan. There was hardly anything vegetarian on the menu. "Um..." said Sarah, "give us a minute would you Betty?"

"Sure," she agreed with a warm smile. "I'll come back in a few minutes dear."

Jack and Shirley both ate juicy hamburgers which was Jack's one triumph of the night. His consolation prize. Sarah had a grilled cheese and fries doused with generous amounts of ketchup.

As he brought his thick cheeseburger to his lips, the aroma of red meat doused with mustard and sweet relish under his nose had him salivating. His teeth were just sinking into it when he heard the hauntingly familiar voice. "Hey Betty, how's tricks?"

With the sound of that voice, at once comical and threatening, his senses of taste and smell instantly withered. He was focused on the shadowy presence arriving from behind. He slumped forward over his plate so the back of the booth would hide the top of his head from the approaching ghost. Jack wished he could just crawl away and die someplace where nobody would see him. But maybe he was mistaken. Maybe it was all this talk about SGW in the late 60s that had set off his imagination. What were the odds it could really be him? But Jack knew it was him and Jack knew there was nowhere to hide. Morty would find him. Just like he did on the metro years earlier.

The steps came closer. Jack expected a hand to grab his shoulder. But the dark figure moved right past him and then veered to the service counter where he sat with his back to the Murphys. All that Jack could see was a slightly balding crown surrounded by disheveled gray curls, a tweed jacket and blue jeans. But Jack could tell it was Morty, just by that dreadfully cheery bounce in his step and the way he played the bongos on the counter as Betty came up to take his order. Morty was clearly biding his time, waiting for the right moment to swivel around on his stool and pounce.

"A friend of yours?" asked Shirley.

"What?" Jack sat back upright and looked at his wife in surprise.

"That man sitting over there," continued Shirley. "You just keep staring at him. Is he a friend of yours?"

"What?" Jack said in a hushed offended tone. "I'm not staring at anybody. Please Shirley."

"Okay Jack, take it easy," his wife responded soothingly. "I'm not accusing you of anything." And before Jack could continue the senseless argument any further she deftly changed the subject. "So Sarah, how do you like your grilled cheese?"

"Ish greaa..." Sarah replied with her mouth full. She chewed a bit more and swallowed before adding sarcastically, "that's why I come here. The best grilled cheeses in town." And then in an effort to keep Betty in their conversation she raised her voice a couple of notches, "Plus the service is excellent."

"My pleasure dear," Betty replied from behind the counter. "Need any more ketchup or anything?"

And once the conversation crossed the counter, the inevitable result was precisely what Jack had been dreading. The man seated between the Murphys and Betty swiveled around on his stool to see the other party in the dialogue. Jack was surprised in spite of himself. He knew it was Morty before he turned around but Jack wasn't prepared to see the face of his nemesis. It was different than in his dreams—not twisted in anger, but mild-mannered and good-natured as always. The most surprising thing was how black his mustache had remained despite the complete graying of his hair and eyebrows. His glasses looked less Grouchoesque without their thick frames, but he still looked like the old Morty.

"Oh my God!" Morty exclaimed. "I don't believe it. And here of all places. Jack, I wouldn't have guessed it in a million years."

"It's been a while," Jack replied sheepishly.

"Yeah it has, ages." Morty enthusiastically counted the years on his fingers. "Jeez, almost two decades, it has to be. The last time was... Oh yeah, on the metro. I was having a tough time back then, Jack. Sorry for my behaviour."

"Oh," said Jack nonchalantly. "Don't worry about it. You know me. My feathers don't get ruffled over stuff like that."

"Water off a duck's back, eh Jack?" Morty laughed. "Oh, well it's good to see you're not sore about it. I was just such a wreck, man. You've got to understand. I was working full time in the stacks at the Redpath Library. You know, over at McGill? And then I was moonlighting on this crazy project with the Québec-Palestine Solidarity Committee..."

"Don't worry about it," Jack repeated more forcefully this time. "Really." Then partly out of politeness but mostly to change the subject, Jack introduced Mordecai Dingleman to his wife and daughter.

"I can't believe my dad knows someone involved in something called the 'Québec-Palestine Solidarity Committee'," marveled Sarah.

"Me neither," Shirley added.

"That was a long time ago," Jack explained.

"Yeah, it sure was," agreed Morty. "In fact, back when I knew your dad, I didn't know the first thing about Israel or Palestine or the Middle East. I had all the religious education as a kid. Learned Hebrew and the whole bit. But by my teenage years I was what you might call a 'ham-on-rye-Jew.' My family bought Israel bonds and all that but I had no idea what it was all about. I knew about anti-Semitism here in Montréal though. Sure was lots of that. So it made sense to me we should have a country of our own somewhere. My uncle Max couldn't get into med school at McGill because of the quotas back in the 50s. That's why my parents insisted I go there. But remember what I said about McGill Jack? Remember?"

Jack shook his head. He remembered but he just didn't want to repeat it.

"Sure you remember, Jack," continued Morty undeterred. "I used to say it all the time, 'McGill can suck my circumcised dick.' That's what I used to say. And then wouldn't you know it? I end up working for the bastards! I've been working the stacks at Redpath since '76. Mordecai Dingleman, a yid from

Sir George, organizing the hallowed tomes of knowledge for the Anglo-Saxon bourgeoisie!"

Shirley, Sarah and Betty were all laughing while Jack smiled uneasily. He bit into his cheeseburger but it wasn't as tasty as it was supposed to be.

"I'm involved in Québec-Palestine solidarity too," offered Sarah. "Although we don't have a committee of that name. There's SPHR, Solidarity for Palestinian Human Rights."

"You're sure you're Jack's daughter?" Morty laughed with a wink in Jack's direction. "I know those kids in SPHR. They're a great bunch. I'm not as political as I used to be now. I gave a bit of money to help with the start-up of the Jewish Alliance Against the Occupation but I don't have time to go to the meetings. I'm working on a novel now..."

As Morty started explaining the concept of his book about Montréal Communist factions of the 1970s, Jack excused himself to go to the washroom. He felt like he was going to be sick. He ran the water and leaned over the sink, looking at himself in the mirror and shaking his head. What the hell were you thinking Jack? he asked himself. The whole purpose of this family evening was to talk his daughter out of the crazy terrorist cult she had been dragged into. Instead he was taking a trip down memory lane with a computer centre rioter turned waitress and Morty Dingleman was telling his daughter what a great bunch of kids SPHR are.

When Jack got back to the table Morty was still talking. "So Jack moved out at the end of the fall term in 68, if my memory serves me. That was one room empty. Then Shelly and Simon get arrested in the February occupation, so me, Benoit and Jennifer had to scrape the money together to pay all that extra rent. Simon's parents ended up covering his end and Betty ended up moving in, so it wasn't that bad. At least I got some good Jamaican cooking. What was really cool were all the meetings that used to happen in our house about trial strategy after the occupation. Remember Betty?"

"How could I forget?" said Betty rolling her eyes. "You were talking the whole time, dominating the meetings, and you weren't even in the occupation. Me and Jennifer ended up doing all the cooking and cleaning. That's why your little commune fell apart dear."

"We weren't very enlightened in those days," Morty admitted.

"I don't feel so well," Jack wheezed as he sat down.

"No you don't look good at all," Shirley agreed. "You're white as a sheet."

"I think we should go," Jack said as he took out some money to pay the bill. "I should get to bed."

"Aw jeez Jack," Morty complained, "we were just getting caught up after all these years. I'm giving you my phone number, and you have to promise to call! We can go someplace nice next time," he said with a wink in Betty's direction. She punched him in the shoulder.

Jack managed to get out the words, "Sure thing Morty." Then Jack settled the bill and went to wait in the car.

His frustration grew as he sat in the car watching the much longer goodbyes through the diner window. His own family was being brainwashed before his eyes, in a mini drive-in movie, and he was a mere spectator, sitting in his sedan, powerless to do anything about it. Sarah he could understand, but Shirley should know better. Finally Shirley extricated herself from the conversation and joined her husband in the car.

"Well that went just fabulously!" snapped Jack.

"Actually," said Shirley, putting her hand on Jack's, "I had a good time. We should do this more often."

"What?! I can't believe—"

"Look Jack, we finally went out as a family and we got to see a bit of what makes our daughter tick. That's what this was about."

"No this was about stopping Sarah from ruining her life. I didn't count on Morty and that waitress interfering! I'd say we're worse off than when we started. Now she's under the mistaken impression that we're okay with what she's doing. I can't believe you laughing at Dingleman's jokes."

"Can I help it if the man has a sense of humour? Come on Jack, lighten up."

At that, Sarah entered the car. "Yeah Jack, lighten up! I can't believe that Morty friend of yours. I would've liked to see what you two were like back in the 60s."

"I was nothing like Morty," snapped her father. "But you seem to be heading down that dangerous road my dear. And trust me, you don't want to end up like him, or that waitress friend of his."

"Her name's Betty dad! And I could do a lot worse."

"You're right, you could!" Jack replied revving the engine and starting into the traffic without signaling. A car honked at them as they jerked to an abrupt halt. "That Betty got off easy. Things have changed since 9/11. You could go to jail now for doing what she did. You'd better watch yourself."

"You know dad," said Sarah much more calmly, "that's the first intelligent thing you've said in a long, long time. That's what Betty told me herself. She told me about the RCMP spies at their meetings and how she sees the same paranoia starting to take hold now."

"It's not paranoia," Jack shot back. "There are terrorists out there. How do you think the World Trade Center got bombed?"

"I guess there are dad," Sarah agreed. "But Betty's not a terrorist and neither am I. You think the RCMP should be following us around?"

"I'm not going to be second guessing the work of the RCMP."

"Oh, you're impossible" laughed his wife. "You really expect us to believe you'd want the RCMP to investigate your own daughter? Really Jack. Get real."

Jack didn't reply. He just drove.

SUNDAY, SEPTEMBER 16, 2001

"I guess you can take the arab out of the gaza but you can't take the gaza out of the arab. It is no surprise that the college with the lowest academic standards in the country would attract the stupidest people in the country."
— HATE MAIL SENT BY STEPHEN G.
RECEIVED ON THE CONCORDIA STUDENT UNION EMAIL ACCOUNT, 12/5/02

MAYBE IT WAS THE MUSLIM prayer beads hanging on the rearview mirror, maybe it was the medical bag in the front seat with his father's name on it–Mohammed–maybe somebody had seen him in the car and thought "that guy looks Arab." It was impossible to know exactly what motivated the attack. But when Ali woke up on Sunday morning, September 16 and went down to the street, the message the vandal had painted on the car beside the smashed window left no ambiguity about his feelings towards people like Ali:

Arab go home!

You don't fucking belong here!!

Ali wasn't an Arab, but that didn't matter. The backlash wasn't too fussy in its choice of victims. It didn't matter that Ali was a McGill University medical student from Iran. He was one of "them."

Just a couple of days ago Yasmin, a Pakistani student at Concordia who wears a hijab, passed a man downtown–not a skinhead with a swastika on his jacket but a well-dressed man in an expensive suit–who told her to "stop terrorizing him" and that if he had a gun he would like to see her dead.

It was not a surprise to Hassan when he started hearing about these cases in Montréal. He had already accumulated hundreds of similar written accounts from the wave of hate crimes spreading across the United States. And he knew the collection was just a snapshot of the unbridled storm of post-9/11 violence. Cases like these were emblematic of the new war on terror. If it was okay for the government to prevent people from getting on a plane and question them because of the colour of their skin, their clothing or their name, if it was okay for the government to lock up immigrants from certain countries indefinitely without any evidence of wrongdoing, if racial profiling was now a legitimate tool in the war on terror, then why couldn't ordinary citizens do the same thing in their own communities? After all, the war on terror was a war without borders. Everybody was expected to contribute. It was our duty to watch, catch, stand up to and fight "them."

Hassan knew exactly what to expect from the reports he had read, but it was different when he actually knew the people being targeted. He didn't think that Ali was more important than the Muslim taxi driver who was harassed in Virginia, but he had met Ali at Friday prayer. He had shaken his hand and had talked to him about how competitive it was to get into medical school at McGill. He laughed at Hassan's joke about how the cabby was going to apply to medical school once he finished his 25-year bachelor degree, so that in another 30 years he could start practicing medicine. Hassan could imagine the look of shock and horror on Ali's face when he saw his car. And it made Hassan realise that it could happen to him, or his daughter, his son, or any of his friends. The us and them dichotomy put him, his family and his friends on the wrong side: the enemy in the war on terror.

Hassan had the kids this weekend. He looked at Katia and Ahmed watching television in the living room as he hung up the phone in the kitchen. In fact, the living room and the kitchen were basically one room separated by a counter. The kids couldn't understand what their father was talking about on the phone because he was speaking in Arabic. Nevertheless, Katia repeatedly turned away from the gunfights and car chases in the movie her brother had rented, to look in her father's direction. Even if she didn't know what he was saying, she seemed to know something was wrong. He had already put a cigarette in his mouth before hanging up the phone. He went out on the balcony to smoke and pace.

Katia left her brother to his juvenile movie and joined her father on the balcony. As she slid open the balcony door, automatic gunfire and screaming invaded Hassan's thoughts. The cries of battle died away as she closed the door behind her. "Why does Ahmed always rent those terrible action flicks?" she asked her father in a perfect québécois French. "The villains are always Arab terrorists. He's going to develop a complex."

"What do you expect him to watch?" Hassan responded in a Parisian French with only a slight Arabic accent. He was careful to blow the smoke away from his daughter but it did not stray very far from their 5th floor concrete balcony before being blown back in their direction. "He's a 12-year-old boy. That's what they watch. Why do you watch your Hollywood entertainment shows about the impact of September 11 on the lives of the stars?"

"That's different." She felt it necessary to be precise on the matter. "That show is mostly just gossip about the personal lives of film and music artists. I like to keep up on that kind of thing." Katia saw his point, but she couldn't deny herself the pleasure of Hollywood gossip. She thought calling them "film and music artists" instead of "famous people" would make them sound more worth watching to her dad.

"Oh really?" said Hassan with mock astonishment. "Silly me, I thought it was American propaganda." He looked away, towards the setting sun above the row housing.

"Fine, it is American propaganda," she admitted. "Sometimes. But I can see what's real and what's Hollywood."

"So teach your brother how to see it too," advised her father. "And while you're at it, teach your whole generation. The post-9/11 generation is going to need some impressive critical thinking skills. I can't believe how bad things are getting."

"This isn't just about what's on TV, is it dad?"

"No it's a lot of things." How much should he tell her? She was bound to find this stuff out in one way or another, but he didn't want to scare his daughter either. He was already scared enough for the both of them. It was tempting to just let her go on thinking that she was a *québécoise*, like her mother. She wore a generous application of makeup like the other teenage girls at her *CÉGEP*, and she didn't wear the hijab or speak with an accent. She didn't even go to Friday prayer. Katia had dark skin like her father, but she could pass for Italian or Greek. Maybe nobody would notice that she was Arab... until they saw the family name on her passport. He could imagine the strange look the border guard would give her, "Katia Mohamed? I thought you said you were Canadian..."

"What, dad?"

"Have you heard about the backlash since the attacks in New York?" he asked.

"Backlash? You mean like people blaming all Arabs for what happened? Yeah sure."

"Have you heard about that stuff happening here in Montréal?" he pressed further.

"Hmm, I don't think so..." Katia had to ponder the question. It was not something she talked about with her friends–they were all non-Arab, non-Muslim *québécois*. "I mean, I think some people might look at you funny now. I guess that's why you stopped wearing your kaffiyeh. But, all the really bad stuff is happening in the US, right? I mean, you're not in any physical danger if you're an Arab in Canada... are you?" What started as a statement of fact transformed itself into a question when she saw the furrowing brow on her father's worn face.

"Well, not exactly." He wanted to protect his daughter from the backlash, but would she be any safer if he kept her in the dark? She didn't have much sense of her cultural identity and Hassan realised he was to blame. How could he expect Geneviève to teach his kids about Syrian culture? If he had been a better husband, they wouldn't have divorced and he would have had more access to his kids. Her grandparents would be mortified to see their granddaughter living such a Western lifestyle.

Hassan should have been there more for her and Ahmed. "Canada is almost a part of the United States you know. We get all the same music and movies." He pointed to her brother, sitting completely absorbed in front of the black box. "It's not quite as bad here, but there is a backlash."

"Yeah dad, that's what I said, isn't it?" his daughter persisted. "It's not as bad in Canada."

"You said Arabs were not in physical danger here," Hassan corrected her.

"So Arabs are in danger?" she asked. "What were you talking about on the phone?"

There was no getting around it. His daughter was zeroing in on the truth and she would expect nothing less. Katia did have good critical thinking skills. Hassan was proud of her. She would be able to deal with this, probably better than he was. "That was a friend of mine from the Muslim Students Association calling to tell me about another friend, not an Arab but an Iranian, whose car was attacked last night. They smashed his window and painted racist slogans."

"Here?" she asked, eyes wide with disbelief. "In Montréal?"

"Yes. Downtown Montréal. And the day before yesterday, the sister of another friend was verbally abused by a well-dressed man in broad daylight. He accused her of being a terrorist."

"Wow," she gasped. "Now I see why you stopped wearing your kaffiyeh." It was now Katia's turn to look at her father with concern in her eyes. Cab driving could be a dangerous occupation.

✳ ✳ ✳

The Manifesto of
Those Who Refuse to Remain Silent

The ugly figure of terrorism was suddenly manifest at the World Trade Center and the Pentagon on September 11, 2001. Very few North Americans recognised their uninvited guest, but the fact of the matter is that the specter of terror has been haunting North America for centuries. Hours after the attacks, the US State Department issued a statement saying, "The worst act of terrorism on U.S. soil was committed on September 11, 2001." This callous and self-serving rewriting of history may have induced historical amnesia on the part of patriotic Americans, but there are those of us who do not forget the genocidal Indian Wars and the terrorism of kidnapping, rape and torture inflicted on countless African people dragged here in chains against their will. Nobody with any sense of humanity could celebrate the senseless mass murder of September 11, but nobody with any sense of humanity could allow "good corporate citizens" to continue their mass murder on a global scale. Africa, Asia, South America, the Middle East, in short the Global South, is increasingly becoming a provider of natural resources and cheap labour for the North, and at the same time, a battlefield and a mass graveyard. Yet many, especially those who enjoy wealth and power, seem ready to call on multinational arms merchants to increase production for the sake of "global security"—a euphemism for the ruthless enforcement of the dictates of US imperialism. Through our actions and through this manifesto, we are calling on all people, but especially the North Americans who live in the belly of the imperialist beast, to make the functioning of global capitalism and US imperialism impossible and unworkable. Only with justice, will there be peace.

"That's very good dear." Shirley was genuinely proud of her daughter's writing even if she didn't entirely agree with the political sentiment of her manifesto. "Really excellent writing. You have the whole manifesto style down pat. I like the way you allude to the *Communist Manifesto*. It takes me back to my university days. But don't you think you could attract more people to your cause if you were less confrontational?"

Shirley saw her daughter's face light up with each compliment. Sarah was perched on the kitchen counter, a seagull waiting for each tidbit with anticipation, hanging on her mother's every word. Then came the downcast glance with the suggestion that she write less confrontationally.

Sarah folded her arms and spoke with staccato intonation, "Dude, I mean, come on. How are we supposed to suggest that people do something about the mass murder being perpetrated by multinational corporations without being confrontational?" The question was much more accusatory than Sarah wanted it to sound, but she had worked the whole weekend putting that manifesto together. Much of the content had been shaped by Hassan's critical notes but it was Sarah who weaved it all into a seamless whole. And she was looking for constructive criticism, not a fundamental questioning of the document's very principles.

"Hmm, I see your point," said Shirley in a reassuring tone. She saw that pushing too hard about the problems she had with the manifesto would risk alienating her daughter. On the other hand, she really didn't agree with it and didn't want to give her the false impression that the first year university student had successfully converted her mother to the revolution.

"But what about the poor indoctrinated dupes like me who don't necessarily believe that CEOs are all murdering swine and that the only way to improve the situation is to make 'the functioning of global capitalism and US imperialism impossible and unworkable'? I agree that a lot of hawks in the United States are using the attacks as a way to increase military spending, and the cries for vengeance are really dangerous. I think a bombing campaign in Afghanistan will probably kill a lot more innocent people and will probably end up causing more terrorism. It's a vicious circle. But I don't necessarily think sabotaging global capitalism is the answer. I mean, what will we put in its place?"

"Oh Mom," Sarah said with exasperation but with a much better sense of humour than she exhibited earlier, "you're such a liberal!"

"Yes I am dear," her mother agreed with a reassuring smile, touching her daughter's knee. "And so are a lot of people. We're your best allies too. Because we believe in the free expression of ideas—even crazy radical ones like yours. We're worried about fundamental freedoms being trampled in the race to catch the terrorists."

"But that's not good enough Mom," Sarah complained. "Free speech is like so important. I'm all for it too. But it doesn't do much to help the vast majority of people suffering in the world because of global capitalism. Try to think about the situation from the standpoint of a Guatemalan peasant. You live on less than a dollar a day, you don't have clean drinking water, and the multinational fruit company you work for, when you're lucky enough to have a job, gets thugs to kill the leaders every time anybody tries to start a union."

"Sure, it's bad for Guatemalan peasants but..."

"Wait Mom, I'm not finished. The predecessor of the company you work for also got US support for a military coup back in 1954 when people tried to change things by voting for a moderate liberal kind of president who tried to institute some moderate liberal land reforms to make the capitalist exploitation you suffer a little less bad. A military dictatorship took the place of the democratically elected government and proceeded to torture, kill, rape and displace indigenous peoples, peasants and union leaders over the next decades. Sound familiar? Just like the situation in Chile the Rodriguezes lived through, eh? History has like repeated itself so many times Mom. And as long as US arms manufacturers, and fruit companies, and coffee companies, and banks continue to make money keeping Guatemalan peasants like you in your place, how do you expect anything to change?"

"Okay Sarah," she was impressed by her daughter's historical knowledge. "You really know your stuff." Where did she learn all this? thought Shirley. Sarah was only in first year at Concordia. "But I'm still not convinced about the whole overthrow of global capitalism thing. It just seems so unrealistic and unworkable. And how can you do it without causing as much death as the capitalistic violence you're trying to stop? The USSR wasn't exactly the workers' paradise it was made out to be now was it? I mean, maybe we need to inform consumers of Guatemalan bananas about the conditions of workers in the industry. If you can provide alternative fair-trade bananas, even if they are more expensive, many people will buy them because they don't want to see those terrible things happen. I buy fair-trade coffee quite often... and I recycle."

Sarah was shaking her head in that oh-mom-you're-such-a-liberal way. "And you recycle?" Sarah was laughing. It was just a giggle at first, but gradually became a roaring torrent. "And you recycle!" she repeated.

Shirley started to laugh too. "Yes I recycle. Don't ask me to explain how that helps Guatemalan peasants, but it's one of those good things we're supposed to do to make the world a better place." The laughter was contagious, as if somebody was tickling her. "Oh, I am a liberal. Don't expect me to change. That's just what I am."

"It's never too late," her daughter insisted. "At least read the rest of the manifesto and think about it. There are lots of examples in there, like the Guatemalan one, from all over the world. Maybe you'll argue that we just need fair trade gasoline and the Tobin tax, and everything will be all right, but then it'll be my turn to be skeptical."

"Okay dear," Shirley was genuinely interested in the text and more than happy to read it. Of course she would read anything her daughter wrote. That's what mothers are for. "But what's the Tobin tax?"

"Oh you need to learn about that Mom," Sarah was grinning and the giggle was starting to trickle out again. "You'll like it even better than recycling. It's like so liberal."

Her daughter's teasing didn't bother Shirley in the least. She would have to look into it... Jack would probably know about the tax. "Now, if you want a more pointed critique," Shirley offered, "I bet your father could give you one."

A look of panic came over Sarah's face. "Don't you dare show him this manifesto mom! This whole World Trade Center attack thing has put him over the edge. I've never seen him so, so..."

"American?" her mother offered.

"Yes. That's it."

"Me neither," confessed her mom. "It's kind of disconcerting. When I first started dating Jack it was his draft-dodging past that I found attractive. It was like he was refusing the unjust war his government was fighting. That's what I thought at the time anyway, but I guess he was just scared. I mean, going to Vietnam was no picnic. I would've been scared too. Anyway, he's more of a patriot than I thought."

"As long as someone else is doing the fighting," said Sarah, making the unforgiving indictment of her dad without thinking of how it would affect his wife.

Tears started to form in her mother's eyes, but there was no anger towards her daughter. She did not defend her husband. "Yes," Shirley agreed, "when somebody else is doing the fighting it's much easier, isn't it?"

MONDAY, OCTOBER I, 2OOI

"They came after the Jews, and I was not a Jew, so I did not object. They came after the Catholics, and I was not a Catholic, so I did not object. They came after the trade unionists, and I was not a trade unionist, so I did not object. Then they came after me and there was nobody left to object."

— REV. MARTIN NIEMOELLER, EXPLANATION OF WHY HE SPOKE OUT AGAINST THE NAZIS AND EARNED EIGHT YEARS IN CONCENTRATION CAMPS FOR LEADING PROTESTANT CHURCH OPPOSITION TO HITLER, 1945

"HAVE YOU SEEN THIS GIRL?" asked the beefy plainclothes agent. The white-haired red-faced RCMP corporal clearly expected cooperation from the security guard. As a general rule, all security guards were cooperative in such matters. Too cooperative, like they wished they could be doing the investigation themselves. So why was this kid taking so long deciding whether or not he'd seen this girl? The agent was holding a photo of Sarah standing in front of some pine trees.

Greg squinted at the photo as if he were taking a closer look. That bought him a bit more time. What was he supposed to do? The investigation was the most transparently political one Greg had ever seen. It was inconceivable that Sarah was some kind of criminal. She smoked dope with her hippie Raging Granddaughter friends, but she was no dealer. The only explanation for the RCMP agent's questions was her politics. What a sick world his mother had brought him into. She had tried to make it better, and he loved her for it, but there was nothing that could be done. Sarah was trying to make it better too, and look what was happening to her. Now she was under federal investigation.

"How long does it take you to know if you've seen her?" the agent was getting impatient.

"Sorry Corporal Boisvert," he apologised, rubbing the back of his head like he was deep in thought. "It's just that so many people come in here every day. Maybe if you could tell me who she might be with, or why she might be coming in?"

He does want to run the investigation, the shit! Well, if it'll help me get some information, it wouldn't hurt to make him feel a bit more important. "Well, her father works here, a Mr. Jack Murphy, you know him?"

"Yes, Mr. Murphy," answered Greg. "I see him pretty much every day. I didn't know he had a daughter." That was the first lie Greg told the RCMP. It wasn't really much of a lie. It was, after all, only a week ago that he had learned about Mr. Murphy's daughter. On the other hand, earlier that morning he had been admiring the rounded topography of his daughter's soft naked form as she slept in his bed. There was a bit of a resemblance. Both had those full dark eyebrows, funny he didn't notice them before. She didn't have the eyebrow piercing in the photo. Sarah's comportment was so diametrically opposed to Mr. Murphy's that it didn't seem right for them to look so much like each other, even if they were father and daughter. How could he be getting so close to somebody related to him? Of course it wasn't her fault her father was such a bastard...

"So you haven't seen her here then?" concluded the corporal, but in the form of a question for Greg to agree or disagree with.

It was true. He had never seen her here so Greg wouldn't be lying. "That's right. She's never come in here." Greg wiped his sweaty palms on his slacks as he sat back down at his desk, hoping the questions were finished. Maybe he could claim he wasn't lying, but there was no getting around it. He had already misled an official RCMP investigation. Greg could be in big trouble. Why did he let Sarah seduce him? Or was it he who seduced her by letting her believe that he was something more than he actually was, that he was not really selfish, that he really did care about child labourers in East Asia, global warming, and the coming war in Afghanistan?

"Good." The corporal's tone was on the upper end of the patronizing scale. "And what about this guy? Have you seen him here?" He asked the question as if he were talking to a 5-year-old child.

Oh shit! It was a photo of Hassan getting out of his cab. Greg did his best to slow the adrenaline rushing through his system. Fighting the urge to react, he rose from his chair at what he hoped looked like a leisurely pace to pore over the new photograph.

"He might have been wearing a scarf," offered the agent. "You know, one of those Arab scarves? It seems he just stopped wearing it recently," then he leaned on the counter of the security desk to tell Greg in a hushed tone, "like he's trying to make himself less conspicuous."

Of course he's trying to make himself less conspicuous you racist fuck. After September 11, what Arab wouldn't? "You think he's a terrorist?" asked Greg.

"I can't talk about that," Corporal Boisvert curtly shot back. "This is not a public investigation. Just tell me whether you've seen him or not."

As soon as he saw the photo of his friend, he felt the bile of lies rising within him. Wasn't it supposed to be easier after the first one? He hated lying for any reason, but lying to cops added another level of stress. It went against the whole security guard persona he had cultivated. As a security guard, he was expected to be fully cooperative with the authorities. Over the course of his whole career, that is exactly what he did. It was strange at first, after all the harassment he had suffered at the hands of the police. A six-foot-six black man walking alone late at night brought suspicion from the forces of order. But once he donned the uniform, his relationship with those authorities changed. Then they saw the blue of his jacket, not the brown of his skin. And he had to admit he liked the feeling of not being a suspect, but rather, one of the good guys. On the other hand, he had never been asked to betray any friends, and there had never been any such racially charged political investigation on the premises. It just didn't seem right for the authorities to be going after Hassan because he was Arab and because of his politics. But it wasn't his job to judge what police actions were right or wrong. His job was to help them do their job, period.

Still, lying to the cops was a candy-bar-stealing guilt: fear of getting caught. There was another kind of guilt that had been much more corrosive to his system over the past few weeks. It was a stealing-from-mom's-purse guilt. He had been feeling genuine shame ever since September 11 when he failed to follow through on calling Mr. Murphy's racism. The more he talked to Sarah, the more he realised his mother was right about some things. There was a line that people just couldn't cross, and Mr. Murphy had crossed it.

Maybe having the courage to lie to the RCMP now was the way to redeem himself for his earlier cowardice. Maybe there was some kind of cosmic order that made Mr. Murphy's cell phone ring at just the right moment, so that Greg would keep his job and get the chance to mislead Corporal Boivert's investigation into the activities of two people he cared about.

"I've never seen this guy before in my life," Greg responded unequivocally. Mom would be proud. It felt good to lie to the Corporal but the satisfaction still came with a strange twinge of guilt and regret, like he knew there would inevitably be a price to pay. Somebody was bound to notice the missing candy-bar sooner or later, but at least he had managed to put the money back in mom's purse without anybody seeing. Still, there was a limit to how far he could go, even when it came to Sarah. He had been willing to play the role of her unseen "consultant" for the past few days, but the RCMP investigation changed everything.

For Greg to remain in the picture, the revolution would have to get by without the help of Sarah Murphy. She would have to let Warmonger Inc. continue to ply its trade without getting in the way. No more half-baked schemes of corporate sabotage. And if she refused, and he knew that's exactly what she would do (in fact, he would be disappointed if she gave in to his selfish demands), they could not meet again until everything had died down. They had planned to watch part 2 of *1900* tomorrow night. Now they would have to wait. How long? Two weeks? Would it be safe then? A month? He didn't want to wait. He wanted to see her now, especially now...

* * *

There were more than 500 people in the Ottawa Government Conference Centre—not bad for a Monday morning opening plenary session. The title of the conference was Women's Resistance: From Victimization to Criminalization—an irony that would be lost on most when the complaint of anti-American "hate crime" would be filed with the RCMP against one of today's presenters.

The Cable Public Affairs Channel was there to catch everything on video, but that has never stopped anybody from being misquoted.

UBC Women's Studies Professor and former head of the National Action Committee on the Status of Women, Sunera Thobani, started off her talk with a question:

"If Canadians are Americans now, what are women of colour to do in this country?"

She went on to forcefully make the following arguments, speaking passionately as always:

> [...]no women's emancipation, in fact no liberation of any kind for women will be successful unless it seeks to transform the fundamental divide between the north and the south, between Third World people and those in the West who are now calling themselves Americans.

> [...]Today in the world, the United States is the most dangerous and the most powerful global force unleashing prolific levels of violence all over the world.

> From Chile to El Salvador, to Nicaragua to Iraq, the path of U.S. foreign policy is soaked in blood. We have seen—and all of us have seen, felt—the dramatic pain of watching those attacks and trying to grasp the fact of the number of people who died. We feel the pain of that every day we have been watching it on television.

> But do we feel any pain for the victims of U.S. aggression? 200,000 people killed only in the initial war on Iraq. [...]Do we feel the pain of all the

children in Iraq who are dying from the sanctions that were imposed by the United States? Do we feel that pain on an everyday level? Share it with our families and communities and talk about it on every platform that is available to us. Do we feel the pain of Palestinians who now for 50 years have been living in refugee camps?

U.S. foreign policy is soaked in blood. And other countries of the West—including, shamefully, Canada—cannot line up fast enough behind it. All want to sign up now as Americans and I think it is the responsibility of the women's movement in this country to stop that, to fight against it.

[...]Consider the language which is being used. Calling the perpetrators evil-doers, irrational, calling them the forces of darkness, uncivilized, intent* on destroying civilization, intent on destroying democracy. [...]Every person of colour, and I would want to say also every Aboriginal person, will recognize that language.

[...]We were colonized in the name of the West bringing civilization, democracy, bringing freedom to us. All of us recognize who is being talked about when that language is being used. The terms crusade, infinite justice, cowboy imagery of dead or alive posters, we all know what they mean.

[...]Events of the last two weeks also show that the American people that Bush is trying to invoke, whoever they are these "American people"—just like we contest the notions of who the Canadian people are, we have to recognize that there are other voices in the United States as well, contesting that—but the people, the American nation that Bush is invoking, is a people which is bloodthirsty, vengeful, and calling for blood. They don't care whose blood it is, they want blood. [...]We have to stop condoning it and creating a climate of acceptability for this kind of response. We have to call it for what it is: Bloodthirsty vengeance.

Thobani received a standing ovation from the audience that day. When writers from the *National Post* and *The Globe and Mail* got wind of the speech, they were not nearly so enthralled. Did she call all Americans "bloodthirsty?" Well not quite, but she might as well have. Close enough for lawyers to defend publishers from defamation suits. Opinion-making writers and columnists all over the country had found a new enemy from within—a traitor to the American cause.

And on the very same day the national press would learn about other enemies from within, which had burrowed deeply into other parts of Canadian academic institutions. The Concordia Student Union had produced a student agenda that was tantamount to a "blueprint for Osama bin Laden's youth program in North America"—more fodder for the media feeding-frenzy.

Just hours after Thobani's Ottawa address, Frank Dimant, the Executive and Vice President of B'nai Brith Canada, gave a speech to a Montréal audience of considerably less than 500 but with considerably more sympathetic ears from the press on hand. The title given to the press conference: "Concordia Student Union Advocates Violence and Anarchy."

"He said what?" Hassan jumped down from the hood of his cab to grab Hakim by the lapels of his jacket. "Don't bullshit me, Hakim. I'm not in the mood today." It was impossible for the little Buddha-like cab driver to intimidate a young man of Hakim's large stature. Looking down at the cabby as his own head wagged back and forth from the shaking he was receiving, Hakim would have found it amusing if the news he carried was not so dire, yet at the same time, so surreal.

"I'm serious," Hakim insisted. Sarah was nodding in agreement.

"Osama bin Laden would hate this agenda!" Hassan exclaimed. "It's queer positive. It gives information about safe sex and safe drug use."

"Well, I think it was a rhetorical question," offered Sarah. "Like, 'Is this the blueprint for Osama bin Laden's youth program in North America?' Obviously it doesn't matter what the answer is. Just asking the question, especially when it's B'nai

Brith, will be enough to grab the headlines and drag all Concordia activists through the mud."

"How can they get away with that?" Hassan was going through the same stage of denial that everybody did upon hearing the news for the first time. It was a hard pill to swallow.

"B'nai Brith is smart," observed Hakim. "They're using the same strategy as Ariel Sharon. Since September 11th Sharon has been painting Arafat as Palestine's Osama bin Laden. That's what B'nai Brith is doing with the CSU. Not that the CSU is anything like Arafat, but, you see, the principle's the same."

"Dude, it's so ironic," Sarah jumped in. "B'nai Brith was one of the organizations that helped defend Jewish entertainers who were brought before the U.S. House Committee on Un-American Activities in the 1950s." After learning about her grandfather's McCarthyist past and then watching *The Front* with Greg, she started to pore through other material on that unfortunate episode of US history. She found, to her great surprise, the organization that was now smearing Concordia activists. "In the 1950s, if you were a Jew or a union organizer, you were a Communist. Now, if you're an Arab or somebody who supports Palestinian human rights, you're a terrorist."

"They're actually telling students to rip out certain pages from their agendas," said Hakim. "They gave out a list of page numbers."

Hassan was staring at them wide-eyed, pulling at the little bit of hair that was left on the sides of his head. So it was actually true. When would the secret police be seizing the CSU office? he wondered.

"I know it sounds weird. But I actually think I totally understand their warped logic. If you look at the pages they have a problem with, it's pretty instructive," observed Sarah as she took her agenda out of her bag to illustrate. "They don't like the poem that the editor wrote at the beginning. Ah, here it is. Because it mentions 'intifada' and it has the phrase 'take up arms for the revolution.' But replace 'intifada' with 'uprising' which is what it means in English, and the poem could be a Bob Marley song. Actually, he totally did an album called *Uprisings*, didn't he?"

"And another thing, they don't like," Sarah continued flipping through the pages. "It's sooo 1984. Here it is, look at this." She held up a collage of planes and a corporate boardroom. "This is a piece of art, a collage, done by a Concordia Fine Arts student. In the background are planes, like the F16s that Pratt and Whitney makes the engines for, you know the ones that bomb Palestinians, and it looks like they're bombing some little people that are uprising down below. Anyway, that's like the background. Then in the foreground you have a bunch of corporate board members sitting around a table. One of them is asking the guy sitting beside him, 'Tell us, is it too late to try this grassroots organizing?' But B'nai Brith looks at this thing and they say it's a representation of planes crashing into a corporate boardroom! They even called it a chilling and bizarre' coincidence that the agenda was produced before September 11. Just like the Splitting the Sky thing. Dude, they're actually saying that somehow the CSU knew about the attacks."

"Then there's Steal Something Day," offered Hakim.

"Steal Something Day?" asked Hassan. "I must've missed that one. What day is it on?"

"That's just it," Sarah replied. "It's so not a date in the agenda, because there's no such day organized by anybody." She flipped through the pages of her agenda once again. "I suppose this is where the 'violence and anarchy' that the CSU supposedly advocate comes from. The article called 'Steal Something Day' advocates a fictional event called steal something day as an alternative to buy nothing day but, excuse me, it's like satire dude, hello. Buy nothing day is one of those wonderful feel-good things that you can do as a consumer to make yourself feel like you're doing stuff to help the planet—like recycling. The idea is to become less consumeristic by not buying stuff on one day of the year. So steal something day is a critique of that idea. It points out that your ability to affect change with buy nothing day is like totally dependent on your consumer power—one dollar, one vote. And it's completely passive as a strategy because you 'participate by not participating.' But with steal something day everybody is equal and it's like totally participatory. Of course steal something day does not exist. It's totally a foil for buy nothing day and a way to poke fun at it. Dude, wake up and smell the irony. But since September 11, irony is dead."

"So they didn't get the joke," concluded Hassan, now calm and collected. Denial passed over him in a brief wave, much like it had with Hakim and Sarah earlier in the day. It should have struck him as the height of absurdity that the CSU was attacked because a satirical article went over somebody's head. After the Splitting the Sky incident, however, it seemed par for the course.

"Unfortunately," replied Hakim, "I think a lot of people missed it. Irony really is dead."

"So when we put all this together," Sarah concluded, "you have a poem, a painting and a piece of satire. Poetry, art and satire, the three pillars of terrorism."

"Rip them out and burn them!" said Hakim, throwing up one hand in disgust while his other reached for his cigarettes.

Hassan laughed, but it was a strange and forced sort of laugh—totally void of humour and joy. He didn't really think it was that funny, but he had to laugh. Not laughing would be admitting that irony was dead. Laughing was an act of resistance—perhaps it was even an act of terrorism, since it appeared that resistance and terrorism were one and the same.

"Did you hear what Lillian Robinson said in response to B'nai Brith?" asked Sarah.

Hakim shook his head.

"She said, 'Jews don't burn books!' I saw her on Global TV of all places. Dude, she's my hero."

"Wow," said Hassan, eyes wide with appreciation. "That's something at least. When the head of the Simone de Beauvoir institute, and a Jew from New York, says that, it's got to take away some of the university's credibility."

"Thank God for Lillian," Hakim agreed.

"Still," Hakim cautioned as he lit his cigarette, "they're calling for an RCMP investigation. Who knows what the RCMP is going to do..."

Just as Hassan was lighting a sorely needed cigarette of his own, he heard the dispatcher calling his cab. "Shit," he said in frustration, looking at the cigarette between his fingers. At times like this he wished he could inhale the whole thing in one go, getting all that lovely nicotine in one convenient pulmonary movement. He took one long puff and then handed it to Sarah, "*un* death stick *pour la madame?*"

"Don't mind if I do," Sarah happily took it from his hand as he leaned into his cab's passenger-side door and picked up his CB receiver.

The dispatcher told Hassan he had an emergency call from a Greg Phillip, and he should call him back right away at this number. Hassan ran to a public phone in Concordia's Library Building, leaving Sarah and Hakim to watch his illegally parked cab and smoke his cigarette.

He returned less than five minutes later, shaking his head with a worried look and another cigarette in his mouth, which he lit as soon as he passed through the doors and stepped onto the sidewalk.

"What's the matter?" asked Hakim. "Everything okay with your family?"

Hassan did not respond, but climbed back up onto the hood of his taxi and continued to smoke, shake his head and rub his eyes. After he had composed himself, he gestured for Hakim and Sarah, who were staring at him with interest, to come closer.

"I just talked to a friend on the phone," said Hassan in a hushed tone, as if he were afraid of being overheard. "A friend that I trust. And he told me the RCMP questioned him this morning about Sarah and me."

"Oh my God," said Sarah putting her hand over her mouth, eyes wide with fear.

"No way!" said Hakim in disbelief.

"Yes," the cabby insisted. "I believe him. He wouldn't bullshit me about this." Greg insisted that they cancel their game tonight, and that all their future meetings be put on hold for the moment. Greg couldn't fake the fear that Hassan heard in his voice. He was taking a big risk telling his chess partner about the investigation, putting his own job on the line.

"What did the RCMP guy ask?" Sarah whispered, looking around to see who might be watching them. De Maisonneuve and Mackay streets were busy as always, full of students talking and smoking. A TV camera crew was unloading its truck across the street at the Hall Building.

"Nothing too specific," Hassan spoke softly to his co-conspirators who had drawn in even closer and formed a closed circle. "He just showed our pictures and asked if we had been seen around your father's office building."

"That's weird," commented Sarah with a frown. "How do they know my father is involved in this whole thing?"

Hassan simply shook his head and shrugged his shoulders in response. "How do they know anything? I don't think any of us would've told them."

"Unless somebody was just bragging..." said Hakim, wincing with pain for having to suggest the idea of an unwitting traitor in their midst. He didn't voice his suspicions about who the loquacious betrayer might be, but he had a pretty good idea who it was not. None of the SPHR crowd would have said anything—they had too much at risk to start boasting like that. It had to be one of the white anarchists. He had lost a lot of respect for their ilk ever since the more-radical-than-thou flag-burning adventurism after the SPHR demo. Hakim knew that none of "his" anarchists were involved in that inadvertent act of sabotage, but he couldn't help extrapolating.

"You could be right," Hassan admitted. "I don't see any other way they could know anything." He lit another cigarette off the butt of his last.

"So should we call everything off?" asked Hakim.

"That's the question," confirmed Hassan with a nod.

Sarah looked back and forth between her two comrades. She bit her lip, choking the instinctive no, no, no that was on the tip of her tongue. Sarah had put too much work and planning into this operation to see it go up in smoke. That's what was happening right before her eyes—dispersion of a political gathering. Her friends were scattering in panic, like they had in Québec City when teargas was fired into a peaceful crowd. She wanted to stop it, to order everyone back into formation. But it was not her call to make. She was not the one taking the most risks. "Obviously, I would like to go ahead, but I guess you guys want to call it off. I don't like it. But if that's what you want to do..."

"Just hold on," Hassan put his hand on her shoulder. "Nobody has called anything off yet, we're just considering all the possibilities."

"Well, consider this," Sarah whispered passionately. She couldn't stop herself. They had to know how she felt. "We all knew the cops would be involved at some point. And we all know what the risks are. As long as they don't stop us from doing what we plan on doing, the rest is irrelevant. And now that we know they're watching we can act accordingly so they can't stop us."

Her two friends looked at each other for a second. "She's got a point," Hassan admitted, but he still had his doubts.

Hakim wasn't convinced. "We need the element of surprise," he insisted. "If they know what we're up to, it could get very dangerous. Imagine if they set some kind of trap. Somebody could get seriously hurt."

"He's got a point too," Hassan turned to Sarah as he took another drag on his cigarette. "Those RCMP boys can get pretty rough sometimes. They deal with Hell's Angels and shit. And right now they think we're all a bunch of al Qaeda terrorists. We could get kidnapped and beat up and nobody would be the wiser. Who'd believe us right now if we cry foul against the counter-terrorism heroes?"

"Okay," Sarah agreed in a calm tone. The novice was able to set aside her own fear by treating the situation as an abstract prisoner's dilemma. It was easier for her to do since she had much less grasp of what being a prisoner really meant. "Let's not jump to any conclusions here. We have no idea what the RCMP's doing. Who knows why they're investigating, what they know, or what they're up to? It's all speculation. And anyway, if we call it off, they're not going to necessarily stop whatever it is they're doing. We could still face the same risks anyway. And we'll have to be looking over our shoulders anytime we do anything political. Imagine if all activists reacted like that every time the cops threatened them in some way. Dude, we'd have no right to protest at all."

"But still," objected Hakim, a little less forcefully this time. "It's the RCMP." He didn't know what else to say, simply because Sarah was right about one thing—they had no idea what the RCMP was up to. How could he convince her that there were terrible risks if he had no idea what the risks were?

"Yes, it is the RCMP," Hassan agreed. "So we've got to be really fucking careful. No fooling around. No more *Mission Impossible* jokes and shit. This is serious now." Sarah and Hakim had never seen Hassan's expression so grave. His eyes were wide open, eyebrows raised high, and he stared long and hard at both of his friends' faces like he was sizing up their capacity to take on this important task.

Hassan tried to synthesize their common position, "We continue with the plan, but we pass the word that the RCMP is asking questions—not via email obviously, but by word of mouth. And we continue with the post-bombing rendezvous at Al-Taïb. We'll re-evaluate things from there. We don't have to decide right away. It probably doesn't make sense to decide in the heat of the moment. Let's think about it. Hard."

"This is so bizarre," said Hakim. "Planning things like this, underground. It's like we're living in a police state."

"That's why I'd hate to call it off," Sarah sighed. "As bad as things are now, if we stop resisting, things might get even worse."

"You're, you're... calling from a payphone?" asked Greg in a breathless voice. He was even more afraid than the activists were.

"Just like Hassan told me to," said Sarah in as reassuring a tone as she could manage. "You think they're bugging my house?"

"Well, they had your photo and they were asking about you," said Greg. "Seems pretty likely they would be keeping close tabs on all your activities."

"Shit," said Sarah. "Maybe we should call this thing off."

"That's what I was going to suggest. Either that, or we stop seeing each other until this whole thing's over..."

"Sure..." Sarah said absentmindedly, not really knowing what she was agreeing to. She knew that if they went ahead with the action, seeing Greg was dangerous for both of them, but mostly for him. If she cared about him, which she really did, maybe it was best to stop seeing him. On the other hand, if this action was so risky that it meant she had to sneak around and use payphones to contact Greg, perhaps calling off the whole operation was the sensible thing to do. Yes, it was sensible. But lots of things were sensible. Her father made sensible investments...

"Sure, you're calling it off, or sure, you're not going to see me?"

"Um... I..." she really did have to decide, but how could she?

"Please Sarah, concentrate," the desperation could be heard in his voice. "This is not a game anymore."

His insistent tone shook Sarah, "A game? Is that what you think this all is?"

"What? Our relationship or your action?"

"Either. Both. I don't know."

"I could ask you the same thing Sarah."

"Dude, our relationship is not a game," she insisted.

"Really? Sure you didn't catch a dose of jungle fever?" He had to say it now. This might be their last conversation before everything fell apart. They had been dancing around it for the past week. Whatever happened, they couldn't pretend their relationship was somehow taking place outside the world where race mattered.

"Yes Greg. I'm sure. Absolutely sure."

"I'm not just one more political trophy to piss off Jack? A romp with a nice virile slave to make massa all angry?"

"No Greg," Sarah said softly. She knew he was scared and upset. And so was she. But she had to try to be calm. If she said the wrong thing now everything could be ruined. Her socio-political world was crashing down around her. The aftershocks were destabilizing her love life too. "You're right about my dad. I'm sure he'd be angry. And normally I do like making him mad... I admit that. I have to admit it. I want to be completely honest about everything here," her voice started quavering. Her voice never quavered. "Normally I do like making him mad. But this is one time where I really wish he wouldn't get so angry."

There was a long pause. Sarah could imagine Greg weighing her response. Would she pass the test?

"Yeah," he finally agreed. "So do I."

There was another long pause. Sarah had to let some time pass before she went any further, placing a bookend after the "jungle fever" discussion, so they could move on to a completely separate one about the action. They were different issues.

"The other thing's not a game either," said Sarah, much more composed now.

"Yeah," Greg grudgingly admitted. "I guess it's not. At least not for people like you and Hassan. You guys are serious."

"Dude, we're all serious."

"You'd better be."

"And that's why I can't just call it off." And she knew it was true. Her agonizing was over and her decision was made. "It's not up to me. It's a collective thing."

"A collective thing," Greg repeated. "Yeah, I suppose that's how you have to call it." That's how his mother would call it. He would suck his teeth disparagingly when his mother said such a thing, but he had no right to do that with Sarah. "So I guess it's goodbye for now."

"Just for now," Sarah promised.

"Just for now," Greg agreed.

And there was one final pause as each waited to see if the other had any last words. None came. They hung up.

"If any of you have ever looked at your FBI file, you discover that intelligence agencies in general are extremely incompetent. That's one of the reasons why there are so many intelligence failures. They just never get anything straight, for all kinds of reasons. Part of it is because of the information they get. The information they get comes from ideological fanatics, typically, who always misunderstand things in their own crazy way. If you look at an FBI file, say, about yourself, where you know what the facts are, you'll see that the information has some kind of relation to the facts, you can figure out what they're talking about, but by the time it works its way through the ideological fanaticism of the intelligence agencies, there's always weird distortion."

— NOAM CHOMSKY, Q&A WITH COMMUNITY ACTIVISTS, 2/10/89

NO THANKS, I DON'T NEED any Viagra, thought Jack as he erased another spam message in his inbox. He and Shirley hadn't had sex in months, and right now that suited Jack just fine.

Spam didn't bother Jack as much as most people. He appreciated the amount of work that must have gone into the collection of email addresses, and how he must have been specially targeted by his age and income-level for various products and services. It was all part of the game—the PR and advertising game that paid Jack's salary. Spam was a primitive hucksterism on the frontier of new communications technologies, like snake oil salesmen in the Wild West. Eventually it would be tamed and integrated into people's daily lives, providing a useful and entertaining service, just like regular advertising. Jack did a lot of business online so he got a lot of spam. He erased it every morning before he went to work.

The high-speed connection wasn't working as fast as Jack's caffeine-enhanced brain this morning so, while he waited for the computer to erase his email, he decided to create some order out of the clutter that Sarah had left in his office over the weekend. It seemed to be the result of a short burst of frantic schoolwork. There were chocolate bar wrappers, bits of crumpled paper, a dictionary, a thesaurus, *Selected Works of Karl Marx*, Noam Chomsky's *Manufacturing Consent*, Susan George's *Debt Boomerang*: anti-establishment propaganda. What was she learning in that Women's Studies program anyway?

Wait a minute, what was this? Beside the recycle bin was a crumpled paper. The title caught his eye, *The Manifesto of Those Who Refuse to Remain Silent*. It looked like it was just the first page of a larger document. There were words crossed out or circled in pen, and plenty of marginal notes. He forgot about his email and read the manifesto rough draft of page one.

With each anti-American leftwing catchphrase he saw Sarah sinking further into the abyss. With each call to radical action, his breath quickened. What would be the price to pay for these transgressions? Corporate mass murder? US imperialism? And was she advocating a strategy of sabotage? "Only with justice, will there be peace," was written in the margin. It looked like that was the slogan to be added to the first paragraph, right after the call to make "the functioning of global capitalism and US imperialism impossible and unworkable." Sounded like terrorism. She cleverly twisted her words to make it seem like she condemned the September 11 attacks, while justifying them as a reaction to American "imperialism." Deception, lies, trickery. Treachery, subversion, treason.

How could Sarah have strayed so far from him and Shirley and their life in Westmount? Had she really become part of this dark underworld of terror? What could make her join the evildoers? His daughter could never stoop to advocating terrorism against people like her own father, at least not of her own accord. It must have been the Arabs she was associating with. He could see their bearded faces whispering in her ears, their dirty hands clutching her wrists. They were brainwashing her.

When Sarah mentioned that Palestinian group, SPHR, during the cumin spice blowup over dinner, alarm bells had been set off in Jack's mind. He found the *Suburban* article, "Rally, terror groups linked." It cited a terrorism expert. And re-reading the *Suburban* article made him remember a story that came out on September 12th in *The Globe and Mail*—a nationally respected newspaper—which cited a B'nai Brith "urgent alert" for Montréal following the September 11 attacks. When he re-read *The Globe and Mail* article, he saw that name again: SPHR "a Palestinian student group at Concordia University." B'nai Brith was warning immigration authorities to stop demonstrators from coming into the country to participate in the SPHR protest because some

...DNESDAY, SEPTEMBER, 2001

'No matter what you may hear from other children on the playground, you need to know you are safe.' *Toronto Grade 5 teacher*

Canadian Reaction   Day of Infamy A:

Muslims fear backlash; Jewish group issues alert

'hile Canadian Islamic groups rned of a backlash against Mus- s after the terror attacks in the ited States, a prominent Jewish up demanded stronger mea- s to keep out pro-Palestinian onstrators expected in Mon- l this weekend.

aired interviews with persons who have used phrases like 'Muslim ter- rorists' and have attributed these vicious attacks to Muslims." While the organisation said there is no cause for panic, it urged Mus- lims in Canada take more caution. B'nai Brith Canada, a Jewish ad- vocacy group, said it was issuing an "urgent alert" to Canadian immi-

president of B'nai Brith, said the demonstration is being organized by a Palestinian student group at Concordia University. She said the university has told the Students for Palestinian Human Rights that it may hold the rally on campus. In a statement, the Jewish group said yesterday's events in the United Stat...

world in the face of the ruthless agenda of terrorist groups, those who fund and equip them, and those who provide them with logis- tic and moral support," it said. Individuals among these [Mon treal] demonstrators may well have links to organizations that...

tacks. He called for "all democra- cies [to] work together to stamp out terrorism. Leaders of several Muslim groups expressed worry that Cana- dians won't differentiate between militant extrem...

lamic Society of North America, which is based in Mississauga, Ont. But while condemning the at- tacks, the Kitchener, Ont., office of the International Islami...

participants may be linked to organisations "that espouse, support or implement terrorist activities." The article quoted a B'nai Brith spokesperson who explained that the university had told SPHR it could not hold the event on campus. Everybody knew Concordia was a bleeding-heart liberal institution. That's why there were so many crazy radical students there. So if Concordia was forbidding Palestinians to hold a demo, there must be compelling reasons for the ban. And now Jack's daughter was being corrupted by these terrorists. This manifesto was evidence of how deeply indoctrinated she had become. How could he get her out of this dangerous cult?

He had to delve into her dark world, to find out how far she had gone. He looked through the rest of the crumpled papers, and went through the recycle bin as well, finding what looked to be five crumpled, ripped and coffee-stained pages from the manifesto. Once Jack had laid out the pieces of the puzzle on the desk, he went over them for clues.

The manifesto itself was one long rant against "US imperialism and global capitalism" which cited historical examples in South and Central America and the Middle East. Some of the sections on the Middle East had what looked like Arabic script in the margins. Jack's heart beat faster just looking at that mysterious handwritten text, and not knowing what it said. It had to be something supporting violent terrorism—otherwise it would have been in English. By the overall structure, it looked like there were supposed to be examples from Africa and Asia as well but those pages were missing. There was nothing about Soviet Imperialism, nothing about human rights violations in China or the horrors visited upon women living under Muslim fundamentalist states. Wasn't she supposed to learn about that in Women's Studies?

Some of the marginal notes were obviously corrections or additions to the text, but others looked like personal commentary not meant to be part of the manifesto itself. The name "Henry Kissinger" was circled and beside it was written "bastard should rot in hell with Pinochet" along with a drawing of flames and a devil's grinning face. On the bottom of a page with numerous George Bush references there were various slogans: "No more Bush-shit," "Stop the Bushery," "More trees less Bush," etc. But what interested Jack most was what was written beside the reference to something called the "Sabra and Shatila massacres" which was circled. The marginal note scrawled beside it read, "Dad's connections = payback. Thanks dad!" with the sketch of a smiley face. What dark meaning was hidden by that cryptic equation? Were the Arabs using his daughter to get to his corporate connections to achieve revenge for some kind of massacre?

Suddenly his daughter faded into the background for a minute as he realised that his own career could be affected by her radical politics. If any of his corporate clients were embarrassed or negatively affected in any way by Sarah's actions, it could have serious repercussions for his business. Just one more reason to nip this thing in the bud.

The father turned investigator spent two hours that morning looking through Sarah's files on the computer. He couldn't find a more recent version of her manifesto, but he found plenty of stuff she had written about the FTAA and US Imperialism in Latin America—papers for her World Issues teacher, no doubt. Jack printed them off, and he printed off the list of web sites she had visited that he found in the cache of the Internet browser.

As the last pages were printing off, he heard the crash of dishes downstairs in the kitchen. That had to be Shirley. She was often clumsy in the mornings as she hurried to make it to work, especially when she had not yet had her infusion of coffee. Unlike Jack, she would never make the switch to a morning person. He looked at his watch—9:05. He didn't have any appointments until 9:45 this morning, but Shirley was going to be late again. It was a good thing she didn't have a real job. Anyway, she wouldn't mind being a little bit later once he confronted her with this. Shirley was always defending their daughter's radicalism. "In our day it was the Vietnam War," Shirley would remind him. "Today it's globalization. She's young Jack. Give her some slack." But once Shirley saw the concrete proof that her little girl was being manipulated by terrorists, she would have no choice but to help him find a way to deprogram her.

When he arrived in the kitchen Jack saw his wife standing over the sink, frantically working on a coffee stain that she had made on the sleeve of her daffodil blazer. "Sorry about the mess, hun," she said gesturing towards some broken dishes on the floor. "Think you could clean that up for me? I'm in rush, late already."

"I'll take care of it," Jack assured her, "but you're going to be even later than usual today. There's something you should know about Sarah."

She stopped rubbing her sleeve, turned off the water and looked her husband in the eyes. "What is it Jack?" she asked with concern.

He held up the papers in his hands. On the top were the wrinkled pages of the manifesto. Shirley took a step towards her husband to get a better look. When she saw the title she breathed a sigh of relief and went back to the sink to continue washing her sleeve. "Honestly Jack. I don't have time for political arguments this morning. I'm already late."

"But Shirley, this is serious!" her husband shouted in anger. "You don't even know what's in here."

"Yes I do Jack," Shirley snapped back. "I read the manifesto. I don't agree with everything in there, but it's nothing to get upset about. It's just politics." She looked at her sleeve with exasperation. The stain was not going to come out but she didn't have time to pick out another outfit.

"How can you say that?" Jack cried with frustration. "Can't you see Sarah's being brainwashed by Arab terrorists?"

She looked up from her sleeve again, and inspected the man that she thought was her husband. She frowned at him. Yes, that was Jack, but something had snapped in that PR consultant brain of his. "You need professional help Jack. I'm going to work." She rolled up the cuffs of her blazer.

"But she's going to become involved with something danger-ous and illegal," he pleaded. "She's advocating sabotage or even terrorism, especially against corporations that I'm involved with."

"Oh Jack," Shirley shook her head as she picked up her bag from the kitchen table and adjusted her sleeves again. "Every-thing's not about you. Get a grip."

"Okay, forget about me," Jack continued as he followed Shirley out the door and onto the driveway. "Don't believe me. Believe the terrorism experts. That organization, SPHR, that Palestinian organization Sarah's involved with. It's connected to terrorism! Our daughter is being brainwashed by a bunch of Arab terrorists!"

Shirley turned around as she was opening the car door and furiously shot back at her husband, "Yell that a little louder Jack, I don't think all of Westmount has heard it yet." And with that, she got in her car and drove off, leaving her husband standing in the garage entrance wearing his slippers and a business suit with a stack of loose papers in hand. Just then a gust of wind blew some of the papers out of his grip, sending him scurrying over the neighbour's perfectly manicured lawn to collect them.

He was grumbling to himself as he picked up the wrinkled, stained and scotch-taped together pages of his daughter's mani-festo. "She thinks I'm crazy, does she? I'll show her who's crazy. Our daughter's in bed with Osama bin fucking Laden."

Mrs. Green from across the street waved at him as she swept off her front porch, "Hello Mr. Murphy. Nice weather we're having." Jack didn't even notice.

Once he had calmed down, put the papers in his briefcase, cleaned up the mess Shirley had left in the kitchen and got ready for work, he started to think about a course of action. Maybe his wife was not too far off when she suggested he get professional help. But he didn't need a psychiatrist. He needed an intelligence expert.

"To criticize one's country is to do it a service and pay it a compliment. It is a service because it may spur the country to do better than it is doing; it is a compliment because it evidences a belief that a country can do better than it is doing. In a democracy, dissent is an act of faith. Like medicine, the test of its value is not its taste but its effect, not how it makes people feel in the moment but how it makes them feel in the long run. Criticism, in short, is more than a right; it is an act of patriotism, a higher form of patriotism, I believe, than the familiar rituals of national adulation."
— J. WILLIAM FULBRIGHT (FORMER U.S. SENATOR), *THE ARROGANCE OF POWER*, 1966

It was beautiful—the most splendid thing that Sarah had seen in weeks. The banner hung exactly where the American Students Association 9/11 banner had been hanging, from the balcony beside the escalator in the Hall Building lobby leading to the second floor Mezzanine. Gone was the US flag and the blind patriotism, mourning only American lives and ignoring the role of US imperialism in producing such a terrible tragedy. The old pennant had been replaced with a new emblem bearing no national flag. Over the background of a B-52 bomber dropping its deadly cargo was the following text:

Our hearts go out to the millions killed as a result of U.S. Foreign Policy:

IRAQ	600,000 Children
NICARAGUA	70,000
GUATEMALA	200,000
EL SALVADOR	75,000
VIETNAM	4,000,000
NEW YORK	5,000

WITHOUT JUSTICE, THERE IS NO PEACE!

Who had dared to hang the United States' dirty laundry in public? Weren't they afraid of being labeled terrorists? You can't tell the truth about that, not now. Sarah's surprise was in large part due to events from earlier in the morning.

* * *

She was up before 9 a.m., thanks to her ungodly Wednesday class schedule, so she had to endure her father having a good chuckle at *The Globe and Mail*'s editorial cartoon at the breakfast table.

Still half-asleep and smiling at her bowl of granola and plain yogourt, she tried to ignore her father. Her mind was not in the brightly-lit Murphy kitchen, but somewhere much nicer in Greg's dingy rundown fourth floor east-end apartment where they had made passionate love less than three days ago. She was coming to the realisation that she couldn't keep to the agreement they had made over the phone. She had to see him. Things were more intense after their exchange whose ostensible purpose was to wind everything down for the foreseeable future. So much had been shared between them in such a short time. It was cliché, but it was true—romances moved at dizzying speeds in wartime. And the one true thing out of Bush's mouth in the past couple of weeks was his insistence that we were living through a time of war.

Sarah's father laughed louder, forcing her back to the reality of the Murphy kitchen. "Even you've got to laugh at this Sarah. It's damn funny!" He brandished the cartoon in front of his daughter's face—a rude wakeup call.

It featured Taliban soldiers in Afghanistan listening contently to the speech given by feminist and anti-fundamentalist Muslim Sunera Thobani. Sarah hadn't heard the speech Thobani gave in Ottawa two days ago and she didn't know the UBC professor was an anti-fundamentalist Muslim, so there was very little she could do to deflect her dad's criticism. According to the *National Post*, Thobani had called all Americans "bloodthirsty." How could Sarah argue in favour of that? American foreign policy was definitely bloody, but Sarah certainly didn't think that all Americans supported or even knew about those policies. It seemed unlikely to Sarah that Thobani was really trying to say that all Americans—every single last one, from CEO to welfare mom—were bloodthirsty warmongers. It seemed more likely that Thobani was offering a more subtle critique of US foreign policy, but Sarah had no evidence to support her position. She had no way to contest the direct quotes from the press.

She tried to argue with her father on the basis of the US foreign policy record alone, but he wouldn't listen. "If your Women's Studies professors at Concordia are anything like Thobani, I understand why you're defending Arab terrorists. Those professors ought to be fired. I'd like to see how long they last in the real world spouting crap like that. Damn tenure! Academic freedom shouldn't be a license to promote dangerous crackpot ideas."

The headlines about the CSU agenda were just as damning:

CONCORDIA HANDBOOK "ADVOCATES TERRORISM"

Pro-intifada handbook sparks outrage at Concordia University

Student Handbook Called "Blueprint" for terrorists

* * *

And now somebody actually had the temerity to hang the bloody and gruesome truth for all to see exactly where the comfortable jingoistic platitudes had been only days before.

Sarah was starting to realise that no matter what critics of American imperialism did or said, no matter how good their arguments were, no matter how much concrete proof they had to back up their position, they would be dragged through the mud and treated as if they were in league with Osama bin Laden himself. It made her angry. It made her want to fight back. And yet fighting back would invite more abuse. It was a self-reinforcing technique for dispersing political gatherings, more effective than crude teargas or rubber bullets: public ridicule and social ostracism. How could activists do anything else but go into hiding?

But now, as the escalator carried Sarah and a tide of strangers towards their morning classes, she saw she wasn't alone in her subversive thoughts. Sarah put her shoulders back and held her head high as she made her way through the rush, more determined than ever to move forward with their plan.

When she got up to the top of the escalator Sarah noticed a girl sitting on a chair between the railing where the banner was attached and the escalator leading from the Mezzanine to the 4th floor. Incredibly, the girl was reading a book. The crowded and bustling thoroughfare was not exactly the most comfortable place to study. As people rushed to make their 9:45 a.m. classes, a traffic jam formed at the base of the escalator. People were waiting impatiently to get on the conveyor-belt of the human resource factory known as Concordia University. The crowd bottlenecked around the poor girl, jostling her. Sarah stood by the railing a few paces away and watched. The young student sitting in the chair patiently waited for the crowd to die down, then found her place in the text and went back to reading.

The girl looked familiar. She wore jeans, a T-shirt and a headband to keep her prolific brown curls from covering her high forehead. Sarah seemed to remember seeing her at an information meeting about the Tom and Laith expulsions, but she couldn't recall her name. "Hi," Sarah greeted her.

The girl had a pained look on her face when she looked up from her book.

"Um, sorry to interrupt your reading," Sarah apologized. "I was just wondering what you're doing here."

The pained look subsided as she breathed a sigh of relief. "Oh, I'm guarding the banner here so that nobody can tear it down."

"Really?" asked Sarah. "Is the university administration giving you a hard time?"

"No," said the girl, putting down her book as she turned towards the security desk below. "At least not yet. We have the banner space booked. We filled out all the forms to reserve the space so that we'd have it right after the booking of the American Students Association ran out. So the admin is supposed to let us keep our banner here, unless they suddenly change the rules just for us. I wouldn't put it past them though."

"Well," said Sarah, her brow furrowing with confusion, "then why do you have to guard the banner? Dude, security is right there," she pointed across the lobby to the glass-covered security desk and the two guards sitting behind it. "Nobody could tear this thing down without security seeing everything."

"You would think so, wouldn't you," she said through clenched teeth. "But every time the banner has been torn down, security, miraculously, 'didn't see anything.' I caught a guy just down the hall yesterday as he put the banner in a garbage bin and I had a big argument with him. I gave security his description, but I don't expect anything to come of it."

"Did he say why he tore it down?" asked Sarah. "I mean, he can't really argue with the facts. It's all true, what you have on the banner."

The banner's guardian sighed and shook her head. "I wish it were that simple. That'd be great if all we had to do was prove our facts were well-founded and then people would say, 'Oh, I guess you're right. Maybe we should stop exploiting people all around the world, and killing anybody who resists.' That guy who tore down the poster was definitely not too concerned about the facts. He kept saying the banner was 'offensive' to him because he's an American."

"But your banner totally includes all the Americans killed in the September 11 attacks," Sarah objected. "You're just trying to put those attacks into context, right? 9/11 didn't happen in a complete historical vacuum. It seems to me, the best way to make sure this doesn't keep happening is to try to understand the global conflicts that generated the terrorism in the first place..."

As the girl sat smiling and nodding in front of her, Sarah realised she was probably just repeating all the arguments the banner's guardian had made to the vandal. "Oh, why am I telling you this?" asked Sarah rhetorically. "You're the one who made the banner. It's really a great piece of work, by the way. It's way cool. We need more stuff like this around here."

"Oh, I don't mind you telling me that stuff," the girl laughed. "Believe me, I really don't mind at all. It's a nice change. There are so many people that get pissed off about this banner. They come up to me and call me all kinds of names and want to argue all day about how it's 'disrespectful to the September 11 victims.' And 'what would I say to the family members of the people who were killed?' And I tell them that I'd say 'I'm really sorry for your loss. We should make sure the US government stops funding terrorists like Osama bin Laden and stops creating the conditions that allow their ideology of hatred to gain followers. That way we can make sure nobody else falls victim the way your son did, or your sister, or whoever.' But it doesn't matter what I say because they're not listening. Anyway, I'm glad you like the banner, my name's Brandi."

"I'm Sarah," she said shaking Brandi's hand vigorously. "Let me congratulate you on an amazing piece of work. It's marvelous, really."

"Oh, it wasn't just me," said Brandi. "It was a team effort. My friend Susana also worked on it. And she's helping me guard it too. We take turns."

"Well, it's good to see there are people who don't think the same way as my father," Sarah offered with a grin. "And who aren't afraid to show it."

"Some others are voicing their opposition to American imperialism tonight," Brandi observed, pointing to a poster on the wall beside the escalator.

The poster read:

America's New War:

Perspectives on War and Imperialism

The event was to take place in the Hall Building auditorium at 7 p.m. Sarah noticed Lillian Robinson's name as one of the invited speakers at the talk. "Wow! Lillian's everywhere. Defending the CSU's 'terrorist blueprint' and now this. Dude, I so hope they don't pull a Sunera Thobani on her."

"Oh, I'm sure she gets her share of hate mail and threatening phone calls," Brandi responded. "Maybe not as much as Sunera Thobani gets right now. But she gets enough. An anti-Zionist Jewish professor has already been targeted by the Committee for the Extermination of Palestine—the CEP. And that was before all the September 11 backlash started! You can bet Lillian will be getting the same treatment."

"The CEP?" asked Sarah incredulously. She had heard about the CEP threats against the CSU, but she didn't know about a professor being targeted as well. "How could a group dedicated to the 'extermination' of Palestinians target Jewish professors?"

"Simple," Brandi replied. "Jews that support Palestinian self-determination are traitors to their people. That's even worse than being a savage Palestinian. After all, the Palestinians can't be expected to know any better."

Hearing the reports given by Hassan, Sarah knew very well about the targeting of non-Western people: Arabs, Muslims, Sikhs and other brown people like Sunera Thobani. But now she realised, anybody who failed to accept the sacred truth of American victimhood, unblemished by any imperialist guilt— even the head of a university department, even a Jew from New York, anybody—could be thrown in as the enemy. An enemy to be "exterminated." It was the ultimate dichotomy as stipulated by the Commander in Chief when he said two weeks ago, "You're either with us, or you're with the terrorists." Sarah had to wonder if things were getting to a point where the

CEP would make good on its death threats. "We"—the civilized world—were getting better and better at convincing ourselves that "they"—the enemies of freedom—were evil.

Sarah was about to tell Brandi that she should watch her back too when a young man stepped out of the line of students filing onto the escalator and leaned over the balcony. He was pulling at Brandi's banner, and right in front of her too!

"Excuse me," said Brandi calmly.

The guy kept pulling on the banner. Brandi had done her best to tightly link her message to the very structure of the school this morning for precisely this reason. It was fastened with conviction. All that Sarah could see was the backside of a pair of dark blue dress slacks and black shoes as the young man bent over the railing, grunting with effort as he pulled frantically at the anti-imperialist banner, but with little success.

"Excuse me!" Brandi shouted forcefully this time.

The well-dressed vandal continued in his efforts, completely ignoring the banner's guardian. The security guards were intensely disregarding the argument about twenty feet in front of them and fifteen feet above their heads. Sarah could not imagine they failed to hear Brandi's attempt to gain the vandal's attention.

Brandi stood up, leaving her book on the chair. Her thin frame was about half the size of the man bent over the railing. She grabbed the arm of his blazer and pulled him upright. "Excuse me!" she shouted again. "But you can't remove this banner. The banner space has been reserved by the Québec Public Interest Research Group."

He glared through a set of thin metal-framed glasses, directly into her eyes. He was breathing heavily from his exertions and his face was bright red. The unlikely vandal had light brown hair, was cleanly shaven, and wore an expensive dark blue suit with a red tie. He tucked his shirttail back into his pants as he asked, "So you're responsible for, for... for this!"

Seeing there would be no help from the security guards whose job it was to ensure student safety, Sarah was ready to intervene. But when Brandi met the vandal's eyes with an icy glare of her own, Sarah could tell the banner guardian had the situation well in hand. "Yes," she answered calmly but firmly. "I'm one of the banner makers. And I'd appreciate it if you would refrain from damaging my work."

"Who let you put this thing up?" he asked incredulously. "This was a memorial to the victims before. Now you're trying to make it about the US government! Don't you have any respect for the victims?"

"I can assure you that all the proper channels for booking the space were followed," Brandi continued. She had obviously rehearsed this rejoinder many times before. "If you'd like to file a complaint about the banner, you're certainly welcome to do so. There's the Office of Rights and Responsibilities, or the Security desk just below us. But I should point out that this banner is still very much about 'the victims,' as you say, the millions of victims who have suffered as a result of US foreign policy. Most of those victims are in Third World countries but that doesn't mean we're ignoring the recent attacks on the World Trade Center. As you can see we include those victims in this long but hardly exhaustive list. And I should also point out..."

"You can't blame all this on the USA!" the young man interrupted her. He was pointing his finger right in her face but Brandi did not flinch. "People die in the Third World because they're poor, and because they have dictatorial leaders, and because of all kinds of stuff. But it's not an excuse for attacking the country that's done the most to help them improve themselves!"

"And I should also point out," Brandi continued from where she left off, "that 'respect for the victims' is not shown by ignoring the role US foreign policy makers had in their deaths. You say people die in the Third World because they've got dictatorial leaders. Well, why do you think that is? Who do you think helped put a lot of those leaders into power? Who do you think supplies them with military hardware? You say those people die because they're poor. Well who do you think forces austerity measures down their throats so they can pay back the US banks, and sell public sector industry to US multinationals?"

"Don't give me that bullshit!" he shouted back. "All that has nothing to do with Osama bin Laden and al Qaeda. You can't excuse the murder of 5000 innocent people like that. It's not like those other deaths you're talking about. We're talking about the cold-blooded murder of 5000 people who didn't do anything to hurt anybody. They were just going to work."

"Oh I agree!" Brandi assured him, and with that he backed off slightly, a puzzled look coming over his face. "Those people who were killed did nothing to deserve what was done to them. And the ideology of the attackers probably had very little to do with the injustices of US foreign policy I've been criticizing. I don't think bin Laden or al Qaeda are trying to win the freedom of the world's poor from the oppressive weight of US imperialism. I think they're going after 'the infidels.' But that doesn't mean the attacks were not at least partially the result of US foreign policy. You've got to understand the US supported bin Laden and his followers when they were fighting the Soviets in Afghanistan, when they thought it was in the US interest to..."

"Oh sure, just blame everything on the USA!" he interrupted Brandi yet again, just as angrily although with a little less energy. "How can you say you respect the American victims of terrorism when you twist everything around to make it the fault of the USA?" And with that he leaned over the railing again and started to pull on the banner.

"Excuse me!" Brandi shouted again. She grabbed his arm and pulled, but this time he resisted, refusing to budge. And his efforts at removing the banner were starting to be rewarded. The string on the left side of the banner was beginning to come loose from the railing.

"Hey, you heard her!" Sarah jumped into the fray grabbing the vandal's other arm. Once Sarah added her strength to that of Brandi's they were able to pull the pro-American vigilante into an upright position. Now he was glaring at Sarah and breathing heavily through his nose and into her face. It made her skin crawl, but she didn't back off one inch.

"This banner's staying right here, asshole!" shouted Sarah. She figured at this point it was her job to play the bad cop. "My friend tried to tell you nicely, and you wouldn't listen. Now it looks like you've got a nice expensive suit there," she brushed a bit of lint off of his shoulder. "And it would really be a shame if it got damaged as you tried to tear down this girl's banner, now wouldn't it? Why don't you just be a good boy and go to your class? Let me guess, commerce, right?"

"You're threatening me?" he asked.

"No, I'm just..." Sarah tried to object but he interrupted her with the answer to his own question.

"You're threatening me!" he yelled.

Sarah let go of the vandal's arm and backed away. A group of onlookers had formed around them, and the guards at the Security desk below had finally taken notice of the conflict. The woman sitting at the desk was pointing up at her, and a male guard was making his way out from behind the booth, walking towards the escalators.

"Look," said Sarah in a calm tone. "Nobody's threatening anybody."

"You people say you're against violence," he shot back. "But you defend the violence of the terrorists and you threaten people who try to protect the memory of terrorism's victims."

"Dude, nobody's defending terrorism," Sarah insisted, "and nobody's threatening anybody."

The security guard stepped off the escalator from the lobby and placed his large blue-clad frame in between Sarah and the vandal. "Everybody calm down," he said in an authoritative voice as he held one open hand up towards each of the parties in the dispute.

With a little encouragement from the security guard both Sarah and the would-be vandal were convinced to go to their classes. The student opted to register a formal complaint about the banner. Sarah would have liked to stay and recruit Brandi for the action she and her friends were planning. The calm and collected banner guardian would have been a useful addition to their team. But Sarah had attracted too much attention with her bad cop routine. She would have to talk to Brandi later. Unfortunately, when Sarah came back in the late afternoon both Brandi and her banner were nowhere to be found.

Brandi would have liked to talk to Sarah as well to tell her what happened after she left. It might have been nothing. It probably was nothing, but the older man in the blue baseball cap and the green jacket didn't look at all like a student or a professor. He was talking to the guard down at the desk, showing him what appeared to be photos, and at various points in the conversation Brandi could have sworn that he gestured up to the balcony where Brandi was sitting pretending to read.

"**Wolf Blitzer:** *Let me read a quote from the New Yorker article [by Seymour Hersh], the March 17ᵗʰ issue, just out now. "There is no question that Perle believes that removing Saddam from power is the right thing to do. At the same time, he has set up a company that may gain from a war."*
Richard Perle: *I don't believe that a company would gain from a war. On the contrary, I believe that the successful removal of Saddam Hussein, and I've said this over and over again, will diminish the threat of terrorism. And what he's talking about is investments in homeland defense, which I think are vital and necessary. Look, Sy Hersh is the closest thing American journalism has to a terrorist, frankly.*
Blitzer: *Well, on the basis of—why do you say that? A terrorist?*
Perle: *Because he's widely irresponsible. If you read the article, it's first of all, impossible to find any consistent theme in it. But the suggestion that my views are somehow related for the potential for investments in homeland defense is complete nonsense.*
Blitzer: *But I don't understand. Why do you accuse him of being a terrorist?*
Perle: *Because he sets out to do damage and he will do it by whatever innuendo, whatever distortion he can. Look, he hasn't written a serious piece since Maylie [sic, intended reference likely the My Lai massacre of the Vietnam War]*

— CNN *LATE EDITION* HOST, WOLF BLITZER, INTERVIEWING RICHARD PERLE, CHAIR OF THE PENTAGON DEFENSE POLICY BOARD AND ADVISOR TO GEORGE W. BUSH, 3/9/2003. DAYS LATER SEYMOUR HERSH WOULD RECEIVE THE GOLDSMITH CAREER AWARD FOR EXCELLENCE IN JOURNALISM. TWO WEEKS LATER THE NEW YORK TIMES PUBLISHED A STAFF EDITORIAL OUTLINING PERLE'S CONFLICT OF INTEREST.

"**IF YOU ASK ME, IT'S** a waste of a perfectly good video cassette," Shirley scolded her husband as he fiddled with the VCR.

"Well, I didn't ask you," Jack replied without turning away from the delicate work of VCR programming, "did I?"

Shirley chuckled to herself and went back to reading her romance novel. She was snug in her pajamas, tucked under a warm quilt on the comfy love seat by the window. Jack had traded his leather shoes for slippers and his blazer for a cardigan, but he still wore his tie and slacks. Until he watched tonight's Presidential address to the joint session of Congress, his working day was not over. His note pad was sitting on the coffee table in front of the couch facing the television, but he couldn't find his gold pen. Where could he have left it? He would have to make do with a regular ballpoint.

When he had double-checked every connection and made a test recording, Jack turned to his wife, lecturing to her above his reading glasses, "This is important Shirley. It's a part of history. It's not just any speech. It's our President addressing the nation—the first address to Congress since the opening act in the war on terror!"

Absorbed in her novel, Shirley was only half listening to her husband. Did he say 'our' President? "Oh, of course it's important dear. I just don't think I'm going to watch it again, or show it to my grandchildren. Dubya is not exactly Kennedy material you know."

Jack sat down on the couch and stared at the muted TV ads in anticipation of the big show. "Oh the old boy might surprise you tonight honey. Since the attacks he's been really on the ball."

"Oh yeah, what about the..."

Jack wouldn't let his wife finish her sentence, "Oh, I know. The crusade thing! Now come on, that's just political correctness crap! Of course the liberals gave him a hard time about that but he was just saying what everybody already knows. This is a war between Judeo-Christian Western civilization and the terrorist hoards who are, let's face it, Arabs and Muslims. Now if I were Bush's PR consultant I would tell him to avoid saying the 'C-word' because everybody in the PR business knows, it's not about truth, it's about image. Public relations isn't about reality, it's about the management of reality. The truth is the war on terror is a crusade. And that's a good thing. It's a moral war for a just cause—a higher purpose. But we live in a multicultural bleeding-heart liberal society, so the image that's projected has to be a bit more nuanced. That's what good PR people do. And I know Bush has some of the best. I wonder how many focus groups tonight's speech has gone through..."

* * *

Tonight, we are a country awakened to danger and called to defend freedom. Our grief has turned to anger and anger to resolution. Whether we bring our enemies to justice or bring justice to our enemies, justice will be done.

Applause...

But nobody in Al-Taïb was clapping. The predominantly Arab crowd watched the big screen TV in somber stillness, almost as if Bush was reading a eulogy at a funeral service, and in a way, he was.

"He's a very scary man," said Hakim over the Congressional applause.

Hassan and Sayed nodded.

"Our grief has turned to anger and our anger to hatred," said Hassan in a hoarse voice, full of irony but devoid of any humour. "Whether we bring the Muslims to justice or justice to the Muslims, justice will be done." He was rubbing his eyes, as if it caused them pain to look at the Commander in Chief. This was going to be a long night. After watching the speech Hassan would have a full graveyard shift ahead of him.

They watched Bush as he thanked Congress for the $40 billion it had liberated to "rebuild our communities and meet the needs of our military" as if the two purposes were one and the same.

Then the President thanked the world:

> America will never forget the sounds of our national anthem playing at Buckingham Palace, on the streets of Paris and at Berlin's Brandenburg Gate.

> We will not forget South Korean children gathering to pray outside our embassy in Seoul, or the prayers of sympathy offered at a mosque in Cairo.

> We will not forget moments of silence and days of mourning in Australia and Africa and Latin America.

And it was true. For the past nine days the entire planet was in mourning for the innocent civilians killed in New York on September 11. There were billions watching tonight just like

Hassan, Hakim and Sayed. It was enough to give Americans the impression that the United States government was a force of civilization and progress in the world.

Then the President, or "our" President, because we were all Americans now, talked about the "enemies of freedom" committing an "act of war against our county" on September 11. No need to go into any historical details. It was as simple as night and day:

> All of this was brought upon us in a single day,
> and night fell on a different world, a world where
> freedom itself is under attack.

No need to talk about CIA financing received by the enemies of freedom in the 1980s. Nobody would remember that anyway. Back then, Ronald Reagan and *Rambo III* called them "freedom fighters" because they were resisting the grip of the Soviet "evil empire" on Afghanistan. It would be far too confusing if the freedom fighters suddenly became the enemies of freedom.

> Americans are asking, "Who attacked our country?"

Who were the enemies of freedom? Al Qaeda and its leader Osama bin Laden were on the top of the Commander in Chief's list, but it was impossible for him to tell Americans who precisely the enemies were. They had been "sent to hide in countries around the world to plot evil and destruction." One place they were surely hiding was the Taliban's Afghanistan. So George W. Bush said a lot of bad things about the Taliban—how they were religious fanatics like al Qaeda, how they wouldn't let people have televisions, and how they oppressed women. And he told the Taliban leaders to hand over all al Qaeda terrorists and give full access to US authorities into any areas where they might be training. The precise ultimatum:

> They will hand over the terrorists or they will share
> in their fate.

The "they" grammatically referred only to the Taliban, but smart bombs hadn't been taught the finer points of grammar. The "they" would likely include a lot of Afghan families who had nothing to do with the Taliban (except for living under the repressive Taliban regime the war was supposed to be liberating them from). Anyway, it was very hard to be precise about who the enemy was:

> Our war on terror begins with al Qaeda, but it does not end there. It will not end until every terrorist group of global reach has been found, stopped and defeated.

Applause...

> Americans are asking, "Why do they hate us?"

It was only logical of course. If they were the enemies of freedom their hatred for us could only be explained by all of the freedoms we enjoyed:

> They hate our freedoms: our freedom of religion, our freedom of speech, our freedom to vote and assemble and disagree with each other.

But Americans did not need to worry that their freedoms might be taken away because the terrorists were predestined for defeat:

> ...by abandoning every value except the will to power, they follow in the path of fascism, Nazism and totalitarianism. And they will follow that path all the way to where it ends in history's unmarked grave of discarded lies.

Applause...

> Americans are asking, "How will we fight and win this war?"

With political power, security agencies, and military might including "every necessary weapon of war." But our President explained that it would be a long war, "a lengthy campaign unlike any other we have ever seen" and it would be fought all around the world, much of it under a veil of secrecy. And over the course of this protracted, indefinite, confusing and largely covert war, countries and regions not within the formal boundaries of the United States would have a decision to make:

Either you are with us or you are with the
terrorists.

That one phrase would be George W. Bush's legacy to the
American people and the world. It would echo through space
and time, affecting how we look at entire nations and religions,
past historical events, and the future. Henceforth there were
only two categories of people: "us" and "the terrorists." Not
only countries and regions, but every single living human being
on the planet would have to decide which of those two categories she or he would fit into. This was the flip side of the slogan
"we are all Americans now." Those who did not sign up for the
American dream would automatically be relegated to the terrorist nightmare. There was no middle ground in the war on
terror:

> This is the world's fight. This is civilization's fight.
> This is the fight of all who believe in progress and
> pluralism, tolerance and freedom.

* * *

The whole us versus terrorists dichotomy had made Shirley
feel uncomfortable. But she was somewhat reassured by Bush's
kind words about non-fanatical Muslims—"our many Muslim
friends"—and his characterization of the war on terror as
"civilization's fight" and a fight for "pluralism, tolerance and
freedom." She wondered if these were the nuances Jack said
were needed to soften the crusade's image. In any event, it was
only a vague unease that was produced by Bush's sweeping
statements against an ambiguously defined "terror." Much more
powerful emotions were evoked by the President's welcome to
the widow Lisa Beamer who sat in a place of honour during
the speech in recognition for the loss of her self-sacrificing
husband on the ill-fated flight 93. Or the President's brandish-
ing of the late George Howard's New York City police shield,
using his self-sacrifice as an example of the future sacrifice
that would be demanded in the war on terror. After hearing
the address, Shirley wiped tears from her eyes and settled back
into her loveseat. She pulled the quilt up under her arms, and
closed her eyes. She knew she couldn't fall asleep—she was far
too agitated for that. She tried to think positive thoughts, about
people coming together in the face of tragedy—just like she and

Carla had found each other on September 11. But images of war—Pinochet, bin Laden, Carla's aunt and uncle, Afghan peasants, bombing campaigns—kept creeping back into her mind. A long, ugly, indefinite and global war. That's what President Bush was talking about. How do they expect to stop the cycle of violence by bombing more people?

"Well nothing too specific about military spending," Jack commented as he hit the rewind button on the remote and put his feet up on the coffee table. He looked over the notes he had taken. "Still, the creation of the Office of Homeland Security sounds promising, plus there was a clear commitment to a strong military. Not to mention the ultimatum to the Taliban, which is obviously fair warning for the upcoming just crusade. And everybody knows that even a fight for a just cause can't be won without lots of planes and bombs." Then as an afterthought Jack mused, "Of course the promise of continued direct assistance to the airlines industry will help with damage control."

"Jack, do you work for a PR firm or the military industry?" asked his wife.

"Both," he answered. He put his reading glasses back down on the table, leaned back and rubbed his eyes. "One of our biggest clients is a military manufacturer, an aerospace firm actually. Up until nine days ago it had huge expansion plans in the civilian sector, but everything is changing overnight. It's great they're getting more military money, but it's a shame the civilian market is shrinking so much. We need to bring consumers back into the fold somehow..."

There was an audible click as the cassette finished rewinding. "Don't you dare play that tape Jack!" warned his wife. But Jack had already pressed the play button before the words had left Shirley's mouth.

"Oh Jack!" Shirley complained. "You're impossible!"

The sound of her voice was drowned out by the loud applause of Congress and then Bush's opening remarks:

> Mr. Speaker, Mr. President Pro Tempore, members
> of Congress, and fellow Americans...

Shirley threw off her blanket in frustration and trudged upstairs to the quiet of their bedroom. Jack watched his President's speech two more times that night, filling in his rough notes with direct quotations. Millions of Americans had seen their President reset the nation's moral compass for the post-9/11 world, and more importantly, so had Mr. Tremblay. The sermon from the joint session of Congress would be a common reference point and a backdrop for a whole new corporate PR campaign. If it could win the hearts and minds of Americans to the imminent crusade, then it could also grease the gears of the military production machine.

* * *

Hassan, Hakim and Sayed were hardly put at ease by the Commander in Chief's assurances that the war on terror was "civilization's fight." When he made this pronouncement, the threesome shared a knowing glance, mouths open in disbelief. They knew exactly what civilization he was referring to and they knew it did not include people like them. In his address, the President had defined civilization as including all those who believe in "progress and pluralism, tolerance and freedom." The words were dripping with erudition, even when pronounced by this lowbrow Texan. Nevertheless the friends knew those words had about as much integrity as Osama bin Laden's 1998 call "to all mankind" made in the spirit of "justice, mercy and fraternity among all nations" two months before he ordered the bombing of US embassies in Kenya and Tanzania. Bin Laden called upon the international forces of "good" to battle "evil" with the same zealous enthusiasm his nemesis displayed tonight.

The President closed his speech with assurances to his fellow Americans of the "rightness of our cause" and of "the victories to come" while calling upon God "to grant us wisdom" and to "watch over the United States of America." There was a moment of silence shared by the three friends while Congress gave the Commander in Chief a standing ovation.

"You're either with us..." said Hakim.

"Or you're with the terrorists," the trio finished the sentence in unison.

"How can he say that?" asked Sayed, his low rumble less subdued than usual. The President's speech was intended to produce resolute acceptance of American power by the Muslim world, but for Sayed, it did the opposite. "So anybody who disagrees with Bush is a terrorist?" he asked incredulously.

"He can say anything he wants," Hassan answered matter-of-factly. "Right now, he can do no wrong. He has a blank cheque and he can write any number he wants on it. He wants Afghanistan? Okay, go ahead Dubya, take it. The world won't object. How can it? This phrase: 'You're either with us or with the terrorists.' It just restates the actual strategic lay of the land in the simplest terms. You can imagine Bush and all his advisors standing around a map of the Middle East, like a huge chessboard, and laughing. They know their advantage is overwhelming. If there is any weakness at all, that might be it: their overconfidence."

"Yeah," Hakim agreed, "I can see how they might see it like that, but we are the terrorists! He's talking about us." He pointed at his kaffiyeh-covered chest to emphasize the point.

Then Hakim felt a hard object pressing into the back of his neck. "I heard that," said a strange voice. "You're under arrest you fucking terrorist. Put your hands on the table where I can see them."

Hakim's eyeballs scanned from left to right, trying, with all the peripheral vision he could muster, to catch a glimpse of the agent pressing the gun just below his cranium. He didn't dare move any other muscle in his body.

For a few brief seconds Hakim was gripped in absolute terror, but it faded just as quickly when he noticed Hassan and Sayed were both smiling at whoever was behind him. Then he heard a familiar voice, "Missed the big speech. Dude, I'm so heartbroken. So what did old Dubya have to say?" But it couldn't be Sarah. That other voice—the voice of the agent—was so hard, tough and dangerous. He could feel it pushing under his cranium like the gun.

Hakim turned around to see Sarah looking down at him with a goofy grin. He wanted to yell at her for scaring him half to death, but he didn't. It would be too undignified.

"You're either with us..." said Sayed.

"Or you're with the terrorists," finished the trio.

Sarah giggled thoughtlessly for a second but stopped suddenly. She looked at her friends and saw that they were not laughing. "He really said... that?" she asked in disbelief.

They nodded.

"Shit," was all she had to say.

"Nicely put," said Hassan.

"That about sums it up," agreed Sayed.

"So we're terrorists then," Sarah concluded.

Hakim could only partially agree, "Well we definitely are." He gestured with his hand to include his Arab comrades. "But you have a choice," he said with his finger in Sarah's face. "Bush wasn't giving us the choice. The choice is for the non-Arabs and non-Muslims. Are you with him, or with the terrorists? With us?"

"Like I said, dude," Sarah replied. "So we're the terrorists then." It was both a restatement of her former position and the choice she had consciously and explicitly made.

"That remains to be seen," Hakim replied respectfully. He was convinced she sincerely meant what she said but he could not be entirely persuaded her decision was final until all of its consequences had been borne. He knew most of these white, pierced, anarchist punks had middle class parents who were probably as radical as them back in the 1960s. When Communist ideology went out of style, they hung it in the back of their closets with their bellbottom jeans. But the injustices of US imperialism and global capitalism continued all the same. And they would continue after the piercings of today's radical youth had healed over. Hakim, his two sisters and their parents would still be barred from returning to their native Palestine. His cousins would continue to face arbitrary arrest and torture at the hands of the IDF occupation force. His aunts and uncles would continue their stubborn efforts at sifting through the rubble and rebuilding their gardens, shops and houses crushed under IDF bulldozers, just to see them bulldozed yet again.

Now, it seemed the Israeli-Palestinian dichotomy was to be globalized. How long could white activists, even white activists like Sarah who really seemed to care what happened to Hakim and his family, be expected to withstand being placed in the terrorists' camp? Would she still be with the terrorists when the knock on the door came in the middle of the night? Why should she, when it was so easy to put down her protest sign and blend into the crowd?

"Well," replied Sarah with the hint of a smirk in one corner of her mouth, "you'll find out soon enough."

"What's that supposed to mean?" asked Hakim. "What are you up to, you terrorist? Look at her," he gestured to his friends. "Look at that mischievous look in her eyes. That's the same one that she had right before she and Alex and Melanie went up to the front of the demo in Québec City. The next thing you knew the fence was coming down. Remember?" And it was true. Hassan and Sayed saw the spark. That was definitely the glint in her eyes right before it was covered up by the industrial-strength gas mask. The three Raging Granddaughters made quite a spectacle, running towards the fence, hand in hand, wearing flowery sun dresses, gas masks, straw hats and army boots—the Raging Granddaughters on the attack!

"You totally can't prove a thing," said Sarah defiantly. "There were, like, hundreds of kids at the fence. They were angry, they were tear-gassed. Like, dude, what do you expect?"

"Ahhh," Hakim sighed wistfully, "those were the days. We'll never be able to organize anything like Québec City again. Everybody's too scared. They're afraid of being called terrorists. We cancelled the SPHR demo last weekend, and who knows if we'll even get enough people to make the 29th a respectable event."

"How about this Sunday's march?" asked Sayed.

"There's a coalition forming," answered Hassan, "but it's not nearly as large as it needs to be. The big unions and citizens' groups are being very cautious. Their memberships all watch that crap," he gestured towards the television behind Sarah's back where various commentators were dissecting the Commander in Chief's post-9/11 oratory debut. The reviews were in, and Dubya vs. Osama was already a fall blockbuster.

"So, are you going to be there?" Hakim asked Hassan. "Or are you trying to keep a low profile now? I noticed you stopped wearing your kaffiyeh."

Hassan glanced at Sarah who subtly shook her head an inch to either side. Then he looked at the floor, with a tinge of embarrassment. "No," he said softly. "Looks like I've got to work on Sunday." There was bound to be an important businessman needing a cab ride from a garage to a corporate office.

"I'm going," affirmed Sayed proudly. "I hear we're supposed to go to the American Consulate. I'm not ready to write Dubya a blank cheque at the moment." The defiant declaration from the soft-spoken Sayed helped his friends overcome their post-Bush-speech-blues.

Sayed and Hakim continued to talk about Sunday's demo and what strategy should be privileged at the American Consulate while Hassan and Sarah went onto Al-Taïb's darkly lit street-level terrace for a smoke.

As Hassan handed Sarah her death stick, she proudly put the gold pen on the plastic patio table. She had been gripping it in her hand the whole time she was in the restaurant. It was the source of her excitement and the object she had pressed into the back of Hakim's neck. "Trade ya," she said.

He picked up the gold cylinder and held it close to his eyes. It was difficult to make out the markings in the darkness:

Jack Murphy, communicator. The pen is mightier than the sword. Love Shirley.

SATURDAY, OCTOBER 6, 2001

> *"The first duty of a revolutionary is to get away with it."*
> — ABBIE HOFFMAN (1936-1989)

It took a little while for him to realise that somebody was tapping on his window. The tapper was very discreet. The sound could have been produced by the wind knocking the rusty wire hanging from the fire escape against the pane of glass. But after hearing the noise for a minute or two Greg noticed its regularity. In fact, the instant Greg heard the tapping he knew what it was, but he couldn't allow himself to believe it. He tried to wait calmly but as the regularity of the click, click, click became more and more obvious his heart beat faster and faster. His mouth went dry. It took every ounce of his self-discipline to calmly press the stop button on the VCR and slowly make his way into the kitchen. He was mostly annoyed, and that was the role he would play, for at least the first five minutes.

As his bare feet apprehensively touched the cool linoleum floor and he looked across the tiny brightly lit kitchen to the window just above his milk crate shelves, all he could see in the darkness outside were some thin fingers lightly tapping with a key or a coin. He couldn't see the face the fingers belonged to, but he suddenly felt terribly self-conscious knowing the tapper could see him clearly. The old steam radiators in his apartment building kept all the residents in a dry heat above the comfort zone, so Greg often spent his autumn evenings in boxer shorts and a T-shirt. He reached over and turned off the kitchen light, turning the tables on the window-tapper. Suddenly Sarah's face appeared out of the darkness, illuminated by the city's ambient light. It was more beautiful than he remembered. Her dimples exquisitely framed that lip-ring-studded smile, expressing the excitement that Greg had decided not to show—at least not right away. But since he knew she couldn't see him, he allowed himself a grin before opening the window to let Sarah in.

"What are you doing here?" he demanded crossly. She handed him a grocery bag and climbed through the window awkwardly, almost knocking over a plant.

She steadied herself by grabbing his arm. "What do you think I'm doing here?"

She was very close now. He felt her warm breath on his neck as she suggestively wrapped the question around him. He almost gave in. But he fought the urge to reciprocate, remaining as cool as the October air coming in through the window. "Somebody could've seen you," Greg replied.

"Dude, relax," she said, rubbing his arm reassuringly. Her icy fingers sent tingles up his spine. "I took every precaution. I'm totally sure nobody followed me into the alley. They probably don't even know you live here. It's not like you're a suspect."

"And I want to keep it that way," Greg reminded her. "That's why we agreed not to meet until after... After your... Oh, I can't even say it. You shouldn't even have told me about it. I don't need to know that shit. The less I know the better." Now he remembered why he had to keep a cool head about him. He still wanted to kiss her, but the fear that kept them apart this past week became strong enough to keep away from her now.

"What's the big deal Greg?" she pleaded. "It'll all be over soon enough."

"Yes it will be over," he shot back, pulling his arm loose from her grip and closing the window behind her. "I just hope for your sake everything doesn't blow up in your face. You're playing with fire you know. We're talking about the weapons industry and secret service men. A bit out of your league don't you think, dude? Believe it or not, people get killed over this stuff."

It hurt to have her idiomatic "dude" thrown back in her face, but Sarah knew Greg was just reacting out of fear. He was afraid this was all just a game to her. She realized that responding to the jab instead of the substance of his argument would be proving his point. Sarah was determined to show that she and her friends were serious about what they were doing.

"We're being careful," Sarah insisted. "No more email discussions or phone conversations, information on a need-to-know basis only..."

"You told me a fuck-of-a-lot more than I needed to know!" Greg didn't need to fake anger now. She told him about her clandestine precautions like a kid promises her dad to wear a bicycle helmet. But this was serious. She had seen for herself the results of his mother's flirtation with revolutionary activism, yet it seemed nothing could deter Sarah from a date with disaster. How could somebody as resolutely apolitical as Greg allow himself to get mixed up with this crazed Palestinian-sympathizing anarchist?

"Yes," she admitted, stepping closer, wearing a mischievous grin. "But that's different."

"Oh really?" he crossed his arms, looking down at her accusingly.

"Yes really," she reached up and clasped her hands behind his neck. The softness of her breasts pressed against his folded arms.

"How so?" he asked. The edge of his voice had softened slightly.

"Because if you told anybody..." Sarah paused to tongue her lip ring.

"If I told anybody, what?"

"If you told anybody..." Her eyes lit up, "If you told anybody, I'd tell everybody you're addicted to *All My Children*!"

"You wouldn't!" Greg laughed in spite of himself. There was no use trying to deny their intimacy. It was ridiculous to expect Sarah to keep him in the dark about her group's plans. Only his inner circle knew about his weakness for daytime drama. His mother had gotten him hooked at the young age of eight in the summer of 1984. They watched it on Mondays—her day off. He would watch it for her from Tuesday through Friday and fill her in on all the juicy details when she came home from work. It was like she was with him all week long. Together, they secretly lived the glamorous lives of a rich and larger-than-life family. Now she taped it, and so did he. They still gossiped over the phone every other night or so. Only his mother, two ex-girlfriends, and now, Sarah, knew his secret.

"So you're the one who should be careful!" She defiantly pulled his head down for a kiss. She loved his sinful addiction. It was much healthier than her death sticks. And it suited him perfectly: a well-educated young man with no degree, a chess-playing security guard and a connoisseur of French cinema who watched *All My Children*.

"I guess it's too late for that now," he mused, speaking more to himself than to Sarah. He knew she was trouble the moment she walked into Stratagème straight from that anti-war meeting. How could he have allowed himself to fall in love with her? Was he in love with her? After just two weeks? He hadn't told her yet but maybe she had already read it in his eyes. He couldn't tell her. Sarah would think it was ridiculous. "Two weeks and you're in love? Whatever, dude," she would say. She was open, genuine, passionate about social justice, audacious, stubborn as hell, and gorgeous—what more dangerous cocktail of personal traits is there? She was like his mother. And people like his mother loved guys like Rocky Jones, not guys like him. He was her infatuation. Her real love was social justice. Despite her white skin and wealthy family background, Sarah had the same self-sacrificing disposition as his mother. Unlike many of his mother's old fly-by-night Jacuzzi-Marxist comrades, Sarah was genuinely passionate about collective self-liberation. Greg could tell by the way she pronounced phrases like "US global imperialism" and "military-industrial complex." For her, they were not catchphrases to show she spoke the obscure language of a secret society. They were the terms she needed to express both the actual state of the world and how she felt about it. She was in it for the long haul, no matter what privileges she would be required to forfeit. He allowed Sarah to pull his face to hers, but just before their lips met he moved his head to the right and put his arms around her waist. Sarah would have to settle for a hug right now. She was moving too fast.

"Want some wine?" she whispered into his ear.

"Trying to get me drunk, eh?" Greg quipped. He looked in her grocery bag and found a bottle of cheap Chilean red with some cheese and a baguette.

"Absolutely," Sarah agreed looking in his cupboards for some glasses. "I want to take advantage of you."

"Well, in that case," he said nonchalantly unscrewing the cap, "want to know what really turns me on?"

"Sure," Sarah turned towards him, a wineglass in either hand, one of them playfully teasing the ring on her lower lip.

He looked into her eyes and spoke in a deep sultry voice, "Knowing that my lover will still be alive, in one piece and on this side of jail next week."

She looked at him adoringly, as if to say, oh, it's so sweet that you're worried about me, and held up the glasses so he could pour. They both knew that nothing Greg could do or say would convince Sarah to move off the runway and let the bombers take off for Afghanistan.

"This whole thing has gotten a lot bigger than you realise, Sarah," he continued, sighing with exasperation.

Ignoring his huffing and puffing, she poured the wine as if they were having a little tiff over what movie to see.

Greg pleaded, "Even the university administration has joined the witch-hunt."

"You mean the rector's call for an investigation into the CSU?" Sarah asked. The call to three provincial ministries to bring the radical leftwing student union into government trusteeship had been made yesterday. Coming on the heels of the B'nai Brith "terrorist blueprint" accusations, the Gaza U terrorists had made headlines again today.

"They could give the RCMP your personal files you know?"

"Sure," she had to admit. Sarah was well aware that Laith Marouf's files had already been leaked to the press to undermine efforts to get him and Tom Keefer reinstated from their summer expulsion. No need to tell that to Greg though. He was already worried enough. "But my records won't tell them much anyway."

"They're out for blood Sarah," he insisted. "You may not look the part, but you're going to be their Osama bin Laden if you go through with this."

"Who?" she asked while putting the glass to her pouting lips. "Little old me?" She was more worried about how the cops would treat Omar, Hakim and especially Sayed. With his dark eyes and full beard, he was definitely the most terrorist-looking of the bunch.

"This is no joke," Greg sat down at the table. "You should've seen that RCMP investigator ask those questions. He's really convinced you're part of some terrorist conspiracy like the 9/11 hijacking. Imagine what they would do to somebody they thought was another hijacker."

"Dude, relax." She sat down beside him and put her hand on his. "Everything's getting blown way out of proportion. That's why you're so upset. It's all part of 9/11 media overload. Boy, it's hot in here." Sarah took off her jacket and reached down to undo her army boots.

"It's not me you need to convince," Greg told her. "It's them. They're the ones who are blowing everything out of proportion."

"Well, I see your point," she grunted as she pulled off her left boot, letting it fall to the floor with a thud. "But there are still some limits." She took a sip of wine as if to amass the energy to pull off her other boot. "Look at Lowy's call, for instance. It's more of a PR move than anything. Urrrmmng," the right boot came off with a thud, louder than the first. Greg glanced down at the floor where the boot had fallen, thinking briefly of the downstairs neighbours. "There's no basis for the government to investigate anything. When you look at the list of reasons the rector gave to the authorities it's just ridiculous."

"That's not the point, it's-"

But Sarah wouldn't let him get a word in, even if she had been dying to hear his voice for the past five days. Once she started offering a political analysis, Greg would have to hear it to the conclusion. It was like talking to his mother. She cut him off and spoke louder, "Like the anti-corporate information the student union published. Lowy says it's illegal, but not because it's libel or slander or whatever. He says it's illegal because it kept corporations away from job fairs."

"Oh, come on!" guffawed Greg. "There's no way he said that!"

"Well, not in so many words," Sarah admitted, sitting back and swirling her cheap wine as if it was a fine vintage from her dad's collection. "But essentially, he did say just that. You see, he cited one of the student union's binding articles of incorporation that states that the CSU must act in students' interests. And since it's in students' interests to have job fairs, and since publishing information about how Concordia's corporate partners profit from death kept some of those corporations away from the University's job fairs, publishing that information must be illegal. Even if that information is true." She smiled triumphantly then drank from her glass.

Greg replayed all the steps of Lowy's argument in his mind, a perfect example of deductive logic he vaguely remembered from his first year philosophy class a half-decade earlier. It was rigorously academic. And it was otherworldly, without connection to reality. But at this point reality didn't matter. Greg was convinced of that. Corporal Boisvert, Rector Lowy, B'nai Brith, all of them were living in a different world. It was a world where this intelligent gentle girl was a terrorist, the CSU was printing Osama bin Laden's blueprint, and SPHR was training suicide bombers. "Okay, Lowy's out to lunch," Greg admitted, "but that just proves my point. Look at what these guys are willing to do to fuck you over!"

"If we're pissing them off," she replied, "we must be doing something right."

That was exactly what Betty Phillip and her friends used to say back in 1969. That's what they said after the charges of kidnapping and extortion were laid against the three black students who dared stand up to Vice Principal O'Brien. That's what they said right up until the riot cops brutalized and strip-searched the occupiers amidst the broken glass and smoke-filled rooms of the Hall Building. Most of them stopped saying it after a few nights in jail and a lot more in the courtroom. But Betty Phillip kept saying it even as she was condemned to life-long poverty and chronic pain. Martin Bracey said it, even as authorities denied him access to medication during his five-year prison sentence. Rosie Douglas said it as he was being deported from the country in leg irons, and if he were alive today, those defiant words would still be on his lips. But most had learned their lesson. What would it take for Sarah to learn, or was she really so much like Greg's mother that she never would?

All Greg could do was offer an alternative interpretation, "Or, you might just be pissing them off."

"Either way," Sarah said jovially, filling her glass again. "It's a lot of fun." She was starting to get a bit tipsy. "Here's to pissing them off," she toasted.

Greg gave her a piercing gaze. Could that be a suggestion of fear behind all that revolutionary bravado? Without acknowledging Sarah's toast, he picked up his untouched glass of wine, went into the living room, and flopped down on the couch.

Soon after, she joined him. Noticing the television screen on but without an image, Sarah asked, "so what were you watching before I came in?"

He handed her the remote and she pressed play. The screen revealed the tortured face of a young man while a matriarchal figure questioned him from the comfort of her loveseat. "You knew she wouldn't stop when you married her. The baby won't change that. What did you expect?"

"*All My Children*!" Sarah exclaimed triumphantly. They both laughed. "I should've known. So tell me the latest," she said as she snuggled her way under his arm.

Forgetting the potential dangers Sarah was facing, Greg filled her in on the latest details. They settled into the couch and allowed themselves a brief escape. More excitement than real life could offer, and none of the personal risks. It captured their attention long enough to forget their political differences. Sarah's hair peeked out from under her bandana, tickling Greg's nose with a sweet odor. He pulled off the cloth and ran his fingers through her thick waves. Her breath quickened. Sarah wasn't used to anyone touching her hair, hidden as it was most of the time. She turned away from the screen and pressed her lips against Greg's—softly at first.

SUNDAY, OCTOBER 7, 2001

"The belief in the possibility of a short decisive war appears to be one of the most ancient and dangerous of human illusions."
— ROBERT LYND (1879-1949), IRISH ESSAYIST AND JOURNALIST

IT WAS A LOW-KEY BOMBING campaign compared to the Gulf War of 1991. Most of the tonnage was dropped in the form of 500-pound gravity bombs from 15 US long-range bombers like the B-2 Stealth bomber, the B-1 Lancer and the B-52. There were also hits from 25 strike aircraft like the Navy F/A-18 and F-14 fighters taking off from nearby US aircraft carriers. And 50 Tomahawk cruise missiles were launched from US and British vessels. But all the destruction was pretty much invisible. Nobody expected to see the bloody and dismembered victims amidst the rubble of their homes. It was understood from the beginning that those kinds of images were out of the question. The US didn't blow up families. Only al Qaeda and the Taliban did that. Nevertheless, the producers of shows like *America Strikes Back* or *America's War on Terror* were hoping for more dramatic images. They needed fireworks to keep people watching. The least the Defense Department could have done was show a few seconds of carefully edited footage of surgical strikes on military installations.

Many viewers must have felt shortchanged by the special reports interrupting regular programming. There were no dramatic scenes to rival the Twin Tower attacks, no palpable semblance of revenge. Speculation from military experts and strategic analysts looking at maps and charts was interspersed with replays from George W. Bush's White House declaration about the commencement of the bombing campaign.

"Dude, it's unreal. Looks like a kid's war game with toy soldiers," shouted Sarah as she watched blue symbols representing US aircraft carriers and bombers, and red ones for Afghan military targets. She was seated on a futon, the closest thing to a couch in the living room of Alex and Melanie's St. Henri apartment. The kitchen was a mere five feet away, so Sarah had to raise her voice to be heard over the running faucet Melanie was using to rinse the spaghetti.

"Yeah," agreed Melanie as she turned off the water and dished out the pasta. "It'll be hard to make people realise the destruction. People are dying."

Alex poured a generous helping of sauce onto each plate. "Still, I think there's a way we can break through to people. We just need to focus on the aspects of the bombing campaign we don't see on TV."

As the roommates joined Sarah on the living room floor, the image of Bush came on the screen again, offering a familiar soundbite:

> At the same time, the oppressed people of Afghanistan will know the generosity of America and our allies. As we strike military targets, we'll also drop food, medicine and supplies to the starving and suffering men and women and children of Afghanistan.

"Oh come on!" Alex pleaded with the television as if she could somehow shame it into offering more realistic commentary. "How many people do you think will venture out to pick up packages coming from the same planes dropping cluster bombs?"

"So they're using cluster bombs?" asked Sarah with a mouth full of spaghetti. "We know that for sure?"

Alex shook her head as she chewed then swallowed, "We can't say for sure. But they used them in the Gulf War and in Yugoslavia. You can be damn sure the Afghanis won't be treated any better."

Months later, Alex's suspicions would be confirmed. There was, in fact, a very good chance that a cluster bomb or two were being dropped over the course of their spaghetti dinner. As her research into the Gulf War and Yugoslavia campaigns had led her to believe, it was the B-1 bombers that dropped the deadly cargo. At least 50 cluster bombs were dropped in the first week of the Afghanistan campaign alone. During the six months that followed, US bombers would drop over 1000 more. The most sinister aspect of the weapon, from Alex's perspective, was its harmless appearance. The little yellow CBU-87 canisters looked kind of like soda cans. That's probably why so many children picked up the seven out of one hundred that failed to explode on impact. As a myopic sickly little girl, one of Alex's favourite activities was collecting little bits of debris carefully gleaned along the beach. Her treasures were worn fragments of green or blue translucent glass, glittering stones and shells. She could easily imagine how naturally curious children would gravitate towards the brightly coloured canisters that had been dropped from the sky. In terms of human casualties, they were probably the most destructive conventional explosives ever designed. Each cluster bomb targeted an area of about 5,000 square metres with its 202 individual submunitions called "bomblets" that tore right through flesh and bone. That meant the US dropped well over 200,000 bomblets during the first six months of the war. In an ironic coincidence, but one that Alex would not become aware of until much later, the humanitarian food-aid packages the Afghanis were being encouraged to pick up were also dropped by US bombers in yellow containers.

"Dude, this is delicious," Sarah complimented her host's cooking. "The zucchini's really tasty."

"Thanks," beamed Melanie. "It's from our garden."

"It seems so strange enjoying this meal while people are being mutilated and murdered," said Alex in her husky serious voice. Melanie's smile disappeared and Sarah looked at the floor, as if she had committed a social indiscretion by complimenting her host's culinary abilities while a volatile mixture of bombs and American rations fell on hungry Afghanis. Their meal became less appetizing.

"We're in the middle of a war," Alex continued, oblivious to the unsavory effects of her gruesome dinner conversation. "And tomorrow we'll be on the battlefield."

"Well," Sarah objected, "I wouldn't go that far."

Alex turned her ghostly face away from the monotonous broadcast and looked directly at Sarah. The glow of the television gave her dark eye sockets a bluish tinge that also reflected from the lenses of her thick glasses. "I know there's a big difference between the suffering faced by Afghanis and what's going on here, but you have to realise we're crossing behind enemy lines tomorrow. And I mean that literally."

"Sure," Sarah agreed. "They're producing the tools of destruction, so by attacking them we're sabotaging the war effort 'behind the lines' but..."

"No," Alex interrupted. "That's not what I mean." Her bony fingers turned the fork full of noodles on her plate. It seemed to be a nervous reaction to keep her hand occupied rather than any effort to prepare food for her mouth. She wasn't even looking at her food. "I mean it literally. When we go to a demonstration, we're on the street, maybe outside a consulate. Sometimes we go into a government office. But we never enter a corporate office, or a bank, or whatever. Those places are protected from people like us. We know there's an invisible line we can't cross. Those offices are protected by soldiers with guns. Of course they're not called soldiers. They're called security guards or cops. But that's just semantics. There will be armed people trying to stop us from doing what we need to do. Like it or not, we'll be in a war zone."

"Okay," said Sarah uneasily. She had never seen Alex like this before. "But there are war zones and, dude, there are war zones."

"When you go into a war zone," warned Alex, "you risk serious injury or death. You're kidding yourself if you think otherwise. Why do you think the RCMP is gathering intelligence about us? We're their enemy."

"Shit," said Melanie. "Is it worth the risk?"

"I guess that's the question," admitted Sarah. Yet again, she was starting to have serious doubts about their operation. Greg had tried to warn her last night but she told herself that was the irrational fear of an overprotective boyfriend. Alex, on the other hand, was offering a disquietingly serious dissection of the entire scenario.

"It's a question that North Americans don't ask themselves very often these days," said Alex. "We usually have other people fighting wars in our place. We send a few bombers who press a button to release a missile on a far away target. The real fighting is mostly done by foreigners on the ground. Other people take all the risks—on both sides of the battle lines."

"I guess that answers the question," said Melanie with a smile, cheerfully accepting the inevitability of their task, like having to wash the dishes after a meal. You can leave them on the counter for somebody else to do, but eventually, one way or another, they will have to get done.

Sarah and Alex were not nearly so cheerful about it, but they accepted the task as well.

"Hey, I went to the Sally Anne today and got some sheets for the banner," said Melanie as she leaped from the floor. "I sewed them together to make a really long piece. And we've got some great red paint!" She left her dinner plate on the floor and ran into her bedroom to get the supplies.

* * *

"Libya's population is just over 6 million..."

Corporal Boisvert sighed with disappointment as the lecturer at the podium pointed to an African country on his Powerpoint presentation. He had so hoped the presentation would end with the tour of the Muslim sects and states of the Middle East. The Corporal was glad to be in this swanky downtown Ottawa hotel with all these important figures from the RCMP, CSIS, the Canadian Military, Canada Customs and Revenue, and the Justice Ministry, almost all of whom outranked him. The only people who didn't outrank him were the constables in dress uniform adorning all entrances, checking people's identification coming in and out of the dining room. And he really enjoyed the fine food and wine—the artichoke salad was delectable. He almost felt like thanking the terrorists in the Murphy-Mohamed cell for making him important enough to get invited to this exclusive affair. But he was getting lost in all the finer details of Muslim religion and Arab culture.

"It's predominantly a Sunni Muslim and Arabic speaking state even though it's in Africa, not the Middle East," the lecturer droned on as the Corporal put some more butter on his dinner roll. "It's leader Gadhafi, seen here..."

"Oh, looks like he had a bad-hair-day there," said the CSIS man at the table beside him with a chuckle. The corporal had a good laugh at that one too. That's what was missing in these presentations, a little humour.

"Gadhafi uses his oil revenues to finance Arab-Islamic revolutions abroad so he's definitely somebody we're keeping an eye on..."

How was all this supposed to help him crack the Murphy-Mohamed cell? With all the experts here, there wasn't one person who could tell him with any certainty whether they were connected to the Muslim Brotherhood or Islamic Jihad or al Qaeda—or Gadhafi, or whoever. These authorities were looking at the big picture, but they didn't seem to realise things didn't look at all the same from his angle on the ground. The big picture, the one in the Powerpoint presentations, had big dark splotches over the northern part of Africa and the Middle East. Then there were arrows going from the heart of darkness to Europe and North America where they connected to little black dots in major urban centres with sizable Muslim populations that threatened to become big black splotches if intelligence agencies didn't get more funding and resources from their governments. But those little black dots, the terrorist cells, in the major urban centres like Montréal, were not immediately obvious to agents in the field like him. Apparently, the corporal had stumbled onto one of those black dots that everybody knew existed in Montréal, but there was no way of knowing how it connected up to the bigger picture. Suddenly Boisvert had become an important intelligence resource that would help these experts connect the dots. This whole situation reminded him a bit of his early days on the force when he was a young constable in uniform. Back then, in the period immediately following the FLQ crisis of 1970, the big picture was one where Russia and China were the big red splotches with arrows going to Europe and North America. There were violent Communists, FLQ separatist cells and treasonous saboteurs everywhere. Unfortunately, the RCMP was only able to find the tip of the iceberg. As the years passed, some questioned whether there ever was an iceberg under all that peaceful ocean to begin with.

"Neighbouring Algeria and Tunisia, on the map here, have more Western-friendly governments but the rising fundamentalism among their Sunni Muslim populations is a serious cause for concern..."

How was the corporal supposed to use this information? He had no idea what the difference was between Sunni Muslims and Shi'ite Muslims. He probably wouldn't even be able to remember all the countries and regions this guy pointed out on the map for the past hour. Still, he was glad to be here. This was where important decisions were being made, and more importantly, where his career was being made. He signaled the tuxedoed waiter to fill his wineglass again.

"These countries are also primarily Arabic speaking, so you can see the importance of recruiting more Arabic proficient agents and informants. We're going to need millions of dollars for language training and recruitment..."

Everybody was talking about increasing funding this weekend, and it looked like a sure thing to the corporal that money would be pouring in. 9/11 was the wake-up call the public needed.

Although the culinary delights were much appreciated, it was a great relief to the corporal when the dinner and the Powerpoint presentations came to an end. It finally gave him a chance to extract professional advice from the real counter-terrorism experts he had met in the focus groups earlier in the day. A bit of alcohol would loosen their tongues and assuage inter-departmental suspicions and rivalries. The real networking at these events always happened over a few drinks after the formal workshops and presentations were over.

"The one I would worry about is Silent Sayed," advised the CSIS man with a hint of a drunken slur. "He fits the type perfectly."

"Really?" asked the corporal with a hopeful smile, happily pouncing on what seemed to be the first concrete piece of advice at the conference. Corporal Boisvert was still not at ease with the higher-ranking men in his company. The atmosphere in the dimly-lit hotel bar was much more relaxed than the formality of the dining room, but even with the confidence of wine and hard liquor in his system, he was still paralyzed by his ignorance of all matters Middle Eastern.

To a casual observer, there was nothing out of the ordinary going on in the bar. A bunch of fat old men in business suits with government-issue photo-tags around their necks—drinking, talking and laughing. Nobody would have guessed they were deciding life and death issues for the whole country.

"Sure," continued the CSIS man, putting his glass of scotch down on the bar so he could gesture with both hands. "He's a devout Muslim. Very quiet and polite. He's studied religion in the Middle East. Do I have to draw you a picture?"

"Yeah," the corporal agreed, "but he hasn't done anything in the group as far as anybody can tell."

"The leaders never do," replied the expert, undeterred by the suspect's outward behaviour. "They take orders from the top, and pass them down through the chain of command. They don't get their hands dirty."

"I don't know," said Boisvert. He wasn't convinced. Something told him Sayed was not leadership material, but he wasn't quite sure what it was that made him think about Sayed that way—as a follower, not a leader. His thoughts were clouded by the alcohol and the contradictory blend of expert opinion. How could every counter-terrorism authority be so sure he was right about the biggest threat, about terrorist thinking and protocols, about the big picture? They couldn't all be right.

"Once the new legislation goes through, we'll be able to make preventative arrests on people like this Sayed character. And we'll be able to hold them indefinitely for a nice long interrogation," commented the Justice man. He didn't quite pronounce all the consonants through the cigar clenched between his teeth. Ignoring anti-smoking bylaws, he lit it and took a few puffs before continuing, "The Anti-Terrorism Act will be introduced in the Commons next week. I doubt the civil libertarian fanatics will let it pass through very quickly though. The US is lucky that way right now. They won't have any problem getting stuff through Congress. The States don't want Silent Sayed extradited for anything?"

"No," the corporal shook his head. "We checked it out."

"Well, keep a close eye on them," advised the CSIS man. "With the war starting today," he gestured to the TV over the bar where military targets on a map of Afghanistan were being bombed by symbolic planes and missiles, "you can bet they'll be on the move very soon."

"That's what all the experts keep telling me," replied Boisvert. "It's amazing how fast the resources have come into place for my operation. In less than a week, I got a team of Middle East experts, authorization for bugs in six possible corporate targets, a tactical unit trained in counter-terrorist measures on call and a bunch of constables working around the clock."

"That's nothing," said the CSIS man. "Wait to see what you get when you crack the Murphy-Mohamed cell. You'll be a hero. Just don't let them blow anything up. Then we'll be on the hook the way the CIA and FBI are now for 9/11. And you'll be the fall-guy."

"Yeah," said the corporal with a self-conscious laugh. "I'll keep 'em on a tight leash. Anything looks suspicious and I'll give it a good yank. Can't be scared of breaking somebody's neck by pulling too hard. It's life and death after all." It was bravado meant to impress his new friends, but Boisvert was also coming to realize that the rules of engagement were changing in the face of a new threat. He had to change with the times.

* * *

"What is it?" shouted Melanie over the chants of the demonstrators, her voice muffled under her gas mask. An object had dropped into the middle of their protest at the corner of Guy and de Maisonneuve, just down the street from the Hall Building. Teargas canisters had been clunking onto the pavement every so often, but this one looked different, and no smoke was coming out of it.

"Could be some of that invisible gas they use," Sarah shouted back. "Better keep these kids away from it. They'll be coughing up their lungs without knowing why." All around them were student demonstrators, most of whom had never experienced teargas or pepper spray. They were getting a crash course today. Lucky for them the street medics were on hand with handkerchiefs and vinegar to make the acrid air a little less stifling. Everywhere they looked, they saw watering reddish eyes, running noses and lips dribbling with CS gas-contaminated mucous coughed up from traumatized lungs. It was Québec City all over again.

Sarah, Alex and Melanie—relatively comfortable under the protection of their tightly fitting gas masks—carefully and calmly took up positions around the bright yellow canister and spread out towards the crowd. It had fallen in the middle of the median park that separated the two lanes of traffic on de Maisonneuve Boulevard—right beside the statue of Norman Bethune. Having given his own life for the Chinese revolution, the People's Republic of China had donated this commemorative statue to the City of Montréal.

The Raging Granddaughters gestured with their arms for demonstrators to stay away from the canister, encouraging people to back away from the traffic island. "There's an invisible gas canister in the park. Everybody get back." They had to yell at the top of their lungs to be heard over the din of protestors, wailing sirens and the thunder of helicopters flying overhead.

Somebody with a megaphone heard their warnings and made an announcement in both English and French that could be heard at a greater distance. "Stay away from the statue of Norman Bethune. An invisible-gas canister has landed there."

Then, out of the crowd came a gas-mask-wearing kid with a helmet, pads, and a la crosse stick—a sort of fusion between a soldier and a lacrosse player. He was part of the Concordia Urban Lacrosse Team (CULT)—an activist group whose members could withstand most normal crowd-control techniques thanks to their unconventional protective devices. CULT was dedicated to the protection of mass demonstrations from police violence.

He ran past Sarah and headed straight for the canister to scoop it up and throw it back toward the riot cops.

Sports fans cheered on the athlete as he jumped over a park bench and dipped his la crosse stick towards the bright yellow canister. But at that moment Sarah recognized the canister for what it was. There was no invisible gas at all, because it wasn't a gas canister. As implausible as it seemed, those were unmistakably the markings of a CBU-87 canister. If he scooped it up it would turn this entire demo into a gruesome bloodbath.

"No!" Sarah shouted. "Don't touch the..."

The stick hit the can. There was an ear-splitting blast as shrapnel flew in all directions. Blood washed over the scene. It splashed all over the visor of her gas mask. And the screams of pain were horrifying. She was afraid to lift her head from the pavement to look at the destruction but she forced herself to get up. She couldn't move. Her arms and her legs wouldn't obey the commands of her brain. "Shit," she said. "I can't move."

Then she felt Melanie's hand on her head. She knew it was Melanie's hand even before any words came out of her mouth. It was a caring and soothing hand. "Sarah, it's okay. Wake up. You're having a bad dream."

Sarah woke up and turned over. She wasn't paralyzed. She was lying on the futon of her friends' apartment.

"Another fucked up dream," said Sarah as she got up.

"It's okay," said Melanie. "Just relax."

As she worked herself up to a seated position, Sarah looked down at her shaking hand held in Melanie's. Both of them were coated with crimson. It scared her for a second, until she remembered they had been painting the banner with red paint.

Melanie felt the flinch in Sarah's musculature. "You're wound up pretty tight. I'll give you a massage." She started to work on Sarah's left arm. It felt so good that Sarah gave up her efforts to raise her body. She turned her back towards Melanie and let her fingers work their magic.

"What time is it?" asked Sarah. "How long have I been out?"

"It's about 3:30 I think," replied Melanie in a careless tone. "Don't worry about that. You can stay over tonight."

"No, I should get back to my place," said Sarah. She knew there was some reason she had to get back. Then she remembered all the stuff on her checklist was in a backpack in her room. She grunted, and forced herself to pull her body away from those soothing hands that had melted into her shoulders. "I really have to go."

She started to pick up her things scattered among the red-stained newspapers, water, rags and paintbrushes. "I really have to get home," she repeated in a tired voice as if she were insisting against the protestations of someone trying to keep her from leaving. "Anyway, it'll take me ten minutes on my bike. There's no traffic at this hour."

She started to head towards the door when Melanie stopped her with a giggle. "Do you really want to go out like that?" she asked.

"Like what?" asked Sarah.

"Look in the mirror."

Sarah went into the bathroom and looked in the mirror. The face staring back at her was grotesque and absurd. There were dark circles under her eyes and stains of crimson encrusted on her chin and nose. There was even some red paint stuck in the hair on her forehead. She looked like the victim of conjugal violence. Surveying the damage, she concluded, "Guess I better take a shower."

"War is capitalism with the gloves off."
— TOM STOPPARD, *TRAVESTIES*, 1974

"Good morning Mr. Murphy," said Greg. It was almost afternoon now—half-past-eleven. Mr. Murphy was never this late.

Jack barely registered the salutation. How could he focus on the minutiae of his daily routine? A bomb had been dropped squarely on Jack's doorstep at 7 a.m. this morning and he was still in shock. The dust kicked up by the bomb obscured his surroundings. Yet there was an unmistakably aggressive edge to the security guard's greeting that forced Jack to pay attention. He could swear that black security guard—Greg was his name, yes definitely Greg—was gritting his teeth. Usually he was so polite. Already slightly off-balance, Jack had trouble collecting his thoughts. "Um," Jack replied in an uneasy and hoarse voice, "good morning Greg."

A teardrop was starting to form in the giant's eye as he looked down at the wretched executive. One look at the disheveled Mr. Murphy was enough to tell Greg that he was right to be worried. Mr. Murphy never came to work unshaven. And look at those pinkish eyes. Those were the eyes of a man who had been crying all morning, probably with a distraught wife. The newspapers had all agreed on one thing—an attack by "Arab terrorists" at the Innomonde Building had been foiled by the RCMP. There was no mention of those who refused to remain silent, no mention of Sarah or her friends. Greg knew there were white women who were part of the so-called Arab terrorist group and they were all unarmed. That information should have been somewhere in the news. It wasn't surprising that the forces of order would take advantage of mass paranoia to cast the non-violent occupiers as Arab extremists, but there still should have been some kind of statement from the other side about what really happened. Hassan was supposed to be the group's press liaison, but the cabby was not even quoted once. And why had all the emergency crews been called in? And the bomb squad? And the "unconfirmed reports" of shots being fired had to be mistaken. But what if they weren't mistaken? What if something had gone horribly wrong? He tried to call Hassan but nobody answered at the SPHR-Concordia office. He called the police station closest to the site of their action–at great personal risk because it could have revealed his efforts to mislead an RCMP investigation–but the Montréal police refused to comment on anything. About five minutes ago, when it seemed Mr. Murphy would not be coming in today, Greg even called the Murphy residence, but Sarah's mother said she didn't know where her daughter was. He could tell she was worried too. She asked Greg to call her if he heard anything. The look on Mr. Murphy's face told him more than anything he read in the papers, but he was still in the dark. Sarah had been devoured. Nothing was left.

"No, Mr. Murphy," Greg contradicted his superior, "it's not." He did it without thinking, without any hesitation whatsoever. And without any regrets.

"What?" Jack blinked his eyes as he looked at the guard, as if the light reflecting from Greg's bald head was blinding him. "I'm sorry, I..."

"No, Mr. Murphy," he repeated, "it's not a good morning at all. Is it?"

Jack stopped blinking and stared at the guard. Then he realised his own dreadfully shabby appearance. His suit and tie were a mess. Had he even bothered to comb his hair or wash his face? Jack couldn't remember. And he didn't really care–not now. He hadn't taken the time to shave, dress properly or even to drink his morning coffee after seeing today's papers. Right there on the front page, along with the latest details on the bombing of Afghanistan, was something deeply wrong– "RCMP Foils Terrorist Plot in Montréal." The more he read, the less he understood and the more he panicked. The Inno-monde Building? Bomb scare? Arab terrorists? They all fit with Sarah's fanatical manifesto and her plan to use his connections for "payback." And Sarah had not come home last night! Heart racing, blood pounding, breath quickening, his whole morning routine suddenly blew apart. Run for cover? Cry for help? Go on the attack? He wasn't supposed to be in the war on terror. What should he do?

"In fact Mr. Murphy," Greg continued in loud but quavering voice, "this might be the worst morning of my entire life." And the tears started flowing.

"Look," Jack said awkwardly moving forward to put his small white hand on that of the weeping giant before him, but then stopping halfway. "I don't know what it is you're upset about. But to tell you the truth, it's not that great a morning for me either. I..."

"And Mrs. Murphy sounded terribly distraught on the phone earlier..." Greg sobbed, wiping his tears with his sleeve.

"Yes," Jack felt the tears welling up within him as well, and a lump in his throat already sore from talking all morning. "She's as much of wreck as I am now..." At first Shirley didn't understand why Jack was calling the police and the hospitals. After all, this wasn't the first time Sarah had failed to call before staying out all night. But then Jack exposed their daughter's cryptic "payback" remarks on the manifesto's rough draft and put that together with his aerospace client in the Innomonde Building. Finally, his wife began to realise that maybe he wasn't crazy. He hoped to God it wasn't too late. The papers reported that Corporal Boisvert refused to comment on whether shots were fired and by whom, or how many suspected terrorists were in custody, or whether the terrorists were prepared to blow up the building being swept by the bomb squad.

Jack was a rat in a maze, and it was only Corporal Boisvert who knew the way out. But he wouldn't talk about Sarah. "National security." "The investigation is still in process."

Wait a minute. Greg called Shirley? Why the hell would the security guard call Jack's wife? "You called my wife?..."

"I needed to find out about Sarah," said Greg, sniffling and drying his face on his sleeve. "I really care about her." Greg loved her. He was sure about that now. When all this was over, he would have to sit down with Sarah and Mr. and Mrs. Murphy, and they would need to have a serious talk.

Jack's jaw dropped as he looked at the man he had walked by every day in an entirely new light. Except for the one day—September 11—where he failed to produce a "good morning Mr. Murphy" Jack had hardly even noticed Greg's presence at all. He was part of the furniture, an automaton. He didn't have a life—no friends, no family, no girlfriend, let alone Jack's daughter... Oh my God. Maybe he was one of the...

"Where were you yesterday Greg?" he asked in an accusatory tone. Maybe this was a way out of the maze.

"Yesterday?... I..." Greg scratched his head, trying to find his bearings.

"Yesterday at about 5 p.m.?"

"I was... um... I was here Mr. Murphy. You don't think I was..." The irony was that Greg now wished he was with Sarah. If he had been there, maybe there was something he could have done to... to prevent whatever it was that had happened. Sarah had made him realise that he really did support what those crazy radicals were trying to do, even if he thought they were deluding themselves into believing they had a chance of changing anything in a meaningful way. But now that they had failed so spectacularly, he had to wonder if he might have made a difference. Greg didn't know what happened, but maybe Mr. Murphy did. The RCMP must have told him something. How else would Mr. Murphy know that Sarah was involved in yesterday's action?

"And are you part of any political groups?" Mr. Murphy continued impatiently.

"Political groups? What do you mean?"

"You know, political groups," he glared at the tearful guard. "Groups that are involved in politics, political parties, interest groups, like SPHR for instance..."

Greg stopped crying, wiped his tears away, and glared back at Mr. Murphy. He was on the anti-terrorist warpath? Didn't he see what the war on terror was doing to his own daughter? "No, I'm not. I know your daughter is though. She's very political. They didn't talk about that in the papers at all though did they? Why do you think that is Mr. Murphy?"

"It's not her fault!" Jack shot back angrily. "She was duped by those... those..."

"Terrorists?" asked Greg. "Unarmed terrorists who wanted to stop children from being blown to bits by cluster bombs?"

"They were attacking people and property in a corporate office," Jack replied, his voice trailing off into a cough towards the end of the phrase. Too much talking and stress. He was coming down with laryngitis.

"Listen to what you're saying Jack."

Jack stopped coughing briefly to look up at the underling who had the temerity to address him by his Christian name.

"You're talking about your daughter and her friends," Greg continued. "Your own daughter. Do you really think she was part of some evil plan to destroy the planet? Even unwittingly? How can you say that? Especially now?"

"Well, I..." Jack said weakly before he started coughing again. How could he say that? Or perhaps the question was how could he say anything else? Admitting Sarah was not in league with terrorists would mean he was wrong about everything, or that everything was wrong. "I... cough, cough, I don't know," he finally admitted. "I don't know."

Jack hoped to God nobody was hurt—especially not Sarah. Why couldn't Boisvert at least tell him that much? "National security" my ass! thought Jack. Boisvert was playing some kind of game, and Jack was going to find out what it was. Time to make some serious calls.

"America's name is literally stamped on to the missiles fired by Israel into Palestinian buildings in Gaza and the West Bank. In August of 2001, I identified one of them as an AGM 114-D air-to-ground rocket made by Boeing and Lockheed-Martin at their factory in—of all places—Florida, the state where some of the [9/11] suiciders trained to fly. It was fired from an Apache helicopter (made in America, of course) during the 1982 Israeli invasion of Lebanon, when hundreds of cluster bombs were dropped in civilian areas of Beirut by the Israelis in contravention of agreements made with the United States. Most of the bombs had U.S. Naval markings, and America then suspended a shipment of fighter bombers to Israel—for less than two months. The same type of missile—this time an AGM 114-C made in Georgia—was fired by the Israelis into the back of an ambulance near the Lebanese village of Mansori, killing two women and four children. I collected the pieces of the missile, including its computer coding plate, flew to Georgia and presented them to the manufacturers at the Boeing factory. And what did the developer of the missile say to me when I showed him photographs of the children his missile had killed? "Whatever you do," he told me, "don't quote me as saying anything critical of the policies of Israel." I'm sure that the father of those children, who was driving the ambulance, will have been appalled by the events of September 11th, but I don't suppose, given the fate of his own wife—one of the women killed—that he was in a mood to send condolences to anyone. All these facts, of course, must be forgotten now."

— ROBERT FISK, "RETALIATION IS A TRAP," *THE INDEPENDENT,* 9/16/2001

"**SO FAR SO GOOD,**" **DAVE** said to his friends as he joined them in the obscurity of their bunker behind the garbage bin in the office building's underground garage.

Sarah's eyes glanced about furiously as her tongue toyed with her lip ring. For a second, it seemed certain they had been discovered. In the blue pinstriped suit and black leather shoes, it took more than a cursory glance for her to pierce the business guise of the McGill grad student. "Get back here, and stay down!" Sarah whispered. A tall blond businessman poking around behind a garbage bin could attract a lot of unwanted attention.

"What's the word?" Sarah asked Hakim as he held the cell phone to his ear.

"He says we're going to have to keep waiting," Hakim answered. "Both the guards are there, and there's nothing to distract them at the moment."

"Okay," said Sarah in a nervous tone. Deep breaths, deep breaths, she kept repeating to herself. Had they chosen the right path in Al-Taïb earlier that afternoon? Should they be going ahead with it? The group had come to a consensus without Sarah pushing her point of view. But now she was having doubts. Too late.

Even Sayed was clear and explicit about his willingness (if not eagerness) to go forward. He said what they were all thinking, "After the bombing started, and I thought about the Afghan people afraid in their homes or in shelters or caves— and I thought about those cluster bombs and all those other weapons Alex and Sarah researched—I decided it was worth the risk." And then looking into the eyes of his comrades he added thoughtfully, "At least for me. I don't want to put pressure on anybody else. It's a personal decision." Everyone had been moved by the basic truth in Sayed's low rumble. They were not convinced. Nobody could be convinced of something they already knew to be true. They were moved. And the decision was made. That didn't stop the discussion from going on for another hour-and-a-half though. There were plenty of risks that needed to be mentioned and evaluated before they could finally move forward as a group.

Since learning that they were "of interest" to the RCMP, they found themselves stumbling through a house of mirrors where nothing and nobody could be taken at face value. Phones and electronic communications were presumed tapped. Strangers and recent acquaintances became suspect. Everybody had the impression of being shadowed, but nobody could say for sure. The description Alex and Melanie gave of their stalker matched fairly closely the description of Sarah's man. Hakim and Hassan had both noticed suspicious cars parked near their homes.

And now that the US-led bombing of Afghanistan had begun in earnest, government intelligence services were sure to be on high alert. The activists' state of alert would have to be higher. But at the same time, they had to maintain their composure. Deep breaths, deep breaths, Sarah kept telling herself.

Right now, anxiety was their worst enemy. Sarah felt a certain responsibility to keep her friends calm. They were a non-hierarchical group, but a commando action was no place for consensus decision-making. This was a situation that called for leadership, and Sarah knew that made her the unofficial commander. She took yet another deep breath and looked over her troops. They were all in position, hidden in the dark recesses of the belly of the beast, ready to move when the word was given. Melanie was perched on a ledge where the corner of the garbage bin touched the stairwell's wall just behind the surveillance camera. She was the lookout since she was the only one with a clear view of the building's exit. Only the back of her hoody, which she wore to hide her florescent blue hair, was visible to Sarah since the lookout's eyes were fixed straight ahead. Alex was right behind Melanie, her arm reaching up to gently rub her friend's back. Omar and Sayed eyed Hakim expectantly as the latter bit his lip and held the cell phone to his ear. Dave was the only one who didn't betray any nervousness. He squatted contentedly at the rear behind Sarah. He was grinning from ear to ear, happy that his initial acting role had come to a successful end. What could Sarah do to occupy her team's anxious minds?

"Let's just go over our inventory one more time," Sarah suggested. They had already checked their supplies at Al-Taïb earlier that afternoon, and even if they found a gap in their provisions, at this point it would be impossible to remedy the situation. Nevertheless, it would keep their minds occupied enough to stop thinking about the policeman's boot set to grind them under its heel.

"I've got two loaves of bread, peanut butter, bottled water, two flashlights, rope…" said Alex, rummaging through her sack.

"I've got lots of toilet paper," said Melanie as she turned her head in their direction for an instant, "and the banner."

"I've got cigarettes," said Sayed to Sarah with a nervous glance in her direction, "for more than one person."

"Okay, Hassan says we should get ready to move!" Hakim interrupted.

The commando team closed their bags and prepared to head out.

On the street in front of the office building Hassan was spying on the security desk through his side rearview mirror. The same redheaded fascist and his bored female colleague from his initial casing of the building were sitting behind the desk. Red had left briefly to take Dave's letter to the mailroom, but his absence was not long enough to ensure success. By the time Dave had left the washroom, Red had returned.

He gave Hakim all the details, speaking in Arabic just in case anybody walking by the busy downtown sidewalk was listening.

Red was taking a phone call. And it looked like his colleague was getting up to leave the security desk. This would be their chance! "Get ready," Hassan told Hakim, "your chance is coming."

When the woman guard disappeared into a corridor that led to the washroom, Hassan gave the order, "Okay go!"

"No hold on," said Hassan. There was a man coming out of the other elevator now and he was heading for the rear exit. "Wait until the guy comes out of the door to the parking lot, then go, fast!"

"Hold on everybody," said Hakim, but Dave had already come out from behind the garbage bin.

A well-dressed middle aged businessman came out the basement door of the building and headed over to his car. He saw Dave standing by the garbage bin. Without missing a beat, Dave continued to play his part, heading over to another car, pretending to look for his keys, finding them, dropping them on the ground. He had chosen a car at random, hoping it did not belong to somebody the man knew. The executive wore an expensive suit so Dave figured the safest bet would be the blue Cavalier, an older model.

As the car door closed and the man started his engine, Hakim told his friends, "Okay as soon as that car leaves, we go!"

As the car left the garage, Melanie turned around and whispered "The coast is clear."

"Let's go," said Sarah. And they ran out from behind the bin, directly past the security camera and through the door.

Dave, who was pretending to put the keys in the car door that belonged to somebody else, was caught by surprise. He ran after his friends, pulling the plug that he had left in the exit's door-latch as he followed them into the stairwell.

"Okay, we're in," whispered Hakim as they ran up the stairs.

Hassan breathed a sigh of relief. "Looks like you're safe," he said in a reassuring tone. Red was still occupied with his phone call. From his sniggering, Hassan surmised it was a personal call.

"Okay," said Hassan as he started his engine. "I'm off to make you guys famous." And he drove off to send the emails and press releases.

If Hassan had stayed parked where he was for another two minutes, he would have seen an unmarked car screeching around the corner and illegally parking in front of the building, its two occupants running through the doors and straight to the security desk.

* * *

Everybody was breathing heavily from running up four flights of stairs as they came to the entrance with the corporate name and logo on the door that, to the activists, had become synonymous with mechanized slaughter. "You go in first," said Sarah, pointing to Dave. "Tell us when to follow."

Dave nodded. They had already gone over the plan at least ten times and had pretty much exhausted every contingency. Still, he had a whole flock of butterflies in his stomach. This would be even more of a challenge than his little escapade with the security guards downstairs.

He opened the door and walked calmly and purposefully into the lobby, like he belonged there.

"Good afternoon," said the receptionist. Her painted face with its pearly smile was a radiant icon of corporate goodwill. "What can we do for you today?"

"Mr. O'Riordon to see Mr. Tremblay," he said as he walked straight towards her desk.

"Sorry sir, Mr. Tremblay has left for the d- Hey, what are you doing?"

Dave was pressing the button on her desk to unlock the door to the offices behind the reception area, "Okay, come on in!" he yelled. "Warmonger Inc. is open for business!"

The receptionist's friendly corporate mask instantly fell away. Her painted features metamorphosed into a look of confusion, which quickly turned to terror as the uninvited guests overran the office.

As the ragtag gang spilled in, Hakim ran straight to the door that Dave was buzzing and held it open for his friends. Dave took his hand off the buzzer and said, "Thank you madame. Have a nice day."

She was already on the phone to Security before Dave had taken his hand off the buzzer. The activist in business drag then went over to the coffee table and picked up the scale F16 model, following his friends past the reception desk as they secured strategic points of the third floor complex.

Sarah made the rounds through the main horseshoe-shaped corridor, peering in all the offices along the way. "Your attention please!" she yelled. "Those who refuse to remain silent are confiscating this space from the war criminals who have been using it to run their operations. We are not holding anybody here against her or his will. You are all free to leave the building."

It was almost five o'clock so there were only five low-level employees left in the third floor complex besides the receptionist. They hastily made their way out of the photocopy room and ran into the lobby and out the main exit, chattering amongst themselves all the way. "Oh my God, who are those people?"

"I don't know. Did you see the guy with the big beard? He looks dangerous."

"Did somebody call 911?"

Hakim and Omar made sure that the main doors were locked behind the employees as they left and then started to set up barricades. Sarah and Sayed worked on the "employees only" door.

Alex and Melanie went frantically from office to office looking for a window that would open to hang their banner from. They finally found one in Mr. Tremblay's office. "Being the boss has its privileges," said Melanie as she took the banner out of her bag. "It figures the only window that opens would be in here." The pair worked together to attach the banner to the desk and roll it out the window. It dropped a full 20 feet, covering the windows of the floor below with an indictment written in blood. People passing by on the street saw the crimson arrow pointing up to the floor where the banner was hanging from. It read:

> **More than a million killed or displaced worldwide since 1960.**
>
> **Ask us about the cluster bombs in our Afghanistan campaign!**

And it had the company's corporate logo, painted red and dripping with blood.

Dave brought in the model F16, and roped it to Mr. Tremblay's desk so that it could be hung from the window in front of the banner.

"Okay, all the employees are gone and the doors are secured. Everybody in the lobby!" shouted Sarah. "We need to have a meeting."

As her friends filed into the lobby she announced, "Congratulations fellow terrorists. We have taken control of a key Canadian outpost of American imperialism!"

Melanie and Hakim shouted "yeah!" and "alright!" Then everyone else joined in with whooping and hollering. It was as much a release of nervous energy as it was a celebration. As they settled into the comfy leather couches strewn among the ruins of the disheveled corporate lobby, they looked around apprehensively. Although the oversized coffee table ornament had been removed, the intimidating images of fighter jets and military helicopters still hovered all around them, waiting for orders to drop their cluster bombs. When Hassan had visited the lobby there were still some commercial aircraft on the walls, but since that time the entire office had undergone a complete militarized makeover to match the company's new PR campaign. The anti-war activists had taken over the office, but they were already surrounded and outgunned, and they knew it. Saying they had taken control of an outpost of American imperialism was pure bravado—a bunch of Palestinian kids throwing rocks at Israeli Defense Force tanks. Now the question was how much of their enemy's overwhelmingly superior force would be used to get them out? Was there anything they could do to minimize the risks to their bodies while holding the office long enough to make a statement about Canadian complicity in an illegitimate and bloody bombing campaign? The question was on all their minds. What next? It seemed too incredible to believe they had actually accomplished what they had set out to do. They were just an insignificant group of activists occupying the Canadian head office of a major multinational military supplier. What would they do to a few young activists? If it had been Afghanistan, they would become "collateral damage."

They needed to take the edge off, thought Sarah. Time for a celebratory cigarette. "Hakim, you'll be glad to know that for this special occasion I've brought an extra large supply of death sticks!" She picked up her backpack and started to rummage around, feeling underneath the papers and the sleeping bag for the carton of smokes—a surprise for her nicotine-addicted comrades who had been keeping her in tobacco for the past few months without any recompense.

* * *

"What are they saying?" asked Corporal Boisvert crouching in the back of the unmarked van with two plainclothes constables and a sound technician. He cradled his head between his hands, feeling the pulse in his temples. His eyes were slammed shut. Why did the Murphy-Mohamed cell have to attack today? The corporal was up drinking until 2 a.m. with important Ottawa bureaucrats and now he was feeling the after-effects. He didn't get back to Montréal until 5 a.m. and he wasn't in bed until 6 a.m.

"Anybody speak Arabic?" asked the technician wearing the earphones as he worked at getting a clear sound from the cell phone signal they were intercepting.

"Shit," said the Corporal. He had assumed all their communications would be in English. The Arabic writing on the Murphy-Mohamed manifesto was determined by handwriting experts to be directly translated by the same hand (likely Hassan Mohamed's) for the benefit of the non-Arabic-speaking Sarah Murphy. Since Murphy seemed to be taking the lead on this operation, it seemed only logical that all communications would be in English so that she could understand what was going on. Maybe the CSIS man was right about Silent Sayed. Maybe Murphy was just a patsy. In any event, there were no Arabic speakers in his unit so there was nothing to be done. They needed more Arabic proficient officers in their ranks. The bigwigs at the conference were right about that one.

"Is the tactical unit ready to go?" he asked.

"Yes Corporal," the younger constable replied with a serious look. Constable Ham was a little over-excited, this being his first plainclothes stakeout. His left leg was bouncing up and down like he had to go to the bathroom. "They're on standby."

"Good," responded Boisvert in a reassuring voice. "Just relax Ham, everything's going according to plan." The one advantage of having a hangover was that it effectively camouflaged his own nervousness behind a veil of nausea. But the fog in his head was putting the already murky facts in this case into doubt. Maybe he had misjudged the scenario. If they were speaking Arabic, maybe his informant had it right: an Arab terrorist cell recruiting an unsuspecting good little white girl.

Everything up to this point had suggested the contrary, but they had relatively little information to go on. That good little girl had threatened an American business student. She had quite the temper, prone as she was to violent outbursts, and her manifesto showed she was a political fanatic. That's why her photo was at the top of the list given to all tactical unit members. Hassan was number two and Silent Sayed was number three. A lot of these dangerous Arab terrorists were real quiet types.

"The white guy is heading for our car," warned Constable Bellini. "Not the van," he said to Ham who was going for his gun. "Our car, the Cavalier. It looks like he's going to open the door... No, now his friends are going in and he's running after them."

"Okay, call in the tactical unit," ordered the corporal.

As Ham called in the tactical unit, Boisvert and Bellini stepped out of the unmarked van to watch the black truck speed to their position in the garage. Its back doors swung open and the armor-clad stormtroopers spilled out and ran to the stairwell door, their faces invisible behind black visors. The lead officer pulled frantically on the steel door but it wouldn't budge. He turned to corporal Boisvert and announced, "It's locked sir."

"Shit," he cursed again. Those were clever little buggers. He had to give them that. Two tactical unit stormtroopers stood ready with a battering ram but the corporal figured the solid metal fire door would be too much trouble to knock down with brute force. He gestured for them to rest easy and felt in his pocket for the card-key to the door's electronic lock. Where had he put that key? "Shit, shit, shit..." he continued to curse as he took out his phone to call the security desk. The line was busy. Just not my day, he thought, and ordered Ham and Bellini to take their car around to the front and let the rest of them in the back way.

When Bellini and Ham opened the fire door, the stormtroopers ran in and up the stairs just as Boisvert had ordered them to do. He was back in the van now with the sound technician, listening to a chaotic clatter. It was impossible to say for sure exactly what his microphones were picking up, but it sounded, from the banging, scraping and shouting, like they might be moving furniture around. That would explain the ear-piercing reverberations and screeches they were getting from one of the bugs under the coffee table in the lobby. Responding to the attack on his nerves, Boisvert pressed his fingertips against his temples to sooth his cranium.

There were too many voices yelling at once to get a clear idea of what was going on inside. The last clear phrase had come through about a minute ago, before the cacophony had begun. It was a male voice yelling, "Okay, come on in! Warmonger Inc. is open for business!"

The corporal thought he might also have heard Sarah Murphy yelling something about not being kidnappers, but he couldn't be sure. There was just too much interference. It was making his hangover more unbearable.

The banging and screeching finally stopped, allowing Boisvert to hear an announcement, "Okay, all the employees are gone and the doors are secured. Everybody in the lobby!" shouted an activist. It sounded like Murphy. "We need to have a meeting."

Immediately after the tactical unit's leader reported, "We're in the third floor corridor, sir." He was breathing heavily from running up the stairs. "What are your orders?"

"Subjects are all in the main lobby." responded Boisvert. "Doors are locked and barricaded." His team would pull this one off after all.

The corporal chuckled to himself as he heard Sarah's announcement, "Congratulations fellow terrorists. We have taken control of a key Canadian outpost of American imperialism!"

She's a total fanatic, he thought. We'll teach her a lesson like her father should have done.

"Battering ram ready to go, sir," said the tactical unit lead officer.

"Prepare to go in," ordered the corporal.

Just before the tactical unit smashed through the door, Boisvert heard Sarah's declaration, "Hakim, you'll be glad to know that for this special occasion I've brought an extra large supply of death sticks!"

JUST DON'T LET THEM BLOW ANYTHING UP. THEN WE'LL BE ON THE HOOK THE WAY THE CIA AND FBI ARE NOW FOR 9/11. AND YOU'LL BE THE FALL-GUY.

The corporal saw his thirty-year career flash before his eyes.

"Change of plan," said Boisvert in a panic. "Subject number one is armed and dangerous. Use of lethal force authorized. Take her out if you need to. She's ready to blow up the whole fucking building! Go in now!"

BANG! CRASH! The door splintered as the full weight of the battering ram slammed into it. Dave, who was sitting on the floor near the barricade, was hit in the head by the coffee table as it flew into the lobby. He was leveled flat by the impact. The reception desk, the main bulwark of the barricade, lurched forward enough for the lead tactical unit officer to step into the lobby. The armoured stormtrooper pointed his gun directly at the lead terrorist and ordered, "Drop the bag now! Everybody face down on the ground with your hands on your head!"

The backpack wouldn't come loose. Sarah's arm was buried to the elbow, stuck in the folds of the sleeping bag. "Fuck!" she cursed as she started to stand up from the couch, her face was crimson with anger. Anger at the cops for busting in so quickly, anger at herself for not listening to peoples' warnings, and anger at her backpack for being stuck.

"I said drop the bag!" thundered the officer a second time. "Now! Drop it!"

She kept trying but it was really stuck. The zip had caught hold of her sleeve. "I've almost got it," she said. "Just give me a second."

Boisvert assumed the worse. That crazy bitch. She's gonna blow everybody up. "Shoot her!" yelled Boisvert. "Shoot her now!" The words came in loud and clear on the stormtrooper's ear-piece, but they were inaudible to the occupiers.

"But sir," objected the team leader. She was on the top of the list Boisvert gave him, but still. She was a white girl, not one of the bearded Arabs.

"Shoot her Dan! Shoot her now! That's an order!"

The shot was deafening. Sarah's neck spurted blood onto those who refused to remain silent and onto the lobby's expensive furniture. Her corpse fell onto the thick beige carpet, right where the coffee table and the F16 had been earlier. Sarah's eyes were open wide in horror, her mouth screaming one last cry of pain before hitting the rug.

"And Abraham stretched forth his hand, and took the knife to slay his son. And the angel of the LORD called unto him out of heaven, and said: "Abraham, Abraham." And he said: "Here am I." And he said: "Lay not thy hand upon the lad, neither do thou any thing unto him; for now I know thou art a God-fearing man, seeing thou has not withheld thy son, thine only son, from Me."

— GENESIS 22

"**GOOD AFTERNOON CORPORAL BOISVERT,**" Jack greeted his guest. "Please sit down." He offered the plainclothes RCMP officer a seat on the comfortable leather chair facing his desk.

"Nice view you have here Mr. Murphy," the corporal complimented his host as he sat down. They were able to see the greenery of Mont Royal towering above the condominiums, foreign consulates and McGill University buildings on its flanks.

"Yes, well I'm glad you could come and see me on such short notice, Corporal," Jack said with a servile smile. "Can I offer you a cup of coffee?" Jack was always a gracious host to everyone who walked into his office—to his clients anyway, since they were the ones paying the bills. The officer could have passed for one of Jack's corporate clients, with his gray hair, potbelly and beef-red face. Only his decidedly less-than-fifteen-hundred-dollar-suit gave him away as something less.

"No thanks Mr. Murphy," replied the plainclothes agent. "Oh, is that a cappuccino machine? Well, in that case..."

How many clients had Jack wooed with the help of a first-class cappuccino? That machine was one of the best investments his company had made. Normally he would call in Janet to make the coffee, but he didn't want her nosing around in his personal business. No need for her or anybody else in his office to know about his wayward daughter. As Jack busied himself preparing a cappuccino for the officer, he commented, "I didn't know the RCMP dealt with terrorism cases. I called CSIS, but they referred me to your office."

"The RCMP and CSIS work together on a number of fronts," said Boisvert licking his lips. "Um, just one sugar please. I'm with the Public Order Program. We were set up in May..."

"Right after that Québec City riot," Jack interrupted.

"Yes, exactly," the corporal nodded. "We work with a lot of different public security agencies to make sure everybody has the information they need to ensure public order. And from what you told me on the phone, it sounds like your daughter may be involved with some radical groups that we're concerned about."

"Right," said Jack, raising his voice so that he could be heard over the noise of the steamer he was using to froth the corporal's milk. "So you're investigating SPHR?"

There was a pause. Then the corporal responded slowly. He seemed to be staring intently at the cup of cappuccino Jack was holding, and there was a look of concentration on his face. He appeared to be choosing his words very carefully. "I can neither confirm nor deny that, sir. All ongoing investigations are confidential. So if we were investigating that group, and I'm not saying that we are, but if we were, I could not talk about it."

"Okay," said Jack, frowning with confusion. He was a little taken aback by the corporal's lack of candor. After all, Jack was acting as a good citizen, providing useful information. He was an important man making a six-figure income, with a big office and employees working under him. It wasn't like he was some informant off the street. "I... I understand that you have certain protocols you must follow in your line of work. Um, here's your cappuccino Corporal."

"Thank you Mr. Murphy," he replied, nodding respectfully to his host. "You must understand sir, these rules exist for public safety and public order. I don't want to keep any information from you personally, but since 9/11 we cannot be too careful..."

"Oh," said Jack, his head wagging a knowing smirk up and down in front of the corporal's face like a signal flag. "Of course. We're in a state of war. I understand it must be very frustrating for the RCMP with all the reporters wanting to know all kinds of information that could put the public in danger." Jack put the offering down on the desk in front of his guest.

"Exactly. Mmm, this is good coffee Mr. Murphy."

Jack sat down across from the corporal, nodding acknowledgment of the compliment.

"So what do you have for us Mr. Murphy, besides such excellent cappuccino?" asked the plainclothes agent.

Jack pulled a file-folder out of his desk drawer and laid it open in front of the corporal. "That's everything I could find. There's part of her manifesto rough draft, some of the web sites she's been frequenting and some other things she's been working on. Latin American politics and whatnot."

As the corporal looked through the documents, he nodded and bit his lower lip as if he were in deep thought. "Hmm," was all that he said before he took another sip of coffee. "This is really good. What kind of machine do you have?" The corporal didn't have the slightest idea what to make of the manifesto or the FTAA documents. He only had a few university courses under his belt from back in the 1970s and almost all of them were in criminology. What did he know about international politics? And the best advice he ever got in undercover training was, if you don't know something, shut the fuck up.

"It's a Krups," Jack responded. "Top of the line. Only the best here. Um, you can see that there's more than a simple political manifesto there." Jack had put on his reading glasses and was reading the papers in the corporal's hand but he was struggling because they were upside down from his point of view. "There's some kind of sabotage agenda there. And look at what she wrote about me in pen there, right beside the happy face."

"Dad's connections equals payback. Thanks Dad!" read the corporal.

Jack flinched involuntarily as the corporal read those words. His ego was even more wounded when he heard it out loud. He had tried so hard to use his connections to her advantage, and this was how she repaid him? By getting drawn into a terrorist plot and forcing him to call the RCMP?

"You see that's right beside the reference to the Sabra and Shatila massacres," Jack pointed out.

"Yes," the corporal nodded and took another sip of his coffee. Sabra and Shatila—weren't those the massacres that SPHR had been focusing on for their demo that had originally been planned for last weekend—the weekend immediately following September 11? Corporal Boisvert now wished he had a deeper SPHR background briefing before meeting Mr. Murphy. When it came to Middle Eastern politics, he was lost. He was positively insecure regarding his lack of knowledge about that region of the world. After 9/11 everybody suddenly expected intelligence officers to be Middle East experts. He resisted the urge to ask Mr. Murphy more about Sabra and Shatila. There would be plenty of time to get background research done by professionals in the field.

"I looked them up," said Jack. "Those were some massacres that took place back in 1982 in two Palestinian refugee camps in Southern Lebanon."

"Yes, that's right," acknowledged the corporal, complimenting the amateur. "Very good Mr. Murphy." Shit, even a PR consultant knows more about the Middle East than I do, he thought. Yet despite his frustration over his own ignorance, the corporal's interest had been tweaked. When a worried parent calls in the RCMP, there always has to be a certain degree of skepticism, but this guy had documentation. There really did seem to be some kind of Middle East terrorist agenda here. "And there's Arabic script here too..."

"That's the most worrying part for me." Looking hopefully towards the professional, Jack continued, "I don't read Arabic, so I have no idea what it says."

"Yes," replied the corporal. "Well, you needn't worry about that Mr. Murphy. Just leave it to the professionals." Of course Boisvert couldn't read Arabic either, but there was no reason to let Mr. Murphy know that. He would be able to get some translators with proper security clearance to go over the document in detail. This could be really big for the corporal's career. Since September 11, the whole focus of intelligence agencies had been radically altered in a decidedly Middle Eastern direction. Corporal Boisvert would have to get with the times if he wanted to advance through the ranks before retirement.

"So what do you say Corporal?" asked the PR consultant and amateur intelligence gatherer. "Can you help get my daughter out of this mess? She's a good girl really. It's just that she's being brainwashed by these Arab terrorists."

"Hmm," said the agent, leafing through the files again. He took another sip of coffee as Jack waited, fidgeting impatiently. "Obviously the specifics of the political agenda of these groups is not of great concern to us. Our concern is public order. And public order is threatened when radical groups of whatever race or religion—but obviously since 9/11 we have particular concerns about Arab and Muslim terrorist or terrorist-connected or terrorist-supporting groups... Public order is threatened when these groups take actions, or plan to take actions, or help others take actions that could jeopardize lives or property or cause economic harm."

"Right," Jack agreed confidently, even without quite being sure what he was agreeing with.

"So when your daughter suggests she might go after some of your corporate connections, that is of great concern to us," concluded the agent.

"Good." There was audible satisfaction in Jack's voice. Finally he was getting somewhere. "So you're going to help get her out of that group—that SPHR?"

"We're going to look into the matter," assured the corporal. "We treat all such cases very seriously."

"Great," said Jack with a gratified smile. "That's just super. So if there's anything I can do to help you out..."

"Well actually," replied the corporal, "we could use a photo of your daughter. Is this your daughter here?" he asked picking up a photo off Jack's desk.

"Well, yes," said Jack more hesitantly, suddenly uncomfortable about giving out something so personal. All the papers were about politics, but this was a photo taken on their family trip to the Gaspésie a year ago. That was the last trip the Murphys had taken together. It was before all the trouble started, with that World Issues *CÉGEP* course.

"Is this a recent photo? Could I take it? It would be a great help."

"Well," Jack said indecisively, "I suppose I could replace it. I think Shirley still has a couple more copies at home."

"Great," said the corporal taking the photo out of its frame and putting it in the file that Jack had given him. "And I could also use a printout of all of your corporate clients."

"Oh that's no problem at all, Corporal." Jack pressed a button on his intercom and told Janet to print off the list for the agent and to come in and clean up the mess he had made around the cappuccino machine. Then he turned to his guest again, and said in a hushed tone, "Of course I don't have to tell you that is a very important and very confidential list. I expect you to protect the corporations on that list with the discretion that they deserve. Our clients depend on us to make sure that they don't get the wrong kind of attention if you follow my drift."

"Of course Mr. Murphy," said the agent. "You can count on our discretion on this matter. Corporate confidentiality is an important part of our mandate. Well, I guess that's everything then. Thanks very much for your help Mr. Murphy. You're a good citizen." He held out his hand for Jack to shake.

Jack took the agent's hand but he held it longer than the corporal would have liked. "Thank you Corporal Boisvert," said

Jack. "So you're going to help me get my daughter back from these fanatics?"

"We are going to look into the matter sir," the agent responded, pulling his hand out of Jack's grip. He was trained to be very careful not to make any commitments about the safety of anybody potentially involved in a criminal enterprise. Such promises, however reassuring to a distraught parent, could cause terrible legal problems if things got messy. For all the corporal knew, this Sarah Murphy could be just as crazed as the Arab terrorists she was caught up with. In fact, it seemed she had written the manifesto of her own accord. "As I explained earlier, we cannot comment on any investigation, if there is an investigation, and I am not saying that there will be one. All investigations are strictly confidential."

"Sure, I understand completely Corporal," said Jack with a tinge of worry in his voice. "But you must understand as well that Sarah is my daughter. She's a good girl. I just want to be sure you're not treating her the same as those Arab terrorists that are corrupting her."

"I can assure you Mr. Murphy," said the corporal in a calm tone, the kind of voice he was taught to use in hostage negotiations, "that our only concern is public order. As I explained, we are particularly concerned about Arab and Muslim terrorist groups since 9/11. We will do everything we can to make sure that these people do not threaten the public order. That includes doing everything we can to prevent harm to your daughter and the rest of the public, including the members of the terrorist organizations themselves."

"Oh, okay," said Jack in a slightly more convinced tone. "I just wanted to make sure we understood each other."

"I think we understand each other perfectly," said the agent as he started to back out of the office.

"Yes, well I hope so," said Jack. And then more confidently, "No I'm sure of it. Yes we do. We understand each other fully, Corporal. If you need anything else, anything at all, don't hesitate to contact me."

BOMB SCARE BOTCHED
Cops Kill Anti-war Activist

By Stuart Martin

On Monday, October 8, it looked like the Mounties had "foiled a terrorist attack" at the Innomonde Building. In the press and on the airwaves, journalists fell over themselves to congratulate the RCMP on its intelligence coup. But on Indymedia websites and activist blogs conspiracy theories began percolating to the surface.

It turned out this time that the conspiracy theorists got it right.

Late Tuesday we learned the Mounties also got their women. There were three white women and one white man amid the "Arab Muslim extremist men" caught in the so-called anti-terrorist operation. And the shocker: a 19-year-old Westmount resident by the name of Sarah Murphy had been shot and killed.

RCMP Corporal Denis Boisvert has been tight-lipped about the details of the alleged terrorist attack and Murphy's death. He says, "There are still highly sensitive aspects of the investigation that are ongoing. I can't talk about them now because it could compromise national interests."

Boisvert would only confirm that Murphy died from a gunshot wound, and that her death was part of an ongoing investigation.

There has been much speculation about the circumstances of this young woman's shooting death. Defense lawyers for the bomb scare suspects claim she was shot for failing to drop a backpack whose most dangerous contents appear to have been a carton of king-size extra-light cigarettes.

Some journalists have cited unnamed sources in the RCMP as stating that Murphy threatened to blow up the building and that she was acting in a "confrontational and irrational" manner.

Journalists have been unable to get the story directly from the alleged terrorists themselves, who are under lock and key. Some would question whether the mainstream press even wants the real story. The RCMP foiling of a terrorist plot was too dam sexy, just the kind of good news story Canada needed after the trauma of 9/11.

But the surprises keep on coming! This reporter was able to get an exclusive interview with one of the alleged terrorist, Hassan Mohamed. Why are you reading this suspect's statements in a Montréal weekly, three days after the fact, instead of on every front page across the country? According to Mohamed, who calls himself an anti-war activist rather than a terrorist, it is because the

RCMP destroyed his press releases and calls to action by hacking into his email.

On Monday, October 8th, the day of the alleged terrorist attack, Mohamed was able to tell me as much before his phone went dead. He was arrested at the Solidarity for Palestinian Human Rights (SPHR) Concordia office in the middle of our interview about 45 minutes after the RCMP ordered the evacuation of the Innomonde Building. Mohamed was not aware of shots being fired or Murphy's death when I spoke to him.

Mohamed spoke to me on behalf of an anti-war group called "those who refuse to remain silent". He says his friends, Murphy among them, were doing an unarmed, non-violent occupation of ██████'s Innomonde Building office for its participation in the US-led war in Afghanistan.

"We wanted to draw attention to the incestuous relationship between the US Pentagon and the Montréal aerospace industry," says Mohamed. "We're not terrorists. The war industry is terrorism and we're trying to stop it through non-violent direct action."

Among the occupiers (or alleged terrorists, depending on your point of view) were three white women (including Murphy), one white man and three Arab men. They were all students at Concordia and McGill.

No firearms were found on any of the occupiers although they apparently had other weapons and have been charged with uttering death threats.

Gilles Blackburn, defense lawyer for Alexis Stewart, says the weapons were eating utensils, merely supplies for the group's planned occupation. And he calls the death threat allegations "absurd".

The idea that anti-war activists were doing a politically-motivated occupation is supported by a rather large piece of evidence initial reports failed to consider – a 6-metre-long banner they hung from the window of ███████████'s offices to protest its involvement in the production of technology used in the Afghanistan bombing campaign. A few eyewitnesses saw the banner before it was unceremoniously removed.

What did the "terrorist" banner say?

a) Down with Western Infidels and all glory to the Martyrs in the cause of Jihad!; b) Al Quaeda rules!; c) More than a million killed or displaced worldwide since 1960. Ask us about the cluster bombs in our Afghanistan campaign!

If they were really terrorists, it should have been a) or b). But it was c). It would appear that Murphy was killed for trying to tell the world about ████████ ████'s involvement in the bombing of Afghanistan, which she alleged includes the use of a rather nasty piece of military hardware – the cluster bomb. This little beauty is an anti-personnel ordinance that can tear through the bodies of anybody standing within about fifty metres of the explosion. Some fail to explode on impact, becoming *de facto* anti-personnel mines.

Xavier Corbeil from the Collectif Opposé à la Brutalité Policière (COBP) says this tragic death is part of a larger pattern of heavy-handed police tactics against activists and members of Montreal's Arab and Muslim communities.

"People of colour, the poor, the homeless and sex workers have always been targeted by police," says Corbeil. "Since 9/11, there is even more targeting of Arabs and Muslims, and the activists who are in solidarity with them. They are perceived as enemies in the so-called war on terror."

With so many questions about the circumstances of Murphy's death, Corbeil and others are calling for a public inquiry into the RCMP's response to Monday's bomb scare. "Nothing we do can bring Sarah back," says Corbeil. "But maybe we can learn from her death."

(See our feature retrospective on Sarah Murphy's life including excerpts from her political manifesto on page 4.)